I0590101

Twin Pines

Twin Pines

Sarah Lengler

Twin Pines

Acknowledgements

Thank you to my fiancé who encouraged me to pick it back up and supported me throughout the journey. To Donna McKeone for being my alpha reader with constructive criticisms and words of encouragement. To all of the beta readers, who read this in its most infantile stages, including Violet Everingham, Matthew Lengler, Carissa Lengler, and Pauline McKeone. And to the editors and everyone involved along the way. Special thanks to my family, without their encouragement and love as a child, I never would have made it.

Twin Pines

Table of contents:

Be sure to check out Shea's Mega Mix playlist on YouTube Music! For the broken, the brave, and the ones trying to find their way back.

Twin Pines

AFTER

I know something I shouldn't, I just can't remember what it is... I don't remember the last year of my life...

Twin Pines

00001 🌲🌲 John Doe

He slams the car into park and hits the button to close the garage behind them. The motor goes quiet as he turns in his seat, checking to make sure she's still breathing. When he sees the rise and fall of her chest, he releases a sigh of relief and steps out, opening the rear driver's side door.

Her feet, pressed up against the door, slide toward him as it opens—like the weakest attempt at a kick he's ever seen. On any other night this might make him chuckle, but not tonight. He grabs her filthy, blood-crusted feet and gently pulls her limp body toward him. As her hips near the edge of the seat, he drops her legs and leans over her, ensuring her nose and mouth are unobstructed.

Blood pours from her head, soaking a trail along the backseat. With no other option, he pulls her right arm with his left, hard enough to lift her torso in his direction. He bends, pushing his right shoulder into her abdomen, pulling and pushing at the same time he lifts her swiftly and messily out of the car.

With her draped over his shoulder, her stench—raw, rotting, unforgettable—assaults his senses. The sound of thick drops of blood hitting the ground follows behind him as he carries her through the garage. Glancing back, he sees her long, matted hair smearing the blood and dust in their wake.

Turning the doorknob then using his foot to nudge the door open, he gets her inside, careful not to drop her. He takes her to the room he has prepared for her and sets her down on the bed, the sound of the disturbed tarp screams into the dark, silent room. He heads to the kitchen, pulling out a bucket, soap and towels. Turning the faucet to nearly full heat, he leans against the counter, waiting for the water to warm.

Pressure builds behind his eyes. He slaps himself—hard—and barks, "FUCK." Immediately regretting it, he rushes to check the cameras monitoring the entire exterior and interior of the house. "All-Clear," he mutters, returning to the now-steaming water coming from the faucet. Grabbing all of his supplies, he heads back into the bedroom, which reeks like an outhouse baking in ninety-degree heat.

Gently, he removes her clothes, leaving her undergarments intact—for her dignity. As soon as the clothes leave her body, he rushes to throw them in the garage, to be dealt with later. He then spends forty-five grueling minutes scrubbing dirt, blood and what he's fairly sure is human feces from her skin and hair. It takes several water changes to get her fully clean.

When the job is done, he stands back from the bed, breathing heavily. One problem solved. But now she's clean, lying on a wet, filthy tarp.

"Shit," he whispers this time, "what the fuck am I gonna do now?"

After staring at her for several minutes, he calmly walks to the bed, tucks the tarp under her on one side, then rolls her over gently. Pulling firmly, he slides the tarp out from beneath her, spraying water and God-knows-what all over himself and the floor. He takes the towel he had ready and wipes her back before setting her down on the comforter. Now that she is clean of feces, blood, dirt, and worse, he gently cleans her scalp wound and covers it with gauze—just in case it hasn't finished bleeding.

By the time he's ready to take watch that night, he's dressed her in pajamas and tucked her tightly under the covers. He flicks off the light and quietly closes the bedroom door before heading to his security den to pull up the cameras. He sits, watching her still form and monitoring the house's perimeter until daybreak. When the sunlight streams through the window hours later, he decides to make coffee, hoping the smell might rouse her from her deep sleep.

He sits at the dining room table, sipping the coffee and dials a friend on a cheap burner phone.

"Hey, I picked up the patient last night," John says when the phone connects.

"Status?"

"Unconscious. No reaction to stimulus."

"Give it time."

"I know."

"Update with changes."

"I will."

"Talk soon."

"Sure," John replies, then snaps the phone in half and takes the pieces into his closet.

Back at his wall of security screens, he sets alarms for short naps throughout the afternoon, each no longer than thirty minutes. When his last nap ends at 7 p.m., the motion floodlight at the front of the house is illuminating the entire driveway. Before leaving the closet, he slips on a tactical vest with several magazines and a 9mm handgun stored within. Silently, he moves down the hall to her room to check her breathing, then exits out the back door.

The door closes with a click behind him. He leans against the house, pulling out his gun, using the dim light the moths hover around to check the chamber for a bullet.

Making his way to the front of the house, he scans his surroundings, keeping his gun near his waist with the barrel pointed down. The closer he gets to the front, the more alert he feels. He stays out of the floodlight's illumination, carefully scanning the entire area. He's so on edge that when a bunny hops across his field of vision, he nearly pulls the trigger. Taking a deep breath, he calms his nerves and completes the perimeter scan, circling around the other side of the house and returning to the back door.

Inside, he grabs a handful of lettuce and baby carrots, then jogs back to where he saw the bunny. He doesn't try to approach it but instead tosses the vegetables near it. He watches for a moment—just enough time to recharge—before hurrying back inside, unwilling to leave her alone for too long.

Night watch brings a little more excitement: a couple of slow-moving cars, and a drunk man who stumbles around for over an hour before collapsing in a bush out front. John calls a cab and watches like a hawk until the man is gone. Afterward, he increases his perimeter checks and peeks in on his guest to change the gauze on her head—it's still bleeding. He briefly considers sewing the wound closed but decides to leave the jagged mound of flesh alone. It'll be easier to figure out the medical stuff if she's awake and eating. When she's awake and eating...

The next morning, he has coffee alone and takes that time to read through some notebooks she had left for him. Taking out another burner phone, he dials the number he has memorized.

"What's the update?" comes through the phone.

"No change, thinking this might be worst-case scenario," John responds.

"Stay positive, it's only been a couple of days. Have you played her any music?"

"No. I will."

"You've got this, take it as it comes. Contact to a minimum now. I'll see you soon."

As the line goes silent, he breaks the phone in half and puts it in his closet. He grabs her iPod, selects a playlist and places her earbuds just barely in her ears. Heading back to the closet, he watches the screens and sets alarms, but sleep doesn't find him. On one of his nap breaks, he hangs his head in his hands, rubbing at his temples.

While sitting with his head in his hands, lost in thought, he hears a sound—a slinky sound, like someone shifting in bed.

Sitting bolt upright, his head snaps to the screens while his right arm reaches instinctively for his pistol. The gun slips from his grip as soon as it's in his hand. She's not awake, but the sound was her shifting in bed.

Twin Pines

00002 🌲🌲 Gregg's Rats

■ ☐ ☐ ☐ ☐ ☐ ☐ ☐ ☐ ☐

Shea Murphy mentally checks through her list as she steps into the garage.

Keys. Phone. Purse. Shit… Coffee

Once she has everything she needs, she starts her Jeep and opens the garage. Growing up and living in rural Ohio, she has grown to love the weather. Today the local meteorologist, Ms. Pantaloons, says there's going to be a high of sixty-five—sunny, cool and crisp.

I wonder if Pantaloons is her legal name. If not, it makes no sense. She always wears dresses

Backing out of her driveway and into the street, her phone automatically connects to her Jeep, and she selects her playlist titled *'Wake the fuck up'*. Her Jeep is nice and warm, but she's feeling a little too toasty, so she rolls down the window to regulate her temperature. The cool air gently caresses her face, helping her to feel more awake and ready for her day.

She doesn't have a long drive to work—just a few lights, a school zone and ten miles later, she pulls into her spot. Her spot marked with a concrete bumper painted with *'Head of Implantables-B2'*. She gets out, grabbing her coffee cup in one hand and the rest of her things with the other, nimbly pressing the button on the key fob to lock the Jeep.

As she approaches the building, she starts to pat herself down.

Key card… dammit

She tucks her coffee between her chest and forearm, then digs in her purse while walking toward the monolith of a building. She hopes she tossed the keycard in there on Friday, when she got off work. Sure enough, she didn't.

She presses the buzzer, the one visitors would use if they ever had any, while looking at her reflection in the mirror-finish windows covering the front of the building. She looks a little disheveled but nothing too bad—although her dark grey dress slacks are a little tight in the butt, as usual for her size US16 figure. Her long dark hair reaches all the way to her waist band, in delicate waves that would look better if they were freshly washed. She slept on wet hair last night leaving it looking a little smushed. Her big brown eyes behind eyeglass frames that are a little large for her pale face, roam over her appearance while she waits for the guard to respond.

She looks up at the camera with a pleading expression. Her hands are cramping from everything she holds, and she wants to be in that building as soon as possible.

Dean, the security guard's voice comes out over the intercom, "Forget your card, Ms. Shea?" His gentle southern drawl, nothing too obnoxious, is just enough to make him sound more respectful than the other guards who work at the desk.

She recognizes his voice immediately, "Yeah Dean, could you please buzz me in? I'm a little bit late and I need to get a ton done today," she says, holding down the coms button.

The door buzzes, and she lets herself into the building, trying not to spill her coffee. Dean is sitting at the security desk just inside the door.

"I buzzed HR for you, ta lettum know you're in the building and to clock you in," he says, focused on the security monitors showing the outer gates.

"Thanks Dean, I think you're the best guard we've ever had," Shea admits. She also thinks Dean is the most attractive guard they have ever had—about six feet tall, hazel eyes and lean build—from what she could see with his long-sleeved uniform and guard jacket. Oh, and a beautiful tungsten wedding band on his left ring finger.

"Oh, I don't think so Ms. Shea, just doin' my duties," he says, flashing her a smile.

"Well, I appreciate it, especially when I can't get my shit together on a Monday morning." Shea had just gotten this promotion a couple of months ago and was hoping she was doing a good enough job so that her tardiness wouldn't make the worst impression on Dax and the other big wigs.

Dean walks around the desk to go get himself another cup of coffee, "I gotta get a cup, Shea. My wife is way too pregnant for either one of us to sleep. I'm three cups in since I've been here, and it's not making a dent."

"Oh Dean, real quick— can I get a temporary visitor's badge for the high security areas, so I don't have to keep asking for a buzz all day? I think we have some left from when Dax had that scientist group last fall."

"Yeah, they're in the top drawer if you wanna grab one, I'll see ya around Ms. Shea."

Shea makes it down to her floor—basement level 2—since her promotion, where some of the more "secret" projects get done. Before her promotion, she was part of a research team for an advertising agency, that used algorithms to advertise products on social media. Now, she is on basement level 2, working on 'implantable hardware for the human body'. Sounds like a weird move, but her education helped it make sense. Her team members were really the ones doing the heavy lifting; she just helps keep them on track and liaises with the companies they're in development with. The company she works for is about to implement the chips her team had been developing, hoping to get rid of the key cards everyone always forgot.

Mostly me… I forget… all the damn time…

The implant would also track their location within the facility. There had also been talks about being able to use the implant to make purchases in the café. Essentially, it would function just like their keycards. They were remarkably close to making this a reality, and Shea was excited for the future development and potential uses for the government and private sectors.

Shea's day went by in a blur, she hadn't been able to leave her office once, juggling calls and video conferences all day, trying to shmooze investors and align schedules as they neared the end of this project. Her coffee had gone cold a while ago, before she was able to have more than a sip, and her bum was starting to ache from sitting too long. A knock on her closed office door pulls her from the focus of work.

"Come in," she says, having forgotten to open her door after her calls. Everyone on this floor knew Shea didn't close her office door unless she was on a call, leaving it and herself open to her employees.

As the door opens, Gregg, the lead developer, steps into her office.

"Hey Gregg, what can I do for you?" she asks, smiling as she surveys him. In her opinion, Gregg looks like a typical scientist, complete with the crazy hair, coke bottle glasses and a wrinkled shirt. Shea appreciates his "mad scientist" look, he pulls it off with his 6'5 muscular frame, perfect white teeth and sharp jaw.

Handsome… okay, he's very handsome

But it wasn't his good looks that made him stand out. Gregg's calm in the midst of chaos and his genuine kindness and caring nature were what made him truly remarkable. He's also the smartest person she knows, but he never rubs it in anyone's face.

"Shea, I've started the trials in 003-006. I thought you should know. If all goes well, we'll be ready for employee volunteers within the next three weeks," he says with an excitement that reminds Shea of a child telling someone about their Lego creation.

"Seriously? Gregg, you are a machine!" she says, standing from her office chair and smoothing out her clothes. Gregg had worked around the clock sometimes for this team, even when ordered to go home he would agree and then be right in that same spot when Shea arrived the next morning.

"I didn't think we would be close to completion until December. Can you show me the method you used for implantation on the rats?" Shea asks.

Gregg walks quickly to his area. His desk is surrounded by little plastic enclosures, each holding one well-fed and well-loved rat. Gregg treats his rats like pets, so, Shea knew if four of these rats had the chip in them, it was already human-safe. Gregg wouldn't take the chance of one of them getting hurt.

He walks over to the enclosures labeled *003: Templeton, 004: Pettigrew, 005: Splinter and 006: Remy*, then turns toward Shea, his enthusiasm palpable. "Okay, so, I actually used a couple of different methods here. I think at least one will be an option for our human volunteers. *003*-has a subdermal implant, right between the deepest layer of skin and the tissues below. I managed to get the hardware small enough that a fairly small needle can be used for deployment."

"Wow, Gregg. This is amazing," Shea says, impressed. "I'm listening, but I'm going to need a written report on my desk before the week is out. I need to pass this information up."

"I already have most of it done, I keep very detailed notes for myself," he smiles at her and slides a nut through one of the air holes in *003's* enclosure.

"*004-* has the same chip but it was implanted into muscle, to test if the chip will still function at that level. *005-* we tried a capsule with the chip inside. The capsule is designed to dissolve, and the chip would move into the small intestine. We would then utilize a command prompt, and the chip embeds in the small intestine. *006-* has a 0.01mm flat chip embedded into the skin, it's almost like a patch but with microscopic needles that embed it. We're unsure if this would really work in the long run, but for a temporary solution, it would be great. *006-* has chewed on the edge of this one, but it is still fully functional at this time. I don't know that this will be a viable option for an animal, but for a human subject it could be."

He walks over to his computer and pulls up the tracking program for all four rats, side by side, looking at their location, heart rate and body temp.

"There it is," he says, pointing to the screen. "We will keep a close eye on them over the next week, one day at a time."

"Thanks for the info, Gregg. I can't believe how far you've gotten in the couple of months that I have been down here," Shea says, truly amazed. While it probably has nothing to do with her leadership, it will make her look great to the guys running the show.

"How are things with Lydia? I saw her looking at you with that dreamy faraway look this morning," she teases, a smile tugging at her lips as she watches the blush rising on his face.

"We've gone out a couple of times. A few of us went out Friday night for drinks and I drove her home. I was a perfect gentleman of course, but she didn't seem as interested as I thought she was," he admits, clearly wanting this conversation to be over.

"She's interested Gregg. Don't give up on her," she encourages him, her tone softer now, feeling a pang of longing.

"Well, I'm going to go email the higher-ups to let them know about your progress. Hopefully, they can notify the contract holders and get us a big-time bonus."

Back in her office, she focuses on sending emails. When she glances at the clock again, it's already 7 p.m. She's been at work for nearly twelve hours, and her stomach is telling her it's time to head home for some dinner. She secures her computer and grabs all of her things—including her ice-cold coffee—and heads to the exit, waving at Dean and Petrie on the way out.

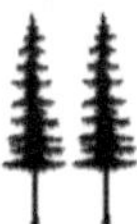

She walks into her dark home and flips on the lights, chasing away the darkness that always makes her a little bit jumpy living alone. Her house isn't large—she doesn't need much, especially since she's hardly ever home. It is decorated with contemporary tastes, black couches, glass tables and several bookshelves filled with some of her favorite books—and several she still needs to read. There is some art on the walls, mostly watercolor paintings by V Rea, depicting different arctic animals. There are pictures of her family, from when she was a child, hanging in the living room in a cluster, but they are all at least ten years old.

Ten years ago, Shea lost everything—both of her parents and most of her belongings, in a house fire when she was seventeen. She was away at University when it happened. The pictures and a couple of items from childhood—that she had with her at University—are all that remain of that life.

She drops her keys in the dish by the door that connects the garage to the living room, right next to the keycard that she forgot this morning. Her socked feet walk her through her living room, down the hall and into her bedroom. Once she gets home, she's usually in pajamas—taking off her bra was the highlight of her day.

After changing into her cozy pajamas, Shea heads back out to the kitchen, one of the largest rooms in her house. She loves to cook. Despite what people might assume from her size, she works hard to make healthy meals regularly. When she bought the house, the kitchen was the main selling point for her—plenty of counter space to hold her precious coffee pot and Truvia, not to mention a large island in the middle.

After heating up some leftover rice and veggies, she plops down onto her oversized black couch with a Stephen King novel, her bowl of food and a fluffy blanket. She settles in putting something on the muted TV she's watched a hundred times before. She'll spend most of her night there. She spends most of her nights there, alone.

OOOO3 🌲🌲 Black & Blue

Shea stirs. Bright sunlight illuminates her closed eyelids, making her head feel like it might explode. She cautiously opens one eye and realizes she doesn't recognize her surroundings. She is in a room with a large window letting in the light. After opening both eyes, squinting against the bright sunlight, she waits, allowing her eyes to adjust to the brightness. Finally able to fully take in her surroundings—white walls, white linens on the bed, no decorations—no personality. Looking out the window, Shea sees a normal-looking suburban back yard with a privacy fence. Her head mercilessly pounds, her bra digs into her sides, she feels faint and weak, with every muscle and bone in her body screaming out in pain. She also feels like she hasn't eaten or consumed any water for at least a week. She gingerly touches her hand to her head and finds her hair matted to her head with something crusty.

I must have been in an accident. Where am I? Why the hell am I wearing a bra?

She gingerly gets up from the bed, testing the locks on the window. She's out of luck, a good old 'landlord special' has the paint gripping the window like a vice. Panic flows through her veins, she isn't getting it open, she's trapped. She works on steadying her breathing and continues to look around, trying to find a way out of the room. The only exit she sees is a door leading to the rest of the house, slightly ajar. Feeling her heartbeat bounding in the wound on her head, she tip-toes back to the bed, checking for any clues.

Hearing a voice call her name and a light knock at the door, a figure steps into the frame. She throws herself back into the bed, tugging her bra out of her skin and pulling the covers up over the thin nightgown.

She panickily and jerkily says, "Who—Who is it? Where am I?"

The door opens fully. A very tall man, looking to be about thirty with a full dark beard and short cropped dark hair fills the doorway. He doesn't look at her when he speaks.

"I put a few towels in the bathroom across the hall for you. I'm sure you want to get that blood out of your hair. You need to get moving if you want to stay ahead of them."

Ahead of who? What the fuck is going on, who is this guy?

"What are you talking about? Where am I? What's going on?!" Her voice rising, each question sharper than the last. Her hands clench into fists around the linen held in them.

"I know you're confused, and you have no idea who I am or what I am talking about, but I'm a friend and I'm trying to help you. You can call me John," he answers, his eyes fixed somewhere outside the window while he says it, continuing to stand half in the doorway.

Her body is shaking. She hurts all over. She feels like she has been hit by a truck. Her left hand is swollen, a small gash on the top of her hand between her thumb and index finger that throbs with her rapid beating heart.

"John huh? Let me guess—last name Doe? Listen I don't know what you want with me, I don't know what's going on." She takes a shaking breath, feeling the fear flood through her system. "Did you do this to me?" she accuses, using her left hand to touch the wound on the left side of her head, her eyes fixed on him.

He steps forward into the room, when he sees her shrink back in the bed, he pauses where he is. His voice is calm and soothing when he speaks to her.

"Shea, please listen to me, there isn't much time, you need to shower and get yourself together. The backpack you gave me is in the bathroom. Maybe it will help you remember something." He looks in her direction this time.

"ANSWER ME!" she screams, her fear fueling her outburst and making her voice crack. Tears blur her vision and slide down her face. "Did you do this to me? Why are you keeping me here? Why can't I remember how I got here?" she asks, feeling more lightheaded by the moment.

John's gaze locks with hers. His brow furrows, jaw clenches and she can tell he is chewing on his cheek.

"Shea, I would never hurt you. I know this is hard to believe and trust, especially with how your memory is right now, but I promise, I have no reason to hurt you. I only want to help you. What can I do to help you believe me?"

"I don't know, because I don't know what's happening! How do I know you?" Shea sobs, on the verge of hyperventilation, "how can I trust you?"

"I am a friend, like I said," he says quietly, stepping a little closer. "We've been friends for a while now. Earlier this year, on the anniversary of your parents' death, I took you out. But I had no idea that's what day it was before I got there. When you got there, you told me all about it, you cried in that bar reliving the pain of your loss, and I sat there like an idiot with no idea how to help," he admits.

She doesn't let go of her panic, but she does feel like his story rings true. It makes sense. A little bit of sense. She decides to be strong and put a sliver of trust in this stranger's story. But due to her thin pajamas, she doesn't want to get out of bed in front of him. Her hand instinctively reaches up to the crucifix on a gold chain she always wore—a nervous habit—but it's not there.

"What is it you want from me?" she asks, cautiously and curiously, her voice trembling.

"Shower and change. The bathroom is to the left, the door is open, and the light is on. There are towels for you, and your backpack is in there for you already, too. I'll be going down the same hall to the right, to get some coffee brewing while you shower. You will have your privacy, I swear," he says, with soft eyes that appear honest to Shea. He walks out the door and to the right, as promised.

She could use some caffeine; she has no idea what's happened, and she feels lost. Still reaching for her cross, she climbs out of the bed and gingerly walks to the door. She feels like she ran a few marathons, pain sparks with each step and a current of electric pain streaks up both legs. She feels nervous about leaving the room she woke up in; she feels some sort of strange attachment to it now. Plus, she doesn't know this guy. What if he tries something? She wouldn't even be able to run.

Why do I feel so shitty? What happened to me?

She looks back and forth down the hall and sees nothing but a light on across the hall. She doesn't see her 'friend' anywhere, so she gingerly hobbles to the illuminated bathroom. Closing the door swiftly behind her, she locks and relocks the door, checking it several times. Looking around she finds two five-pound dumbbells under the sink and shoves them against the door, thinking that on her way out she could use them as weapons.

Her eyes immediately find the large, camo hiking style backpack sitting on the toilet, she grabs it by a strap and hauls it onto the counter. Catching a glimpse of herself in the mirror, she brings her hand to her mouth, where a stifled gasp escapes from her lips. She looks horrific—her hair is a rat's nest, she has two black eyes under a gash in her hairline on the left side of her head, with several other bruises that look like they are in different stages of healing on her face. Seeing blood around her mouth she turns on the faucet and uses her hand to scoop some into her mouth, swishing, she notices something is off. Getting close to the mirror with her mouth wide open she sees that where two of her teeth used to be, is now just raw, barely healed gum.

My teeth, seriously! Is he holding me captive?

Closing her mouth, she wipes it with the back of her hand and steps back from the mirror. She notices that it looks like she has lost weight, but not much.

Stay focused, backpack!

She unzips the backpack and starts pulling things out. On top is a deed to a cabin in Alaska, under the name Fay Lynhart and a passport with the same name, but with Shea's picture. She sets these on the counter and continues to search through the pack. A set of keys, none of which look familiar to her, on a keychain of a bear with Alaska engraved on the bottom. A pair of jeans, clean bra and underwear, tank top, plush hoodie and thick wool socks are next, with at least a week's worth of outfits below that. There is a large makeup bag and a toiletry bag—that includes full-size shower 'condiments', a razor, a whole box of tampons, etc. At the bottom of the bag is a small leather notebook. When she opens it there are several contact names on a list titled 'safe'. All the locations seem to be around the same area in Alaska.

This doesn't make any sense

She is about to close the notebook and put it away, when she realizes there are other pages written on within. She turns to the first page she finds with writing and it's a list of berries that are safe to eat in Alaska. Next, mushrooms that are safe, then several more reference pages of all sorts of other survival-type information. When she gets to the last page that is written on, Shea reads,

Shea,

Trust John- with your life if needed.

-Shea 00015

Setting aside the clothes and toiletries she stuffs the rest back into the backpack. She'll trust this supposed note from herself for now—even though the numbers don't make any sense. She turns on the water in the shower, letting it run until the room fills with steam. Stepping under the hot water brings her blood to just beneath the surface of her skin, immediately flushing her body red—highlighting the menagerie of bruises she is covered in. She scrubs her skin and hair until she's certain all the dried blood is gone, then sinks to sit in the shower until she feels like she's suffocating from the buildup of steam. Turning the dial to the off position, she stands and reaches one of her hands out of her warm sanctuary to the towel rack and grabs the oversized towel that is waiting there for her.

She wrings out her hair while standing in the shower, the towel wrapped around her body, tucked into her armpit. Once dry, she carefully brushes all the knots from her hair before slipping on the clothes she had apparently packed for herself in another life. She doesn't bother with the make-up—what's the point? It won't hide the black and blue of her face; if anything, it would probably just make things look worse. She takes the weights from in front of the door and slides them under the lip of the cabinet, to be used another day if need be.

Checking to make sure she has all of her things (including the weird sleeping clothes she had been wearing) packed back into the backpack, she throws it over her shoulder and cautiously walks down the hall, drawn by the smell of coffee.

00004 ♯♯ Call Me Todd

Shea can't help but marvel at the progress her team has made in the past month with the trials on Gregg's 'pet' rats. A company called Crowned Skull Laboratories had dumped a large sum of money into the project two weeks ago, and they were hoping to expedite the research into human trials this coming week. While the future of this project hinged on Gregg and the efforts of the team, Shea feels cautiously optimistic as she watches them parade into the conference room.

"Thanks for the bonus, Shea, we all know you didn't need to do that with the money and could have kept it all for yourself. Or put it back into the department for the next project." Dena leans in too close—her breath coffee-sour, her perfume a sharp burst of Clinique Happy. Dena was a wonderful employee, and maybe even someone Shea could call a friend, but she wasn't used to people invading her personal space.

Shea offers Dena a warm, knowing smile, her expression empathetic, as she continues to count heads entering the room. Shea had been lower-middle class growing up and knew what a bonus could mean for a family. With Dena's husband and two kids at home, Shea imagined the money was helpful but also knew that Dena's family probably hadn't experienced much struggling on her salary.

Is everyone here…

"Okay people, if you could all grab a seat. There should be plenty. Dean brought some extra chairs up from the café for me this morning," Shea says, from the head of the table, hoping she projected calm and authority. As watches everyone take their seats, she spots a face in the crowd she doesn't recognize, in a chair pulled to the back corner of the room.

"Excuse me, sir. Could I ask who you are? I haven't seen you on B2 before, and as our discussion will be of a top security clearance manner…" Shea's voice trails off as the man stands and nods down to the badge clipped to the lapel of his suit coat.

"Of course, Miss Murphy, I don't think we've been introduced. My name is Todd Donoghue, CEO of Crowned Skull Labs. Dax told me I could sit in on the meeting today, considering you will be discussing a project I'm funding, correct?" His question was punctuated by a raised eyebrow and a crooked smile. Shea got the impression he wasn't used to being questioned.

"I am so sorry, Mr. Donoghue. Of course you are welcome to sit in on our meeting, it'll save me from sending an email later." Shea smiles and nods.

It would have been nice for Dax to give me a heads up

She glances to her secretary, Danielle, and asks, "Could you please add Mr. Donoghue to the email list for the meeting minutes?"

"Of course, Miss Shea," Danielle answers, standing up and heading to the back corner to have Mr. Donoghue type his email into her laptop.

Shea greets the entire group, then begins the meeting by reviewing the results of the rat trials, expressing her gratitude for all of the team's hard work, especially the long nights spent working on this.

"I want to be clear—those bonuses were not a gift," Shea says. "These are because of all of the hard work you all have put into Project Salt N' Vinegar." She smiles and looks at Mr. Donoghue, who returns her look with a half-smile. Maybe he got their attempt at humor or maybe he thought she was silly. Either way, even just the half smile lit his face up and caused Shea to stumble over her words.

"Uhhh, yes, so. Moving forward, Gregg, do you think the medical supplies you need for human trials will be in by the fifteenth of this month?" Shea asks, looking out over her employees, searching for the disheveled genius that had made this project a reality.

Gregg stands and addresses the whole room, "All orders have been placed to McKesson. Our lab has perfected the version of the chip we will be implementing and will have five hundred ready by next Monday, which of course is the ninth. In reality we could begin with volunteers a week from today, the tenth. So that we're all on the same page, it will be a subdermal implant. All of the other chips performed great, but for the application we are looking to use it for, chip *003* made the most sense. We've also placed an order for the manufacture of the transdermal patch, for visitors and anyone who prefers not to have the implantable chip, though key card access will remain available."

Clapping erupted from the room, beginning with Mr. Donoghue. Shea stands and claps, smiling until the applause dies down. Then addressing the team, "I am amazed, yet again, by this team. I could never take all the credit, especially not in front of Mr. Donoghue, but this projects success is entirely because of you." She glances around the room, her smile genuine as she reaches down to a stack of papers on the table in front of her. "I would like to be the first volunteer to get the chip, not only because I can never remember my key card," she pauses for the laughter around the room, "but also because, as your leader, I feel like I should be the first to go through it. Now, who has questions?"

She looks around the room, noting several raised hands and the intense gaze of Mr. Donoghue. Her right hand nervously reaches for the crucifix that hangs around her neck.

He's looking at me like he's trying to read my thoughts… or like I have a booger hanging, I'm hoping for neither

"Okay." She scans the room and points to a lab tech to her left. "Russ, go ahead."

"Thank you, Miss Shea. I just want to make sure I'm not required to get the implant, right?" he pauses, then continues, "like, I could still use my key card?" he asks.

"Yes, Russ, that's correct," she says to him directly, then looks out to the whole team, "remember guys, this is not mandatory. You can absolutely opt out. Anyone who is interested can grab one of these written consent forms on their way out. Just turn it in to HR when you're done." She sets the papers on the edge of the table. "Any other questions?" She looks around the table, but no hands go in the air. "Meeting dismissed then."

Almost every employee grabs a form on their way out of the room.

"Miss Shea, I'll send these minutes out as soon as I am back in my office," Danielle says, picking up a form. She is the last person in the room, other than Mr. Donoghue.

"Thank you, Danielle. As long as it is done by the end of the day, today," Shea replies, her gaze drifting over Danielle's shoulder to the handsome man in the back of the room.

"Well done, Miss Murphy. It appears your team has great admiration for you, and I can see why," Todd says, his voice carrying a subtle hint of flirtation.

"You flatter me. I wouldn't be anywhere without that crew of people that just left," she says, not in false modesty, but honesty. Her job isn't incredibly difficult—not with a team like this. At least she was qualified for it though, with a degree in Technical Management.

Todd absentmindedly fidgets with what appears to be a family ring on his right ring finger. Shea's attention is drawn to the motion, as she has a similar habit with her necklace.

"Mr. Donoghue…" she starts, deliberately keeping her hands busy, so she doesn't reach for her necklace.

"Todd, please. Call me Todd," he interjects, still fidgeting.

"Well then, Todd, I'd like to invite you to come back next Tuesday for the start of our volunteer trials. I don't know if you'll be able to fly in again, or if you'll even be willing to so soon, but it would be an honor if you would join us," Shea says, nervously stacking the papers that were left on the conference room table.

"Of course, it would be an honor for me as well, Miss Murphy. I have a few things to work out with Dax and the lab anyway, so I'll probably just stay in town and get some other work done," he answers.

"Oh great! I'll keep it a surprise for the team." Shea smiles. Gathering her laptop, folders and loose paper, she excuses herself. "Well, if you'll excuse me, I have a ton of things to do before we really get going on Tuesday."

As she walks to her office, she feels exhilarated. She had only been in this position for a few months and had blown through the projections that Dax had set for her team when she first started. As for this new development with Todd—she was still on the fence. She wasn't sure if she was more intimidated or impressed by him.

Nowhere to go but up.

Twin Pines

00005 Friend or Foe?

She walks down the hall, toward her 'friend,' with her backpack slung over her shoulder. He's sitting at a dining room table with two cups of coffee sitting in front of him, a first aid kit placed to his side. He is currently flipping through a notebook, and she hesitates barely moving, unsure what she should do. Trying to trust the page in the notebook, or rather herself, she timidly walks closer.

This guy is so big that he could crush me in a second

Shea clears her throat, sets her backpack down on the carpeted floor next to a chair and plops into it. She wants a coffee, but asking for it feels like too much and getting it from the kitchen herself feels even worse.

At least I remember how I take my coffee

"I already put two Truvia in for you, and don't worry it's French vanilla, I know you hate hazelnut," he says, pointing to the cup closest to her with his notebook, still not looking at her.

Shea stays silent for a while, frozen in her seat. Almost as if reading her mind, he says, "It's not poisoned. Want me to prove it?"

"Oh, no, I just...sorry," she stammers, sliding her mug toward her, taking a small tentative sip of the coffee.

I wonder if he has my necklace...and phone...and Jeep!

He speaks, pulling her out of her daydream. "There is a lot we need to go over, I have a satellite phone for you, under the name you gave me. I'm double-checking the lists you gave me to make sure I have everything before we leave," he says, never looking up from his notebook.

Why won't he look at me...

She sips her coffee as her eyes rove around the room. There is no other furniture in her field of vision—which seems to cover the entire rest of the house. Something else that covers the entire rest of the house is carpet, it's everywhere. There's no TV, no art on the walls, not even a couch. It's eerily empty. Just the dining room table she sits at and four chairs. She is trying to remember something, anything. She feels like there's something tickling the back of her mind but it won't come forward.

Is John a friend or foe...

"Ow, for fucks sake," she yelps, reaching her hand toward a sharp pain in her head. Her hand is swatted away before it can touch the stinging sensation, which pulls her the rest of the way out of her thoughts. Her 'friend' has the first aid kit open and is holding something to her scalp, where she had been bleeding before.

Shea shrinks away from him and again reaches for her cross, which isn't there.

"I need to clean the wound and see how many stitches I need to throw in," he says casually, like he's about to braid her hair, not dig at a wound with a needle.

"Um excuse me? How many, what? You need to throw—where?" she asks sarcastically. She heard exactly what he said, she just can't wrap her mind around it. This stranger wants to act like he is helping her, but he could have been the one who caused it.

"Shea, this wound is deep. I have no idea what conditions you were under recently. I probably shouldn't stitch it closed because of the risk for infection, but I have a course of antibiotics that you will take twice a day, and we will cross our fingers and hope," he says, while gently prodding the wound with a gloved finger.

"Ow, would you quit fucking touching it? Where's the numbing shit? Where's the pain meds? Screw antibiotics!" She's trying to stay calm as he continues to prod the wound, but she's decided to take her chances running her mouth.

He probably would've killed me already if he wanted to…

Her 'friend' stops prodding and moves to her side, where she can see him. "Shea, I only need to throw in a couple of stitches, you will need more injections to numb it than if you just deal with it," he says.

He grabs her left hand, pulling it from her coffee mug to inspect it. "This should heal fine on its own and with the antibiotics you should be covered for infection. I'll just clean it and leave it be," he says, turning her hand this way and that. She watches him and notices that the glove on his left hand is split open, right over a ring on his 'ring' finger.

I wonder where his wife is, maybe he hurt her…

He drops her hand momentarily to open an alcohol swab.

Alcohol swab…

Twin Pines

00006 00015

Shea arrives at work a little earlier than usual, with her keycard clipped to her smart ladies' sport coat lapel—not that she will need that stupid keycard after today. She's dressed like she's going to an interview, she even straightened her hair, which is now neatly pushed behind her ears. She's pacing the area near Gregg's desk, waiting for him to show. He said he would be here by 7:15 a.m.

Gregg arrives looking a little less disheveled than usual. "Sorry, Boss, let me just grab my supplies, and I'll meet you at the 'implantation station'. What do you think? Too corny?" he asks, while grabbing a pair of large gloves and his other supplies.

Shea starts walking toward the privacy dividers that had been set up the night before. They surround tables with vinyl chairs set on either side. The dividers look like Chinese silk screens, but not as pretty. These had that medical, light blue, sterile look to them. Shea pulls out one of the chairs and sits in it, placing her hands on the table.

Gregg brings over all the supplies and arranges them in front of Shea, on top of a paper drape. "You will be getting chip number 00015. I'll assign it to your personnel file as soon as it is implanted, so you can start using it immediately," he says, while lining up all his supplies. He dons his gloves and opens the alcohol swab, the sharp scent of alcohol permeating into the air. He gently takes her left hand, and asks, "Are you okay? Do you need a minute?"

"Oh, Gregg, I'm super excited. I'm just thinking about how crazy today is going to be," she replies, relaxing her left hand into his gloved one. He slides the alcohol swab across her hand, leaving a cold snail trail in its wake. As he waits for that to dry thoroughly, he assembles the needle for implantation.

"Okay, so the lab did all the hard work for us, they have put the tiny chip—smaller than a grain of rice—into this syringe with a small amount of sterile saline for ease of injection," he explains, admiring the syringe. "Your body will absorb the saline no problem and the chip will remain where we place it."

"Alright, Gregg, I'm ready when you are," Shea says, watching him uncap the needle.

"You will feel a little pinch, but it shouldn't be anything too bad," he reassures her, while using his left hand to gently hold her left hand flat. He slides the needle in an eighth of an inch and depresses the plunger on the syringe. Shea feels a small pinch when the needle enters her skin, followed by a light burning sensation when the fluid enters her hand. He makes sure the plunger is depressed all the way, then slowly slides the needle out and places a band-aid that he had already opened onto the injection site.

"Wow, I barely felt a thing, you're really good at that!" Shea says, as she inspects her left hand and the small BB-sized bump that's there, covered by a small round band-aid.

"Thanks, Miss Shea, I have been working to perfect the technique to make it as easy as possible on my victims, that's why your chip number is 00015. I lost a few to practice and then put 00014 in my own hand early this morning. That's why I was running a little late—I had to check for myself that it opened all the doors that I have access to and that I could buy my breakfast in the café," Gregg says, while he is putting all the trash on to the paper drape. He crumples it up and holds it in his fist as he pulls his gloves off over it and drops it into the closest garbage can.

"Did it?" Shea inquires.

"Did it, what?" Gregg replies, looking down at his hand-held computer, already assigning her chip to her in the system.

"Gregg, did the implanted chip open all of the doors and work in the café?" Shea asks, standing and smoothing her outfit. She grabs her keycard off her lapel and looks at it.

"Oh, yeah, it was a breeze. The team working on that side of things modified all of the keycard sensors to work with this technology," he says, walking with Shea over to his station. "Picked myself up a muffin." He reaches for the cinnamon swirl muffin he bought in the café, opens the packaging and breaking off a large piece, pops it in his mouth.

"I know you will be busy today, but I need you in the meeting. The CEO of Crowned Skull Labs will be here, and I want to go over some of the security issues that I'm thinking we need to address while we're there," Shea says, still holding her ID card.

"Yeah, I have it in my e-planner. I hired a few nurses and had them trained in the implantation process. They'll be here at 8:30 a.m. to start setting up. I took it out of my personal budget, since I never hired an assistant like you told me to, I have the extra money to pay the nurses for a couple of days," Gregg says, in between bites of his muffin, which was well on its way to being done.

Does he think I only care about the bottom line?

"Gregg, I have no questions regarding your spending. Your budget still has enough room to purchase a whole floor at the hospital if you choose to. Did you feel like I pressured you about money?" Shea asks honestly. She respects Gregg and feels they have become good friends, she hopes she doesn't come off as being all about the money.

"No, sorry, Shea. I've just been looking at spread-sheets and how I was going to do this for the past week," Gregg says, while looking at her through his thick lenses. "I knew you wanted everything in place for the CEO guy today, to make a good impression, and I just wanted to make sure I had your back—that's all," Gregg says, blush rising in his cheeks.

"Oh, I totally get that, I felt like my fucking eyeballs were going to melt out of my head lately, staring at a screen all day," she says with a smile, holding his gaze. "I think that is the first time you've called me 'Shea,' instead of 'Miss Shea,'" she smiles larger, as he looks away and blushes.

"I'm sorry, Miss Shea. I think I should probably get to work now, so that I can be at that meeting," he says quickly. Gregg's cheeks flare red and it rises into his ears.

"Don't apologize," Shea says as she walks away. Turning back toward Gregg, she says, "I think we're good enough friends that you can just call me Shea. I don't feel like your boss most of the time anyway. I think if anything, you should be my boss, so how about we call it equals?" She means every word and hopes he will take her seriously.

Gregg's eyes widen, mouth slightly agape. She can tell he takes her seriously, when he says, "Thank you Shea, that really means a lot to me. I don't know about equals, but if you say so, I'll take it." He flushes again and looks down at his desk.

Shea walks back to her part of the floor, utilizing her hand to open doors along the way.

This is really handy

She chuckles to herself as she arrives at her office. She walks over to her desk, clips her ID badge on the edge of her lamp, staring at it, she hopes there will be an answer to her concerns.

Her office is boldly in the middle of the floor plan, an odd design she thought at first, but now she sees how perfect it is. She is available to everyone equally. Due to its location, the outside of her office had been decorated by her secretary Danielle—who is actually a talented artist— to look like a giant fish tank. Danielle did a great job and painted coral reefs and tropical fish all over the cube, everyone loved it. The door to her office was painted to resemble a stone fish hide—though sometimes Shea thought it looked like Squidward's house too. Inside is her large desk, several filing cabinets, a bookshelf full of terminal binders, a computer with multiple monitors, her laptop, and two plush chairs across the desk from where she sat, for visitors.

Sitting in her office chair she glances at her computer monitor, and is shocked to see that it's already 9:00 a.m.

How long have I just been sitting here daydreaming, empty-headed...

Shea walks to her office door and scans the floor. The entire floor is bustling with activity. Not wanting to let her team down, she quickly sits at her desk, changes into comfortable slip-on sneakers, then charges into the fray.

Peeking into Danielles office she sees her secretary smiling, talking on the phone. "Danielle, can you go prep the conference room please? I want info packets for each employee, a legal pad, and a bottle of ice-cold water. Also, don't forget Todd Donoghue will be here too," Shea orders, without waiting for Danielle to even hang up the phone, and promptly walks toward Gregg's team.

"Of course, Miss Shea. I'll get it all prepped now," Danielle calls after her from the doorway. Looking around, she steps back into her office.

As Shea approaches Gregg's implantation station, she can see that everyone is moving quickly, working like a well-oiled machine. Employee volunteers go behind the curtain to Oz and come out not even a minute later, with the next employee ready to head in. Shea quickly sees where she can be of use. Gregg and the nurses are held up by having to assign the chip, ensure it is assigned to the correct employee, and then they still have to clean the station before the next implant can be installed.

Shea looks around, dons a pair of small gloves and grabs a container of sanitizing wipes. She enters the first station, quickly balling everything up like she saw Gregg do, and taking off only one glove over it. She then uses the other gloved hand to grab a couple of wipes, wiping the chair and table down quickly but thoroughly. She finishes by throwing away that glove and the wipes. Before she leaves the station, she calls for the next employee, telling them to sit in the chair and that the nurse will be right with them. As she turns to take her wipes and leave, the frazzled nurse turns and mouths *'Thank you'* before getting back to work.

This routine continues over all five stations for the next hour. Toward the end, Shea feels like she has it down to a fine science. It's Gregg who breaks her out of her trance-like cleaning state.

"Hey, Boss, it's 10:15, we're late for the meeting, and that CEO guy has been here for at least a half an hour, watching everything. He just went into the conference room."

"Son of a bitch, I should have set an alert on my phone, let's get over there—like yesterday." She feels red in the face and not as put-together as she did this morning, but it was worth it to feel truly helpful.

OOOO7 🌲🌲 No Whiskey?

John cleans the wound on her hand, telling her it would be best to place a butterfly stitch over the wound, just in case. Shea watches quietly and intently, sipping her coffee—which she has now unfortunately reached the bottom of. The coffee had been a good distraction from the tremor in her hands and the sweat pooling in the small of her back.

"Hey, John, can I pop over to the kitchen and make a cup of coffee? My head is still throbbing a bit, and I think more caffeine will help," she asks, looking over to the kitchen in this older home. It has a window-like bar on this side, and she can see into the other counter, where her addiction awaits her. Shea assumed the house was old because of the thick coat of dust across the top of all the base boards and the khaki-colored Berber carpet that was darker toward the walls and more of a gray where there was foot traffic that covers every inch of the house.

"Naw, I'll get it. Here, hand me your cup," he says, immediately reaching out his hand for it.

"I don't expect to be waited on hand and foot, I mean, I am sore, but I can make a cup of coffee. Or is it that you don't want me in your kitchen alone?" she asks, on full alert, note be damned.

"I'm sorry, Shea, but yeah kind of. Look, I know you don't know me and I'm dealing with that, but I know you. We are friends after all, and I know you are going to try to do something reckless, like put a knife down your pants, just in case I am actually the bad guy, In the end, we'll just end up back here, at the table, with me cleaning a wound on your thigh instead," he tells her calmly.

Knife down my pants, why didn't I think of that?

"I was not going to do that! I am trying my hardest to trust you, I really am. I just really want another cup of coffee. I don't care who gets it, to be honest," she says with tears in her eyes. She looks at him and the sadness seems to grow, until large tears fall silently down her face. She puts her head down, trying to breathe.

After just a minute or two, John grabs her chin gently, turning her face toward himself. Saying in a quiet, calming voice, "Shea, I know this is a lot. You're doing an amazing job, even better than we both thought you would. Just bear with me, okay?" he asks, gently brushing his thumb along her jaw.

"I don't think your wife would like you touching me like this. Can I please just have a coffee?" she asks, with a little venom in her voice. She feels upside down, her emotions flipping all over the place.

"Sure thing, Shea," he says, grabbing her coffee cup and heading toward the kitchen.

Shea watches him through the gap between the cabinets and the bar, to ensure no foreign substances make it into her drink. He returns from the kitchen with her cup and gently sets it down next to her.

"Thanks. I'm sorry I was snappy, I don't know what the hell is going on with me," Shea admits, trying to keep her voice from shaking.

"Yeah, I understand," he says in a clipped manner, reaching for gloves and a small sewing kit.

"Um… you don't have actual stiches?" she asks.

He shakes his head and proceeds to gather the rest of his supplies.

"What do I look like, a fucking teddy bear with a boo-boo?" Shea exclaims. She can't believe what she is seeing.

Where's the whiskey?

Mr. John Doe looks at her and cracks up laughing, he even has the audacity to bend over and hold his side. As he begins to pull himself together, Shea says, "What, I'm not joking, no numbing shit, no pain meds, no whiskey, and a sewing kit from 1994?"

John continues to laugh as if there is some kind of joke Shea has missed.

"What is so funny, man? I'm feeling left out," she says, truly looking into his eyes for the first time. They are a color she cannot describe, blue and green and seafoam. His face is more handsome than she'd initially thought, making her feel more embarrassed about her behavior now.

"Shea, I'm sorry, but what we got is what we got, together. We didn't think we would need to waste space on another thing when we were already packing the sewing kit, and what's funny is that even when you don't know what is going on, you are still you. You are who you are. Also, I do have whiskey, that you did plan for," he says, heading to the kitchen.

She feels dumb founded, it sounds like she and 'John' must have been really great friends before, and wonders if she ever met his wife.

"Here," he says, handing her the bottle of Crown Royal. "You going to put it in your coffee, or you want a shot glass?" he asks, pulling a shot glass from behind his back that reads, *Twin Pines*.

"No, thanks, I'll put it in my coffee, Irish style. Where we're going, we don't need…shot glasses," she says, filling the top two inches of her mug with whiskey and places the bottle to the side.

"But you have no idea where we're going," he says, a glint of mischief in his eyes.

"I was making a joke," Shea says, sipping her coffee.

"I know." His mouth barely a smile but his eyes don't meet hers. He stands in front of Shea, tapping his toe while she drinks her coffee.

Shea chugs the coffee, it is fresh and still plenty warm. She doesn't mind though, as she feels the warmth of the whiskey already entering her core and spreading through her extremities. She sets the mug on the table and looks to John with a steady, 'I'm ready' gaze.

He approaches slowly, not making any sudden moves, which Shea appreciates because she is still very wary of him.

Putting on a pair of gloves and getting the needle ready with alcohol and a lighter, he casually looks down at her. Her face is uplifted to him, watching his every move.

"What color you want?" he asks her upturned face.

"Surprise me," she says, feeling more relaxed now.

"Alright," he says, looking at the sewing kit, he picks up a spool of teal colored thread and cuts off about twenty-four inches before putting it back.

Shea continues watching as John threads the needle. She wonders how much this man truly knows about her, because that is the color she would have picked for herself.

He seems to know me so well

Shea keeps her mouth shut as he approaches her wound with the needle, without realizing it, she bears down and holds her breath in anticipation of the pain.

"Shea, you need to relax and breathe. You're going to pass out if you keep that up," John tells her. His voice calm but firm.

Shea lets out her breath and takes a new one, a few new ones, and tries to calm herself. "I'm sorry, this is just making me really anxious for some reason."

"I can imagine," he responds, then asks, "is it okay to start now?"

"Yeah, yeah, I'm fine, I'll be good."

He places himself closer to her, positioning one of his legs in between hers, so he can get as close as he needs. He begins the first stitch and Shea remains unmoving—not making a sound. She can feel the initial prick of the needle, then feels his fingers gently pull the needle through her scalp. Next comes the incredibly long length of thread, that vibrates the tissues as it goes through, the sensation makes her clench her butt cheeks together.

Moving to the second suture, it takes him longer to go through the second bit of skin. She feels the needle slide through her scalp, then him tying it, cutting the thread and moving to the next. Shea has remained stoic, unmoving and silent. At the next suture it becomes more than she can bear. She reaches down, grabbing the edge of the seat on either side, so tightly that her knuckles quickly turn white.

"Are you okay, Shea?" he asks, as her head dips down lower toward his leg.

"I'm fine. Keep going." The response comes through Shea's clenched teeth.

So, he does, and they don't stop until the job is finished. "Alright Shea. That's all. We're all done," he says softly, smoothing her hair away from her face.

She immediately sits up, looking embarrassed. She looks over at the whiskey bottle still sitting on the table.

"I'm sorry, no more. You need to be in the right mindset for the kind of day we're going to have," he says, putting away the sewing kit. "Also, usually I would put some sort of bandage on this to keep it clean and dry, but I knew you would freak out if I shaved your hair, so we just need to make sure it stays clean and dry without a bandage."

"What if I wore a cloth headband to cover it up?" Shea asks, feeling her heartbeat bounding in the wound and wanting to make sure she follows his instructions.

"Yeah, that'll work. Great idea," he says, taking all of his gear out of the room, along with the bottle of whiskey.

Shea opens her large backpack and rummages through it until she finds one of the headbands she saw earlier. Pulling it out, she slips it on and adjusts it to cover the whole wound. The headband feels a bit '70s style to her, she glances at her reflection in the compact mirror and thinks it would actually look cute—if only her face weren't covered in bruises.

John walks back to where Shea is sitting, and says, "Hey I'm going to have to leave you here alone for a few minutes while I go grab us some lunch. I had it delivered to an abandoned house down the road, I just have to grab it. Just know, there are cameras and alarms for your protection, please tell me you won't try to leave."

"I won't. I promise," she says, feeling the sense of emptiness from her stomach that has been nagging her all morning, reaching new heights.

I'll just have to escape later...

00008 🌲🌲 Danielle

Shea and Gregg walk together to Conference room A.

Shea stops just shy of the door, taking a moment to observe the employees enjoying the water—she knew they would—and Todd, sitting at the table this time, is looking at her and smiling.

"Gregg, I'm going to go in first, okay? Wait until I say your name to enter, please," she says, and without waiting for a reply, she walks into the room.

She can feel Mr. Donoghue's eyes on her as she walks to the head of the table, where she stands, looking around the table at her employees.

"Today has been a monumental day for Project Salt N' Vinegar, as you can see, you have the stats and projections in front of you, but what you don't have in front of you is the knowledge that none of this would have been possible without the hard work and dedication of our lead developer."

"The man who stayed late and came in early to ensure this project took off without a hitch. Not only that, but he also had the forethought to arrange for the employment of several nurses for today and tomorrow, to see this goal come to fruition."

"He has been running his tail off all morning to see this accomplished, let's hear it for our one and only, Greggory Marsh."

The room erupts in applause, accompanied by hoots and hollers. Shea can feel the pressure of tears, when the CEO himself stands to give Gregg a proper standing ovation. Her eyes begin to well up and she tries to hide it with a large smile. As Gregg walks into the room with his head down, she can see that he is trying to hide his emotions as well. His face is beet red, and she watches as a single tear falls and lands on his glasses. He raises his hand in thank you and takes his seat to the right of Shea. He looks up at her, nodding in gratitude, then shifts his eyes and furrows his brow in a pleading expression.

"Alright, alright, let's settle in now," she says, trying to gain control of the room. She notices Todd is still standing, watching her with a half-smile and raised eyebrows, fiddling with the ring on his right hand.

"Everyone, I think you all remember Mr. Donoghue, the CEO of Crowned Skull Laboratories," Shea says, waving a hand in Todd's direction like Vanna White. "I believe he would like the floor to kick off the meeting today. Mr. Donoghue," she says, nodding to him while pulling out her chair and taking a seat.

Mr. Donoghue clears his throat and looks around at the employees gathered at the table. "Thank you for having me today, Miss Murphy and team." He smiles at her, and it feels genuine. "In all my years at Crown, I truly feel that this is the best investment we have ever made," he says, to quiet applause and whoops from around the room. Shea blushes and gives him a shy smile when he glances her way.

"That being said, I hope there are other projects we can work on together, in the future."

Todd turns slightly, his entire body facing Gregg, as he says, "The geniuses that have worked on this project can expect a healthy bonus.

Especially a one Mr. Marsh, who will receive the rest of his budgetary funds as his bonus."

Gasps ripple around the room and those sitting closest to Gregg jostle his shoulder and mess with his hair. Shea sits slack-jawed for a moment, but feeling Mr. Donoghue's eyes on her she quickly brushes it off and reaches out to put her hand on Gregg's arm. With his hands covering his mouth he looks over at her and just shakes his head.

Shea feels the need to say something, knowing Gregg must be uncomfortable with the attention. She looks at Todd, and says, "This is very generous of you, Mr. Donoghue. That's life-changing money."

"Absolutely it is, it's given because of the hard work of Mr. Marsh. The sheer determination he put in to get this project where it is today, while only spending a fraction of the budgetary funds, is nearly impossible. That kind of determination—ensuring the project does not bankrupt those involved—is quite literally unheard of in my business. Mr. Marsh is a valuable asset to this team, and I feel the need to treat him as such."

He smiles at Gregg, then at Shea, and adds, "Oh, also, everyone, please call me Todd. We're one big family here, right?" Extending his arms out toward the others in the room.

"Thank you, Todd. I feel like I was just doing my job, but I appreciate it nonetheless," Gregg says, his voice soft. Shea watches him with curious eyes. This is the most she's ever heard him say in a meeting.

Todd flashes his megawatt smile at Gregg, then turns to Danielle. "Danielle, that is your name, correct?"

"Yes, yes sir, Todd, um, yes that is my name." Obviously caught off guard she stumbles through basic communication and looks like she just ate something bitter.

"Great. Well, Danielle, I am sure you and your team here, all recognize the hard work that every one of you put into today, correct?" he asks, with a mild edge to his voice. It surprises Shea, whose eyes are now moving back and forth between Todd and Danielle.

"Yes sir, everyone was doing everything in their power to make everything run smoothly today," she says, her voice still on edge.

Where is this headed?

"Well, rightly so, although I must say Gregg's team, those nurses, and your very own department head, Miss Murphy, really kept things moving, wouldn't you agree?" Todd asks. He spins his ring.

"Yes sir, though everyone has different tasks, and I think everyone was working as hard as possible to keep things moving," Danielle answers, her face growing more pale by the second.

"Right," he says. Then, he scans the room, his gaze landing on each employee. "I saw this young lady stocking supplies that were needed all morning, and this gentleman here keeping a running list of everyone who was waiting and passing those names off to this woman here, who would then look those names up in the system to ensure with absolute certainty it was the right clearance assigned to each person's chip. All the while, your lovely Miss Murphy, was darting from partitioned area to partitioned area, cleaning messes and offering support to the nurses." His eyes remain locked on Danielle as he speaks.

What is he getting at?

"Riiiight?" Danielle says, her drawn-out response dripping with annoyance as she fidgets with her pen.

"So, tell me why, when your superior asks you to—what was it?—set out the paperwork, legal pads, and water, including yours truly, is it that you stayed on your phone call? The one with a man you're having an affair with, for another forty-five minutes in your office?" His accusation causes those who weren't looking in Danielle's direction turn their heads in shock, waiting for her reaction.

"I…that's…I didn't…" Danielle stammers, the rise and fall of her chest labored.

Shea stands, and firmly says, "Mr. Donoghue, while I am sure you have made observations since your time here, I am unsure how you could have come by such information regarding my assistant."

Todd's attention shifts to Shea, and she feels like a deer caught in the headlights, a heat rising in her chest. "Miss Murphy, I don't claim to believe I know more about your employees than you, but I did observe Danielle today, and one only needed to pass in front of her office to overhear her conversation. I apologize if you feel I've crossed a line, but she explicitly said to whomever she was on the phone with that she hoped his wife found out about them so she could move in with him," Todd says, maintaining eye contact with Shea throughout.

Shea looks between the two and finds herself speechless. Her attention settling on Todd, she notices a muscle just above his very chiseled jaw that seems to be dancing as he looks back at her.

He looks so angry, I'm not sure if I'm into him or terrified of him…

Todd smiles at her and says, "Not only that, but she spent the last few minutes she had before this meeting, doing what was ordered to do initially, leaving yours truly out of the setup. Requiring me to ASK her for what should have already been done." Todd turns to Danielle. "Is that not correct?" His posture is rigid, he fidgets with his ring.

What the fuck!

"Todd," Shea interrupts his questioning, "I am so sorry this has been your experience today. I should have been more on top of things, but I don't know that this is the best way to handle this."

"Miss Murphy, this is not a reflection on your performance, but on hers. This may not be the way you would have addressed it, but she needs to tender her resignation immediately, or you can fire her if you must. That kind of insubordination should not be tolerated, especially considering the way I saw you running around here today," he says, taking deep breaths.

Danielle looks up at Shea, face full of desperation. Shea sighs, standing her ground. "I don't fire employees after just one mistake, sir. I need Danielle for the minutes, and I will talk with her later about this, but now is not the time."

"No, you do not need her for the minutes," Todd says, moving slightly to the right. Behind him, there is a woman typing furiously at a laptop. "I had my own assistant brought in after what I observed the last time I was here, and after looking at last week's minutes. They simply aren't up to the level this kind of work requires," he says, matching Shea's stare. "This is not in isolated incident. If you'd like, I can call Dax to get the phone records, to see just how many times this has happened."

After seeing Todd's secretary, she glances over at Danielle, who hasn't written a single thing on her legal pad. As Shea thinks about it, she hasn't seen her type anything either.

This guy is being a total ass, but I think he might have a point…

"I'm sorry Danielle," Shea says, her voice firm. "There is a certain standard and attitude we strive for here and today was a testament to the fact that the entire team sees this, except for you. I appreciate the work you've put in and there will be severance, but I need you to leave your laptop and go pack your things," Shea says, already pushing the security button under the table.

"You can't do this! He's lying! I do my job!" Danielle argues, standing so quickly that her chair topples to the ground behind her.

"Everything okay, Miss Shea?" a lovely, dark-skinned, six-foot-five, loaded with muscle man, named Petrie asks from the doorway. He got this nickname because of his tender-hearted nature, and because everyone loves calling the largest man in the company the name of a cute little dinosaur. He even got a 'tree star' tattoo on his forearm a few years into his employment.

Shea can see Danielle's appalled expression out of the corner of her eye. "Thank you, Petrie. Can you escort Danielle to her office to pack her things, ensuring she takes no company property?" She says, her gaze scanning Danielle's hand, investigating if she has gotten the chip yet, not seeing one she says, "And make sure you take her keycard, ensuring there are no other keycards in her possession, please."

"Yes ma'am, right away. Let's go miss," he says, ushering Danielle out of the room.

Shea plops in her chair, feeling a weight settle heavy in her chest. She knows there are things on the agenda they need to discuss, but she's suddenly feeling too emotionally exhausted to deal with it.

An affair… not doing her job… why haven't I seen this?

"I'm sorry, Miss Murphy, I just couldn't ignore how well everyone worked together this morning, but her blatant disobedience and lack of ambition just really sat wrong with me," Todd reports, his posture having relaxed a bit.

"Please, call me Shea," she says, then sighs, pushing her glasses further up her nose. "It's okay, that really was inappropriate on her part."

Todd nods, taking his seat, signaling to her that it's her turn to lead.

"Alright, everyone," Shea says, standing up. "After all that I'll keep this as brief as possible. You have all the information you need in the packets in front of you—or at least, you should. Danielle printed them, but I honestly don't know anymore." She pauses, feeling a huge weight on her heart for what transpired. She wishes this could have been avoided but doesn't see how.

"What I want to discuss, really only concerns Gregg, Todd and I, so everyone else, back to work. Make sure you are helping those nurses, please," she calls to them as they quickly file out of the room, likely heading down the hall to get a glimpse of what's happening in Danielle's office.

As the room clears, Todd and his secretary move closer to where Gregg and Shea are sitting.

Gosh I'm a jerk, I didn't even see her the whole meeting, sitting back there behind Todd, Who, come to think of it, is pretty broad…and muscular looking… and has a great jaw line… Henrey Cavill, who?

As they sit in front of Shea, she leans in closer to the blonde woman and apologizes for not knowing she was there, while extending her hand to shake.

"Pleasure," the small blonde says. "Names Tina," she smiles genuinely at Shea. "And don't worry about not seeing me—that's how Mr. T likes it. More discreet you know?" Tina finishes, settling back in her seat.

"I pity the fool," Shea mutters, noticing the blank faces around her, she flushes with embarrassment. She slowly sinks into her chair, just as the room erupts in laughter.

Laughing, Todd gets out, "Sorry it took me a second to remember what Tina had called me."

Gregg shoots a wide grin at Shea. She knows he loves breaking the tension with something awkward.

"Alright, let's do this. I would love to get out of here early today and I feel like that is never going to happen," she says, beginning to really feel a headache. "My concern here is security. I got my chip and was able to walk away with my ID card and the chip. Couldn't this lead to people giving others their keycards to get in here? I mean I don't think our employees would do this, but we really need to cover all our bases. Also, without an ID badge, there's no picture to match a face to a name. How do we know when someone from a different area comes in, or even a visitor?" Shea finishes, looking toward Gregg.

She realizes Todd is also waiting for Gregg to solve the problem.

I need to take Gregg out one night… as a thank you

"Those are great concerns and ones I had myself while working on this project. So, when you activate the new chip on the computer, like we've been doing all day, those employee's keycards are automatically deactivated. So, there is no risk there—they're just inert plastic cards now. The ID issue is relevant, but I spoke with Dean, and when someone needs a visitor patch or just uses the patch, there will be a screen down here displaying their pictures. Dean said he will be down sometime this week to install four, fifty-inch screens, all around B2 and every other level. It will make it easier to verify someone's identity, as that is a legitimate concern. There are other security problems we have thought about also, like the risk of stolen chips. That's why they are numbered, and that number is immediately linked in the employee's file, so if some go missing or someone has a chip that wasn't registered with us, it wouldn't work in here first of all, and we'd know who to blame," Gregg reports, looking confidently at Shea, and then Todd during his explanation.

"I should have known I had nothing to worry about," she says, smiling at Gregg.

"Boss, you should probably punch out early, your face is getting that scrunched up look it gets, when you get one of your bad headaches and you're miserable," Gregg says, blushing slightly.

"Yeah, I think I will. Why don't you go back to the grind, Gregg? I'm really depending on you to manage in my absence," she says, wincing as the pain in her head gets drastically worse.

"Sure thing, Shea. I'll text you later to check on you," Gregg says heading out the door.

Shea turns to Todd, offering him the best apologetic look she can muster, and tells him, "I'm so sorry, I wanted to go over some things with you, but honestly, it has all been emailed already anyway, and you were here for the meeting, so you're up to date." She takes off her glasses to rub the bridge of her nose, hoping the pain will ease.

"I'm sorry you're not feeling well, Shea. It's probably just from all the adrenaline earlier," Todd says softly, while motioning his secretary to pack it up. "I was hoping that I might also text you later to check on you, if that would be okay?" he asks, back to spinning the ring around his finger.

"Oh, well, yeah, that would be okay. My number is in my email signature, so really, you already have it anyway," she says, hoping she can leave soon and still be able to drive.

I wonder if this was triggered by getting the chip, probably not but..

"Miss Murphy, gather your things, I'll have my car take you home, and they'll get you in the morning, so you don't have to worry about your car. I'm planning to stay here in your absence, to lend a helping hand, so I won't need the car for several hours anyway," Todd offers.

"Oh, I can't. That's too much—I really can't," Shea protests, not used to anyone trying to take care of her.

"Yes, you can, and you will," Todd says softly, reaching out his hand to help her stand.

"Let me help you gather your things, and I'll walk you to the front, where the car will pick you up. You look like you are really hurting. This is the least I can do, after I caused a scene in the meeting today," he says, supporting her, he holds her close to his chest. She can feel the chuckle in his voice, as he adds, "Plus, you are a favorite investment of mine. I need to ensure you're safe."

"Okay, but just this one time," she agrees, yawning, in pain and exhausted.

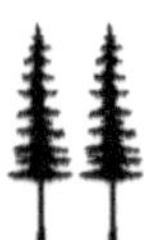

"Miss, do you need help into your home?" a voice Shea doesn't recognize asks, while gently shaking her shoulder. Her eyes flutter open, and she realizes she is in a luxury town car, which is currently parked in her driveway.

What the hell, the last thing I remember is Todd walking me out, oh no did I fall asleep on him? DID HE CARRY ME?!?!

Shea quickly tells the driver that she can, in fact, walk on her own, and makes her way to her front door. At least her headache has eased up a bit. Letting herself into the house, she doesn't even bother turning the lights on, she just heads straight to her room, puts her phone on the charger, and climbs under the covers. Within seconds, she's asleep again.

She wakes up to the sound of beeping and a glow from her phone. Groggily she rolls to the side and grabs her phone, finding several text notifications and one missed call.

Text from Gregg at 7:00 p.m.:

> Just now leaving work

> How u feeling

Text from Gregg at 10:20 p.m.:

> Heading to bed, hope all is well

Missed call from Gregg at 10:30 p.m.

Text from Todd 'Crown' at 7:30 p.m.:

> Hello Miss Murphy, I hope you're feeling better

Text from Todd 'Crown' at 9:30 p.m.:

> The car will be at your house at 7

> See you then

Ugh what time is it?

She looks at her phone's time display—3:00 a.m. is shining back at her. "Well, might as well get a few more hours," she mutters to herself, after putting her phone down and rolling back over.

Twin Pines

00009 🌲🌲 Poop & Snoop

Shea sits in the same seat, at the dining room table, watching John leave through the door that leads to the garage. She waits, listening intently for the unmistakable sound of the large two-car garage door opening and closing. As soon as the sound stops, she springs to her feet, up and racing to the bathroom. She thought she would explode if she had to sit there for one more second.

She barely makes it to the bathroom, flinging the door closed behind her and reaching the toilet just in time to make her deposit. She has every intention to snoop through the house, so she needs to be quick about this—she has no idea when he'll be back. Looking around, she sees that she, in fact, did not close the bathroom door. One of the weights she shoved under the cabinet earlier is sticking out just enough to make the door bounce back open. If he came back through that garage door right now, she might literally die.

Finishing up, she stands at the sink, washing her hands. She catches a glimpse of herself in the mirror, and grimaces, hating what she sees. Maybe a nice long braid will fix part of the problem.

I shall call this chapter of my life 'Poop & Snoop'

Twin Pines

As she giggles to herself, she goes back to the dining room table and takes a more thorough look at her backpack. Finding a hair tie almost immediately, she braids her long hair and secures it neatly. With that task out of the way, she rummages through various things that her past self so lovingly packed for her. There really isn't much—she feels like she has already seen all of this, so she packs it back in the bag. Turning the bag toward her, she now notices several zippered pockets in the front that are hidden under flaps.

That's nifty

While deciding which one to open first, Shea can feel her heart beating in her chest, pounding really. She takes deep breaths through her nose and blows them out through pursed lips. She shakes her arms to repel the energy and continues with the task at hand.

In zippered pocket number one she finds several tubes of Carmex, her favorite lip balm. Taking one out and using it, she already feels more like herself.

In zippered pocket number two she finds a couple of Life Straws.

I guess I thought I'd be drinking from puddles

In zippered pocket number three...she freezes as she looks down at her hand. In it is a handgun of some kind, marked with Security-9 on the slide. She slowly and carefully slides it back where it came from, feeling two small boxes beneath it. She assumes they contain ammunition.

Did I think I was going to be drinking out of puddles while working for the CIA?

In zippered pocket number four, she pulls out three envelopes. Opening the heaviest one first, her crucifix and chain slide out onto her awaiting hand. Setting the envelope down and covering her mouth, she lets the tears flow. Shea loves Jesus more than anything, but that chain and crucifix were a gift from her mother for her sixteenth birthday—something she could never replace. She holds the chain out in front of her to make sure the crucifix is facing the right way and then works the clasp to secure it around her neck. Already, she is reaching up to hold it.

After giving herself a moment to cry, she wipes her eyes and opens envelope number two, which feels thicker than the other one remaining, so why not? Pulling out the contents she realizes it's all the pictures she had of her family—folded and a little worse for wear, but she has them.

I swear, past me is trying to kill me-me

Her eyes are leaking again but she places the pictures back in the envelope, tucking them in the zipper pocket for safekeeping. The last envelope she has in front of her she opens and pulls out a sheet of yellow legal paper. Opening the paper, her eyes catch the neat handwriting within. It's a note from her past self—another attempt to help her out, she assumes.

Shea,

Remember when Dad took you to get your wisdom teeth out, and you reacted so badly to the anesthesia that you lost a whole week of your life? And you never got it back? We assume this is kind of like that, though I have no idea what the state of your memory is, or your functioning, really. I guess you're awake if you're reading this. So, we think you might be able to remember.

John and I have strategically placed 'reminders' for you, in an attempt to be as gentle as possible in assisting you in regaining memories. Have patience. Do everything he tells you and for the love of God, Shea, keep your head on a swivel. Be patient, if you've lost your memories, we can't just tell you everything. Something about not creating false memories.

Good luck. You can do this.

Shea 00015

P.S. Don't ask about his wife. She's gone

P.P.S. There are pain meds in a tampon, DO NOT GO HAM!

Reading the letter several times, Shea nods to herself, then puts the letter back in its envelope. Adding it to the pocket holding the pictures, then zips the pocket shut.

There's only one more zipper pocket left, and with little ceremony, Shea opens it and pulls out it's contents. In it is her old iPod and a set of ear buds. Putting only one of the buds in, she turns on the iPod and presses the shuffle button.

First up on her playlist is: *"Black" by Pearl Jam*. Tucking the iPod in her hoodie pocket, she grabs the trash she pulled out of her backpack, and limps slowly to the kitchen to throw it away. She walks back and looks for the tampon, finding it, she takes only one tablet of the Percocet 10/325. Sliding the slender bottle back into the tampon and placing the tampon in her bag.

Remembering she drank all her coffee, she looks in the fridge for a beverage. Finding a Sprite, one of her favorites, she pops the can open and takes the tablet.

Then, realizing John had already been gone for at least ten minutes, she gathers herself and heads down the hallway she came from this morning. Moving as fast as her aching body will allow she begins looking for a master suite. The guest bedroom and bathroom she knows, and there's only one other door in this hall.

She approaches the door and tries the handle. It opens, to her surprise, and she steps into the room. She knows he probably has cameras on the inside of the house, too, but she doesn't really care. She needs something—anything—to help her. She knows the letter said that they were already trying to help her, but it was with kid gloves. She can handle something real.

Looking around, she sees the room is nearly bare. The bed is huge, its comforter and sheets are done in shades of turquoise and teal— her favorites.

It matches his eyes…

In the nightstand drawers, she finds several different 'GO' phones and a pocketknife.

This is the kind of knife I can put in my pants…

She picks up the knife and opens the blade, noticing it's engraved with something she can't quite make out. All she can read is the word 'wife'. She doesn't know what else it says, but thinking it's from his dead wife, she decides it's better not to take it. Moving to the dresser, she opens one drawer after another, all empty. Walk-in closet, empty. She's about to leave when she sees a photograph on the wall, hidden behind where the door has opened.

♫Black♫ plays in her ear

Getting a better look at the picture, she sees a cute blond-haired little boy hugging the neck of a beautiful juvenile Rottweiler. They both look so happy, out in nature surrounded by trees. She wonders if this is

John's son, or nephew. For the first time, she starts to think about what John might have had to give up just to help her, and she feels incredibly guilty being in his room. The longer she looks at the picture, the more homesick she feels.

Walking back to the dining room table, she sits, waiting, drinking her Sprite. She hears the next song start up, *"Chicken Head" by Project Pat*. She starts rapping along, when she hears the garage door shut. A few seconds later John walks through the garage door, carrying a ton of Chinese takeout containers, giving Shea a look that says, "I'm glad you're still here."

"What? You sharing all that food?" she asks.

"*Project Pat*, was it?" he asks, walking over, with a small smile.

"How did you know?" she asks, surprised. She didn't think she had the music that loud.

"There is a specific way you move your head while rapping along."

"Are you calling me a chicken head?" she asks, feigning disbelief. But deep down, thinking he must have been her friend, he knows so much about her, even her playlist habits.

"I wouldn't dare, I know how seriously you take the playlists," he says, plopping all the delicious-smelling Chinese food onto the table in front of her. "Do not eat out of the carton. I'm going to grab plates and forks real quick, you can wait two seconds."

"I dunnooooooo, I'm reallllyyyyyy starving. I might die," she says, sliding low in her seat.

He hustles and is back over to her before she can even sit up in her chair properly, "Impressive, sir."

"Why thank you. Now let's eat. We need to get on the road within the hour."

The road?

00010 Rejected

BEFORE

■ ■ □ □ □ □ □ □

Sure enough, there it is—the town car, as promised by Mr. Donoghue, and right on time.

When Shea got up this morning, she felt back to her normal self. She showered and got ready for work as usual, but she might have spent a little more time perfecting her hair, and she had applied maybe a little extra highlighter—just at the end of her nose. She also made sure to text both Gregg and Todd—letting them know she had come home and gone straight to bed, thanking them for their concern. Her Band-Aid had fallen off in the shower, and now, looking at her left hand, all she could see was a tiny red dot, where the needle pierced her flesh—almost like nothing ever happened.

Man, that's cool

She's securing the lid on her coffee cup—and as always—making sure she has everything she needs, when there is a knock at the door. Looking out of the front window, she sees that the driver of the town car is standing next to the car's back door, so who could be knocking? Shea grabs her things—as she was planning to walk out the door anyway—and walks toward the door. She opens it wide, absolutely not expecting what she sees on the other side.

Todd stands there in a freshly tailored suit, a tie with hints of lavender, fidgeting with his ring as always. Next to him, Gregg is in a pair of nice slacks and a teal-colored polo shirt, his hair slicked back, his face is pinched as his eyes roam over Shea.

"Okay, you have to tell me how this happened," Shea says, smiling at both men from her entryway.

"I was about to leave with the car from the office, and Gregg was already there, working away. He seemed so concerned about your safety that I couldn't just leave him there. So, he came along to get you," Todd explains with a half-smile, glancing over at Gregg as he spoke.

"I'm sorry Shea, it's just… you were in so much pain yesterday, and I never heard back from you, so I was worried," Gregg says, the usual flush missing from his face.

"Don't apologize. That's very sweet—of both of you—to come pick me up this morning. Are we ready to get going?" she asks, looking between these two men in front of her—both attractive in their own way, both being incredibly sweet to her. She also notices, maybe for the first time, that Gregg and Todd are about the same height—very tall, at least a foot taller than her five-foot-three frame. She must not have paid much attention. Todd always seemed imposing, just with his mannerisms and personality. But Gregg, she thought, was maybe always hunched over a little bit or something.

"Yes Miss Murphy," Todd says, as he turns sideways and raises his arm toward the car at the end of her driveway. At the same time, Gregg offers her his hand, to help her down her front steps.

"Well, a girl could get used to this. Keep it up boys, you'll spoil me rotten," Shea says, smiling at both of the gentlemen.

Gregg holds her hand, stepping when she steps, guiding her down the stairs. Todd remains on the top step, standing there with his arm in the air, kind of awkward. Shea notices Gregg watching her feet as she floats down the stairs. When she's back on solid ground, she catches Todd staring at Gregg. She can't read Todd's expression, but she does notice Gregg's body language change—his silhouette becoming more hunched in on himself.

"Thank you so much, Gregg. You're such a gentleman," she says, turning to him and winking as he releases her hand, placing his own in his pocket as he walks next to her.

"Miss Murphy, if it's okay with you, I'd like to ask Gregg to ride up front with the driver so that you and I can discuss some things, privately," he says, looking down at her and messing with his ring again.

"If that's okay with him. If you are around today, we could always talk in my office later, and please, just Shea," she answers, not wanting to make Gregg uncomfortable, but thinking some time alone with Todd might give her a chance to figure him out.

Oh, shit—I forgot, he carried me

"I'm fine, thanks, Shea," Gregg says, climbing into the front seat.

"After you," Todd says, as they arrive at the driver holding the door for them.

"Actually, I don't mean to be a pain, but this skirt cannot 'slide over'," she says, looking down at the tight black pencil skirt made from tweed, or is it wool, either way.

Todd's eyes light up with amusement. "Have I told you how funny you are sometimes, Shea?" He walks to the open door and steps in, awkwardly sliding over with his long legs filling the cabin.

"I wasn't kidding, this thing will get all wrapped around me and I'll be stuck in it," she says, ducking into the car and sitting next to Todd. She reaches over her shoulder for her seat belt and hears Gregg softly laughing in the front seat.

As soon as the driver enters the vehicle, Todd asks, "You know where we're going, correct?" Leaning slightly forward toward the driver.

"Yes, Sir, Mr. Donoghue, we will be there momentarily," the driver responds as he looks in the rear-view mirror at Todd.

"Great, thank you," Todd responds, pressing the button to put up the privacy partition. He turns his body in his seat slightly toward Shea, and looking at her, says, "Now, Shea, how are you? I'm hoping you're feeling better, you certainly look it."

Shea feels a slight flush creep into her cheeks and ears, and for a moment, feels guilty for teasing Gregg all the time. "Thank you so much for your help yesterday, Todd. I don't know what came over me, but I appreciate that you were there to rescue me. I am feeling much better today, though." She takes a breath and holds her crucifix before continuing, "I am feeling a bit embarrassed though." She looks down at her lap, where her purse sits.

Before she can continue, he reaches over, barely touching her chin, he turns her head toward him. He looks into her eyes, and says, "There is nothing to be embarrassed about, Shea. I am glad I could be your knight in shining armor."

"I just, I know I'm not the lightest person, and I know you somehow got me into the car and sent me home. And well, thank you. But I won't make a habit of it," she says, trying to hold his gaze and not look away. She takes a sip of her coffee trying to quell the rising embarrassment.

"Shea, you are as light as a feather, and it was no trouble at all. I called Gregg for assistance with doors, and we got you in the car with no issue," Todd says reassuringly.

"Gosh, you guys really are my heroes," she says, thankful for the company she keeps. "You must be pretty strong then, huh?"

"Oh, yes. I make sure I keep my body in peak condition at all times, never know when you'll need to call on your strength," he says. "Have you not noticed?" he asks, while spinning his ring on his finger.

"Well Todd, it's really hard to 'check someone out' when they're always wearing a suit jacket," Shea says honestly. Not that she hasn't tried.

"Ah I see," he says, chuckling. "Well, I'll have to show off my gray button-down today then, huh? I took my coat off yesterday, when I jumped in to help, but you were already gone, so you missed it," he says, definitely flirting today.

Shea feels the need to change the subject, she has no idea what is going on today. Maybe she has some extra pheromones or something, but she's been single for way too long. She has no idea how to really flirt with this guy.

So, instead, she says, "Oh, why did Gregg have to help you out of the building? Have you not gotten your chip yet?"

Shea can see she catches him off guard, and he looks down at his left hand, "As much as I love investing into these things and furthering the science, I prefer my privacy. Besides, when I go back home, I won't have any use for it, so I find it wasteful."

Should I be worried about my privacy? Come to think of it I only felt bad after I got the chip yesterday...

"Oh, that makes sense, so when are you going back home?" she asks, hoping she doesn't sound like she is tired of having him around.

"So quick to be rid of me, Shea?" he says, smirking. "I figured I would stay to help out through the transition, but something recently came up. I'm pursuing an acquisition, so whenever that works out, I'll be out of your hair."

"An acquisition, huh?" Shea says, stomach tightening, suddenly feeling like she's in the lion's den. "Well, we're glad to have you, honestly."

The car pulls in front of their building and Gregg steps out, squinting in the sun. He feels so awkward. Should he wait here for them or leave them to it? He decides to stay, looking at his reflection in his door's window, he checks his hair and then smooths his shirt for any wrinkles. Feeling like he is looking at least better than usual, he backs up and puts his hand on the door handle to help Shea out.

Pulling open her door, he notices Shea has a slight flush to her face. In that moment, Gregg's fantasy of him and Shea ending up together dissolves. He offers his hand anyway and she accepts it, stepping out into the sun, a smile directed at him.

Shea holds Gregg's hand a second longer than necessary, squeezing it once before letting go. Walking alongside him, she leans over and bumps her shoulder against his… well elbow, let's be real. He looks over at her and she is beaming up at him.

"Hey, I love your shirt. This might sound weird, but you are really valuable to me, and I appreciate you. Not only as a coworker but as a friend. If you're up for it, I'd like to take you out to dinner tonight, just as a thank you. If you can't tonight, we can make it another night," she rambles out at him.

Gregg acknowledges her question with an index finger in the air—the universal sign for "hold on a second." Gregg waves his hand in front of the card reader, opening and holding the door for Shea and Todd, then enters the building himself. The last thing he wants to do is turn her down, but it wouldn't be fair to Lydia. And if he were single, it would probably never turn into a real date anyway. He likes Lydia—she's really smart and loves his rats, but Shea is just his dream girl. He'll have to decline; better just keep her in his dreams.

Gregg hears Shea say, "Aw Dean, you have to show me pictures! Aw, what a sweet angel, looks just like his daddy." He sees her look around and when her eyes land on him she gives him a playful, "well, come on" face. He passes Todd to catch up to her, continuing to open doors for her on the way to B2.

After a while, she looks over at him, and in a firm, but slightly hurt-sounding voice says, "Hey, I guess you won't be able to join me tonight. If you'd like to go another night let me know." Too frustrated at himself to say anything, he just walks to his desk.

Todd follows her into the office, a bit presumptuous, but Shea doesn't mind. He sits in one of her visitor chairs, but then immediately stands, looking at her with a smirk. She is just... standing there with her bum on her desk watching him. She can't help it—he moves so gracefully. Holding her gaze, he slowly unbuttons his suit jacket, slipping it off, he folds it neatly in half and lays it over the back of the chair. All the while, she is noting every bulge of muscle through his arms and back. This man isn't ready just for anything—he is ready for everything.

Todd chuckles, "Like what you see, Shea?" he asks, while sinking into the chair, eyes still on Shea, keeping her firmly in place.

"I'm so sorry," she says, shaking her head in an attempt to clear the thoughts that were now flooding it. She walks around to her chair, behind her desk, and opens the agenda on her desktop.

"Shea," he begins, leaning forward slightly, "I was wondering if you would be okay with me maybe texting you, in a friendly way? If not, don't worry about it. I just figured I'd shoot my shot, before you end up falling for someone else," he says, pulling and pushing his ring off and on his finger.

"Yeah, that would be fine, Todd." She smiles at him, slightly distracted, and then continues to look at the agenda in front of her.

Her phone dings as she is investigating what time the nurses will be in today. Digging her phone out of her purse she unlocks it and goes to her notifications.

Text from Todd 'Crown' at 7:32 a.m.:

> You look very beautiful today

> Are you free for dinner any night this week

She looks up from her phone and chuckles, glancing up at Todd. "Yes. I'm free every night this week."

"Okay then, perfect, I'll pick you up at your house tonight at eight, does that work?" he asks, his hands are lower than her desk so she can't see if he is fidgeting with his ring, but she assumes he is.

"Yeah, that sounds great, thanks Todd." She looks over to Gregg's area and sees him looking in her direction with an unreadable expression on his face.

What is going on today?

"Todd, feel free to use my office as your own. I need to do a lap and see what we have in store for today," she says, locking her desktop and bringing up a generic one. Not that he doesn't know everything that is on there anyway, but at this rate, he'll be adding himself to her planner before she returns.

"Thank you, Shea. I do need to make a bunch of calls, actually. Could you close the door on your way out?" he asks, standing.

"Oh, sure. I'll be back," she says, smiling up at him.

As she makes her way past him, he reaches out and brushes a stray wave out of her face. It feels intimate to Shea, and she starts to blush again.

This guy is awfully presumptuous. . .

She quickly exits her office before anything can be said or done further. She walks straight to Gregg—because if she is honest, she doesn't do a lap, ever. She just talks to Gregg about what is going on. As she approaches his desk, Gregg starts straightening things on his workstation.

"Hey Gregg, long time no see," she says, watching his rats run around in their enclosures.

"Yeah, no kidding. What can I do for you?" he asks.

"Is everything okay, Gregg? Did I do something to offend you?" she asks sincerely.

Gregg takes a deep breath and looks down at Shea. "No, you haven't done anything at all. I'm just trying to get moving—the nurses will be here soon, and I still need to set up all the supplies. Look, about dinner… I already have plans with Lydia, is all. I also don't want her to think anything is going on."

"Gregg!" she squeals. A huge smile spreading across her face, when she says, "I'm so happy for the two of you! I totally get it, I would hate to ruin anything you have going on."

"Thanks, Shea. Sorry I didn't say so earlier, I just didn't know how to explain it, is all," he says, cheeks slightly pink as he looks away.

"Oh okay. I totally understand. Do you need any help from me today?" she asks, sticking her pointer finger in Templeton's cage.

"Uh, I don't know yet, but I can let you know when I know," he answers.

"Perfect," she says, walking back toward her office.

Aw crap, I don't have a secretary

Shea decides to walk down to the secretary's office, after noticing the door is slightly ajar. When she gets to the door, she hears whale sounds coming from inside, and the lights are all off. Pushing open the door, she sees a small blonde woman, sitting cross-legged in the middle of the floor. She isn't meditating, she has a laptop in front of her and she is hunched over it typing quickly.

"Oh. Hey, Tina. What are you doing in here?" she asks at a half-whisper in an attempt not to startle the small woman.

"Miss Shea, hey. Mr. T saw that you were in a bind and wanted me to fill in for as long as you need. So, you were never without a secretary. Pretty thoughtful if you ask me," she says, still hunched over, with just her head lifted toward Shea.

"Oh, that's awesome, I really appreciate it, Tina" she says.

"No problem. I like a change of scenery every once in a while, anyway," Tina says smiling, continuing to work on her laptop.

Shea nods and turns on her heel, putting the door back the way she found it. Arriving back at her office, she sees that the door is still closed. She doesn't want to be rude, but all of her things are in there, including her coffee. Her phone dings as she stands there indecisively and she pulls it out of her cardigan.

Text from Todd 'Crown' at 8:12 a.m.:

> > **You can come back in when you're ready**
> > **I'm too lazy to get up and open the door**

Shea chuckles and opens the door to find Todd sitting behind her desk with his shirt sleeves rolled up, talking on the phone.

"…yeah, that'll be fine. Tell Marcus I'll be back when I'm back. I'm working on a couple of acquisitions here. After that the plan is to leave," he says into the phone while looking at Shea. Hanging up, he stands and offers Shea her chair with a smooth, practiced motion, before settling back on the visitor's side of the desk.

"Thanks for Tina. I really appreciate that," she says, getting settled in her own chair.

"Oh yeah, no problem. I have to make sure you're taken care of," he says, leaning back casually in the chair. His tone hinting at something.

He spends most of the day there, in that chair, only leaving to buy them lunch in the café and then returning. Shea feels uncertain about Todd. He seems to be charming enough, and undeniably handsome, but there is something about him that feels a little controlling. She just can't quite get her finger on it. She'll just have to wait and see how dinner goes.

OOOll ⫘ So, Hell then?

John hands Shea a fork, a napkin and a plate. She snatches them from him greedily, it feels like she's been starved, and she loves Chinese food. John starts opening some of the cartons, setting certain ones in front of her and other ones in front of himself. Shea sits a little taller in her chair to lean over and peek into her cartons. Inside are her favorites: General Tso's chicken, house Lo Mein, crab Rangoon and sweet and sour dipping sauce.

Curious, she asks, "What you got over on your side?"

John smiles and tips his cartons toward her so that she can see inside them. Shea sees that he has sweet and sour chicken, house fried rice and Rangoon, as well. Inspecting him from across the table, she watches him take his seat, then asks, "How did you know these were all my favorites?" Opposing feelings of unease and familiarity pulling her in differing directions.

John looks up from his task of emptying the carton of rice onto his plate and says in a way that sounds genuine to Shea, "I keep telling you, we're really good friends."

"I know. I know. I'm just trying to wrap my head around the idea that a man I feel like I've never met before, knows me better than anyone I've ever met before," her voice cracking slightly under the admission.

John's expression softens, leaning back in his chair, he offers her reassurance, "It's not gonna happen overnight, Shea. You've only been awake for a few hours. Give yourself some time. What happened to you was traumatic. I don't have any expectations about you regaining memories in the first place. So, if you're starting to remember some things, then that's great, but it's not gonna happen quickly. Try not to rush it."

She looks at him as while mixing her General Tso's chicken in with her Lo Mein, ensuring she incorporates it all for the perfect bite. When she finishes chewing and swallowing, she asks, "So, you do know what happened to me?"

John's gaze sharpens briefly, as if he really wants to tell her what happened—but for some reason he can't.

"Why are you keeping this from me, if you know what happened?" she presses.

John exhales, meeting her eyes, he says, "It's not that I don't want to tell you, Shea. It's just that I don't know everything. The bit I do know, you asked me not to tell you. There's a lot going on, and you knowing more of it, or me telling you more of it, won't necessarily help you remember. All it will do is make you think I'm making up a story to get you to go along with what I want you to do," with conviction and confidence.

"I really have no reason to trust you… other than so far you have proven to be a gentleman, and kind, and past me seems to think that my life is safe in your hands," she says, while twirling the noodles around her fork. "I just want to know what happened to me." Her voice falters, but she steels herself. "The last thing I really remember is working on Project S & V and getting my chip implanted, which someone has obviously removed. I don't remember anyone there though. It's like everything is behind a smoke screen."

"Well, at least we know where you are as far as what you remember. If you start to remember anything else you need to let me know, okay?" John says to her, his tone is a little firmer.

She is now dipping her Rangoon into sweet and sour sauce, leaning over her plate to eat them so she doesn't drip sauce all over her hoodie. Deep down, she knows John knows more than he's telling her. He knows at least some of what happened to her, and wonders if he knows the whole story and he's just not telling her. She feels angry at him for keeping this information from her, but she also needs him because she has no idea what happened over the last... "Okay, you know where my memory ends, but I don't know how long ago that was. How much do I have to remember after that?"

John looks at her, brow furrowed, and head tilted, his expression softening with sympathy. "It's been almost exactly a year since then, Shea."

She sits silent and motionless for a moment, not even eating her food.

What did I get myself into?

She looks to John with new resolve. "A whole year of my life is gone, and you can't even give me the highlights? You not telling me anything doesn't make me trust you. It feels all too convenient that you're the key to my survival. I'm going to work as hard as I can to remember everything."

"That's what I want to happen, Shea. I want you to remember the last year of your life. I want you to remember all the things that we've gone through, and what you've had to endure," he says it like he means it, and it makes Shea stop her little interrogation.

As she continues eating her Chinese food in silence, her mind races, trying to summon the last thing she can remember. "Wait, here's something I remember—looking at a fancy chandelier that looked like Saturn. But I don't remember where I was or who I was with," she says, looking at John expectantly.

"Okay, at least we're getting somewhere."

Shea looks at him and believes that he wants her to remember, so she is going to try everything in her power to do that. As they both finish their meals, John begins to clear the table and gather the garbage. Shea gets out of her seat and grabs the rest of the garbage from the table, and helps him take it all to the kitchen.

"Thanks, Shea. Why don't you go ahead and make sure you've got everything in that backpack. Then put it by the door to the garage."

"Sure, no problem," she replies, walking over to where her backpack rests, next to the dining room table. She picks it up and brings it over to the garage door. "Where are we going? If I may ask?"

"What, you don't wanna make sure you didn't leave anything in the bedroom or bathroom? Once we leave here, we won't be back. We're heading to the airport. I'll tell you more in the car," he calls to her from the kitchen, his butt resting on the kitchen counter, his hands braced on either side.

"Yeah, I went through it earlier, so I'm pretty sure I'm all set. But there is one thing," she says, walking into the kitchen, she bumps him playfully out of her way with her hip.

If I'm stuck with him anyway, I might as well have some fun

She opens and closes every cupboard door, searching for one thing.

He chuckles as he says, "It's in the cupboard on top of the fridge. You won't be able to reach it, and I don't have a stool. So, is there anything you'd like to ask me?"

Shea exaggerates an eye roll in his direction, then flashes him a sickening sweet smile. "Could you, big strong man, get little ol' me, a tiny defenseless woman, the whiskey from the cupboard on top of the refrigerator, please?"

Continuing to chuckle, John steps over to the fridge and opens the cupboard above it. Inside, there's not just one bottle of whiskey. Shea notices there are several—maybe four. She can't really tell because she doesn't have the best vantage point, but she hopes he pulls them all down.

"I know what you're thinking Shea," amusement in his voice. "And yes, there will be more packed but here's the open one for your backpack." He hands her the bottle of Crown Royal, there's not much missing from the bottle, so it should last her a while.

She takes the bottle from him, her fingers accidentally sliding across his hand. She immediately thinks about how soft his hands are—almost no callouses, maybe he had a white-collar job... before. She slides the bottle into an empty zippered compartment in her backpack and leaves the bag by the garage like John requested. Turning back to the dining room table, she notices that John is in his bedroom—probably grabbing that knife she saw earlier.

As he comes back down the hallway, she sees he's carrying a medium-sized black box with a lock, a passport and other paperwork. When he gets closer to her, he says, "You should have a passport in your backpack under the name Fay Lynhart. You'll probably have some other documents too, but the only thing you'll need right now is the passport."

"Yeah," she nods, "I did see one in there with that name but my picture, you want me to grab it?"

"Yeah, I've got a couple of things for you. I'm gonna grab them from my safe while you do that," he says, as he walks toward the master suite, stopping to set his documents on the kitchen counter on his way there.

Safe? I didn't see a safe...

She pulls the passport from her bag and walks back over to the dining room table, sitting down to wait. A moment later, John walks out carrying a purse. She recognizes it as the last purse she was carrying... before. Bringing it over, he sets the purse in front of Shea, then sits down across from her.

"Past you packed this for you, I'm sure she put things in there that she felt you were going to need. Go ahead and go through it, then add the passport to the purse. I'm gonna lock your firearm in this TSA-approved lockbox, then load the bags in the car. I'll leave the placement of the key to you."

Shea snatches the purse and pulls it closer to herself. It's a regular, brown leather, messenger style bag, that has some dark spots from wear and tear. One of those spots is from when she got Carmex all over her finger and wiped it on her bag, a decision she regretted soon after.

Slipping her hand inside the bag, she rummages around. Her fingers first land on a small bottle of hand sanitizer. Pulling it out she sets it to the side, the label says the scent is eucalyptus. Next, she feels a small makeup bag, that she pulls out and opens. It contains what it always has, tampons, hair ties, emergency mascara, a small mirror, and a mini brush.

Continuing her search, her hand brushes against her wallet. She pulls it out quickly and opens it. Hundreds of dollars are tucked inside, along with a debit card and a photo ID, bearing the same name as her passport. She studies the ID closely; it's a recent photo, not like the one on her old ID, which still sported the photo she took for her learners permit. The old ID, the one she always renewed online, had been replaced with a much more polished version.

Gone are her insurance cards, Costco membership card and the old student ID—that she always carried just because. Placing the wallet to the side, she does one more sweep with her hand to see if she missed anything, maybe another note from her past self? But no, nothing else.

Turning the bag around she opens the zipper on the front and pulls out a tube of Carmex and a pair of Costas sunglasses. Looking at the sunglasses, she has a sudden realization. She reaches up, touching the skin around her eyes, then sits back. Looking around the room, her vision is clear, sharp even—like it is when wearing her glasses.

"John!" she calls from her seat. "Hey John!" she says, a little louder this time.

He bursts through the garage access door, eyes franticly scanning the house, his hand instinctively atop a firearm that's holstered at his side.

Concern etches his face as his eyes rove over her. "What is it? Is everything okay?"

"Yeah, I'm fine. I just realized I'm not wearing my glasses, and I feel like I can see pretty damn well," she says, looking to him for answers.

"Ohh, yeah," he says chuckling, "I'm surprised you just now realized. It was part of a program you were in. Glasses were kind of a liability, so they paid to have your eyes fixed."

"What?!" Shea exclaims, her eyes wide with surprise. "That's awesome! It must have been a really cool project, and I got my eyes fixed on top of it?" she asks, looking up at him from her seat.

John nods, as a sad smile turns into a real one. "Yeah, it was a really cool project, and now you don't need glasses."

She looks at him, an apology written on her face. "I'm sorry for making you worry and interrupting you. I just had no idea."

"Oh, no problem. I'm just glad you're okay. Are you about finished going through everything? We need to leave soon."

"Yeah, I was just wondering if I could have a phone?" she asks, shoving all her items back into her purse.

"I'm sorry, Shea," John says, shaking his head. "I won't even be taking a phone with me. But we did make sure to load all of your favorite playlists onto your iPod. I'm sorry, we just can't have any contact with anyone once we leave this house. We have to be very careful. Don't worry—if there's an emergency, we do have a satellite phone. But the less we use it, the better."

Shea nods, her voice resigned. "Okay, at least I have my music. It's not like I have anybody that I could call anyway," she says, pulling her iPod from her hoodie pocked and slipping it into the purse.

"Are you all done with your backpack?" John asks, from the doorway to the garage.

"Yeah, thanks," she replies, picking up her purse and slinging the strap over her neck to wear it cross-body. She starts to walk to the garage also, but pauses, glancing back at the kitchen counter. Sure enough, John's passport and paperwork are still sitting there. Grabbing them, she takes a peek inside his passport, she's stunned to see that the name listed is *John M. Doe.* She can't help but laugh, slipping the other paperwork—maps, codes and airline ticket information—inside the front cover.

Carrying the stack of papers, she heads toward the garage. As she steps out, she sees that John has already loaded all the bags in the trunk of a Mini Cooper. He has also placed an unopened Sprite in the cup holder, on the passenger side. He is currently leaning over the engine, checking the vehicle's fluids.

"Hey, John, you left these inside. I thought you might want them. Are we leaving nowish?" she asks, walking around the car.

Looking up at her, he grins and closes the hood. "Well, we wouldn't get far without those, now, would we?" he says, taking the documents from her. "Yeah, if you're ready, I'm going to do one final sweep of the house. I'll be right back."

It suddenly hits Shea that the garage is about a million degrees, and she's in a hoodie, thick socks and snow boots.

John jogs back into the garage and closes the access door. Sliding into the driver's seat, Shea watches him look her up in down. She removed her hoodie while he was inside and is now wearing a tight, black spaghetti strap shirt over her hot pink bra.

She continues to feel his eyes on her, so she glances at him, and says, "What? It's hot as shit in here. Get some A/C going. Are we still in Ohio?"

John chuckles, turning the key in the ignition. "No, we're not. Yes, it is quite hot. Shea packed for where we're going, not where we are."

"Oh, okay. So, Hell then?" she asks, messing with the vents, trying to get some of the hot ass air that is now pumping into the car to blow on her face.

He laughs. "No, but close. Hell adjacent. We're in Florida," he says, opening the garage door and pulling out onto the street. He sets the

GPS for the airport, and off they go. As soon as the garage opens, Shea is hit with a huge culture shock that leaves her speechless. They're near the ocean, surrounded by palm trees. Shea also notices John's vigilance in keeping his head on a swivel, as if always scanning for threats.

And my retinas are burning...

Shea grabs the sunglasses that were packed for her, and she can now see exactly why she would need them. She continues to take in the scenery, looking around at the marinas and the different vibrant flowers. All the while holding her crucifix tightly in her hand.

"Are you nervous?" John asks, glancing at her for a second, before focusing back to the road.

"Well, yeah. I mean, I've never been to Florida. Well, I have, but I don't remember any of it. And now, before I can even set foot on the sand, I'm gone like a fart in the wind to God knows where. Oh, also, bad guys are probably after us."

"Didn't you look at the paperwork?" he asks, his eyebrows pulled up high in surprise. His eyes suddenly darting to the rearview mirror and back to the road several times.

"Well, yeah. I saw the stuff about Alaska, but I didn't know if that was where we're headed right now," she says. In an attempt to calm the anxious energy in the car, she asks, "Oh, by the way, what does the M stand for in John M. Doe?"

"It is where we are going right now, once we get to the airport we'll be on our way. Hence the thick socks," he says smiling. "And it's 'Motha' Fuckin'...John Motha' Fuckin' Doe."

Twin Pines

00012 ⫲ Silk & Velvet

Shea drives her Jeep home, and parks in the garage.

Getting into the house, she turns all her lights on and tosses her keys into her dish. She only has about an hour, and she's determined to start getting ready right away. She chooses a low-cut red dress, although red is not her favorite color, it does make her skin look ethereal. The dress is made of a silky material that slides against her skin. It falls to her mid-calf on one side and her knee on the other. She re-wets her waves and controls them with several hundred bobby pins into a nineties-style up do.

While she's slipping on her red silk wedges with red silk laces that wind up her calf, she hears a car stop at her driveway. For the second time today, she is picked up by a town car.

I thought he said he was picking me up?

Carrying a small black clutch instead of her usual handbag, she walks out the door and down the driveway. A different driver than this morning stands outside the rear passenger car door. Shea smiles and thanks him, looking into the cabin of the car.

"I'm sorry, do you happen to know where my date is?" she asks the driver, who's still standing in the open doorway.

"Yes, Miss Murphy. His hotel is closer to the final destination, so he thought it prudent to arrive at your house first. We will then pick him up, and then head to the final destination," he says, not moving an inch from his position at the door.

"Oh, okay, sounds great. Thank you," she says, and drops herself smoothly into the seat.

Let's not have any free shows tonight, girl

As the car drive further into the city, lights begin to illuminate from everywhere at once, tall buildings, hole-in-the-the wall bars, and even what looks like a carnival in the distance. After a while, the car pulls up to a huge hotel with a luxury fountain out front and its own impressive lights. Looking around in awe, Shea notices a man walking toward the car. He's dressed in gray dress slacks and a tight, short-sleeved, black t-shirt. He opens the car door and slides in next to her.

She knows she saw his figure earlier, but this is something else—the way his shirt sleeves are perfectly rolled up to the middle of his biceps, the black Ferragamo loafers, and the Versace black-and gold-watch on his wrist. The man has style and he's dripping with sex appeal.

Before she can complement him, he says, "Wow, Shea, you look absolutely ravishing, good enough to eat."

"I could say the same about you Todd. You look very handsome. Good for eating, also," she says, then shakes her head.

Get it together. He just makes me so nervous

He chuckles and says, "Stay just the way you are, Shea. You're one of a kind."

Shea knows that at this point her face probably matches her dress, so she just looks out the window to compose herself.

"Where are we going tonight?" Shea asks, after the butterflies in her stomach calm a little.

"There's this great fine dining place, but it's like a hole-in-the-wall, not many people know about it. It's called, 'Nouvelle Amour.' I've been there a couple of times with my business partner, and their food is amazing. It's not all French like you might think, they have a ton of different choices."

"Nouvelle Amour? What does that mean?" she tries to pronounce it as smoothly as he had.

"It means 'New Love,'" he says, holding his hands in his lap.

Presumptuous?

"Oh, that's cool. Thanks for taking me out tonight," she says, looking at him through her lashes and smiling.

"Thanks for accepting. Can you do me a favor and I'll do you the same?" he asks.

"I want to know what it is before I agree," she says, reaching her right hand up to pull her crucifix into her fist.

"Alright, can we just try to relax and be less nervous around each other? I know I'm struggling because I just keep thinking I want to be closer to you. But I'm going to try. Can you do the same?" he asks, his body shifting toward her.

"Yes, I'm sorry. I just haven't been on a date in a long time. I'll try to relax," she responds, hoping she can keep to her word though still keeping her guard up.

The car pulls in front of the restaurant, and Todd's right— it's a hole-in-the-wall. From the outside, it looks like you could go in there to buy bags of ice. As they exit the town car, Todd walks around to Shea's side and offers her his hand. Grasping her clutch in one hand she (as) gracefully (as possible) plants her heeled feet on the pavement and uses the help of Todd to stand. He smiles at her and retains her hand as they walk toward the building.

Once inside, it's like stepping into another world. The room is spacious, with booths lining the walls—no tables of chairs in sight. Each booth has its own walls and even an archway over the heads of the patrons, so it is very private. They are more like personal cubbies than booths. The lighting is soft, but there is a huge chandelier in the middle of the ceiling that reminds Shea of Saturn, in a sparkling, crystal light fixture, kind of way.

They are seated at a booth on the outer edges of the dining room floor. Todd relinquishes her hand so she can sit first. Shea notices this booth is unlike any she's ever seen at a chain restaurant. It's a semi-circle with only the opening cut out, with the table in the middle. As Shea gets in and slides in a bit, Todd gets in on the opposite side but slides all the way to the back, only a foot or so from Shea. The bench is covered in a luxuriously soft velvet, the color of red so dark it's almost black, and Shea is petting it like a dog.

"Like the fabric?" Todd asks, with a smirk.

Shea immediately stops petting the seat between them, realizing she must look like an absolute weirdo, and stops her hand from then reaching up to her necklace. "Uh, yes. It's very soft."

"Don't stop on my account," he says, leaning into the space between them, with his hands on the table, folded together.

"I've just never felt velvet this soft," she says, also leaning slightly into the space between them, but her hands are now resting on her lap.

A server appears in the small gap that is the entrance to the cubby, holding two paper menus. Handing one to both Todd and Shea, he smiles and asks what he can get them to drink, and if they would like to hear today's specials. Todd leans forward a bit, ordering a bottle of Château Lafite Rothschild 2009, an appetizer of calamari, and to speak with Adeline. He hands the menus back to the waiter.

Are we not eating?

"Yes, sir. Right away," the waiter responds before he leaves to fulfill Todd's orders.

Shea looks to Todd and asks, "What if I don't like stupid expensive wine or squid?"

Leaning even closer to her, he says, "You seem like the kind of woman who has never truly been wined and dined. That's all I'm trying to do. Should I have not?" he asks, so close now that she can smell whatever cologne he is wearing, and it's delicious. She has no idea what it is, but she imagines it's a blend of melted gold and the essence of Jeffrey Dean Morgan, or something.

"Actually, I love calamari and ridiculously expensive red wine," she takes a breath, hesitating for a moment. Unsure if she should be offended by his comment or not, she decides to take the honesty route, saying, "And no, I've never really had someone take me to a place like this or try to impress me by asking for the Chef." Shea assumes that's who Adeline is.

The look he gives her is a mix of lust and respect, smoldering even. "Smart girl. But she's not just a Chef—she is a Michelin-star chef, and this is her restaurant."

"How do you know her?" Shea asks, curious about this man's habits.

"Well, we knew of her before this place. Crown offered to invest in a restaurant of her own, we dabble in lots of things, this is another one of my favorites," he explains, his arm now casually draped across the back of the seat, his fingers very gently stroking her shoulder.

Shea shivers violently and Todd chuckles. "Do you want me to stop?"

"No, it's nice. I like it," she says, looking into his eyes. She's telling the truth, but part of her feels like the chill wasn't entirely from pleasure.

I will not go back on my word dammit!

He continues his gentle touches and conversation when the same waiter approaches, placing a pair of burgundy-style wine glasses in front of them, then presenting the bottle of wine atop a linen cloth to Todd. Todd nods, and the waiter sets it on the table closest to himself and begins the fine art of opening the bottle. After removing the cork with practiced ease, he offers it to Todd on a small plate. Todd picks up the cork, and places it an inch away from Shea's nose. After she has had a chance to sniff it, Todd brings it to his own nose and gives a crooked smile in Shea's direction.

After Todd gives his nod of approval, the waiter carefully pours less than Shea thinks she could spit into Todd's glass for tasting. He smells the inside of the glass and swirls it before drinking it all at once. With another nod, the waiter is satisfied enough to pour the wine into their glasses. Then, he finishes by setting the bottle on the table, out of the way.

"Your calamari will be out shortly, and Addi says she will deliver it herself," the waiter informs, while making a small bowing motion.

"Thank you," Todd says, glass of wine in one hand and continuing to gently touch Shea's shoulder with the other.

"So, Shea, what do you like to do when you're not running things down on implantables?"

"Honestly, I don't really have much of a personal life. No real friends or family, no dating life—usually," she admits. " I do love cooking and I like to read until way later than I should on work nights, but otherwise I am kind of a bore," she says, looking at him. "Not like you anyway, I'm sure you have a Rolodex of friends, and a lively personal and dating life." She tries to not sound jealous.

"You, Miss Shea, are anything but boring, I promise you that. As far as my social life, I have a lot of 'friends'," he says, utilizing air quotes to accentuate his point, "but they aren't the kind of friends I could call to move a couch, you know? And, honest to God, this is the first date I've been on in over a year. I'm always super busy with work and I tend to attract a certain kind of woman that doesn't tend to suit my tastes," he says, gently examining the bobby pin creation atop her head with his fingers.

"I can imagine, your expensive tastes are pretty obvious. And don't kid yourself, you would never move a couch, even with friends," she says, giggling softly. The wine has definitely gone to her head.

"I have moved a couch before!" he says, in mock outrage.

"Knock, knock," they hear from the opening in their little cocoon. Both Todd and Shea look over like they were caught with their hands in the cookie jar, making Addi giggle. "I didn't mean to startle you, but in my defense, I have been standing here for a full minute waiting for my chance to interrupt."

Todd gives her a mega-watt smile, and says, "Addi! How have you been? Sorry about that, I was lost in this one's eyes," he says, tipping his head in Shea's direction.

"Would you stop it," Shea says, flirting. She swats her hand harmlessly against his chest, which is very muscular and unyielding.

Oh God, who am I?

Todd catches her hand and holds it in his, as smoothly as if he's done it a thousand times before.

"Okay, you two are sickeningly sweet. Cut it out for a sec while I'm here, will ya?" Addi boasts a big, beautiful, genuine smile at the two of them. "Also, Todd, I've been fantastic. This place is turning into everything I dreamt of."

"I'm really glad to hear that," he says.

"Alright, here is your appetizer," Addi says, setting the large plate of Calamari between the two of them. "I think I'd better get back to it, don't bother ordering, I'll make something special for the two of you," she says, winking, then turning and walking away.

I hope she means delicious-special... and not shit all night-special

"She seems really great," Shea says, pulling her hand from Todd's and reaching for the lemon on the plate of Calamari. Squeezing it with both hands, she moves it over the calamari in circular motions. As she places the lemon back on the plate and turns to look at Todd, he is already there, ready with a small plate to hand to her.

"Thank you, I didn't even see her put these on the table," she says, taking the plate from him. She's starving and serves herself a hefty portion. Noticing that she's the only one serving herself, she looks over at Todd who is watching her with curious eyes. "Are you going to eat some of this, or did you order it just for me?"

He smiles, "I was just enjoying watching you work. I was hoping you would be willing to serve me up a plate as well," he says as he passes her another small plate.

"Of course, I can," she says, "give me that."

She takes the plate, giving him the same amount she took for herself. Handing it to him she pulls her own plate closer to herself and begins to dig in. "This might be the best calamari I've ever had," she says in between bites.

Shea feels relieved to see that Todd is also enjoying the calamari—there's nothing like being the only one eating to make you feel like a fat girl.

As they settle into comfortable silence, eating their appetizer and sipping their wine, Shea is glad she took Todd up on his offer. This is the best date she might have had in the last four years. Trying her luck on 'Plenty of Fish' had only caught her bloated carcasses claiming to be men.

When the waiter comes and clears away the dishes, he places new silverware in front of them. The salad that is served is different from any salad she has had before, and it's delicious. Baby greens with Israeli couscous, dried cranberries, candied nuts, feta cheese, olives, carrots, cucumber and a balsamic glaze. There is some conversation between them as they eat, mostly just Todd flattering her and her thinking how unreal this all is, and if there might be a motive.

The bread course follows, and Shea thinks there must be a slice of every kind of bread on the planet in this little basket. The main course is again served by Addi and consists of sixteen-ounce cuts of Wagyu A5 steaks with red wine reduction sauce and a side of potato confit. Shea takes bite after bite of juicy steak with amazing flavors, the bath of juices on her tongue boasts an undertone of brown sugar, while the potatoes were perfectly crunchy on the outside and delicious cheesy clouds on the inside. She can see why the woman has a Michelin star.

Shea is the perfect amount of full as she walks around the restaurant, taking in the ambiance. Todd told her to go ahead while he settled the bill, one wasn't even dropped at the table. She doesn't know if that's how it's done in expensive restaurants or if it's that Addi fed them on the house. That bottle of wine cost more than a month of mortgage for Shea, so she assumed there had to be some kind of bill.

Todd saunters over to her, holding out his hand. When she doesn't slip her hand in his, he slowly, quietly laughs, then says, "Let's get you home, I've been hogging you to myself all day."

He helps her get into the car and as they pull away, she looks at the world around her, while he pulls out his phone. "I apologize for this, but my partner is emailing me, I can't ignore it, or it will turn into a phone call."

"Oh yeah, no problem. I have some things to check myself," she says as she looks at her phone and notices how late it is. "Wow, it's later than I thought."

Text to Gregg at 11:30 p.m.:

<   How did your date go tonight?

Sitting there, looking for those three dots that signal he is writing a reply, she wonders why she decided to text Gregg at this moment. After she's had this wonderful date with this wonderful guy.

Text from Gregg at 11:32 p.m.:

>   It was great, just got home actually

>   Heading to bed tho, c u tmro

Shea sighs to herself and puts away her phone. The car is almost to Shea's house when Todd apologizes, and says he wishes this had not ended the way it did. Shea says that it's fine, even though it doesn't feel fine, because the date—otherwise—was really great. She tells herself that if they were to date, eventually she'd come to terms with the fact that he is a busy CEO, but maybe just not tonight.

Parking parallel to the end of her driveway, the driver opens her door and helps her out. Todd gets out and walks around the car to walk her up the driveway. "I had a great time. Can we maybe talk tomorrow about doing something?"

At her door she fishes for her keys, she says, "Yeah if you'll be on B2 tomorrow we can do that."

"Great, my car will be here at seven to pick you up," he says, grabbing her hand to kiss it, saying good night.

"Hey, Todd, I like the way you are assertive sometimes, but I can drive myself. It gives me time to wake up to the music that I like and get cool air on my face. I'd just prefer in the future for you to ask, not command," she says, then turns to her door, taking a few deep breaths.

Calm down, why am I so irritated

"I'm sorry, Shea. I was just trying to take care of you is all."

"I know, that's why I talked to you about it. I had a great time, see you tomorrow," she calls over her shoulder, walking in the house.

Behind her, she hears, "Shea, wait a second, I forgot, I have something for you." As she turns, she sees him jogging to the car and grabbing a long black bag. He jogs back and hands it to her. "Here, I thought you'd like the rest of this."

Peeking in the bag, she sees its the rest of the bottle of wine he'd bought. "Oh wow, are you sure?" she asks, knowing how expensive it was, and not wanting to owe him anything.

"Yeah, kind of like a souvenir," he says, again playing with his ring. "Well, goodnight then, sleep well."

He walks back down the driveway as she walks into the house, closes and locks the door, and turns on the kitchen light.

Putting the black bag on her kitchen counter to be dealt with another time, Shea walks to her bedroom, already unlacing her heels on the way. As soon as she is in the privacy of her bedroom, she pulls her dress over her head and pulls off her bra.

Ah finally

Putting on her comfy pajamas she then proceeds into the bathroom to remove the—what was it 5,000? —bobby pins from her hair. Using the time to reflect on why she could be feeling uneasy in Todd's presence.

Twin Pines

00013 ♣♣ To the Moon

Shea sings along to the radio as they speed down SR 528 on their way to Orlando International Airport. John keeps laughing at her, but she doesn't care. She doesn't really know him anyway. He reaches for the knob, turning the volume all the way down.

"Hey, I was listening to that!" she whines.

"I know, I think everyone in the state of Florida knows," he says, smiling.

"Alright fine, we will just sit here in silence… fun."

"No, I turned it down because we'll be at the airport within fifteen minutes or so, and there are some things we need to go over before we get there," he says. She sees him glancing at her out of the corner of his eye, making sure she is paying attention.

"Like what? The baggage claim is not a carousel, don't take your shoes off on the plane, or how about urinal cakes aren't real cake?" she retorts. She is feeling sassy in this heat—it's probably a good thing they're leaving after all.

"I know you're not an idiot, Shea. I'm being serious," he says, his voice tinged with concern.

"I know, John, I'm listening."

"When we get to the airport, before we even get out of the car, I would like you to put your headphones in, hood up, and bubble gum in your mouth. I need you to act like the most disinterested teenager you've ever seen in your life. Don't even people watch, just stay disinterested," he says, his voice pleading with her.

"Why do I need to do that?" she asks, genuinely curious. She was still biding her time until her escape, but he wasn't too bad to hang out with.

"Because, Shea, the people we are running from have access to things like cameras and facial recognition. Flying as far below the radar as possible is key," he says seriously.

"You're right, if you told me the story, I probably wouldn't believe you. Fine, I'll do as you ask."

"I'll be wearing a hat pulled low on my forehead, and it's also why I am just wearing a plain flannel and jeans—nothing that sticks out too much," he says.

They are getting closer to the airport now, she can tell because of how bad the traffic is becoming. She takes her iPod out of her purse and puts in her earbuds. "Should I not actually play music, so I can be more aware of my surroundings?" she asks him.

"That's really smart. Good idea," he says, pulling his baseball cap out of the backseat and placing it on his head. He has not pulled it low yet, though. She thinks it looks like he is ready to go chop some wood, in a hot way.

He reaches into the glove box. Her knees tilting away from his potential touch. He pulls out a pack of Grape Bubblicious, handing it to her. She glances at him, then shyly smiles as she opens it and deposits a chunk of gum into her mouth. "I'll go through this whole pack before we even board," she says, around the copious amount of saliva flooding her mouth and the large wad of gum. "This stuff has intense flavor for like two minutes, then it's like chewing on a balloon," she says, shoving the rest of the pack into her purse

He chuckles, "Yeah, so I've been told."

They have been going around in circles for literally five minutes—this place is so stupid. Finally, they get where they need to go. Finding a parking spot, John gets out, taking several minutes to canvas nearby spots and watch for other cars. Coming back to the car, he lets Shea out and starts to unload all of the baggage.

"What about the car? If we're never coming back?" she asks.

"We don't have many friends left in Florida, or I'd give it to someone. So, I figured I'd just leave it. Maybe, eventually, one day, we'll come back," he says with little to no emotion.

He closes the trunk, tossing the keys in just before it closes. When he looks up, he can see that Shea doesn't understand the brief. "Shea, hood all the way up and over your forehead, and tuck your braid in," he quickly orders.

"Okay, I can pull my hood lower, but my hair is too long and too thick to… what was it you said? 'Tuck it' comfortably. It'll get all bunched up and uncomfortable. I don't see you 'tucking' anything," she says.

This heat is killing me with the sass, focus, Shea!

John laughs and shakes his head. "You are really embodying this teenager thing. May I help you tuck it and see if that is comfortable?" he asks, glancing at his watch for the time.

"Sure, if it's important, I won't be an asshole," she says, turning her back to him and looking down to hide her face. She feels anxious about him touching her, but she isn't scared.

John steps up behind her, and before he does anything, he asks, "Is it okay if I put my hand in your hoodie?"

"Yes, thanks for asking," she says, her anxiety decreasing exponentially with John's careful actions.

Using his left hand to grab the bottom of the hoodie, he stretches it out a bit. Then, with his right hand, he reaches up to the nape of her neck. His fingers, whether on purpose or by accident, Shea has no idea, gently skim her back, sending a pleasant chill down her spine. When he reaches her neck, he feels around for the braid. Finding it, Shea feels him gently pull it toward himself. Once he has all the hair, he lays it straight down her back and puts her hoodie back in place.

"Comfortable?" he asks.

"We'll see, so far so good," she says, then blows a huge bubble in his direction. Her anxiety now at a more manageable level.

"You should have been an actress," he says, picking up her backpack. He puts it on his back, and carries the two large duffels he packed for himself. She watches as he scans the parking garage in all directions.

"What and leave no chance for any of the other gals?" she says in a transatlantic accent, holding her fingers up in a pantomime of smoking.

"You're right, you're TOO talented, that's the problem," he says with a smirk. "Oh, where's that Sprite I put in the car for you?"

"I drank it. The can is in the car," she says, pointing at the passenger side window.

"Shit. Okay, I guess it doesn't matter now anyway," he says, looking in the window, then checking his watch.

"What doesn't matter?" she asks, curious.

"It's just that if you drank it, there could be DNA or fingerprints. I should have thought about it sooner. We should be out of here before they locate the car anyway," he says.

"Are you serious? This is how serious this is?" she asks, that anxiety ratcheting back up.

"I'm very serious. It's okay, though. We'll be okay," he says, looking around. Seeing no one, he asks, "Oh, hey, do you want anything from this bag before we check it?" He flings his head toward the bag on his back.

"No, I'm okay, Thanks though," she says.

"Alright, this is a really long flight, so I want you to be sure. You won't have access to this bag for like, twelve hours," he says.

"TWELVE HOURS! Where are we going, to the fucking moon?" She hollers at him, incredulously.

"Shhh, no yelling. And no, but it is a long day," he answers, again looking around. "But we will be gaining a few hours, so that's cool."

From Hell to the Moon…

"Still no. I don't really have much anyway."

"Did she give you any like… letters or pictures?" he asks.

"You mean, did I? Yeah, I did. Why?"

"Pull that stuff out, please, and put it in your purse," he says.

"Okay, but why?"

"Shea worked hard to get you those things, and if this goes sideways, I would rather you have them on you," he says.

He puts the bags on the ground next to the Mini Cooper and slides the backpack toward her. Reaching through the top, she pulls out the small notebook and closes the bag back up. Unzipping three zippers before she finds the right one, she reaches in and pulls out the envelope of pictures and the other envelope, with the letter in it. Zipping it back up, she steps back from the backpack, and slides the envelopes into the notebook, then slides that into her purse.

"All done," she says.

"Oh, before I forget, here's that key for your lockbox. I put it on a stretchy band so you could put it around your wrist. I would like you to keep it close, just in case," he says.

"In case what?" Shea asks, feeling her anxiety flair again. She grabs the band, pulling it and the small key onto her wrist.

"We just can't be too careful, is all," he says.

"Alright, fine," she says.

"Good, because we need to get moving. It's only a couple of hours until our flight," he says, putting the large backpack back on and picking up the duffels.

"See that sign over there, that's where we are heading," he says, pointing with his chin.

"Come here," she says, walking over to him anyway. She stretches her arms high above her head. "Let me fix this for you, since your hands are full." She grabs his shoulder with one hand and the baseball cap with the other, feeling him tilt his upper body toward her to make it easier. Finally, she adjusts the hat for him so that it's lower on his forehead.

"Thank you, I can't believe I forgot about that," he says, then looks around one last time.

"No problem. Past me told me to trust you with my life, so I figure I should earn your trust too. We should have each other's backs, right?" Shea says, backing away from him.

He nods at her, his face looking haunted.

00014 Acquisition

Shea wakes up to her alarm the next morning, hating herself just a little bit for being up so late. She has to take a shower this morning. After that updo last night there's no salvaging her hair. She plans on just doing a nice little side braid, to save herself some time. After starting the coffee, she steps into the shower, sighing loudly as the steaming hot water runs down her body. After what feels like a year, she steps out onto a fuzzy mat and flips her hair into a towel that she piles on top of her head. Pulling her robe around herself, she pads to the kitchen to pour a cup of coffee to sip while she is getting ready.

Dressed in a coral-colored, silk button-down blouse with black slacks and a black cardigan, she stands in front the mirror applying her make up. She tries to accomplish a neat braid that starts on one side of her head, circling around the back, and hangs on the other side. Once she's happy with her appearance, and has a travel mug of coffee, she is finally ready to head out the door.

Depositing herself and her things into the Jeep, she starts it and opens her garage. Her phone connects to the Jeep almost immediately, and she taps play on her, *Time to Kick Some Ass* playlist. Up first, *Who Do You Think You Are by The Spice Girls.*

When reaches her desk, she puts her things away and checks the time—7:55 a.m. Opening her agenda, she quickly realizes the last couple of days have set her back a little too far for her liking. Time to put her nose to the grindstone, or whatever that saying is. Pulling up her email, she drafts one to Gregg, asking him to come to her office when he has time to give her, but also as soon as possible. Now that the project has pretty much wrapped up, there is a lot to go over.

Pulling out some of the things she's going to need, she places all of it in a pile on one of her visitor chairs. Walking down the hall, on a recruiting mission, she can see that the secretary's office is dark, but that doesn't mean Tina isn't in there. She knocks a couple of times and opens the door slowly. Tina is in the same spot Shea last saw her, typing away.

"Hey, Tina, what are you working on today?" she asks.

"Good morning, Miss Shea," Tina responds, sitting up straight and stretching with her arms up overhead. "Although I'm on loan, there are still things I have to make sure I stay on top of for Mr. T."

"Oh, of course. Sorry I disturbed you," Shea says, turning to leave the room. She really needs to look at some resumes.

"Wait, Miss Shea, if you need assistance, Mr. T made it very clear that you are my top priority. All this other stuff is kind of like busy work—makes me go cross-eyed," Tina says, smiling and crossing her eyes at Shea. She stands in one fluid motion, picking up her laptop and closing it, she carries it like a baby.

"Thanks, Tina, I could use your expertise today," Shea says, turning on her heel and leading Tina to her office.

When they arrive at Shea's office, Tina takes a quick inventory of what is set out and Shea sees a flicker of recognition in her eyes. Tina looks at Shea and says, "Hey since this is going to take up a lot of space, why don't you grab your laptop, and we go set up in the conference room? I have a small printer I can bring in there too, to make it even easier."

"Actually, that sounds fantastic. Thanks so much again for helping us out," Shea says, grabbing her laptop. She steps around her desk and starts to add things from the pile on the chair, to on top of her laptop. Trying to balance it all, she ends up spilling half of it.

Leaning over to pick up her mess, Shea notices that Tina is standing there with a small cart, smiling down at Shea. "Don't worry, Miss, I will get all of this, don't worry about it," Tina says.

"Where did you go? I didn't even notice you left," Shea says, starting to think that Tina is a literal fairy princess, or genie, or elf, or jinn…you get the idea.

"Sorry, Miss. I had this in the office that I've been using. I figured today it would come in handy," Tina says, pointing to one of the shelves on the cart that holds a small printer and a few reams of paper.

"Can you just come work here?" Shea smiles at the woman, the secretary of her dreams.

"Whereas that would be super fun, I do have to get home to my beloveds."

"Beloveds?" Shea asks, maybe she's in like a thruple or something.

"Yeah, my ferrets. They're my babies, and I miss them terribly. Luckily, their grandma does a great job babysitting for me while I'm gone."

"Oh, I can totally understand that. You're their mama after all."

Shea puts her laptop down on her desk and starts gathering supplies from the pile and stacking them on the cart. Tina joins in, and they get it done quickly. Shea grabs her laptop, and together they walk over to the conference room.

Once inside, Shea immediately signs into her laptop, she sends another email to Gregg, correcting the location of their meeting to conference room A. She then pulls up an email to all the department leads, asking for their final budgetary reports and all progress notes, from the very beginning of the project. When she looks up, Tina has organized all the supplies and is plugging her own laptop into the printer. Todd is standing next to Tina, looking over her shoulder while removing his suit jacket and draping it over the back of a chair. Gregg is leaning in the doorway looking in on the scene.

"We're doing this today, Shea?" he asks from his spot, as soon as her eyes land on him.

"We have to, Gregg. I searched high and low, but Danielle never started a terminal file. So, we have to go all the way back to the beginning and I can't do that alone," she says, a bit of desperation creeping into her voice.

"That woman was an imbecile," Todd mutters, now rolling up the sleeves of a deep green button-down shirt.

"I think we can all agree on that," Shea says, noticing that Tina is peeking at her laptop screen.

"Can I help you?" Shea asks her.

"Sorry, I didn't want to interrupt, but the leads are sending you what you asked them for. Can you just forward me those emails and I'll start printing all the stuff we're going to need?"

"Oh, yeah, thanks," Shea says, forwarding the emails to Tina. She then sees that Gregg is still standing in the door frame.

"Gregg, is there something more imperative you need to do? Because if not, get your laptop and get your ass in this room, please," she says, already feeling overwhelmed and they've barely started.

"Yes, ma'am," he says, turning and jogging back to his desk to grab his laptop.

"Well, good morning to you too, Shea. I like this boss lady side of you," Todd says, smirking at her as he loads paper into the printer.

She winks at him, feeling glad he's here in this moment, and that he is actually helping for once. "Thanks for stepping in Todd, I really appreciate it."

He spins the ring on his finger and smiles at her. Grabbing the label maker, he starts to make the labels he knows they will need. Gregg sits down closest to Shea at the table and is emailing things to be printed straight to Tina. They work together in perfect unison, getting the proper documents in the proper files to wrap up Project Salt N' Vinegar.

At around 1 p.m., Shea says, "Hey guys, we've been at this for hours. We're almost done, we only have a little more to do. So, why don't we take a break for lunch and then regroup?"

"That sounds like a great idea," Todd says. "How about I pop down to the café and grab everyone lunch, on me? And then I'll bring it back up here," Todd says.

"Sounds great Mr. T," Tina says in between licking her finger and flipping through pages.

"Yeah, that would be great, thank you," Shea answers as she sticks dividers into a file.

"As long as you get me a plain muffin, the rats love them," Gregg adds, balancing his chair on its back two legs.

"No problem, Gregg. I'll be right back," Todd says, already walking to the door.

After lunch they dive back into the project and have it finished around four o' clock. "Thanks so much for your help, everyone. There's no way I could have done this without you," Shea says.

A chorus of "No problem!" resounds from her comrades. Shea smiles and stacks the two, four-inch binders on top of her laptop. "Alright, why don't you guys pack up and head out for the day?" She walks out of the room and down to her office. Placing the binders where they go on her bookshelf, then plugging her laptop in to charge.

She hears a knock at her open door and looks up to see Todd leaning against the frame, fiddling with his ring, looking like he just stepped out of GQ magazine.

"Hey, come in. Sorry we didn't really get to talk today, but all of that needed to be done, for my employer as well as yours… or for you, I guess," she says, tilting her head slightly.

"I understand. I was just coming in to see if you would like to bring the bottle I gave you last night over to my hotel tonight," he says, stepping closer. "I'm in the penthouse, it's huge, I have a full kitchen and everything. I'd like to cook for you," he says, moving to stand next to her. "No funny business or anything, just dinner… maybe a movie."

"Sure, I was planning on heading out of here soon. Could we maybe do it earlier than last night?" she asks, her voice tentative.

"Let's say like six?" Todd suggests. After she nods in agreement, he adds, "Oh, and Shea, something has been bothering me. Remember at the meeting a couple of days ago, when I gave Gregg his bonus?"

She nods in answer, curious where this is going.

"Well, at the time, I didn't want to discuss yours with the group there, I felt it inappropriate, given that you're the department head," he says.

"Understandable," Shea says, not wanting to get her hopes up too high.

"Here's the thing," he continues. "We all know Gregg basically ran the show—not to say you didn't do an amazing job, don't take that the wrong way—but according to Crown, the 'talent' has already been given a bonus."

"Oh, okay," Shea says, with one hand wrapped around her crucifix she uses the other to take a sip of her ice-cold coffee. Nervous energy pinging around inside her body.

"However, due to the talents of Gregg and yourself, I'd like to discuss something with you." Taking her hand and looking in her eyes, he says, "Crowned Skull Laboratories would like to offer the two of you a package deal. Meaning both of you have to accept it or it's off the table."

He pauses only for a second then continues, "Crown has their, well our, hands in a lot of different pies—from restaurants to innovative cancer research to advancements in prosthesis, we're all over the map. It's how we fund our more classified projects, by using the profit of other, smaller ventures."

"Okay…" Shea responds cautiously. She pulls her hand from the heat of his and reaches for her crucifix for comfort or out of habit, either way.

"So, that being said, there is a project that I can't give you specifics about—not even the project code name—but it is along the same vein of what you've been doing here." Todd's voice taking a more serious note as he continues, "I'm hoping to keep Gregg doing exactly what he's good at, while expanding your role a bit more. If you were to both agree, Crown is prepared to offer each of you a sign-on bonus of $100,000, cover whatever relocation fees that are involved, and pay you double your current annual salary."

He stops for a moment, his eyes searching her face, which she attempts to keep stoic and unreadable.

"Why does it need to be both of us?" she asks.

"Because, like it or not, you motivate him, and you feed off of his intelligence. The two of you have a symbiotic relationship, and I think splitting that up wouldn't be the best investment."

She takes a moment to weigh his words. "You said relocation… where would we be relocating to?" she asks, knowing she can't ask Gregg to do this, he's just getting serious with Lydia.

"The east coast of Florida, where our main headquarters is located. Where I am most of the time," he says, no wink in his eye, but one in his voice.

"Okay, let's push that dinner to 7 p.m., I need to talk to Gregg. Have you told him about this yet?" she asks, shrugging off a chill that starts at the top of her shoulders and works its way down her spine.

"Yes, I talked to him earlier when I went with him to feed the rat gang. He's probably been waiting to talk to you since then," he answers.

"I'll go grab him and send him in here. Then I'm going to head out so I can pick up some ingredients for dinner. I'll see you at my spot at 7?"

"Yeah. I'll be there. I might not have time to change or grab that bottle though."

"That's fine. You look gorgeous as you are anyway," he says with a devilish grin. "Is there something else you'd like to drink? I can pick it up when I'm at the store."

"Sure, I like Crown Royal if you're offering," she says, smiling at him.

He chuckles. "Crown, nice."

"Get out of here," she says, waving her hand in a shooing gesture with a tight smile.

She watches Todd approach Gregg, who turns to look at her office. He then immediately starts walking in her direction, walking straight into her office and sitting himself in one of her visitor chairs. For a moment, he just stares at her, like he is waiting for her to speak first.

"So, Todd told me he spoke with you about the offer?" Shea asks, not really knowing where to start.

"Yeah, earlier when we were feeding the rats. Templeton tried to bite him," he chuckles. "I want to see what you think first, though."

"Gregg, I don't want to influence you with my thoughts; that isn't fair. We need to talk about it together."

"My mind is already made up. I just want to know what you think," he says, confidently.

"Wow, already? It's only been a few hours," she says, shock showing on her face.

He nods at her and she begins to talk through her thoughts.

"Okay, well, let's stick to the facts. Fact number one, a hundred thousand a piece is a huge sign on." He nods at her words.

"Fact number two, covering all moving costs, is also really generous." He nods again.

"And doubling our salaries…" she says with a small smile. "I mean we could live great lives near the beach, soaking up the sun every day after work."

Gregg nods again. Shea continues, "Fact C, we don't even know what we will be doing." Gregg nods. "And I can't be the reason you leave your home. Things are different for you, you're in a relationship and you have family here, I can't ask this of you," she says.

Feeling tears well in her eyes, knowing what she would be asking him to give up. She can't let him do it, even if he wants to, she can't ask this of him.

"Shea, any decision I would make wouldn't be for you, no offence. But I do have a lot to think about, like you said Lydia and my family." He leans forward in the seat, and says, "But, from what I know about Crown, we will be working on something really similar, maybe just more advanced." Looking her right in the eyes, he continues, "We're going, Shea. You have no reason to stay here, and although I do, I will figure it out. It's not like we wouldn't be able to come visit, and we wouldn't be leaving tomorrow, anyway. And it's not about the money. Well, not all about the money. The technologies coming out of that company are cutting edge. I'd love to have my name on a part of that," he finishes excitedly.

Shea can tell that he's actually really pumped about this. "Alright, alright, maybe we should go. We can talk more about this tomorrow. Remember, because we're wrapping, tomorrow will be a 'holiday'. I'll call you in the afternoon, we can talk logistics and timing. Since you've already decided, I'll grill Todd later to help me make my decision," she tells him, wondering if this really is the best move for her.

"Sounds great. I'll talk to you tomorrow, then," Gregg says, standing up from the visitors chair and heading back to his desk.

Shea grabs her things and drives over to Todd's hotel. Once in the penthouse, she looks out of the grand windows which wrap around the entire floor. She gives herself a tour, visiting several rooms: a living room decorated in gold, a master bedroom, two guest bedrooms, a full kitchen, a bathroom the size of Shea's entire house, and so on. She feels like her feet are getting sore just from walking around the suite. Heading back to the kitchen, she watches the man work. He seems to know his way around a knife.

As she's watching, he asks, "How would you like your whiskey?" He opens the fridge to reveal he has picked up Coke and other mixers at the store.

"Actually, I'm feeling a little drained. Can we make coffee in this giant kitchen?" she asks, smiling at him.

He smiles back and presses a button on an industrial-looking machine. "I already prepped it. I had a feeling."

"Getting to know me so well already?" she asks.

"You can be a pretty easy read sometimes, and it feels like I've known you forever," he says, tossing the onion he was chopping into a large skillet.

Shea smiles, fully aware that she tends to wear her emotions on her sleeve.

Known me forever?

A chill creeps up her spine. She knows she wears everything on the outside, not really great at hiding her feelings. He turns and pulls out a mug, grabbing the whiskey, he pours about two fingers into the bottom of it. Looking over his shoulder, he sees Shea nod in agreement. Taking the mug to the coffeemaker, he slides it under part of the machine, and the coffee starts pouring into the mug.

"Oh, do you do cream or sugar—or both?" he asks.

Knowing he probably doesn't have Truvia, she just asks for two sugars. When she finally gets the mug into her hand, it feels like the coffee is boiling, so she leaves it on the counter for a while to cool down. As Todd cooks, she relays her conversation with Gregg and the decision that Gregg has come to.

"I'm still not sure. This is a huge move. I don't really have anyone here, but I'll have absolutely no one there."

Todd looks at her earnestly, and says, "Well, you'd have Gregg and me for one. And you'll meet a ton of new people at Crown. I'm not trying to talk you into anything, but I mean, what do you have to lose?"

"I know, it is an exciting opportunity, I've just always lived here, ya know?"

"You can always come visit, whenever you like. I think you're gonna really love it in Florida. though."

"Well, I don't want to ruin Gregg's chance, and I don't think I'll ever get a better offer… Why not take a chance? I'm in."

Todd's face lights up, his expression ecstatic. Dropping his cooking utensils, he runs around the bar to where Shea is, picks her up, and twirls her around.

"Well, I guess you're glad we're going then," she says, giggling, still in his arms.

He slowly lowers her to the ground and leans his face close to hers. Whispering in her ear, he says, "You are so beautiful, will you be mine?" As he trails the tip of his nose down toward hers, she feels the flush spread up her face and moves her face away from his.

"We'll see," she says softly. "I like spending time with you, I just have a lot to think about and do at the moment."

"Well, I'm here for you either way, Shea. Whatever you need."

Throughout the evening, while he cooks, she attacks him with questions. He seems happy to answer the ones he can and keeps chuckling at her enthusiasm. Apparently, they will be working near where the Kennedy complexes are located. They have about fifteen days to get everything in order before the leave. As soon as she told Todd their choice, he had Tina draft resignation letters for both of them, so they'd have those days to pack and find a place.

He asks her how they think they will get all their stuff to Florida.

Shea shrugs. "Well, we didn't talk about that. I was thinking U-Haul, I guess."

He looks at her in disbelief. "A U-Haul? Are you nuts?" he asks, raising his eyebrow.

"Well, I don't think so, but I have been hanging out with you a lot lately," she says, smirking.

Chuckling, he says, "Good one, but seriously, with a U-Haul it's going to take you way longer. Which means you'll be wasting a ton of time, when you could be spending it with me."

"Oh, I see your intentions now. So, what would you suggest?" she asks.

"Well, depending on how much stuff the two of you have, you could share a pod, or get two. Doesn't matter. We'll have them shipped before you leave, so it'll be there when you arrive," he says.

"Okay, but I still need to get there. What do I do? Climb in the pod?" she teases.

"No! What are you talking about?" he asks, sitting back in his seat, laughing. "Did you finish that coffee?" he asks.

"Maybe."

"Oh, okay. Well, to get there, I was thinking I could fly you down on my private jet. Not a command, just an offer. Gregg would obviously be welcome, too."

"Ohhhhh," she says, smiling at his generous, offer. Part of her starts to wonder what sort of strings are attached to all of this. "Thank you, Todd, for everything."

00015 🌲🌲 Butterfly Effect

Shea begins to walk toward where he had pointed her.

Looking at him beside her, she wishes she could remember who he really is. "That hat makes you look very handsome."

"Oh, so I'm ugly without it?" he smiles mischievously and looks over at her.

"No, I just mean, it looks good on you."

"Oh, okay. Thank you," he says. He starts out for the airport entrance, Shea sees he is walking in a way that puts himself in between her and any cameras or people. Watching this her trust in him increases. Any man who would put himself in front of the firing squad to help you, is a good man.

As they walk across the crosswalk, John is slightly in front and to the left of Shea. A beautiful, brightly colored butterfly circles the two of them. Shea is so entranced that she just stops walking, standing there watching it. John, who always has one eye on her, stops a foot in front of her and turns toward her. She is grateful that he has allowed her this moment. The butterfly flies close to Shea's face, then loops around and lands on the bill of John's hat. Shea gasps and covers her mouth with her hands.

The butterfly stays there, slowly opening and closing its wings for several seconds, then flies away. John had been going cross-eyed trying to see the butterfly on his hat. When Shea sees him look at her again, it is through tears that blur her vision and cascade down her cheeks. Even though there are tears, she feels truly at peace in this moment. John waits for her, but the crosswalk time is ticking down. Looking at him, Shea smiles and starts to walk again.

Standing just outside the airport, John puts down the duffle bags and waits for her. He asks, "Are you okay?"

"Yeah," she says, wiping the tears from her face. "When my parents died…" she sniffles. "At the funeral, I was inconsolable. I felt like I was so alone in this world." Looking up, trying not to cry, she continues, "My grandmother, who died soon after, stood beside me holding my hand as we watched the caskets lower into the ground. We were the last two people there." She takes a deep breath. "As they were being lowered, I saw a butterfly fly by, it was beautiful. As I watched the butterfly, the caskets disappeared into the ground," she sniffles again, feeling the tears welling in her eyes. "The butterfly circled and came to land on my glasses. It sat there, doing the same thing that one just did on your hat. My grandmother noticed, and we both watched it for as long as it stayed. When it flew away, she told me that butterflies, through the years, have been the symbol of many things. But one of them is that it's your loved ones who have passed away, visiting you, telling you they are okay on the other side. Another was that they can sense good in people, landing on them for a little break because they know the person won't hurt them."

"So, which one was it, do you think?"

Past me told me not to say anything, but…

"For you, I can see the butterfly feeling safe with you…" she trails off.

"Or?" he asks.

"Or, maybe it was your late wife, showing you her love," she says.

He smiles in heartbreak, and says, "That's a nice thought, thank you. Do you need another minute?" He watches her put the sleeves of her hoodie over her hands and wipe her eyes.

"Nah, thanks for letting me have a moment," she says.

Getting into the airport, John leads Shea over to an escalator, then down a long line of different airlines. Shea feels bad for John. He's been carrying all those bags, and they had to have walked a mile by now.

Finally, he stops in front of Delta Air Lines. Keeping his head down, he goes to the kiosk to print their tickets and baggage tags. Once he has done that, he looks over his shoulder at her and tilts his head toward the line. She steps to meet him, and they wait for their turn. Shea is trying her hardest to look disinterested, like she was instructed, but she also has a strong urge to reach out and hold on to John, the only person she has in the world.

They slowly make their way to the counter. When they reach the desk, John turns to Shea, and she rolls her eyes. Taking one earbud out of her ear, she asks, "What do you want?"

"I need your passport, sweety," he says, showing his face only to her, upon which is pride in her performance.

She continues to give him a bored expression, shoving her arm in her purse, she feels around and finds the passport. Grabbing it, she flippantly shoves it in John's direction, all without breaking eye contact, or her bored expression.

John takes it from her and turns to deal with the ticket agent. Placing the bags one at a time to be weighed, he completes the task without a hitch. He turns, grabbing the sleeve of Shea's hoodie, and they walk toward security. She rips her arm out of his grasp to better play her part, resuming her teenage trudge next to him as the head into the security line. A sense of unease starts to creep in again. Their passports are fake, and the people in front of them are getting theirs scanned.

What if ours don't scan?

She begins to reach for her crucifix and John catches her hand, pulling it gently down to her side. He lingers, keeping her hand lightly held with his thumb and forefinger. She wants to ask him about the passports, but this is John, he has to have seen it too.

Stepping up to a TSA agent behind glass, John hands over both passports and continues to hold onto Shea with his other hand. The agent looks at the passports, then at the two of them. Since both of their faces are partially obscured, the man says to John, "Faces up, both of you." John immediately lifts his hat slightly and looks at the man. The agent nods and looks at Shea, who slides her hood back a little and looks right at him. Satisfied, he scans both passports without incident and hands them back to John.

Merging back into the line for security, John stands facing Shea. "Hey, can you put both of these in your purse? I don't want to keep mine in my pocket and have it shape to my ass cheek," he asks, handing her the passports.

"Sure," she says, trying her hardest not to laugh. She slides them into her purse, closing it after she's done.

Making it through the maze of security, a tram ride, and a bathroom break later—where Shea briefly considers bolting but ultimately decides against it—they arrive at their gate with about an hour until their take off time. Meaning, they don't have to wait very long at all to board.

Overhead they call for first class and sky priority. John stands and holds his hand out to Shea. She takes it, and they get in line behind a few other people. He takes the tickets out of his shirt pocket and hands one to Shea. He watches her inspect the ticket information, and gestures for her to stand in front of him. They both scan their tickets and walk down the jetway to the plane. The more people that surround them, the more alert John becomes. He is constantly watching Shea and anyone around them, scanning for signs of danger.

She reaches out a hand, grabbing just the sleeve of his shirt, near his forearm. He carefully keeps his arm in the same position so as not to spook her. She continues to hold it until they are in their assigned seats. Sitting first, Shea puts her purse under the seat in front of her. She appears to be searching for something, finding a napkin she spits the gum into it and places it into the seat back pocket.

"Turned ballon?" he asks from his seat next to her.

"Yes! I knew it would happen, I don't know why I'm disappointed," she says with a smile in his direction.

John takes the opportunity to slouch in his seat and drop his head toward his chest, slowing his breathing. He knows that to everyone else it will appear as if he is sleeping. He can feel Shea shifting in her seat, so he cracks open an eye to watch as she leans her head against the window, closing her eyes. As he listens for her breathing to even out, he feels her hand grab his sleeve, gently pulling his arm toward her.

John, of course, allows her to do whatever she is trying to accomplish. He feels his hand fall into a warm lap, and Shea hugs his forearm. He adjusts himself in his seat to be more comfortable, still appearing asleep. After a few moments, he feels her head drop against his shoulder, and hears deep, steady breaths in his ear.

This is absolutely killing him. He wants so badly to tell her what has happened, and who he is. But, at least she's warming up to him.

Twin Pines

OOO16 🌲🌲 How dare you!

■ ■ ■ ☐ ☐ ☐ ☐ ☐

The rich aroma of coffee and bacon brings Shea out of her slumber, accompanied by the sound of two grown men debating which Power Ranger is the best.

Is this real life?

She swings her legs over the side of the large bed. When she stands, it dawns on her that she's still wearing the clothes she had on yesterday—clothes she wore to work. The events of last night come flooding back, she chuckles and then groans. He did it again. She ate his delicious meal, she'd probably never had a Philly cheese steak so good. She had more Crown, and they decided to watch a movie. Cuddling up to Todd on the couch, she then passed out on his shoulder before she even saw the opening credits.

Which means he carried me in here!

As respectfully as ever, he had deposited her into a spare room, alone. One that was equipped with a bathroom. After getting her morning business over with, she stands at the sink and tries to control her hair.

Noticing a small, travel-size, mouthwash on the counter, she uses that too. Feeling better prepared to see what all of the commotion is about, she leaves her suite.

Walking down to the kitchen she is overwhelmed by breakfast aromas. She spots Gregg and Todd, side by side, behind the counter, competing to see who can roll a better breakfast burrito.

"Hiya guys," she says, stepping to the bar.

"Good morning, sweet girl," Todd says, as he passes her a steaming mug of coffee.

Taking a sip, she looks at Todd with her eyebrow raised. "Gregg came over this morning, we were talking about everything you and I discussed last night. We're excited to talk about it all together, but Gregg brought up something about your coffee. He said that you were just too nice to ask for what you really wanted. So, we went to the grocery store so he could show me, and while we were there, we got all of this. To cook breakfast," he says, waving his arm over his cooking surface, covered in breakfast ingredients and Truvia galore.

"But why did Gregg come over in the first place? Not that I'm not glad you're here, I am. I just wasn't expecting this."

"Oh, well. I forgot about the holiday today, so I went to work, and since no one told me they'd sent in my resignation for me," Gregg says, side eyeing his buddy, Todd. "Basically, I was escorted off the premises by Dean and Petrie," he says with a smirk. "I figured since I was up, I'd pop over and see if I could talk to Todd some more, about everything."

"Ohhhh, bad boy, now, huh?" she says. "Oh, no, what about the rats?"

"I like where your concerns are at, Shea. My boys have been given a great life, and although I wish I could continue to do that, alas, I cannot. So, Lydia loves the rats actually, and she got permission to take them home. She'll be able to continue to give them a better life, as long as the chips in them are either removed or rendered inert," he says, placing a breakfast burrito on a plate in front of Shea.

"Whoa, you're gonna just give my girl your burrito like that dude? Right in front of me too?" Todd says in mock-offence.

Grinning, Gregg says, "Well, your burrito is looking a little limp over there. I didn't think you'd be able to deliver."

"How dare you?" Todd retorts. Then Shea watches as Todd picks up a tortilla and threatens to slap Gregg with it.

This must be an alternate universe…

Looking at the two of them, Shea can see that Gregg is dressed in his usual wrinkled green shirt and khakis. Todd, on the other hand, is wearing pajama pants and a loose t-shirt.

Didn't they go to the store?

Shea makes an exaggerated motion of wiping her eyes and blinking several times at Todd, emoting like an old school cartoon character.

"What is it, sweet girl?" Todd asks, amused.

"Did you wear pajamas to the store?" she asks, in mock humiliation.

"What? No! Never! You know me better than that, sweets. I just wanted to be comfy when we got home is all. Should I get dressed?" he asks, suddenly looking self-conscious.

Chuckling, Shea says, "No way. You look hot."

"Oh, okay, thanks."

"Can we get back on track here? I'm leaving my rats, my girl, and my family—you can't leave me out too, I'll shrivel up and die," Gregg says.

"Oh, don't worry, we'll be like the three musketeers," Shea says, holding her coffee mug aloft, she says, "to new beginnings!"

After their cheers, Shea looks over at Gregg, and asks, "So wait, did you already talk to Lydia?"

"Yeah, that's how the rat thing came up. I tried to offer a long-distance relationship, but I'm not gonna lie, I think she was more worried about the rats the whole conversation," he says. "So, we just went ahead and called it. We'd only been kinda serious for like a month, so no big deal… for her at least, ha-ha."

"Aw, I'm sorry, Gregg. If you're having second thoughts, remember, if you don't want to go, we don't go," Shea says gently, reaching for the burrito he gave her.

"No way, I'm going. Maybe I'll meet a hot Latina down in Florida," he grins.

"Be careful, those magnifying glasses you wear on your face are gonna pinpoint the sun's rays and boil the fluid inside your eyes, and then they'll just deflate inside your head," Shea warns, nonchalantly sipping her coffee.

"Shea, stick to logistics. I'm the scientist remember?" Gregg smirks, and then extends his fist to Todd, expecting a fist bump, but Todd just shakes his head at Gregg.

"I'm trying to get her on my side, sorry man," Todd says

Shea smiles, then quips in a pirate accent, "Respectable ladies over impeccable matey's." She giggles along with them at her rhyming skills.

She is suddenly overwhelmed with gratitude that these two weirdos might become her found family. It's still early, but it looks like the three of them could do great things together.

"So, guys, we need to make plans for the day. We only have, like, fifteen days, right? And a lot to get done. Well, Gregg and I, at least."

"Don't leave me out, I took the next fifteen days off so that I can be helpful. Maybe move a couch or something," Todd says, squinting his eyes at Shea as she eats another man's burrito.

Shea whips her head at him, and laughs. "Oh, so we are couch movin' friends?"

He wipes his hands on a towel and comes around to her side. Bending down to get his face level with hers, he drops a peck on her cheek. When he's done, he says, "I'd like to say I am more than a friend, so I'd move anything you needed. And yeah, Gregg's a couch movin' friend."

"I don't know what it means, but it feels significant. So… ditto dude," Gregg says.

"What about me, Gregg?" Shea asks. Todd stands behind her, with his hands on the back of her bar stool.

"Oh, duh, that's a given. Definitely would move a couch for you. Though I don't know if you have it in you to move one, though," he says, smirking.

"I could move a couch!" she says incredulously.

"Now you know how it feels," Todd says, looking down at her and sticking out his tongue.

"Alright, fine. We're all movers for each other. Whatever. I need a shower, a change of clothes, and to start researching, and get boxes to pack, and get someone to clean out my office, because I don't want to be escorted off the premises," Shea rambles out, ticking each task off on a different finger, suddenly overwhelmed.

"Tina's got you, your stuff is in your kitchen," Todd says.

"How'd she get into my house?" Shea looks over at him, a little nervous.

"She found your spare key. She's very tricky, that one. I wasn't meaning to intrude on your personal space, but she didn't want to leave it out in the rain," Todd says.

"Always so thoughtful," she says, a bit sarcastically. "But don't you think that's something I should make the decision on? I mean, it is my house and my things, right?" Feeling that odd shiver make its way down her spine.

"Shea, it was just a split-second decision early this morning. I didn't want to wake you. It's not that deep—I just wanted to help."

Feeling unmoved on her opinion of the breaking and entering, she just nods and gives him a thin smile. "So, what are you dorks gonna do while I'm hard at work?" she asks, one hand on her hip.

"We're coming with you," they both say at once, before looking at each other and bursting into laughter.

"Did you guys rehearse that or something?" Shea asks.

"No," Gregg says between gasping laughter. "Swear… it just happened."

"Alright, are you gonna, like, ride with me or take your own vehicles there?" she asks the still chuckling men.

"We're all stuck like glue, so if you wanna drive, we'll ride," Todd says. Shea feels like he's trying to correct his earlier efforts in making decisions for her.

"Alright, I'm gonna use the ladies' room. Meet back here in five?" she says, nodding toward Todd's pajamas.

Her best friend and… her… friend?…The three musketeers

Shea slides into her Jeep and tosses her purse in Gregg's lap—he called shot gun. As she starts her engine, she pulls up her playlists. While on the toilet this morning, she made a new playlist titled *Couch Movin' Friends*. Hitting play, she reaches for her seatbelt. *Friends in Low Places by Garth Brooks* roars through the Jeep.

OOO17 Plate o' Bacon

John's arm is tingling, Shea has been asleep on it for hours. He isn't super comfortable, but he doesn't care about that. He had kept his head down, appearing to be fast asleep to the flight attendants and anyone else on the plane for the entire flight. About half an hour ago, he felt Shea's head fall back a bit, tilting her face toward the ceiling of the plane. Luckily, because of the early hour, the lights were still dim on the plane.

The flight attendants had started serving breakfast from the back of first class about a minute ago. He hopes they'll just skip over their row, but if not, he hopes they just tap his shoulder and leave Shea to rest. Even though he doesn't know what the last couple of months were like for her, he assumed she needed her rest.

He can now hear the flight attendant a couple of rows back, speaking in whispers about quiches or pancakes. As she gets closer, John makes sure he is settled deep in his sleep façade. Hearing breathing in front of him, he tries to remain calm in hopes that the flight attendant will just move on.

"Miss Lynhart," the flight attendant whispers, while gently shaking Shea's shoulder. "Miss Lynhart," she says, just as softly. Tapping Shea's shoulder more aggressively now.

Watching from a slit of space between his eyelids, he watches Shea wake up and startle. Shrinking away from the stranger in her face, she puts her head down, and murmurs, "Is there a problem?" She looks over John, and when he chooses to remain still, she pushes forward. He is choosing to let this happen, believing that she isn't in any real danger.

In whispered tones the flight attendant asks, "Miss Lynhart, I just wanted to see if you're, okay? Do you need any kind of help?"

"No, I'm great, why do you ask?" she replies, her voice also at a whisper.

"Well, it's just that the other flight attendants and I noticed your face and head. Your headband slipped back while you were sleeping. I just wanted to make sure you weren't in some sort of trafficking or abuse situation. Has this man hurt you?"

John holds back a reaction, but Shea seems calm, her voice steady. "John? No ma'am, he saved me," Shea says, pausing for a moment. "He is trying to help me escape an abusive ex. I would have probably died if it weren't for him."

John is surprised by her response. He thought she might reach out for help, but instead, she stuck with him.

The flight attendant gasps. "Do you think your ex is following you?"

"We can't be too careful," she says, her voice quivers slightly. "That's why I've been trying to keep my face hidden, but I guess I can't control how I sleep."

"Oh, I'm so sorry, miss. It's good you've got someone in your corner. Not everyone has that kind of luck. He's good to you?" she asks.

"Better than I could have ever imagined a man could treat me, and that's the truth," Shea says.

"Well, I know he's been pretty deep asleep, but do you think he'd want anything? We're serving breakfast as our dinner entrée. Can I get anything for you?" the flight attendant asks politely.

"Actually, if I could get a cup of coffee with Truvia, if you have it?" Shea replies. "While you're getting that, I'll try to wake him and see if he wants anything. What are the breakfast options?"

"Well, we have quiche or pancakes, both are served with a side of bacon and toast with your choice of jam," the flight attendant explains. "But I'm sorry, we don't have Truvia. We have Splenda though."

"Ew, no thank you," Shea says, the smile evident in her voice. "I'll just take regular sugar, two please."

"Okay, I'll get some of the other passengers their meals and then circle back. Sound good?"

"Perfect, thank you so much for checking on me. I wish I had someone like you when I was being abused," her voice soft and sincere.

"Sweetheart, it'll be okay. It sounds like you are on your way to a new life, thanks to this one," she says. John's barely open eye catches a glimpse of the flight attendant gently rub Shea's shoulder and then nod her head in John's direction.

After the flight attendant walks away, Shea reaches over and shakes John's shoulder to 'wake him'. He stretches and yawns—both are real, and both help minimally with the kink in his shoulder. Looking at Shea, he grins. "Good morning, Jennifer Aniston. How did you sleep?"

Shea looks over at him, and it appears her eyes go unfocused, and she tilts her head to the side. Without warning, she reaches out and pulls him into a hug, whispering in his ear, "I don't know how I'll ever be able to repay you. Thank you, John. Not all of that was acting."

When she leans back from the hug, he tilts his head back down, feeling moisture in his eyes. The flight attendant returns, bringing Shea a coffee and two packets of cane sugar. Placing them in her cup holder, she looks to John to discuss breakfast options. "Hey, I know you heard her, but what do you think about breakfast?" she asks. "I guess now that you're awake you can put the order in yourself."

Reaching into his breast pocket, John pulls out two packets of Truvia and hands them to Shea.

"What?" Shea asks, mouth slightly agape.

"Yeah, well, I know it's what you like, and they don't usually have it on planes, so I just figured I'd carry a few," he says. It was the least he could do.

Taking them from him, she dumps them in her coffee and stirs it in with the wooden popsicle stick provided. "So, are we eating, or… starving?" Shea asks with a playful grin.

"Yeah, we can eat, what are you going to get?" John replies, letting her be in charge.

"Hmm," she muses. "I've never really been one for pancakes, so I think quiche. To be honest, if I could just get a plate of bacon, that's what I would order."

"Same," John says, smiling down at his hands in his lap, reminded of the Shea from before.

They snicker together as the same flight attendant walks past them to the galley. When she walks back toward them from the galley, John and Shea's smiles widen, nearing them with two plates piled high with bacon. Setting them down in front of the pair, she offers them maple syrup, which Shea greedily accepts.

"The rest of the cabin has had their fill, so don't worry about it being unfair," the flight attendant says with a wink.

"I want to thank you, ma'am," John says, with a slight southern accent. He doesn't need the accent but it's one of the things that past Shea put in place for remembering. "This little lady told me about the help you offered her, and I can't tell you how happy that makes me, knowing that there are people in the world still trying to make a difference."

"It was no problem at all. I'd like to thank you for what you are doing for her. You two take care of each other, okay?" she asks.

"Of course, ma'am."

"Yes, ma'am, we will," Shea responds.

"Alright, you two dig in, we won't be in the skies for much longer."

As soon as the flight attendant walks away, Shea grabs John's arm, which was on the way to his mouth. She halts his eating of the bacon.

"What, what happened?" he asks, confused.

"Your accent. I've heard one just like it before," Shea says, her voice dreamy.

John looks at her, not getting his hopes up. "Yeah, I'm a real Matthew McConaughey," he says jokingly.

He watches her closely as she looks back at him, then past him—or through him. She sits like that for a couple of minutes, and he has no choice but to maintain eye contact while also eating bacon with the arm she wasn't currently clutching.

Finally, Shea appears to come out of it and puts a hand to her mouth.

"Are you okay? That was kind of weird," he says, always trying to lighten the mood.

"I know who had that accent," she says, while dipping her bacon in maple syrup. "Not only that, but I remember what he looked like, too."

"Really?" John asks. If so, this is something, because everything else she has remembered has had no faces associated.

"He named his son Jude, after the Beatles' song. Baby Jude had heterochromia—one blue eye and one green. His wife is gorgeous, she was a pageant girl. Dean—his name is Dean, and he probably buzzed me into the building a hundred times, carried chairs for me regularly and was always respectful. Oh, and Petrie, oh my gosh!" she exclaims. "Why can't I remember the important stuff?"

"It'll happen, this is good Shea. Something must have triggered those memories. Hopefully, eventually, the rest will follow."

"Yeah," she says, holding her empty plate up so she can get under the tray table to her purse. She pulls out the small notebook that her past-self left for her, and asks, "Do you have a pen?"

"I don't, but I can do this," he says, pressing the call light for a flight attendant. When she arrives, he asks her for a pen, giving her their plates at the same time.

Once she has the pen, she gets to work jotting down the events, names and faces she remembers.

John sits back into his seat with his head down and his hat pulled low. He contemplates quietly if—when—his will be the face she remembers? And when it happens, how will she react?

00018 I'm the CEO

A couple of minutes down the road, all three of them are scream singing the song, helping Shea feel seen, and hopefully helping Todd understand her need to drive herself.

After several other "friend" themed songs, Shea pulls the Jeep into her garage. All three pile into her living room, and Shea hands the two men her laptop and the TV remote.

"Start looking at Pods or properties—maybe close to the beach. I'll be back after my teeth, and I feel clean." Walking away she slips into her room and closes the door.

On top of her dresser, she sees a vase of at least thirty long-stemmed roses. After glancing into her bathroom to ensure she is alone in her room, she then walks over to the flowers and takes the large card from the bouquet.

Shea,

Welcome to the team!

Xoxo Tina xoxo

Shea buries her nose in the delicate, velvety, coral-colored roses and takes a deep breath. A small smile lights up her face as she heads to her bathroom.

Oh, maybe Tina will be my secretary now

Shea showers and re-braids her hair. After her teeth are brushed, she heads to the kitchen to make some coffee. On her island, she sees a banker's box filled with her things from the office. The box doesn't hold many things, just a family picture, some lotion, a nice set of pens and highlighters and a card-sized envelope.

This card is signed by a lot of people from B2, offering well wishes, and goodbyes. She eyes Lydia's signature, and a personalized note, *"Please don't break his heart."* Shea's head feels fuzzy.

Why would Lydia write this? Gregg has never even shown any interest, and I... well...

"Hey, sweets, everything okay?" Todd asks, gently stroking the arm that is still on the banker's box.

"Yeah, everything's fine. Did you guys actually get anything accomplished?" she asks, turning to pour herself a cup of coffee.

"Yeah, when you're done, come see," he says, walking back to the couch.

She planned to tell him about the flowers from Tina, but she figured they had more important things to discuss. Walking to the couch, she plops down between the two boys—Todd had slid over when he saw her coming. Gregg, who is typing away on her laptop, glances over at her.

"Hey, how long of a commute are you looking to make?" he asks, still typing.

"Well, I hadn't thought about that. I suppose I won't have my Jeep, so, it depends on whether I buy a car or not."

"See, that's what I was thinking too. I was also thinking, that maybe just for the beginning, until we get more settled, that maybe we could rely on each other a little. Like, share a house and car, just until we get used to things there," Gregg says awkwardly.

Shea responds immediately, "I think that would be a great idea, Gregg. We'll probably be hanging out all the time anyway."

Gregg grins, clearly relieved. "So, I found a couple of houses for rent close to the beach, but it depends on how much of a commute you're willing to make," Gregg says.

"I'd say like thirty minutes, maybe," she responds.

"That's what I thought too. Look at this listing. It looks awesome. A little bigger than we will need, but we could both have our own bedrooms and maybe our own offices too," Gregg says, sliding the laptop in front of Shea, the listing showing on the screen.

"Oh, wow, this is gorgeous. And really expensive," she says, looking at the four thousand dollar a month price tag.

"Yeah, but Todd says the first and last and all that is part of our moving expenses. With my new salary, plus that bonus, I don't think it'll be any trouble," he says, looking at her.

"Is that true?" she asks, turning her head to Todd.

"Sure is, on other occasions it's been a down payment for a house. This is no different," he says.

"Wow, okay. Did you look into anything else?"

"Yeah," Todd says, reaching for the laptop from Gregg. He pulls up a website that caters to moving purposes. "See this website? They'll deliver a twenty-three-foot trailer to the driveway, then move it to Gregg's so he can load his stuff and then they'll drive it down to you guys' new place—all for the low low price of seven thousand dollars"

"Holy shit! Seven thousand dollars?" Shea asks, eyes widening.

"Yeah, but it's the best option and you don't need to worry about that because it's part of relocation," Todd says, "meaning I'm taking care of it."

"I feel like this is all too good to be true. I haven't even seen an offer on paper yet, and I'm feeling anxious. This is all so much money—how can you justify this to your company?" she asks.

Todd smirks confidently. "Well, I'm the CEO, so I do what I want first of all. Second of all, there has been an official offer in your work email for a couple of days—which I'm sure you just haven't checked. And third, Shea, I dumped a few million dollars into Project Salt N' Vinegar. Not only have we profited in just the couple of days since we started marketing them. But, we've profited nine-hundred million dollars. And we now have technology that will help other scientific research at Crown. I make smart investments and when I know what I want, I spend whatever resources I need to in order to get it. You two are, no offence meant here, a great investment."

"I guess I need to check my work email then," she says, the chill at her back yet again.

"I guess so," Todd replies.

After Shea finally checks her work email, she prints and reads the offer.

This is the Employment agreement between Crowned Skull Laboratories and Shea Murphy of Merrit Island, FL.

Both parties agree to the following terms and conditions:

1. Employee will faithfully, to the best of their ability, carry out their duties and responsibilities.
2. As Director, it will be the employees duty to perform all positions' essential duties and job functions.
3. As compensation for services provided, the employee will be paid $80/hour base pay.
4. Benefits will be provided if the employee chooses to partake.
5. It is understood that the first [90] days will be a probationary period. If employment is deemed unsatisfactory within that time, sign-on bonus ($100,000) and moving expenses (est. $25,000) will be void, requiring repayment.

6. Paid time off requests will go directly to Todd Donoghue, CEO.

7. Termination of employment will be at the discretion of Crowned Skull Laboratories. Attempts from the employee to end employment will be discussed, but are not guaranteed.

8. Contract length is (2) years, with discussion of renewal in (18) months.

Without much thought she signs the offer, making it officially official. Apparently, Gregg had signed his right away—try hard. The boys are busy. Todd is on the phone with the trailer company, bribing more than one person in an attempt to get the trailer delivered today. While Gregg is being driven around in a truck, instead of the customary town car, to track down all the boxes in town. Shea's job is to call a realtor to get things moving on a rental, as well as searching for used car lots in their new area. In hopes that they can have a car delivered to their new address, when they get one.

An hour later, the realtor emails Shea several "matches" to look through with Gregg, when he gets back. She also found a car lot with great options and had them email her cars in their combined price range, which they had agreed on earlier. So, all in all, things were moving along quickly.

Since she needs to wait for Gregg to get back to do anything further, she decides to bother Todd. She spots him pacing the driveway, having what seems like a heated conversation. She walks out of her front door and down the driveway to meet him as he heads back toward the house.

"...is there someone else I can speak with, STEVE? I'm really not used to hearing the word 'no,' and today will not be the day," Todd says, sighing as he nears Shea. Bending down, phone still to his ear, he softly brushes his fingers down Shea's cheek and kisses her. "No, I do not want the number for another company."

Shea stands there with his hand stroking her cheek. A long pause passes, before Todd says, "I don't think you are hearing me..." Before he can finish his sentence, Shea reaches up and grabs the phone from him.

"Hello, who is this?" Shea asks.

Through the phone, she hears a gruff, deep, manly voice reply, "This is Steve. I'm the owner of Trekking Trailers. Who am I speaking to?"

"This is Shea. I am hoping to become a patron of your company. Can you explain to me what's going on, Steve?" she asks into the phone but watches Todd, who is now rubbing her shoulders.

"Look, I told your guy, I just don't have any twenty-three-footers in the yard right now. There's nothing I can do about it. He can call another company or choose another size," Steve offers.

"And you offered both of these options to him?" Shea asks, raising an eyebrow at Todd.

Todd whispers, "What—what's he saying?"

Shea shoos him with her hand and continues listening.

"I tried, he didn't wanna hear it. He offered me twenty grand to 'find one today,'" he says.

"Well, that sounds like him. What would those other sizes be?" Shea asks, still eyeing Todd, who is shaking his head in front of her.

"For today? I got a forty-eight-footer, a fifty-two-footer and a twenty-five-foot," Steve says. "Honestly, I don't want a bribe, I want customer satisfaction, but I just couldn't meet his demands. It's not possible."

"Well, how about this, Steve? You deliver that twenty-five-footer today for the same price as the twenty-three, and you'll have customer satisfaction," she says. "On top of that, there might even be a cash tip in it for you. We need to get this started today—I have to relocate in fifteen days, and it would really help me out, Steve."

Todd stares at her with his jaw dropped.

"You know what, alright. I'll be there before 5 p.m. Your guard dog already gave me the address and payment information, so we're all set," Steve says.

"Thank you so much, Steve," Shea says, hanging up the phone. Handing it back to Todd, she stands on her tip-toes, grabs his shoulders, and whispers in his ear, "More flies with honey…honey." She then kisses him on the cheek and steps back.

Staring at her like she's an alien, he backs up a foot and drops to his knees. Arms straight in the air, he bends his torso forwards and backwards, chanting, "I'm not worthy, I'm not worthy."

She laughs, but what's even funnier is the fact that Gregg just got back and witnessed the whole thing. Walking over to them, he claps Todd on the shoulder, and says, "Dude, same. At least you realized it early in the relationship."

Once back inside, Shea shares the rental listings and car options, sitting thigh-to-thigh with Gregg on one side and Todd on the other. After only twenty minutes of discussion, Shea and Gregg decide on a smaller home with a fairly unique layout. The house has a large great room and kitchen in the middle of the floor plan, with a master's suite off either side. There isn't a garage, instead it has a carport or awning. Plus, a large pool in the backyard.

The rent will be three thousand dollars a month, which is well within their budget. Shea immediately calls the realtor to lock it in. Once the rental is secured with the realtor, Shea passes the phone to Todd. He pulls out his wallet, accessing an AMEX black card. Knowing they should give him privacy, Shea and Gregg walk down the driveway to get the boxes out of the truck. They only unload a few bundles before Todd jogs down the driveway, handing Shea back her phone.

"She's still on there. She has some questions," he says.

"Hello?" Shea says, bringing the phone to her ear.

"Shea, I just wanted to confirm your move in details. Mr. Donoghue has paid for the first, last, security, and pet deposit, just in case.

With the move-in date being in fifteen days, he also mentioned a trailer and a car delivery. I just need to know the dates so that I can be there to ensure everything goes smoothly."

"Yeah, of course. We're getting the trailer today, and I assume we'll be packing it up for several days. We haven't picked a car yet, that's next on the list, so why don't I email you when I know more?" Shea replies.

"That works, even if it's just the day before, I can work it out," the realtor promises.

"Oh, well, I'll try to give more notice than that. Thank you so much," she says, ending the call.

"Alright, Gregg," she hollers at him excitedly. "We got it!"

He's over with Todd unloading boxes, so Shea begins to jog over to them, just as he's jogging her way. She crashes into his chest with her face, right before he picks her up by the waist and jumps up and down. She laughs so hard she thinks she might pee herself. Then Todd comes up behind her, wraps his arms around both her and Gregg, and jumps with them. After about thirty seconds, they're all laughing too hard to continue and break apart, panting.

"Okay, guys, we've got to keep on track. Gregg, come pick a car with me so we can line that out too. Then I'd like to stop by your house so we can decide who's shit we like more," she says, smiling.

00019 †† Feelings

John's been watching Shea write things in her notebook for a while now, wondering what she might be remembering. "Hey, are you really remembering that much stuff?" he asks.

She looks at him, and smiles. "No, I mean just Dean and Petrie. I drew his tree star." She holds the notebook up, showing him.

"What else have you been writing about, then?" he asks.

"Oh, a potential song list for Alaska. I feel like I need to get songs about the sun and the dark, because of, how, like, the sun is there," she explains. "Once I get a phone, or computer, or whatever."

"As always with the playlists, what do you have so far?" he asks.

"I've got *Here Comes the Sun by the Beatles, Sun Is Shining by Bob Marley, I Believe in a Thing Called Love by The Darkness, Dancing in the Dark by Springsteen, Crawling in the Dark by Hoobastank*, and *The Sun Will Come Out Tomorrow by Annie*," she rattles off.

"Wow, quite the mix," he says. "Do you ever think that if you're thinking of it now, that past Shea might have thought of it too?"

"No, I generally don't really think about her-me at all. I don't think about that version of me, it's like a mental block," she admits.

"Just a thought, I know she prepared for things as best as she could. There is a chance that she made a playlist too," he says.

"Do I even have all my playlists, though? I mean they were on my phone, on YouTube music. Did they all make it to my iPod?" she asks, unsure.

"Yeah, they're all there. She made sure of it," he answers.

Shea pulls the iPod out of her hoodie pocket, turns it on, and selects the playlist option. Scrolling through, she recognizes some, and notices some new ones. Sure enough, there is one titled *Alaska Adventure*, clicking it, Shea looks at all the songs OG Shea had picked—some are the same, and some she's glad 'past her' found. Going back to the playlist screen, she scrolls through, seeing if she can glean any information from the playlists. Seeing one called *Couch Movin' Friends*, she wonders what it means. Trying to remember, she slips into a meditative-like state.

She can remember feelings of anticipation, excitement, and love, but no specific events. The feelings overwhelm her, and she reaches out for John's arm—but he's not there.

Looking around the first-class cabin, she can't see him anywhere. She has always been very independent but maybe whatever happened to her changed that. She feels like her heart is beating way too fast, and yet none of the blood containing oxygen is reaching her brain. She feels a sharp pain in her chest, a cold sweat breaks out on her upper lip, and drips down her lower back. She leans back in her chair, beginning to see spots.

Her flight attendant friend from earlier notices Shea's distress, so she walks over to her.

"Are you okay, miss?" she asks, squatting down so Shea can see her face.

"I don't know where he is. I didn't see him get up," she gets out, jerkily.

"Oh, okay, I saw him go into the bathroom just a little bit ago. He'll be back soon, just try to take some deep breaths," she says, standing and gesturing at the lavatory door.

"Thank you," Shea mumbles, pulling her notebook back out.

What am I four years old? Panicking like that…

A few seconds later, John opens the lavatory door, squeezing his large frame out into the aisle. Nearby is the bacon flight attendant, she gives him a come here gesture with her index finger curling toward herself a few times.

Shea continues scribbling in her notebook, trying to calm the panic as she waits for John to return. As soon as he sits back down in his seat, she reaches out and grabs his arm. "John, oh my gosh, guess what?" she says.

"Me first. I'm sorry I didn't tell you I was leaving. You were like in a trance, so I didn't think you would notice. So, what did you remember?" he asks, turning his body more toward her in the seat.

Overhead, they hear, "Ladies and Gentlemen, on behalf of myself and all the crew, we would like to thank you for choosing Delta. We are currently beginning our descent and should be at our destination shortly. The local time in Seattle is currently 7:01 p.m. and the temperature is 46 degrees Fahrenheit. As you can see, the captain has turned on the seatbelt sign, which will remain on for the remainder of the flight. So, if you could please find your seat, fasten your seat belt, and put your seat back and tray tables in the upright position, flight attendants will be moving through the cabin to collect trash shortly."

As soon as the announcement started, Shea had whipped her notebook around to face John, handing it to him so he could read it while the flight attendant was talking.

Now that the announcement is over, John is staring at Shea, finally, he says, "You remember all of these feelings?"

"I remember these vividly, but I can't see any faces or anything, just glimpses of feelings," she says, readjusting in her seat. Her whole body hurts and she is trying to not let it show on her face.

John chuckles. "Well, I'm glad you're getting stuff back. It'll only be a matter of time before it all comes back to you."

"If I am in so much danger, are any people that might have been with me— those responsible for some of those feelings—in danger too?"

"They're all safe, and when you remember everything, you will know what happened with them," he says.

"Well, there's nothing else I can really do. Hey, for the rest of the flight, do you wanna listen to a playlist called *Firey Black Hole?*" she asks, passing him an earbud.

"Oh, that one is pretty brutal. How about *Across the Universe*" he says.

"Okay, now playing…*Let it be by Carol Woods and Timothy Mitchum*," she says, leaning her head against the side of the plane to better watch the descent.

After a smooth landing, Shea grabs her purse and shoves her notebook and the borrowed pen inside as they walk off the plane. Keeping their heads down, John leads Shea to a gate that doesn't currently have a flight and is therefore empty. He stops suddenly, startling Shea. She raises her hands instinctively and presses them against his chest. He grabs one of her wrists softly, running his thumb softly over the sensitive skin, while he bends at the waist and speaks into an area several inches above her ear.

"I'm sorry that I startled you, but I need you to listen," he says softly.

She nods her head, and he continues, "We took a commercial flight here, but that can't happen again. From this point on, we are 'disappearing'. There can't be any paper trail, and as little camera exposure as possible. We're going to walk out of the exit closest to us, to the area where the planes park. Hugging the building, we have to make it around to a small airline, where a private jet will be waiting for us."

She nods again, he continues, "This is very important, keep your head all the way down. If they can prove we were here, they can potentially find us."

Shea stays close but lifts her face, and says, "How are we getting a private jet?"

"A package was dropped for me somewhere along the path we need to walk. As long as I get that, we'll be fine.

Twin Pines

00020 The Nerd Show

"Don't you want to keep your stuff for when we, like, get our own places?"

"Gregg, we won't have the room, and honestly, I don't see myself needing my own place anytime soon. I've been on my own for such a long time, I'm excited to have two couch movin' friends that I can count on."

Gregg and Todd both smile at her, and Gregg says, "Yeah, I don't either. You can pick whatever you want most. I don't really care."

"Okay, Todd, can you please get the rest of the boxes, so that poor driver can go? Just while we're looking at cars, then we'll be out to help."

"Yeah, anything for you…honey," he says, giving her a devilish grin.

"You liked that, didn't you?" she asks, walking away.

Once Gregg and Shea are back in front of the laptop, she pulls up the email with about twenty cars attached. Weeding through too big or too small, they land on a beautiful, orange 2022 Lexus NX 350 AWD with a luxury package. It only has eighteen thousand miles, and after contacting the dealership, they got the price down to forty thousand dollars. They'll even deliver it the day before they arrive.

Shea didn't want Todd involved in this part, because it isn't relocation, technically. Gregg generously puts up the whole amount, since Shea doesn't have a ton in savings, and she has a lot to figure out. She has to wait until the last minute to sell the Jeep—she already has it listed, but won't sell until the day before they leave, in hopes that with those funds, she can pay her half. Or whenever that bonus goes into her account. She's worried about it, but Gregg isn't—he got that huge bonus—forty thousand dollars is chump change in comparison. She sends the confirmation off to her realtor as soon as the dealership sends it.

"Well, look at us go," Shea says. Peeking out her front window, she sees that the truck is gone. Todd is now standing in the middle of her lawn, watching a twenty-five-foot trailer back into her driveway.

Gregg must have been watching, too, because he stands and heads out the garage door. Thinking that the men have that covered, she walks into the garage and starts grabbing the box bundles and carries them into the house. After about fifteen minutes, she has several bundles in her living room and is searching for the packing tape she knows she has. Walking out into the garage, thinking it must be in there, she begins opening the drawers of her Craftsman tool boxes until she finally finds the one she needs. In the same drawer is an old leather notebook she hasn't seen in years. She takes it out and decides maybe she will document her journey.

Glancing out into the yard, she doesn't see Gregg or Todd. She hollers in no particular direction, "I'm leaving in five. Be ready!"

Todd comes in from out front with Gregg in tow. "Where are we going?"

"I don't know. I think we should check out Gregg's place before I just start packing all my stuff."

"Okay, let's do it. Should we grab dinner on the way?" Todd asks.

"Sounds good to me," Gregg says. "I'm starving."

"You're starving? I only got a couple of bites of that burrito this morning," Shea says.

"Oh, yeah, let's go then," Todd says. "Are you going to chauffeur us, honey?"

"Duh," she says, walking out the front door.

Their *Friend* playlist starts up as soon as she starts the Jeep, and they head in the direction of Gregg's house. On the way, they pass a hoagie place, grab three, and get back on the road to Gregg's. Shea has never been to his house before, when they pull in, she sees that he lives in a duplex.

"Gregg, this is so cute. I love your little shutters," she says, putting the Jeep in park. She grabs her things, and gets out.

His shutters are a watery whitewash, and they are only about six inches wide. They look cool because they span the entire five feet of the window in height. They were kind of odd, but whimsical.

Gregg walks to his door, unlocking it, then suddenly, he feels self-conscious. What if she thinks he's a nerd? He opens the door wide; either they're really his friends, or they aren't. "Well, this is it, my humble abode."

Todd and Shea walk past him, setting all their things down on his beautiful, natural wood coffee table with raw edges. It was commissioned, with the middle cut out and replaced by a kind of map, from *Game of Thrones* that's encapsulated with resin.

"Wow, Gregg. You have some super cool stuff. We're definitely taking your coffee table," Shea says, looking around the room.

"Oh, you like it?" Gregg asks, surprised.

"Hell yeah! I love *Game of Thrones*, man. Maybe we can have a rewatch marathon. I've already watched it like three times," Shea says.

"I've never seen it," Todd says. By Todd's facial expression, Gregg can tell that he feels both pairs of eyes snap in his direction. "What? I just never had the time," he mutters.

"Well, that settles it. We're definitely having a re-watch-athon. As soon as we're in our brand-new awesome house, with the gigantic TV that is over there on that wall. Sitting on Gregg's couches with our feet up on that coffee table. Because apparently my house is garbage," Shea says, surprising Gregg.

"What? Don't say that! I honestly thought you wouldn't like my stuff," Gregg says, now feeling pride in his choices.

"Are you kidding? Your couches are the kind that move around and have all the pillow combinations. We could turn it into a bed-like couch! Plus, your TV is way bigger, and I didn't even know I wanted a table like this, but here it is, and I do," Shea says excitedly, flinging her arms in different directions depending on what she was talking about.

Gregg chuckles, "Well, it's all ours now, right, roomie?" he says, moving her purse and the other things they brought, so that they could eat at the coffee table.

Thirty or so minutes later, the gang is full and walking through Gregg's house. He and Shea go through everything that would go in the common areas and decide to take all of Gregg's living room furniture, including his TV, as well as his glassware and ultra-sharp chef's knives. With a plan of attack, Gregg is breathing a little easier and thinks Shea is too. Through it all they chat about how excited they are about their move.

"Well, I think I'll go home and get some stuff packed then, and list my furniture on Craigslist or something. We have a lot to do," she says.

"Shea, take a breath," Todd says, gripping the tops of her arms. "We've all done plenty today, and since I knew you wouldn't accept the help, I already scheduled a moving team to come pack both of your places. Since we're here right now, they can start here, if that's okay with you guys," Todd announces like they've just won a door prize.

"Are you kidding?" she asks, eyes wide.

"I didn't want to order or overstep. I can call it off. I just wanted you take some of the stress off of you. I mean, you still have to go in and hand off Project SNV," he says to Shea.

"No, man, this is awesome! Thank you. I'll probably need to wrap up all of my swords myself, though," Gregg says, walking into his office where said swords are displayed. "I'm gonna need a lot of bubble wrap."

As he starts planning how he'll pack them, Gregg hears Todd and Shea mildly arguing from the room he just left. Todd didn't seem to understand boundaries, and Shea was going to get sick of repeating herself. He would keep trying to go with the flow and be there for Shea every step of the way.

He takes his very sharp swords down off the wall and lays them along the wall on the floor, waiting to be wrapped up and packed. While surrounded by his swords, Gregg is lost in his happy place. The doorbell brings him back to reality, and he thinks to himself, "No need to rush, Todd and Shea are right next to the door."

The doorbell rings again.

"I'm coming," Gregg calls, putting down a sword and heading toward the front door, which Shea and Todd are literally right next to. Todd is holding Shea up by her butt and they're making out. "Oh, don't stop on my account guys. I wasn't just handling sharp objects or anything."

Shea breaks away from Todd and slides her legs to the floor. She pushes Todds hands away and turns toward the open front door, "Sorry, Gregg."

He nods at her, then looks out to see who rang the bell.

"Hello, my name's Ashley. I'm from the company 'We Like to Move-You Move-You', I was hoping to find a Greggory Marsh, Shea Murphy, or Todd Donoghue," she says, looking at all three of them now.

"Present," Shea says.

"I'm Todd," he says, raising his hand in a wave in the girl's direction.

"Gregg," he says, pointing to his chest.

"Okay, great. I just need one of your signatures on this form, and quick question—have you gotten any packing supplies yet?" she asks, passing a clipboard through the threshold.

As Gregg signs the form, he says, "I did get some boxes, but they aren't here, unfortunately."

"Again, I probably overstep. But I had Tina go grab some of them and load them in that truck we used earlier. It should be here any minute," he says, fidgeting with that ring.

Shea reaches over and playfully slaps him on the shoulder. "Bad Todd, Bad!"

All three of them laugh, then Gregg realizes they are being jerks. He looks at Ashley, and says, "I'm so sorry. You guys can come in. The boxes we have will be here shortly."

Ashley and her team walk into the house, looking everywhere at everything, starting some sort of inventory. Gregg sits down with Ashley, letting her know what they will and won't be taking. Ashley lets him know they can pack what they won't be taking, to sell or donate it, if he wishes. She also informs him that when they pack each box, there will be an inventory and picture attached to the outside of the box, with a digital copy as well, so they know what is where. She also tells him that she saw his swords in the other room and explains that they have special boxes with foam that forms the box's contents, to keep them safe. By the end of the conversation, Gregg feels very confident in their abilities. Ashley excuses herself to get to work.

Sitting around the coffee table, finalizing plans, Shea looks to Gregg, and asks, "What are the swords from, like *Lord of the Rings?*"

"Yeah, and *Game of Thrones, He-Man, The Hobbit, and Deadpool*," Gregg says, feeling like he's putting his 'nerd' on display.

As Todd just sits listening, probably not knowing most of the words Gregg is saying, Shea is listening intently with a smile tugging at her lips. "No way, that's so cool! So, you have, like, the glowing one Bilbo had? What about Longclaw? Oh, and a Nazgul Sword?"

Gregg chuckles. He cannot believe what he is hearing—Shea thinks he's cool. "Yeah, actually, all three, and many more."

"When we get to the house, I hope you'll display at least some of them in the common area, they're really cool," she says with a childlike excitement.

"We can see what works when we get there, for sure. Especially if you actually like them," Gregg says, his previous worry turning to pride in his 'nerd side.'

The three of them talk while Ashley and her gang work in the background. It was mostly Shea and Gregg describing the plot of *Game of Thrones* to Todd. He now has the opinion that the Lannister's suck—big surprise. They plan to go into the office the next morning, to finish things up before going to Shea's house to pack.

Feeling tired, Shea leans back against Todd and promptly falls asleep.

Twin Pines

00021 Head down

"**Keep** your head down, watch your feet," John says, taking Shea's hand and leading her out of the nearest door. Stepping to the right, he walks as close as possible to the outer wall of the airport without touching it, pulling Shea behind him. They walk at a normal pace for John, but a fairly quick pace for Shea. Some airport employees pass them with luggage, and others pass on their way to direct planes. As they pass under their first jetway, Shea thinks of the luggage that they checked on their flight.

"Where are our bags? Please tell me we're getting our bags," Shea whispers.

"Our bags will be on the airplane. I thought of everything. Don't worry, just keep moving," John replies, looking around the corner before moving forward.

Shea continues to be led by the hand around the building. With each person they pass, she worries that the gig is up, but they keep moving. At one point, they have to squeeze between some equipment and the building. As they do, John leans over, retrieves a canvas backpack from the ground, slings it over his shoulder, and resumes walking.

The small gate for the private jet is within view when an airport employee in an orange reflective vest, carrying cone-like flashlights approaches them. He's the guy who directs planes, telling them which way to go. John continues to move, continuing to drag Shea along behind him.

"Hey, what are you guys doing?" orange-vest guy calls to them.

John looks back at Shea, and whispers, "Just keep moving, don't engage."

"Hey, you two! You can't be over here. This is a secure area," he says, getting closer to the pair.

Shea drops her head even lower and puts all of her trust in John. From near the private plane, a man in a suit walks over to orange-vest guy and speaks in his ear. Orange-vest guy nods and walks away, returning to his duties. John continues walking, and the man in the suit meets them where they are.

"All is handled, Mr. Doe. Follow me to the plane. Can I take your bag?" the suited man asks.

"Of course," John says, handing over the backpack. "Are all pre-flight checks completed?"

"Yes, sir. As soon as you board, we'll seal the cabin and be ready for takeoff," man in a suit says, his eyes moving to Shea and lingering.

"Hey! Eyes forward friend. I appreciate our relationship, but I will not tolerate you or your crew staring too closely at my dealings. Do you understand?" John asks, his question laced with malice.

"Yes, sir. I didn't mean to offend, it's just, there's some fresh blood dripping down her face. I apologize sir," the suited man stammers.

John stops, grabs Shea's face, and tilts it up to the fluorescent lights overhead. He grimaces, looking at the man in the suit, he says, "My apologies. I just can't be too careful." To which the man in the suit nods.

John refocuses on Shea, leaning in close, he says, "Your stitches have opened. Don't worry, I have the kit in my bag. I'll fix it on the plane." He takes his hand and wipes the blood off of her face, and says, "Pull your headband down a little more, to cover the wound better until we get onto the plane."

Shea reaches up and adjusts her headband. John nods and continues the trek to the plane. He leads her directly to it, then up the stairs and onto the private jet. He deposits her in front of a chair near a table and asks the man in the suit where their bags are.

"They're in the bedroom, sir, in the closets. Is there anything else I can get for you?" he asks.

Shea looks up at John with pleading eyes. "Yeah, can I get some coffee and a couple shots of whiskey?" John asks.

"Right away, sir. Anything in the coffee?" suit man inquires.

"Do you have Truvia?" John says.

"Yes, sir. Anything else?" the man in the suit asks.

"Do you have a first aid kit on board?" John asks.

"Yes, right away. Gather what you need from your bags, and please take a seat. We'll begin taxiing shortly," he advises John.

John hustles to the back of the cabin, then returns with his supplies to sit with Shea. He drops them on the table and lets out a sigh of relief. Shea looks over to him from beneath her hood and can see the exhaustion on his face, but his gaze is still warm and kind.

"Why are you so nice to me?" she asks quietly, unsure if she is even allowed to talk yet.

"Because, you've always been good to me, and I care about you," John replies, avoiding her eyes.

"Oh, so I've risked everything to get you across the country to safety, while also cleaning your wounds along the way?" she asks sarcastically.

"That's closer to the truth than you realize. You don't give yourself enough credit, Shea. You are a force to be reckoned with, and I have always been on the right side of your wrath," he says, looking at her this time and smiling.

He could be on the cover of some Alaska Wilderness magazine

"Oh, okay," she says, looking down at her hands as the suited man returns with the requested items. Every part of Shea's body feels like it's in a vice, and her head is on fire. She glances at the man in the suit, and says quietly, "Thank you so much for all of your help. John is just super tired and grouchy, but I appreciate you saying something."

"Madam," he nods at Shea. Dropping the requested items on the table, then sensing a moment of privacy is needed, backs out of the room.

"Okay, as soon as we're at altitude, I'll take care of that wound. Why don't you drink your coffee and whiskey until then?" John says, sliding the mug and shots toward her while pulling the first aid kit toward himself to pick out what he needs.

Shea doesn't waste any time. Knowing what this is going to feel like, she decides not to pour the whiskey in her coffee. Instead, she quickly shoots both shots, grimaces, and then sips her hot coffee.

Once they reach altitude, John's out of his seat, moving quickly to fix Shea's sutures. Between the shots and her exhaustion, she doesn't have the energy to put up a fight. When he finishes, he pulls off her headband, and asks, "Do you have another one of these? This one is soiled and shouldn't go back on the wound."

"Yeah, I'll go find my bag and grab it," she says, getting up from the table.

Seeing her reflection in one of the mirrors lining the bedroom, she pushes her hood all the way back and examines John's handiwork. There are strings going this way and that, anchored in angry, red, swollen tissue. She grimaces, deciding to wait to put the headband on until John can have another look at it.

I haven't taken the pills... Pills!

Shea quickly reaches into her bag, grabbing her special tampon, she opens it and takes two pills this time. She is incredibly sore from whatever happened to her, and being on a plane for that many hours was not helping, at all.

Returning to her seat, she tells John, "I never took any of those antibiotics. And this," pointing to her head, "looks really red and swollen. It also feels like it's on fire, and I'm worried it might be infected. I don't know how close it is to my brain, but I figured you might want to take another look."

Rubbing his eyes, John gets up from the comfortable position he's in and stands over Shea.

"Where did Todd go?" she asks, curious.

"Breakfast and coffee, of course."

"He's always making sure we're fed," Shea says, walking toward the bathroom.

Shea sips her coffee with two sugars, while driving toward her house. Todd is sitting next to her, breaking off pieces of a chocolate croissant and feeding them to her. Gregg is in the backseat, eating an apple pastry.

Today's plan starts with a visit to Shea's house so she can get dressed, then head to the office and do whatever paperwork is needed. After that, the movers are going to meet them back at Shea's, to pack up her stuff and load what's going to Florida into the trailer. Depending on how long that takes, they might call Steve to move the trailer over to Gregg's so they can get it fully packed and on its way to Florida as soon as possible.

"Oh, also, I wanted to let you two know," Todd says looking between Shea and Gregg, "you'll probably want the moving truck at least a few days in front of you, if not a week. So, if you would like to come stay at the penthouse with me, you can go ahead and list your houses. That way we'd be ready to go whenever you guys feel like you have everything all wrapped up. If we leave a little early, you'll have time to unpack and get settled, maybe even hit the beach, before you start at Crown," Todd announces.

"Shit, I have to list my house. I feel like you're my tour guide, Todd," Shea says.

Gregg chuckles from the backseat. "I listed mine two days ago."

"Try hard," Shea slings over her shoulder playfully.

Arriving at Shea's house, she runs to the shower, cursing that she needs to wash her hair. She finishes in what she thinks must be record time and emerges from her room dressed in a lady's pant suit, hair done, made-up on, and perfumed. As she walks out to the living room, she can see Gregg and Todd leaning over her laptop.

"Whatcha doin' fellas?" she calls to them.

Immediately, Todd answers, "It was his idea."

Gregg chuckles, "What happened to bro-code, dude?"

"She doesn't like it when I make decisions without talking to her first. I figured you might be safer," Todd admits.

Gregg looks over at Shea, who gives him a look of confusion. "Alright, nothing is set in stone, so if you don't appreciate the gesture, then just pass on it, okay?"

"Okayyyyy," Shea says, now more confused.

"I called my Realtor—the one who listed my house—she already has a couple of offers she's looking into. I wanted to help you out, so," he looks over at Todd, then continues, "Todd and I went around and took pictures of the house—not your room yet, of course. Then my realtor looked up what you still owed, plus the pictures we have, and gave us a number she might be able to list it at, today. I can't list it obviously, you have to do that, but I figured I could do some of the leg-work for you. Here's the number," he says, turning the laptop in her direction.

Leaning over, Shea looks at the number provided. It seems astronomical, but she would walk away with close to one-hundred and fifty thousand dollars. She straightens herself quickly, and Gregg stands with her. Looking up at Gregg, she puts the side of her face against his torso and reaches her arms around his waist. That's when she can no longer hold it in—the flood gates open. Gregg holds her gently and rubs his large hand up and down her back. She feels him bending down to try to see her face, but she has it smooshed up against his torso.

"Shea, I'm sorry if I did something wrong. I just wanted to get the information for you, since we don't have a ton of time, is all. I feel terrible," he says.

Shea wipes her eyes with one hand while she holds him with the other. She doesn't even know how to explain this outburst. Once she feels somewhat pulled together, she relinquishes the warmth of Gregg's hold.

When she sits, a glass of water and a pile of tissues are placed in front of her. Looking at her guys, she smiles. At the expression, they take it as a cue that it's okay to sit.

"Thank you, Gregg. Both of you, really, I appreciate this," she says, dabbing her tears with a tissue. "I was dreading it, to be honest. You can tell her to send me the paperwork and get whatever photos you need. I think it's better if I'm not involved, actually."

She looks down at her hands, which hold a tissue. Again, wiping her tears, she continues, "When my parents died, there was a lot of investigation, but they never really found out how that fire started or how they died. It took years, but after they finally wrapped up their investigation, the insurance process started. I was leaving uni and looking for a job around that time. After I got the job here, I started looking for a place. I was young, with barely any credit or funds and then the various insurance agencies paid out, right around that same time. I took the money and paid off my student loans, then I decided to put about half down on this house and fill it with furniture. I bought my Jeep, cash, and then put whatever was left back into the house," she says, with a painful sigh.

Shea watches as Todd looks to Gregg, his face asking 'What does that have to do with selling the house?' She watches Gregg shake his head at Todd, then he grabs one of Shea's hands in his.

"Shea, I'm so sorry. I didn't know any of that. I was just trying to help. I feel like I overstepped. Please, forgive me," he says.

"Nothing to forgive Gregg. You helped me more than you know today, now I feel more ready to relocate," Shea says, squeezing his hand once, then dropping it as she stands. "Now, give me just a second to fix my face, and then we can get out of here. You can come with me, to take those pictures if you want. I'll just move when you need me to."

"Miss Murphy, Mr. Marsh. Good to see you both. We'll be meeting with each of you separately today. Miss Murphy, I'll have you in my office, and Mr. Marsh, you can head into Dax's office—he's expecting you," Beth, Dax's secretary, says.

Gregg gives Shea an odd look, but makes his way over to where Dax's office is and walks in. Beth turns, her back now facing Shea, and heads to her own office. Shea assumes she's meant to follow, so she does. Beth takes a seat behind her desk and waves a hand to her very own visitor chairs, silently inviting Shea to sit.

"Miss Murphy, thank you for coming in today. All we really need to do is make sure your NDA covers everything you've worked on, with the exception being discussing the chip with Crowned Skull Laboratories. A couple of other forms here state that you're not owed anything by this corporation, and of course, the 'exit interview' paperwork," Beth says, stacking several sheets of paper together. "Shouldn't take long—there's nothing we really need to discuss."

"Oh, okay. Easy then," Shea says, picking up the pen provided and signing the stack in front of her. When she finishes, Beth gathers the paperwork and walks Shea to her door. "Thank you for your time. Good luck on your future endeavors."

Shea steps out the door into the lobby, an odd feeling lingering about the meeting. She waits for about fifteen minutes, and Gregg is still in Dax's office. Taking out her phone she texts Todd.

Text to Todd 'Crown' at 11 a.m.:

> ‹ Hey honey =)

> ‹ What are you up to?

Ugh, I need to change his name in my phone.

Text from Todd at 11:02 a.m.:

> Meeting Ashley for Gregg, you guys almost done?

Text to Todd at 11:02 a.m.:

< Yeah, I think so, I'm just waiting for Gregg

Text from Todd at 11:05 a.m.:

> It might be a minute, they're definitely trying to retain him

> He won't be swayed, he's solid

Putting away her phone, she sits back and waits. After another fifteen minutes, Gregg finally emerges from Dax's office. She watches as Dax walks out the door with him and shakes his hand, with a shoulder grab to boot. Gregg just looks uncomfortable with the whole exchange, and when he finally approaches Shea, he looks down at her sitting there and gives her a subtle hand signal. Shea reads it as 'get the fuck up now. We need to go.'

She pops up out of the chair and has to jog to catch up with him.

As the climb into the Jeep, Shea asks, "What was that all about? What happened in there?"

"Oh my gosh. He kept throwing counter offers at me. He told me I could be the head of a department, which I obviously don't want. Then they said they could 'review' the offer Crown gave me to see if they can compete, and even tried to hint that they would 'dispose' of my rats if I left. But the rats are already in their new home, and I'm excited for our new beginning. Then, with like fifteen minutes left, Dax had to take a call—it was Todd. I don't know what Todd said but you should have seen Dax's face. After that, I had to sign a ton of paperwork, which I made sure I read carefully, after that kind of behavior," Gregg vents.

"Geez, mine took like two minutes—max. I signed stuff, and she told me good luck in the future," she says. "Oh, by the way, why is Todd meeting Ashley for you? He didn't elaborate over text."

"Well, last night you crashed pretty early. So, Todd and I kind of helped the crew with packing, just for a little while. I got to talking to Ashley, and she mentioned they only had a limited number of vehicles for the business. Since we're pretty much glued at the hip now, you chauffeuring me around and all," he says with a wink. "I thought selling my vehicle a little early wouldn't be a big deal. Plus, Todd promised he'd just always have a town car on call," Gregg says, chuckling. "Must be nice to be that kind of rich. Anyway, Todd ended up buying my car from me as part of 'relocation,' and he was meeting Ashley to hand over the title and keys."

"Oh, well, I guess that goes to show me, I shouldn't pass out early at the slumber party," she says.

"Don't be jealous. Todd says they could buy your Jeep, too, if you're interested," Gregg says.

When Shea opens her front door, she's shocked into immobility at the threshold. Ashley's crew is wrapping things in bubble wrap in every corner of her house. Todd rushes over, quickly explaining that he'd been there to observe, that everything was fine. Shea tries to explain again about making decisions without talking to her first, but he just shuts down. Todd tells her that he feels like Gregg can do the same things and it's fine. Explaining that Gregg didn't actually make any decisions for her, instead just got her useful information—means little, apparently.

By the time she got home, her furniture was already gone, pictures packed, books packed (including the one she was currently reading), and most of her clothes packed. Shea feels a little frantic about her pictures being gone, but then she sees a box labeled with a picture of her pictures and the inventory, next to the front door. She feels perturbed and tired, and she doesn't like it.

Seeming to sense her unease, Gregg says, "You should go pack a backpack. Just like four sets of clothes, toiletries, your make up—that kind of stuff. They didn't even leave my razer unpacked."

"Good idea, thank you, Gregg," she says, heading to her bedroom.

The next half an hour, Shea sits amongst her things, picking different outfits for the rest of her time in Ohio and her new life in Florida. Once she is satisfied that she has gotten at least the essentials—toothbrush, some deodorant, etc.—she hauls the backpack out to her Jeep, just in case Ashley wants to pack a random backpack.

She starts looking for her comrades, but she doesn't see them in the house, and she doesn't see them outside, so she walks into her empty garage. Well, almost empty. Todd and Gregg are sitting on the floor with a box in front of them, which is currently balancing Shea's laptop.

Shit, that's what I need to pack, where's the charger?

Clearing her throat, the men are startled and turn toward her. "Hey guys, whatcha doin'?"

They both stand to their full imposing heights. "Well, Shea, we were checking your offers so we could plan when we might be able to leave," Todd admits. "We weren't going to accept anything or make any decisions—just looking things over."

"What did you find?" she asks.

"Our realtor sent us both a few offers today to see if we'd like to accept any of them. You also got an offer on the Jeep, a good one too. So maybe you want to look those over? I also emailed our realtor in Florida and asked if we could move in a bit early. She said to just email her when we leave here, and she'll have the keys and paperwork ready for us," Gregg says.

"Wow, okay, well, give me my laptop," she says, giving them 'gimmie' hands.

The rest of that day was spent getting the trailer packed and accepting offers. Shea's house was fully packed, and Ashley's team had already loaded everything on the trailer while Shea was on the phone with her realtor. Shea accepted an offer that put one hundred seventy-five thousand dollars in her account, marking the start of her new life. She also accepted the offer on the Jeep, and after cleaning out her personal belongings, handed the keys over to its new owner shortly after.

Steve came to pick up the trailer and set off for Gregg's house. Ashley and her team followed behind, with Todd, Gregg, and Shea following in a town car.

After Ashley's team loads Gregg's belongings into the trailer, they leave Todd, Gregg and Shea sitting in the living room, on Gregg's couch.

"Well, friends, this is the real test. Are you ready?" Shea asks, rubbing her hand on the couch, then patting it.

"I was born ready," Todd says, standing and flexing.

"Anything for my CMF's," Gregg adds.

"CMF?" Shea asks.

"Couch Movin' Friends. Duh," Gregg says, and now he is getting up and flexing.

They are both ripped. Holy shit, maybe I can't move a couch

Shea stands, smiling and nodding at each of them. The guys position themselves on either side of the couch, bending over they slip their hands under it. They lift it up so that the armrests are in front of their faces. Shea laughs, because of her height discrepancy with both men—they are holding it at around Shea's shoulder level. So, trusting the strong men, she bends a little and stands under the couch, pressing her upper back against its bottom.

Gregg and Todd chuckle as they walk out of the front door and up the trailer ramp. Inside the trailer, Shea steps out so she doesn't get squished. As they lower the couch, Shea puts her hands under the bottom of it to make it look like she helped.

With that done, Todd calls out, "Okay, Ashley, we're done doing our weird thing."

Ashley and her team wink into existence just outside the trailer, holding moving blankets, cardboard, bubble wrap and packing tape.

Twin Pines

00023 🌲🌲 El-cap-ee-tan

Using his fingers, he brushes the hair away from the suture line and tilts his head this way and that, inspecting the wound. Tsking, he puts his hands on his hips, worrying his bottom lip with his top teeth.

"What, what is it? What's wrong?" Shea asks, her voice thick with concern.

"Okay, so when I got to you, there was a small burr hole through your skull under the obvious wound." John sits in the chair next to her, spinning it back and forth ever so slightly. "I was expecting that, though, and had prepared with the necessary tools to…well, plug the hole, for lack of a better term"

"Everything was sterile, and you were unconscious for a few days following. I didn't suture you up right away because I didn't know what the sharp instrument was, that was used to make the incision, or the conditions of your environment when it happened. I'm still waiting for you to remember that, so you can tell me. I didn't see any signs of infection when you woke up, so I decided to go ahead and close it," John admits.

"And now?" Shea asks, trying to take in everything he just said.

"And now, it appears to be infected, you're right," John replies, opening up the first aid kit in front of him. "We will start the antibiotics right away. Because there is no odor or pus, I'm going to leave the sutures for now. Without them, the wound is jagged and gaping, leaving your skull exposed, which we do not want where we're going. But I will warn you, if this doesn't start improving, I might have to cauterize it," John finishes, not looking at Shea but at the first aid kit.

"I understand," Shea says, suddenly feeling lighter than air. She reaches over and stops John's chair, placing her hands on the armrests she holds him in place. She maneuvers, to place her face in his line of vision, once he is looking at her, she scoots her chair as close as it will go to his. John looks confused as he places his hands over hers on his armrest. Glancing at his hands—seeing his wedding ring—Shea sobers just enough to realize she might be crossing a line—she doesn't know how long it's been since he lost his wife, and she's unsure if she's pushing him into something he doesn't want.

Having no clue what came over her, a blush creeps over her cheeks, and she pulls her hands out from under his and turns away.

"What? Do I have bad breath?" John asks.

"No, I just… I'm sorry. It would be inappropriate of me to presume or overstep. I can't lose you. I literally have no one else," Shea gets out, feeling vulnerable.

John is quiet for a long moment, so Shea decides to sneak a peek at him from the corner of her eye. He sits in his chair with his hands in his lap, his right-hand fidgets with the ring on his left. His gaze is fixed on Shea, and she doesn't know what it is—between the pills, whiskey and infection—but at that moment, she is hit with an intense wave of nausea.

Holding her hand to her mouth, she stands quickly, pleading with her eyes for help.

"In the bedroom, next to the first closet on the left," he says, assuming her need.

After Shea tosses the very few cookies she had in her stomach, she washes up and splashes her face with cold water. Staring in the mirror, she still sees a bruised and broken woman. But now, that woman also has dark circles the color of plums and a face so pale she could be considered translucent.

"Are you okay?" Shea hears as soon as she opens the bathroom door. John is sitting on the bed waiting for her, and as soon as he sees her, he rushes to her side.

Ugh, did he hear all that? I'm so embarrassed

Holding her around the waist, he helps her back to the table, where a charcuterie board is waiting. It's covered in various meats, cheeses, olives, dried fruits, and crackers. There's also a glass of ice water and two pills.

"This looks great, sorry about everything before," Shea says, feeling awkward that she got so close to him. "What are the pills?" she asks.

"They're the antibiotics we talked about. I'm going to have you take a couple of different kinds in hopes we get it knocked out," he says, picking up a bandage.

Shea sits back in her seat and eats a couple of crackers before trying anything else. Feeling her nausea abate, she takes the antibiotics and eats a piece of cheese, all while John is working on getting the bandage he has made onto her head. After he has it placed, he hands her the headband for her to put over it.

When Shea pulls it over her head and starts to slide it up her forehead, John takes it from her hand. She looks up at him, confused, unsure of what happened.

"You were going to drag it over the bandage. I'll do it," he says, very carefully lifting the headband over the bandage and placing it, just so.

"Yeah, this is great and everything, El cap-ee-tan, but I kinda need my ears for hearing, and listening, jamming out, et cetera," Shea teases.

John laughs, turning his head to see that he had accidentally left the headband over both of her ears. Fixing it, he asks, "Is that better, first mate?"

"Wait a sec, I want to be skipper," Shea pouts.

"But you just called me El cap-ee-tan. We can't both be captains," John says.

"A skipper isn't a captain, is it?" she asks, her mouthful of ham.

"Yes," he chuckles.

"Well, think of something better than first mate, then," she demands.

"Okay, what about deputy?" he asks.

"Naw, then you'd have to be Sheriff, and I'm liking El cap-ee-tan," she teases.

"Okay, what about lieutenant?" John says, packing up the first aid kit.

"That would be cool, then you could call me L.T., because I can never remember my 'name,'" she says, using air quotes.

"Sure, no problem, L.T. Now, we're safe on this flight, so we can both sleep. Do you want to take the bedroom? I can sleep out here on this couch," John offers.

"Oh, yeah, okay," Shea says, getting up from the table. But pauses, turning back to John, she says, "Actually, I don't want to be alone. And although I barely know you, past me and current me feel like we can trust you. Can you please just lie with me?"

"Are you sure?" he asks, tentatively.

"Yeah, super sure."

"Okay, you go in first and get cozy. I'll be in shortly," John says.

Shea hobbles into the bedroom, kicking off her shoes and shrugging out of her hoodie. She pulls back the comforter and sheet, then drops herself onto the bed. She lies there, watching for John for only a couple of minutes. When he enters, he slides off his shoes, placing them neatly in front of the closet, then glances at the bed. With a soft chuckle, he slides in next to her, pulling up the covers.

Shea had pulled the covers on his side as far down as she could, signaling he didn't need to sleep over them for her. Now, with him in bed next to her—with his weight and body heat—she feels her whole body fully relax. Just before she drifts off, she hears the deep, even breathing of an exhausted man.

Sometime during the flight, Shea's eyes flutter open briefly, half alert, she recognizes they must have found each other in the middle of the bed. She clings to his left arm, while he lies on his left side, his right hand resting on Shea's side— in the place her figure dips in beautifully, while she is on her side at least. In the dim light, she realizes that their faces are so close to one another's, they are literally breathing each other in, before slipping back into sleep.

Twin Pines

00024 DNA

They decide to stay at the penthouse for four days before they take Todd's private jet to Florida. Tracking the trailer on the app that Steve had shown them, they think four days should be plenty of time.

They become ever closer, day by day. The three of them doing (almost) everything together. Gregg saw Shea in jeans and leggings for the first time. He continually had to remind himself that he didn't have a snowflake's chance in hell with her.

Their houses were sold, their vehicles sold, and their belongings are waiting for them outside their new house, alongside their new car. They are ready. The day is finally here—in a couple of hours, they will be boarding Todd's private jet. All three of them did their morning kitchen routine, where Shea drank her coffee while Todd and Gregg cooked breakfast. Now, they were all double checking their packing, ensuring they were leaving nothing behind. Three bags and a purse sit by the front door, waiting.

"Damn girl, won't you be cold?" Gregg hears Todd say from the kitchen. Peeking around the corner, Gregg sees Shea in a jean skirt and a top that ties around her neck. He watches as Todd stalks over to her, devouring her with his eyes from a short distance.

Gregg feels the need to intervene, on whatever is about to happen. He's not jealous, he just wants to get going. "Cover your nakedness, I'm coming out," Gregg calls, trying to sound fun and jokey.

He sees them turn toward him as he walks down the hall. "Are we all ready to head out?" he asks.

He's made sure to wear jeans and a T-shirt that aren't wrinkled. The T-shirt says *The North Remembers*.

"Ah, I love your shirt!" Shea squeals. "Look what I have," she says, pulling a cropped gray hoodie over her head.

He reads it as soon as she straightens it out — it says *Thankee, Sai*.

"That's so awesome. How did you know I've read *The Dark Tower* series?" he asks.

"You said something one day that made me think you had — plus, we pretty much have the same taste in everything," she admits.

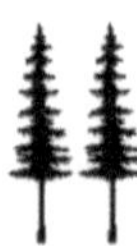

The three couch-movin' friends collect their bags and embark on an adventure to a private jetway. Shea and Gregg make sure to soak in the whole experience—sipping champagne, reclining in massaging seats, and napping in oversized chairs.

Meanwhile, Todd stays busy on his phone and laptop, orchestrating everything behind the scenes: a team en route to unpack their trailer, other arrangements for their new home, and secure access programmed at Crowned Skull Laboratories. He's already sent in their

DNA—making sure they'll be able to enter the most restricted areas of the facility.

And as they laugh and lounge just a few feet away, Todd watches them quietly.

He can't wait to see their faces when he finally tells them the truth.

When their plane lands, Shea and Gregg shoot up, hardly containing their excitement. Todd lingers for a moment, packing his electronics in his black leather backpack. As the plane door opens, stairs are revealed, leading down to the hot pavement. Todd catches up to Shea and Gregg just before they get off the plane.

"Guys, I hate to say it, but I have to stop by the office to get them going on all of your paperwork," Todd says.

He is met with a "lame" called out from Gregg, and a pouty face from Shea. "Listen, I won't be long. I'll meet you at your new house. The town car will take you straight there. There might be some movers unpacking the trailer, so don't freak out."

Twin Pines

00025 Wait Here

"**Sir,** Madam, we are beginning to make our descent into Anchorage. The local time will be approximately 9:35 p.m. when we land. The current temperature is forty-nine degrees with light showers and mild winds. We'd like to thank you both for choosing to fly with us today, and we hope to serve you again with future travel needs." The intercom crackles then goes silent. John opens his eyes to see Shea looking up at him.

"Uh, sorry about that," he mutters, pulling his arm gently from her grasp and standing. "I didn't realize I'd get so close while I was sleeping."

"You have nothing to apologize for, that was probably all me anyway. I've always done that monkey cling thing," she says, also standing and grabbing her boots.

"Yeah, I've noticed. I've never asked about it, but that does seem to be your go-to move," he says, curious if he'll finally figure out why.

"My go-to, huh?" Shea smirks. "Yeah, you could say that. I'm guessing that's not the first time I've monkey-clung you?"

189

John nods in answer. "Yeah, figures. When I was a kid, whenever my dad left the house, I would cling to his leg. He would walk around acting like I wasn't there. It always cracked me up. As I got older, it just got funnier to me, because he would use obvious effort to walk."

"I can imagine," John chuckles. "So, how did that develop into what it is now?"

"When I got my first boyfriend and I didn't want him to leave, I'd do the same thing—wrap myself around his arm trying to hold him in place. But, the tighter I held him, the farther away he seemed to drift," she says, her tone soft. "After dad died, I stopped doing it. It was too painful. But if I have done this with you before, it must mean something. Maybe I just feel safe with you or that I feel absolutely secure in the knowledge that you will take care of me and never leave me," she says, looking into his eyes when she does.

"Shea, I…" he starts, he has to be careful about what he says. "I can't talk about our history. In time, you'll remember. But yes, you can trust me with anything. And I think I'm kind of proving that I'll never leave you, right?"

"Yes, I just wish I remembered. John, you are obviously a big part of my life. Even though my memory is gone, my subconscious knows… it knows you're important."

John stands there, his gaze locked on hers, unwilling to look away first. They feel the plane's descent and it breaks the spell. They both sit down on the bed to put on their shoes, and John moves to the main sitting area for landing. He watches Shea stay in the room to take a swig out of her bottle of Crown before coming out and sitting in the same chair she sat in before.

As the plane continues its descent, Shea adjusts her headband and tries to tuck her braid back into her hoodie.

"Here, let me help," John says.

"Thanks, it got all bunched up while I slept," Shea says.

As he fixes her braid, the plane touches down in a dark, cold, rainy, new land. John grabs all of their bags, and although Shea offers to carry her own, John would hear nothing of it. As he walks toward the stairs, Shea following, the man in a suit approaches John. He speaks close to John, updating him on a team he had dispatched to the area, then hands him the canvas backpack.

Once they reach the bottom of the stairs, John pauses and turns to Shea. She walks up to him and can't help herself—she immediately starts giggling. She tries to stifle the sound, unsure what their current status is, but the sight of John, carrying two duffel bags, her hiking pack, and the canvas backpack he had dropped over his head—looking like it was trying to aggressively choke him from behind—was just too much. His hat, which must have been knocked out of place by the falling canvas backpack, was crooked and sticking up almost straight. The whole scene screamed exhaustion.

As she was trying to pull herself together, he takes the time to rearrange everything and get himself organized. Once she's wrapped up her fit, he swings one of the large duffel bags at her thighs, making her stumble sideways. They smile at each other, and John asks, "Alright, are you about done?"

"Yeah, sorry, but I needed that," she says.

"How big of a nip did you take?" he asks, placing his hands on his hips, narrowing his eyes slightly.

Shea takes a dramatic inhale, then says, "How dare you accuse me…but seriously, how did you know?"

"Well, your pack is a couple of pounds lighter, and I've seen you tipsy before. This is close. Whereas it's cute and all, I need you to be able to focus," he says.

Shea did have a few pulls from the bottle of whiskey, so she smiles at him, and says, "Do you really think I'm cute?"

"Oh, man, this is not the time or place, Shea. We need to get moving," he answers, kicking himself, knowing how Shea can be.

"Okay fine, I'm over standing in the rain anyway. What's the next move?" she asks.

"There's a truck in the parking lot—an older 7.3L F-250. We just need to find it and we're outta here," he says, turning and walking toward the lot.

"Um, okay, but what color is it?" Shea asks, having no idea what the vehicle he described looks like.

John chuckles and looks down at her walking next to him, "It's blue, with a greyish colored stripe down the sides."

"Oh, so, older meaning—like nineties?" Shea asks.

"Yeah, inconspicuous—that's the goal," he says.

"So, once we find it, what are we doing next?"

"We find a hotel. We need showers, hot food, and sleep. Just for one night," he says.

"And tomorrow?"

"We have a day of travel ahead of us, which is why we need some quality rest," he says, pointing to a truck a bit in the distance. "I think that might be it there."

"Well then, let's go. This might be light rain, but it's chilly. I'm cold," she says, her arms crossed tight against her chest for warmth.

John glances over at her, noticing that her headband has slipped a little, pulling at the bandage he applied earlier. The wound looks angry, red, and swollen. "Hey, fix your headband and put your hood up, okay? We need to keep that wound dry."

Shea fixes herself as they near the truck. John places their bags— except for the canvas backpack—into the bed of the truck, feeling around the wheel wells, until he finds the key attached to a note on the third one.

He unlocks her door first, helping her up into the truck before walking around to the driver's side.

As he passes around the rear window, Shea is hit with the memory of a song. Scrambling to slide over, she reaches over and pulls up the lock on the driver's side door. John smiles at her through the rain-covered window and climbs in beside her.

"The Ataris, huh?" John says, placing the backpack between them and turning his body toward her.

"Yeah, you know that song?"

"Of course, I do. I know you, don't I? Have you ever seen the movie that part of the song was taken from?" he asks.

"I don't think so, but I bet it was a good one," she says.

"We'll have to watch it sometime," he says, putting the key into the ignition and backing out of their parking space. "There's a hotel fairly close that's nice. I already talked to them, and they won't ask for a credit card on file."

"Sounds good. Lead on." She says, settling back in her seat.

When they pull into the hotel parking lot, John asks Shea to stay in the truck while he runs inside. He grabs the canvas backpack and walks toward the hotel. Shea is left to be bored out of her mind—no phone, no book, nothing to pass the time. She decides to listen to *Your Boyfriend Sucks by The Ataris* on her iPod, since they'd just talked about it.

John walks out of the hotel a couple of songs later and holds a single finger up at Shea, no, not that one, the one signaling for her to hold on. She continues to look around outside at the green trees and wildflowers, scrolling through her iPod for the perfect song. She doesn't realize that she has completely stopped paying attention to anything other than her iPod. Until there's a loud tap on her window, she squeals and jumps. Her head jolts up to peer through the rain covered window.

Twin Pines

00026 🌲🌲 Thoughtful?

■ ■ ■ ■ ■ □ □ □ □ □

All three of them exit the plane and head to two different town cars. Gregg and Shea spend the entire ride to the new house pointing out things that they see from their side of the car. Gregg grows even more excited when they pass by some of the landscaping they saw on Google Maps, which is now starting to surround them. The town car pulls into the driveway, next to the large trailer that is parked there. Shea and Gregg grab their bags and head to the side of the house to check out their new car, before making their way to the already open front door.

For a moment, they just watch the people with boxes streaming into their house. Then, an idea strikes Gregg. He throws his backpack down on the threshold, and steps closer to Shea, taking both her backpack and purse from her hands, placing them next to his. Shea looks confused but doesn't protest as he lifts her off her feet and into a bridal carry. She wraps her arms around his neck and smiles up at him, pretty much making his entire year in that moment.

"On this day, I proclaim this 'Casa SheGre'. May there be many memories of fun, tomfoolery, and re-watch-athons. This is only the beginning," he says, while stepping over the threshold.

When they get inside, they see that all of their living room furniture is already set up, and there are boxes everywhere.

"As much as I love feeling light as a feather and all, I do still think I'm probably causing compression fractures all up and down that long spine ya got," Shea says, from his strong, competent arms.

He looks down at her face, noticing she is holding herself up with her arms around his neck, he drops the arm behind her back, of course, she squeals. He brings that hand up and pushes Shea's glasses up her face, and then pushes her fly aways behind her ear. All the while, she just continues to watch him with curious eyes.

"Okay, are you trying to prove how strong you are? Because I will never question you again. You're holding me up with only one arm. You're like Thor in my book," she says.

He slowly releases her, letting her slide down his body. Once her feet are on solid ground, he says, "If I'm Thor, you must be Mjolnir, because lifting you is effortless, and you make me feel worthy." He instantly blushes, angering him at his body for its betrayal.

She chuckles. "Alright, alright. Let's go pick out our bedrooms and see where we're going to put your sword collection."

They leave their shoes by the door and take off through the house, giggling like children the whole time. Gregg offers Shea the room that is closer to the beach, with windows facing the sunrise. Her reaction to which, is to squeal, place her hands on his shoulders, and jump up to give him a kiss on the cheek.

They direct the gang of people where to set up each bedroom set, and Shea starts to look for their new coffee maker, courtesy of Todd. They unpack boxes as they find them, and eventually the moving people finish up, taking the trailer with them when they leave.

Later that evening, Gregg and Shea are still going strong. They've been across the house from each other for a couple of hours, working on their respective rooms.

Todd walks up to their front door, carrying a ton of Chinese takeout and a collector's edition Blu-ray bundle of *Game of Thrones*. Walking into the house, he brings the takeout to the kitchen, and puts the Blu-ray set on the coffee table.

"Sheeaaa, Greeeegggg," he sing-song calls out in both directions. The house isn't very large, but Shea likes it, so he figures he will probably be here a lot.

Gregg comes running out of his room, wearing a pair of swimming trunks and a long silk robe, holding a thin sword above his head. Like a nerd ready for battle. Shea follows from the other side of the house, dressed in a one-piece bathing suit with a short silk robe, holding a matching sword in front of her. Like a scared rich lady that never wears pants.

"Okay, please tell me this was planned," Todd says, chuckling, holding his hands up in surrender.

"What was planned?" Gregg asks, lowering his sword arm and getting closer.

Todd leans his head toward Shea, who stands there with her sword arm relaxed by her side, watching Gregg intently.

They both burst out laughing, pointing at one another. Gregg walks over to her, grabs the sword, and places them both on some sort of holder that is set up in their great room.

Turning to Todd, he says, "We talked earlier about going swimming, but we never took a break. I gave her the sword earlier, just in case she felt unsafe being alone on the other side of the house. Great minds, I guess."

"Wow, I leave you alone for a few hours, and you're morphing into the same person," Todd says, with a grin. "I brought takeout, and I found a nice box set of *Game of Thrones*—I figured we could start our watch-athon before we have to go to work every day."

Shea walked over to the counter, while Todd was talking and is unpacking the takeout containers. "What kind of Chinese did you get?" she asks, as she lifts the containers out of the plastic bags.

"I'm pretty sure there's one of everything on the menu there, so there should be something you like," Todd replies.

"Man, you didn't have to do all of this, thank you," Gregg says, now opening the containers.

Coming around to where they are inspecting the contents, Todd pulls out the paper plates and plastic silverware he bought. Setting three plates on the kitchen counter, he watches Shea look and smell the containers. She finally decides on a couple of different containers.

"What'cha got?" he asks, gently bumping his shoulder (elbow) against her shoulder.

"Well, my favorite—General Tso's chicken," she points to one, then the other, "and house Lo Mein." She then grabs a third container and places what looks like fried wontons on her plate.

"What's that?" Todd asks, pointing with his chin.

"Rangoons. They're stuffed with like cream cheese and sometimes crab."

Gregg has also made himself a plate, then looks at Todd, and asks, "Hey, man, you want anything in particular from over here? I can put it on a plate for you."

"Oh, thanks, I think I'll do beef and broccoli with white rice, if you could, that'd be great," Todd answers.

"Nice, that's what I'm having too, brotha," Gregg says, sliding a plate to Todd.

"I'll bring the whole container of Rangoons in case anyone wants to share," Shea says.

"We don't have any drinks," Gregg says, peering into their empty refrigerator.

"Yeah, I didn't think about that," Todd says, pulling out his phone.

"Neither did we, obviously," Shea sighs, making eyes at her empty water bottle.

Todd can feel the weight of their stars as he stands against the counter, typing on his phone.

"Dude, you don't have to jump to spend money every time we need something. We don't expect that," Gregg says, sounding earnest.

"Yeah, Todd, don't worry about it. I heard the tap water is good here anyway," Shea says, lightly placing a hand on his arm.

"No, it's fine. Earlier I sent Tina to the grocery store, and I never told her to deliver the groceries. I didn't even think about it when I bought dinner and the show. She'll be here in a couple of minutes—she doesn't live far from here," Todd says.

The three of them carry their plates and plastic silverware to the coffee table. Luckily, the movers that set up the living room had already hooked up their electronics. Gregg grabs up the Blu-ray set and takes the plastic wrap off, opening the first disc, he pops it into the player and presses play. As the incredibly long intro song plays, they all dig in.

A few minutes later, they hear what sounds like a few heavy kicks to the front door. Todd immediately rises to answer it.

Thoughtful or rude?

Tina walks in, her arms weighed down with at least six plastic bags on each side. As Todd reaches out to take the bags, Tina just whips her head back, and says, "Trunks full, sir, I can make it with these." Todd and Gregg step out of the house as Tina slides off her flip-flops and heads to the kitchen, depositing the groceries on the stove. She then slides all the Chinese containers further down on the counter to make room for the rest of the groceries.

Gregg and Todd walk back into the house with a case of water each, and the rest of the bags shoved onto their forearms. They stack the waters on the floor at the entrance of the kitchen and drop the bags onto the counter next to the Chinese food, completing the unloading of the groceries.

Shea walks over and closes the front door, since they couldn't. Turning to Tina, she says, "Thank you so much girlie! Do you want some Chinese? We have plenty."

"Sure, just a little though, I don't want to keep them in the carrier too long," Tina answers.

"Keep what, where?" Shea asks, confused.

"Oh," chuckling, Tina turns around.

"Oh, my goodness! They're so adorable," Shea exclaims, walking up to Tina's back and sticking her fingers through an air hole grommet. There are two ferrets in a plastic/acrylic backpack, that Tina is currently wearing. As Shea wiggles her finger in the air hole, they rub their noses on it and then go back to digging at other air holes.

Tina stays, sitting on the floor near the coffee table, eating some Chinese, while Gregg and Shea shoo Todd out of the kitchen, so they can unpack all the groceries. Tina picked up a lot of great stuff, with several different beverage options for them. They work side by side, organizing the fridge and pantry, both pleased with their partner's efforts.

Almost finished, with only one bag remaining, Gregg grabs it and opens it. He lifts the contents up out of the bag and shows it to Shea, it's a bottle of Crown Royal.

"Alright, now it's a party," Shea says with a grin, grabbing a can of Coke out of the fridge. "Who wants some?"

"No, thank you," Tina calls from the front door. "I'm outta here, guys. See you in a few days, at work." She waves and heads out.

"I'll take two fingers, on the rocks," Todd says, from the couch.

"You think it'll mix well with a Capri Sun?" Gregg asks.

Shea whips her head in his direction, and gives him a look that says, "are you serious."

Gregg flushes a little, and says, "I mean, I'll have it the way you take it, Shea."

Shea pours the drinks and passes them out on her way back to her spot on the couch, between her two guys. Her Chinese is mildly cold, but she doesn't care. She presses play on their show and finishes her dinner—and a few drinks.

Shea is being carried to her new room, half-asleep she has no idea who it is. Curious, she reaches for his hair. Her fingers sink into a soft, fluffy mane, and she knows it's Gregg. In her mind, it doesn't really matter which one of them it is, because she trusts them both, but since it's her house with Gregg, she's glad it's him.

As he begins to lay her down on her bed, Shea grabs for the front of his shirt—but ends up with a fistful of chest hair. A grunt is the only reaction from Gregg.

She whispers, "Gregg, please stay with me. I won't be weird. I just want your company… please."

She opens her eyes just a little, catching a glimpse of Gregg swaying slightly on his feet. "Shea, I don't want to give Todd the wrong idea. He's our boss, remember? Plus, he'll be back in a little while, he just left to shower and pack a bag," he says softly, into the darkness, his hand resting gently on Shea's arm.

"Okay, so just sit with me for a few minutes, until he gets back. No big deal," she says, mumbling against her pillow.

I hate feeling like I need him, but I know he's a safe guy to need

"Shea, I really…" Gregg starts, but falters.

"Please, Gregg. I've always been alone. I don't want to be alone anymore," she begs.

"Alright, fine," he sighs, sitting down on her bed and lying next to her, on top of the covers.

"Thank you, Gregg. You're my best friend," Shea says, her voice thickening with emotion. She reaches out and grabs his arm, the one closest to her, pulling it toward herself, she hugs it tightly.

Gregg is frozen, his arm currently cuts right in between Shea's breasts, and his hand is tucked in between her legs, close to her body. He reminds himself that they are friends, best friends, all three of them. Plus, Shea is only clingy with him because she feels safe with him.

A few minutes later, Gregg hears her breathing deepen. He softly whispers, "Good night, Shea," before he scoots to the edge of the bed, silently slipping out of her door.

He leaves mostly for his own safety. He has no idea when Todd will return, or how he would react to seeing Gregg in Shea's bed. Fortunately, he escapes with plenty of time to spare—Todd doesn't come back until sometime in the morning, dressed and ready for the day.

"Hey man," Gregg says, pulling the ingredients needed to make breakfast for three from the fridge.

"Hey, did you end up carrying her to bed?" Todd asks, a slight laugh in his voice.

"Yeah, she was out. I thought about leaving her on the couch, but it was our first night in the house, so I thought she deserved to sleep in her bed," Gregg answers.

"Yeah, but the couch is kind of like a bed, right? That's one of the reasons she picked it, wasn't it?" Todd asks, now leaning casually against the bar.

"I mean, yeah—I just thought she'd be more comfortable in her room, I guess," Gregg responds, breaking eggs into a pan.

"I'm just saying you don't really need to be carrying her all around town, now do you?" Todd asks, giving Gregg a look he's never seen before. There's a shift in Todd's demeanor, a tension that Gregg can't decipher, before Todds mask falls back into place.

"Hey, will you turn on that coffee pot? I'm going to go wake her up so we can start the day's festivities," Todd says, then walks to Shea's wing.

Twin Pines

0027 C.I.A

Looking out the window, she sees a man dressed in a nicely tailored suit, smiling at her.

Knowing she has been told to trust no one, she is instantly on high alert and pissed that her bag is in the back of the truck. Smiling back at the man, she says, "Yes?" through the window.

The man brings up his right hand, revealing a gun. With it he rolls his wrist, signaling for her to roll down the window.

Shea feels hot and her mind is moving slowly. She's panicking, heart pounding in her chest. Trying to buy herself some time, she acts like she is trying to roll down the window, but it's not moving. "I'm sorry, sir. It seems to be stuck," she says again through the window, and prays he doesn't get an itchy trigger finger.

"I'm not that stupid, Ms. Murphy. Please, roll down the window. This will go a lot smoother if you cooperate," he says.

"Can you tell me what your business is?" Shea asks, trying to stall until John can come back.

"ROLL DOWN THE WINDOW!" he shouts at her.

She uses his outburst as an excuse to inch closer to the driver's side door, feigning fear. As she reaches the door, the man hasn't realized what Shea is going to attempt. Using this to her advantage, she contorts her face into one of pure terror. With her back to the driver's side door, she tucks her feet in close to herself on the seat, hugs her knees, and drops her head onto her arms.

"Ms. Murphy, no one is going to rescue you. If that's what you're thinking, your caretaker has already been dealt with. So, just get out and we'll take you home," the man tries convincing her.

Shea had been hoping John would be the white knight, but her plan changed as soon as she realized she was well and truly fucked. Reaching her hand to her crucifix, she asks God for strength, speed and to please be with John.

Oh yeah, and please don't let me get shot

All the while, she is slowly inching backwards, so her back is pressed tightly up against the driver's side door.

"Ms. Murphy, this is your final warning. I am not allowed to kill you, but I can hurt you. If you won't come with me, I'll bring someone here that I'm sure you'd really *love* to see," the man says with an evil sneer.

Good use of sarcasm, evil henchman sir, now where is that handle

For Shea, everything that happens next feels like it all goes so fast. She feels around behind her back for the door handle. She looks to the man, who is now holding the gun aimed straight at her through the passenger window, laughing. In one fluid motion, she uses the hand behind her back to pull the door handle while pressing her left elbow into the steering wheel, depressing the horn. Midway through her maneuver, Shea thinks she doesn't need just any white knight, she has a strong feeling that she's the white knight.

Using the momentum from the weight of the door and pushing off the seat cushion with both feet, she lands on her feet outside, just a second later. Ducking quickly behind the side of the truck, she takes a peek under the vehicle. The man is walking around the front, heading straight for her position. She throws a booted foot up onto the back wheel and boosts herself up into the truck bed.

She looks to the hotel for a split second and sees John running—he had parked the truck far away due to its length. It's going to take him a while to get to her. Shea's attention snaps back to the man, who is now behind her, still on the ground, holding his gun in a chopping-like position, aiming to knock her over the head with the handgun.

"You got another thing coming, buddy," she mutters under her breath, grabbing her pack and tossing it off the other side of the truck. She jumps down behind it, twisting, tearing pain rips through her ankle in the process, but she still moves as fast as she can.

She can see that he is now moving toward her around the back of the truck, so she drags her pack to the front of the vehicle and begins feeling around for the zipper pouch she needs. Her mind goes from racing to a focused calm, she feels like something takes over her, like maybe she was in the CIA.

If I weren't so miserable and scared, I just might wonder...

She finds and unzips the proper pouch and immediately feels the bulky gun case. Remembering that the key is on her wrist, she thanks anyone who will listen and unlocks the case. The sound of footsteps closing in causes her heart to gallop. She shoves her backpack under the truck and crawls under herself, while she pulls out her security 9 handgun. She presses the mag release and checks it to see that it's full. Quickly slamming it back into place, she tries to pull the slide but realizes the safety is on. Pushing the toggle to deactivate the safety, she gently pulls back the slide and verifies there's a bullet in the chamber. She releases the slide and stands, now on the other side of the truck, and turns toward the gunman.

She's just in time, he's right on top of her, ready to hit her with the gun. Holding her gun straight out in front of her, she backs up a few feet to put some distance between them.

"What're you gonna do, sweetheart? Shoot me? Please," he mocks, the sneer back on his face.

"I wouldn't normally. No. But you're threatening me, and I am not going anywhere with you," she says, with her back straight and feet shoulder width apart.

"This isn't the Shea I remember. What happened to you?" he asks.

"Well, I don't remember you at all, or what happened," she replies, her voice strong and unwavering. "So, why don't you put down your gun, because if it's knowledge you want, I don't have it."

"We assumed that might be the case. Don't worry, we'll take you where they can restore all your memories for you."

"We?" she asks, looking around, but keeps her gun and one eye on the man in front of her.

The man chuckles, and she feels an arm slide around her neck from behind, while another tries to force her arms down. She knows what she needs to do but doesn't want to take the life of another human being—even a shitty human being. So, she keeps the gun trained on the man in front of her with one arm, while using her other hand to shove her finger deep in the man's eye, who is holding her.

All of a sudden, the man and Shea are tackled from behind, she is sprawled face down on the ground and can feel the man being pulled from her.

Sitting up, still holding her gun, she sees John holding the second man in front of himself like a shield. "If either of you says one word, I will rip out your hearts with my bare hands. If either of you—or any others—come for her again, I will kill every last one of you. You will leave here with your lives tonight, but I'm not taking any chances," John says, in way that makes her shiver in fear—fear of him.

"If you think—" henchman one starts.

"Nope, not a word. You're already blowing it, man," John cuts him off sharply. He glances down at Shea on the ground. "Are you okay?" he asks.

"Yeah, fine," she says quickly.

"Good. We can't stay here now because of these ass hats. Safely keep your weapon on you and toss your bag back in the bed, and get in the truck," John instructs.

"What about this guy?" she asks. Pushing her gun out toward the one holding a gun on John.

"Don't worry about me," John says, watching her put her gun in her waistband, and toss her backpack back into the bed of the truck.

As she starts to get in the truck, John says, "Oh—and Shea? That was the most bad ass shit I've ever seen. I'm glad you're okay."

A smile breaks across her face as she settles into the seat. She watches out the window, wondering what John is going to do. As she watches, she realizes, that she is not even close to John's level of badassary. Looking away, she puts earbuds into her ears and selects a song to drown out the gurgling screams.

Twin Pines

00028 🌲🌲 Days Off

She's lying in her bed, eyes closed, still wearing yesterday's bathing suit, when she hears the footsteps of someone walking into her bedroom. The sun is streaming through her window, warming her exposed skin. The footsteps stop, and then she feels the mattress give next to her, as someone sits down. They brush the hair from her face, and her eyes pop open. Seeing Todd, she smiles and puts her arm over his lap.

"Get up, sleepy head. I want to test out your new pool today, and it looks pretty sunny out there," Todd says.

"Shhh, headache," Shea mutters.

"Coffee is made, and Gregg's making breakfast. Come on, sleepy," he says.

"Fine, go away. I'm getting up," Shea replies, watching him walk out of her room.

She's reluctant to move—but she also knows the men in this house are *super* annoying, so she does it anyway. After washing her face, brushing her teeth, and finally taking off the bathing suit she's been wearing for close to twenty-four hours, she begrudgingly puts on a bra and a sage green sundress.

Realizing her hair is full-on frizz city, she wets the roots, brushes it through, and does a quick braid—flicking it over her shoulder when she's finished.

Feeling more awake, she skips out to the kitchen and greets her boys.

"Mornin', Shea, I made you a couple of eggs, some sausage and toast, you want the apple jelly?" Gregg asks, handing her a plate. "Oh yeah, and I made your coffee, I see you looking for a mug. Are you really that spoiled already?" Gregg teases, smiling.

"Ah, yes, please. You are the best! And no, I'm not spoiled. I just have the most amazing roomie ever, who accurately anticipates my needs," she says, sipping the hot coffee.

"Yeah, yeah. I know. I'm a giver, go sit and eat," he says, grinning.

"You guys gonna get a room or...?" Todd says, in a way that sounds like he's joking, but feels like he isn't.

Ignoring him, Shea says to Gregg, "What about you? Are you gonna come sit and eat?" She looks over at Todd, who is soaking up golden egg yolk with his toast. "Apparently, Todd already had breakfast."

"Yeah, mine is made. I'll come sit," Gregg answers.

After breakfast, the team gets the whole kitchen unpacked. It's a priority—mainly because Gregg *tried* to turn the sausages with a plastic fork, which led to melted plastic and ruined sausages.

With that accomplished, Shea convinces Gregg to hang all of his swords in the common area. Luckily, Todd is there to help, since they start mounting them pretty high up on the walls. Per Shea's request, Gregg hangs the sword of "her husband," Jon Snow, in a place of honor above the TV.

Gregg and Shea both finish their rooms and bathrooms—instructions given to Todd to unpack the other décor they decided on for the house, and the couch blankets, which are stored in a secret cubby of the ottoman Gregg brought. When Shea finishes unpacking her boxes, she meanders into the living room, inspecting Todd's progress. Seeing no more boxes in the area, she walks over to Gregg's room.

"Hey, bud, how's it going in here?" she asks him, leaning in.

"Great, just finished the last box of bathroom stuff. All done in here. And plenty of time to still have lots of fun today," he answers.

"Sweet, maybe we will just start with a swim in OUR POOL!" Shea exclaims.

"Yeah, I'll change and come out," he says.

"Wait, have you seen that box? The one with all my pictures in it?" Shea asks, quietly, shyly.

"No, I saw it at your house, waiting to go into the trailer, but I haven't seen it since then," he says.

"Yeah, me either. I haven't seen it, and I think all of our boxes are unpacked that are here. I'm starting to freak out a little bit," she says.

"Well, did you ask Todd? He's been unpacking too," Gregg suggests.

"Yeah, I know. I just felt weird asking him because he's paid for so much, and I really do appreciate it... I don't want him to think that I don't," she admits. "To be honest, I haven't seen it since it was sitting by the front door in Ohio."

"I'll ask," Gregg says. "It's important, I'll talk to him."

"Thanks, Gregg. I'm gonna go change into my suit," Shea says, walking out of Greggs room.

As she walks by the kitchen, she sees that Todd is in the process of making margaritas.

"Todd, it isn't even noon, what're you doing?" she asks, walking into the kitchen and putting her arms around his hips.

"Well, sweet thing," he says, bending down to kiss her lips softly. "I thought it'd be nice to have a swim in the sun with some frozen margaritas. Am I wrong?" he asks, smiling against her lips.

"Well, I guess not. What could be wrong about that?" she murmurs against his lips.

Todd reaches down and slides his hand up the back of her skirt, squeezing her bum as deepens the kiss. She can feel that her bum is in the breeze.

Gregg clears his throat from a distance and breaks the kiss. Todd, however, just looks Gregg right in the eyes and keeps Shea exposed.

"Like what you see, Greggy?" he says, with a devilish grin.

Meanwhile, Shea is squirming, desperately trying to bring her skirt back down. She's embarrassed, blushing, and struggling—and Todd just keeps staring at him. Shea resorts to punching him in the chest. She stares at his face but can't read his expression.

If this asshole doesn't let me go RIGHT NOW, I'm aiming for the jewels

"Dude, can't you see she isn't into it? LET HER GO," Gregg says loudly and confidently.

"What? Oh, I'm so sorry, Shea. That hasn't happened in a long time," Todd says, releasing her immediately.

"WHAT THE FUCK TODD?!" Shea screams in his face—at his chest, let's be real.

"I'm so sorry, please forgive me. I wasn't doing it intentionally. Please, I'm so sorry," he begs.

"What do you mean it wasn't intentional? It looked pretty intentional, dude. The way you were staring at me and doing that..." Gregg steps toward Todd, his voice raised in defense of Shea.

Todd looks between Shea and Gregg. "Guys, I really didn't mean it. When I was a kid, up until I was like sixteen, I had really bad absence seizures, where I would just freeze in whatever I was doing. I haven't had one since then, that I know of, but I'm pretty sure that's what just happened. Please forgive me."

Shea studies his face for a moment and feels that he is telling the truth, so she grabs his hand, and says, "It's okay, Todd. I understand, I'm just embarrassed. You didn't hurt me or anything."

Shea looks over at Gregg with pleading eyes, and because he cares more about her than Todd's ego, he says firmly, "Todd, I'm sorry, but no. When I walked out here, you looked right at me and asked me if I liked what I saw. Even if that was all that happened, that was still inappropriate. I know Shea won't stick up for herself with this because she doesn't want to ruin our day, but I don't care about our day. I care about Shea, and this cannot stand."

Holy Shit, did it just get hotter in here or is it just Gregg? My knight in shining armor!

"Gregg, man, I'm sorry. I know it wasn't funny, and it doesn't look great for me, but I swear I wasn't trying to hurt her," Todd says, his voice tinged with regret.

"Why are you apologizing to me? What the hell is wrong with you?" Gregg shoots back, his voice sharp.

"Alright, enough. Guys, this is not a big deal. Can we just move on? I want to hang out at the pool. So, since you are both in your bathing suits, I'm gonna go put mine on and take my glasses off, so we can have some margarita pool time," she says, trying to diffuse the tension.

She decides to wear a different suit than yesterday—that one had been great to lounge in because it covered a lot, so it was easy to unpack wearing it. The one she would be wearing today would not be ideal for many strenuous activities—well, maybe one. The suit was a beautiful teal color, crafted entirely of two-and-a-half-inch straps. It reminded her of the white strap outfit Lilu Dallas wore in the *Fifth Element*. After getting it on and adding a cover-up that ties on the side, she stows her glasses in their case and heads out of her bedroom door.

"Sunblock!" Gregg hollers through the house.

Oh yeah, I'm as pale as a ghost, I would burn badly

"Thanks, Greggy!" she called back.

After they are all sun screened up, they head out to the pool. Todd carries a large, oddly-shaped pitcher and three equally-strange cups, while Gregg carries a docking station with speakers that fit Shea's phone.

Shea carries three towels, sunblock, and her phone. The house had come with a set of four lounge chairs and a patio table. They drop their things on the table, and Shea goes about picking a playlist while Todd pours the margaritas, and Gregg re-applies sunscreen to his nose.

"Why does that pitcher and cup set look so weird?" Shea asks, docking her phone.

"It has gel insulation. In this Florida heat, these margaritas would melt super-fast. This keeps them at least cold—if not frozen," Todd replies.

Gregg takes the towels and puts them on the three lounge chairs he has dragged together. "Yeah, it's hot as hell out here. They'd definitely melt—hell, I feel like I might," he jokes.

Shea walks over to her chair, faces both of the men, and slowly unties her cover-up, revealing her bathing suit and skin beneath. The only sound in the patio is the music Shea chose, softly playing. Gregg's skin turns a shade of red that would rival ketchup, and Todd has a look of hunger in his eyes.

Mission accomplished

"Alright, where's my margarita?" she asks, with her hand on her hip.

Todd brings her a cup, and kisses her sweetly, "Mmmm, sunscreen," he murmurs with a grin.

A few pitchers of margaritas, three sunburns, and a pizza delivery later, the couch movin' friends showered and changed into comfy PJ's. Queuing up the third episode of their show, they pile onto the couch next to each other, eating their pizza. Shea talks Todd into a foot massage and uses Gregg's lap as a pillow—Todd can better reach her feet. Gregg glances over at Todd, who returns a single nod before focusing back on the show.

The next few days blur together—the three of them adventuring to the beach, local restaurants and bars, and spending their nights curled up on the couch watching *Game of Thrones*. As their carefree, work-free days begin to dwindle down to nothing, Todd starts to spend less and less time at 'Casa SheGre', turning his focus to preparing for their arrival at Crowned Skull Laboratories.

Shea wakes to fingers wiggling on her upper thigh. Startled, she squeals and jolts backward into her bed. Hearing a low chuckle, she looks up to see the blurry outline of a sleepy-looking Todd. She reaches out and slaps his arm. "What the heck kind of a way is that to wake someone up?"

"Well, some might say it's an erotic way to be woken up. Personally, though I'd love some morning Shea, my fingers were asleep. Your head's been on my bicep for hours. Plus, we have to get up, shower and get ready. It's your first day at Crown!" he says excitedly. "Oh, and—plus plus, Gregg's been up for a couple of hours already, and I think he made a freaking quiche for breakfast. So, let's go, my little Khaleesi," he says, leaning in to kiss her cheek.

Shea hops out of bed and heads to the restroom. She is a little hungover from their adventure to a Con yesterday, but not too unbearable. As she washes her hands, she glances up at the mirror above her sink. She sees why Todd called her Khaleesi—her hair, sprayed silvery blond, and covered in intricate braids.

This shit better wash out, ugh, and on my first day

She had planned their group costumes for them—Gregg was on board immediately, but Todd took some convincing. Gregg dressed up as the one and only, Shea's 'husband,' Lord Commander John Snow, complete with sharp replica sword. Todd dressed up as Khal Drogo, complete with a super long braid and temporary tattoos. They'd taken a ton of pictures on their phones, and Shea wanted to print one out to put on her desk—if she even has a desk.

Trotting out to the kitchen in her pajamas, she follows her nose to the mug on the bar, which is heaped in whipped cream. "What's the occasion?" she asks Gregg.

Gregg turns to her with a plate that holds her breakfast and sets it down in front of her. "Well, winter is…almost here," he chuckles. "Even if we can't tell with the weather here. I thought a nice peppermint whatever would be nice with some whipped cream."

Shea giggles. "Got it, thank you, Gregg." Then whispering, "You know you're my favorite, right?"

"AND YOU'RE MY FAVORITE TOO, SHEA," he yells in the direction of Shea's room.

"Ugh, get a room you two. Actually, get in the shower. Shea, your hair's silver, and Gregg yours is black—still looking like a crow," Todd laughs and plops down at the bar for his slice of quiche.

"Yeah, we need to get ready," Gregg says, eyeing Shea's hair.

"You've been up for a while—what have you been up to?" Todd asks.

Gregg hands him a plate, and says, "I got some emails from the team earlier, and I was brushing up on what today might hold. I'm super excited."

"NEEERRRRDDDDDDD," Todd teases with a mouthful of Gregg's quiche.

Shea sips from her coffee cup and watches Gregg walk into his bedroom. She chuckles at Todd and turns on her heel, leaving him sitting there—shirtless, covered in fake tattoos, shoveling in his breakfast. He chuckles at her retreating back.

The silver washes out just fine. Shea puts her hair in a fancy clip—she normally always wears it down, but she hasn't quite figured out the right product ratio to combat the frizz she has in Florida. She applies a full face of makeup and slips on a salmon-colored silk blouse with a black tweed pencil skirt. She adds a shimmering lotion in the place of pantyhose and slips on a pair of sensible three-inch patent black stilettos. Packing a larger purse, so she can carry a pair of sneakers in case her feet get angry, she takes it and her mug out to the kitchen.

Gregg stands there, dressed in clean, pressed, tailored black slacks and a barely blue, almost white, long-sleeved button-down. The shirt is also tailored and is tucked into the pants neatly, and his belt is Gucci. Shea's mouth seems to fill with saliva—she may not know how to tame her hair in the current humidity, but it seems Gregg has mastered it. His curls are beautiful, perfectly defined, and she feels like she doesn't recognize the man in front of her. She takes a moment to take him all in, and he stands there, motionless, the whole time. When she finally gets to his face, she sees blush spreading across his cheeks and ears, but he smiles at her and then glances down at himself.

"Gregg, I don't even know what to say. I mean, Daddy status," she playfully flirts, grinning.

"Geez, Shea, come on, I was doing so well," he says, placing a palm on his cheek, like he can feel the heat there.

"I'm just being honest with you, bud. You look good enough to make me want to learn some science."

"What about me, Love? What do I make you want to learn?" she hears, coming from in front of Gregg's room.

Turning her head toward the voice, she sees an Adonis in pinstripes. Todd is slowly walking toward her, wearing a three-piece, tailored, pin striped suit in black with blue pinstripes. Shea hears a quiet, almost resigned, "always gotta steal my thunder," from Gregg.

Todd must have heard him, too, because he smirks and says, "See, Gregg? You should let me lend you my clothes and pick out your outfit, every day."

Deflating slightly, Gregg glances at the clock, and asks Shea, "Are you riding with me, or the Greek statue this morning?"

"You, of course. Don't be silly," Shea says, having a clarifying moment that she needs to stop messing with Gregg so much.

Gregg hands Shea a travel mug—like he just can't help himself—then walks around the bar and to the front door.

"Well, I'm not just gonna leave you here in my house. Do you need a ride, or are you good?" Shea asks Todd, walking over to him and kissing his cheek.

"I'm good, I have a car coming. I can wait outside though, no big deal," he responds, and they head out the front door. Shea turns to lock the door behind them.

Gregg has already pulled the SUV around, with the A/C blasting. Shea hops in the passenger side, immediately pulling up her playlists, preparing to jam.

Gregg reaches over and touches her hand.

"What's up?" she asks, looking up at him.

"I just wanted to tell you…you look amazing today. With your hair up like that and your glasses, you look very studious," he says.

"Oh my, Gregg, are you saying I look like a naughty librarian?" she asks with a playful grin.

"Yes, actually," he says confidently, looking Shea in the eye when he says it, without a hint of embarrassment.

Shea's blush starts on her chest and creeps its way upward, into her neck and face. She's at a loss for words, which is a rare occurrence for her. But she doesn't need to say anything, when she looks back over at him, he says, "Shea, I asked Todd about the box that is missing. He says he has no idea where it is. I pulled up Ashley's tracking program, and it shows that the box in question is box number 142. It was scanned in as being on the truck that night, before we both saw it in the house. But it was never scanned again, so according to them, it was never delivered. I left her a voicemail, so hopefully she will have some answers for us soon."

"Oh man, thanks so much for doing all of that for me, Gregg. I was just expecting you to talk to Todd and drop it. I want you to know how much I appreciate you. You're the only family I have, and you've never let me down," Shea says, hoping her sincerity comes through.

"You got it, beautiful. You know I'll always be here for you. This is only the beginning, right?" he says, smiling over at her.

Twin Pines

00029 | Disassociating

On the road to a different hotel—this one in the opposite direction of where they need to travel tomorrow. Shea looks over at John, he had cleaned all the blood off with hand sanitizer, but Shea still feels a little freaked out.

"Where'd you learn to do that?" she asks.

"Same place you learned to do what you did tonight. Did all of that feel like it came naturally?" he asks.

"Yeah," she admits. "I didn't even know I knew what a safety was. But I don't think I could've done what you did. Once the second guy showed up… I knew I was in real danger of death, and I still couldn't pull the trigger."

"I didn't think you would—unless you absolutely had to. What I did protects us without taking a life. They'll live, and I'm sure they'll report back to whoever sent them via email or text—but it also sends a message," he says, putting on his blinker to pull into the resort.

"If these people that are after us are as bad as you say they are," she says, slowly, "why leave them alive? Couldn't they bring more bad guys with them next time?"

"The people we're trying to get away from aren't at their best right now—especially with us gone. It'll take a while for them to regroup and get more guys up here. And honestly? We don't have the time to hide a body. Or deal with the police it would attract if there were any witnesses. We need to get to where we're going, without a hold-up, my way is easier," John answers, giving Shea more information than she thought he would.

"That does make a lot of sense," she agrees quietly. "I'm sorry I didn't really believe you about our situation. That guy that screamed at me… the way he looked at me—like he knew he couldn't kill me, but he would do every painful thing he could think of to make me suffer—I'll never forget it." Her whole upper body spasms in a violent shiver.

"Apology accepted. It does seem unreal. I'm sorry I wasn't there sooner. From now on, I'll do everything in my power to protect you from them."

"I gotta say, your way? There was so much blood! And the noises they made? Absolutely horrifying," she says, making gagging noises.

"Yeah. Cutting out someone's tongue is pretty fast and easy, but it is a horrible mess," he says, pulling in and parking the truck closer to the building this time. "You're not waiting in the truck again, I just want you to look tired and bored—like at the airport."

"Okay, but will that even matter? They know what the truck looks like, right?" she asks.

"Yeah. A replacement is being delivered while we rest. They'll junk this one immediately," he assures her.

A replacement…

They walk into the resort together, Shea clutching the back of John's shirt (yes, it's a clean one). At the desk, the woman working seems unwilling to book a room without a credit card.

John leans in, voice calm but firm, "I'll put ten thousand dollars down in cash if I need to. That should cover any damages."

But she is still hesitant.

Knowing, at this late hour, there probably isn't anyone else they can talk to, Shea realizes that it is up to her. She's always been able to cry on cue, she just thinks about her parents. So, she puts her head down and begins to silently cry. Once snot is running down her face, she peeks up at the receptionist.

She puts her acting skills to work again. "I'm so sorry we can't use a card. We just flew in and then we were held at gunpoint. We got lucky—they didn't take our cash or our lives, but they took all our plastic," she heaves out, hyperventilating and sniffing the whole time.

"Oh, goodness, you poor thing. It's against our policy, but we do have promissory notes. If it's just for one night, I don't see how it could be an issue. Alright, sir, let's do a five-hundred-dollar cash hold, plus the nightly rate. We'll both sign this note, agreeing that you'll pay more if needed, and the resort will return the five hundred if it isn't needed," she says, handing the form to John.

After they sort out payment and Shea receives a tissue from the woman, they grab their bags from the truck and head to their room. Inside they find a king-sized bed and a beautiful, breathtaking mountain view. Shea and John are both so utterly exhausted that they collapse onto the bed, staring out of the window for a while. Shea notices that there are fire pits on the ground level, surrounded by stunning views.

Maybe, in another life, we could enjoy a night by the fire together

"Alright, enough disassociating. I'm going to go grab a really quick shower so that I can have clean hands to examine your sutures. Can you please take everything out that you'll need for your shower, so we can get both of ours done fairly quickly?" he asks.

"Yeah, I can do that. But how are we going to keep my sutures dry, though?" she asks.

"I'll wash your hair for you. There should be a shower cap in here," he says, rummaging through the cupboards in the bathroom. Finding it, he holds it up and puts it on the counter. "I'll help you put it on when the time comes. It should do the trick."

Before he leaves, Shea, sits on the couch, watching as he locks and relocks the door, even peeking out to check the hallway, before one final lock. When John finally gets in the shower, Shea digs through her bag, looking for the tampon. Once she finds it, she takes a couple of the pills inside. She turns the heat up a few times, feeling like the cold is in her bones—maybe from the rain earlier. No matter what she does, she just can't get warm, so she gathers all the blankets from the bed, wrapping herself up in a cocoon.

When John comes out of the shower, half-dried and only wearing loose, plaid pajama bottoms, Shea is nowhere to be seen. Frantically looking around their room, he finds her in the middle of the bed with every sheet and blanket cocooned around her, moaning softly.

"Shea, I don't know what's going on, but I'm coming in," he says, ripping at the blankets to find her in the middle.

"Please, I'm so cold," she moans, teeth chattering, her voice hoarse.

"What else is wrong, Shea? You're cold…what else?" he asks, gently turning her head to assess her wound.

"A little nausea, shaky, weak… need rest," she murmurs.

"I know you need rest, Shea, but we need to figure out why this is happening. Please, just let me look at you," he says. "Hopefully it's just the adrenaline wearing off, but we need to be sure. You need to be well to travel."

"Okay, John," she replies, reaching her arm out of her cocoon and placing it on his leg.

"I'll cuddle you and keep you warm all night, okay? But first…" he says, gently grabbing the headband and trying to pull it back.

Shea tenses, sucking air through her teeth as her eyes spring open.

"Sorry, sorry," he says, trying to figure out what the problem is. As he pulls, he realizes the problem, when pus and blood run down Shea's forehead. "Shit," he says, reaching for his bag containing the first aid kit. Pulling it out, he rushes back over to her side, wiping the blood and pus from her face and finally removes the headband. The infection has indeed escalated. He touches the back of his hand to her forehead—she's burning up.

"Shea," he says, shaking her shoulder. "Shea, I need you awake, just for a little while. Are you awake?"

"Yeah, yeah, I'm awake. What is it?" she says.

"I'm going to have to give you more antibiotics. I have an IV set up that I'm going to use to administer it. I also need to give you something for the fever. Have you taken anything that I don't know about today? I need you to be honest," he says.

"Past Shea gave me a stash. I took two," she says, falling toward sleep again.

"Shea, what did she give you? What are you taking? Where is it?" he asks, shaking her lightly.

"Tampon," she mumbles.

"What was pre-amnesia Shea thinking, not telling me about this? What the hell is it?" he mumbles to himself the whole way to Shea's backpack. On top of the bag, is an open tampon with something inside— she must have just taken it. He picks it up, trying to figure out how to remove the plunger and get to the small bottle he can see inside. Once he gets it, he reads the small label and then puts it all back together. Grabbing four ibuprofens from the first aid kit, he fills a glass with water and goes back to Shea's side. She is sleeping fitfully when he wakes her, but she cooperates as he guides her into a sitting position to take the ibuprofen. After several panicked minutes of trying to wake her, she is finally awake enough to swallow the pills without choking. After, she rests her head against John's shoulder.

"Thank you, John. For everything."

"You're going to start feeling better soon, from the Tylenol in the pills you took and the ibuprofen I just gave you. But there is still a lot to do. Are you still awake?" he says.

She tilts her head back to look up at him, her eyes barely open.

"I know all you want is sleep, beautiful, but I need a couple of things from you," he says. She nods weakly. "I need to give you a bath, clean off any germs and dirt, wash your hair, pull the stitches, leave the wound open, and run an IV of antibiotics. I need to hear that this is okay, Shea. I won't touch you without knowing it's okay," he says, trying to remain calm, but he is terrified.

"I trust you, John... I trust you," she says, looking up into his eyes.

00030 †† Coffee Break

■ ■ ■ ■ ■ □ □ □ □ □

"**So**, do you think we'll even be working in the same building?" Shea asks.

"Well, this is a much larger enterprise, so I don't know, but we'll see each other all the time, I'm sure," Gregg answers. "Plus, we live together, dork. I'll be there to hand you your coffee every morning."

"My hero!" Shea croons.

"I guess we don't have long to wait to find out. There it is," Shea says, pointing to a large building up ahead on their left with a massive 'Crowned Skull Laboratories' sign on the side. Shea had never seen the logo before, but she thinks it's super cool. The words "Crowned Skull" are stacked on top of "Laboratories," and the words are beneath a skull wearing a crown, with a snake slithering out of its eye socket.

"Yeah, and that's just the main building. They own a ton of acreage over here, with multiple buildings and hundreds of warehouses on campus too," Gregg says, pulling into the gate access.

"Good Morning," a cheerful voice comes from inside a guard's box. "How can I help you today?"

Gregg leans out of the window to better see and hear the man in the box, "Good morning, Gregg Marsh and Shea Murphy, here for our first day."

"Yes, of course. I have your badges here," the guard says, passing them through the window. The pictures on the badges are from their last place of employment. "Just know that your chips and keycard all have the same access, so if you lose the card, let us know immediately, for security reasons. But you will still need to wear your keycard, even though your chips are functional, for easier immediate recognition and verification of your identities."

"Thank you," Gregg says, taking his keycard and using the attached lanyard to slide it over his head. He passes Shea hers, and she does the same. They look to the guard, who hasn't said anything further, and the gate is still down.

"I'm sorry, did I miss something?" Gregg asks.

"Sorry, I wasn't sure if you'd know how to proceed. You will use your key card in the small reader right next to your vehicle. If the two of you ride together regularly, please ensure you both swipe, even if the gate has already gone up for the first time. The gate will stay open for fifteen seconds per swipe. Not only is the swipe for security reasons, but it's also for payroll. If your keycard is swiped inside without a gate swipe, it will clock you in at the time of the first swipe," he says.

"Whenever you are ready, please proceed. Continue on this path, it wraps around the building. Behind the building there are visitor's spaces where you can park. Head into that building from the door closest to your parking spot, and you'll encounter the front desk. Tina will be able to help you from there."

"Got it. Thanks," Gregg replies.

Gregg slides his keycard though the reader, then extends his hand out for Shea's. Once both badges are scanned, he pulls through the gate and around the building. Parking, he and Shea walk side by side to the entrance, Gregg grabs the door and ushers Shea in first, following her in after. The room they entered is sterile—white walls, large white tiles, and in the middle of the floor is a large desk made of white marble. The room isn't very large, and all the 'walls' inside are made of glass, offering clear views down hallways and to what is beyond this room. Behind the desk stands a beautiful, petite blonde.

"Hey guys! You two look fantastic!" she says, as she walks around the desk to meet them.

Shea greets Tina with a big hug, and—awkward as ever—Gregg sticks out a hand to shake. "It's great to see you, Tina. Is this where the CEO's secretary hangs out?" Shea asks.

"Oh, yeah. Whereas I do perform duties for Mr. T that one would consider secretarial, I actually run this entire building. He brought me along to help you because he trusts me to get things done. It's one of the reasons that I run this building," she says.

"Wow, I'm sorry, I didn't know. I feel like I've said things that are unfair to you," Shea says.

"Don't worry your gorgeous head about it. Now, I have some paperwork for you both to fill out. You can sit over here on the couch, and I'll take it from you when you're finished," she says, handing them both a clipboard.

Sitting on the very white couch, they fly through the questions. Shea finds them odd—especially the one about her parents—but she answers them all honestly. When they finish, Tina ushers them to a cozy conference room on the same level of this building.

"Alright, you two, there are two more hires for today—both medical personnel. You won't see them around much, but Mr. T wants to do all the onboarding at once."

Waiting in the room, they see Tina deposit two more people, who sit together at another table. Oddly enough one is tall and handsome, and the other is much shorter, thick, and female. Gregg looks over and chuckles. Standing, he reaches over, offering his hand to the man. The four of them make introductions and are chatting when Todd walks into the room. The others' backs are turned toward him, so he winks at Shea and then brings a single finger over his lips. It seems he wants to surprise them.

"Good Morning, ladies and gentlemen, and welcome to Crowned Skull Laboratories. You all have different roles here at Crown, but we are still a team. Though you might not work with one another regularly, there will be times when your paths cross. Your seat choices are aptly split, as Shea and Gregg will be working on the same project, while Katie and Matt will be working together on another," he says.

"Tina will be handing each of you very specific binders for your position. Some of the materials are top secret and therefore will need to stay on-site at all times. There's a lot to go over, and today will be a long day of protocols and learning your new positions. Katie and Matt, I'd like you to follow Tina, who will take you to building five, which is our medical building. Gregg and Shea, you can follow me, you are both in building twenty-five."

Walking out of the front door of building one, there is a golf cart waiting on the sidewalk. "Sorry for the long trek, but the two of you are working on our most top-secret project. Therefore, it is housed in the building farthest away from building one and the outer gates, right in the middle of all of our property," Todd says.

"When you're driving in, it's the building with the silhouette of two pine trees. I got you guys one spot because I know you're riding together, it's the first spot by the door. I apologize, Gregg, but because of Shea's title and the fact that she is—within the structure of Crown employees—technically a few levels above you, her name is on the spot," Todd quickly gets out.

"Yeah, I'm cool with that. I like a woman on top," Gregg says, grinning at Shea, who is sitting next to Todd in the front of the cart. Shea reaches back and slaps his upper thigh. Gregg's eyebrows shoot up, to meet his hair line, while Shea blushes and turns back around.

"Hey man, what do we call you at work?" Gregg asks.

"Gimmie a second, I wasn't done. I don't know if you really looked at your badge or the binder Tina gave you, but your title is Director Shea Murphy," he says, pulling into building twenty-five.

"Director of what?" Shea asks.

"We can't discuss that outside of the building, but soon," Todd responds cryptically. "And Gregg, I think it is best to stick with Mr. T like Tina does—keeps it professional but also has a level of familiarity," he says, stepping from the cart.

As they all step out of the cart, Todd continues, "Oh, and Gregg, in case you were wondering, your title is Project Manager of Nanoelectronics, Greggory Marsh."

"Dang, look at you go!" Shea exclaims, always his cheerleader.

Walking up to the door, Todd explains their ability to use their chips or keycards for admission into the building. Once inside, they're required to stop for a daily photo and temperature check. Todd explains that this building is a sick-free zone, and even the slightest sniffle means they must call in.

Walking past this, Gregg and Shea can only see a long hallway. Todd turns to them, and says, "Eventually you'll both work on a different floor, but there are things you both need to learn and do, prior to that. So, Gregg you'll be going to the second floor and Shea—you'll be at the front desk for a little while, working like Tina."

Todd leaves Shea at the desk to read through her binder.

It's not really MY desk, so I won't decorate it...

After an hour passes, Shea feels like she needs a cup of coffee. But she left hers in the SUV—not wanting to get in trouble on her first day. Now her coffee is like twenty miles away and unobtainable at the moment. Flipping through her binder, she finds schematics of the first three floors. There's a kitchen on her floor, down a hallway behind her, two doors on the right.

Leaving the desk, she finds the kitchen and sees the same coffee maker she has at the house. Todd barely ever drinks coffee, but he does have good taste. Shea visits the machine and makes herself a cup. When she opens the door to head back to the desk, she hears "llloooooo, hhheeelllooooo, is there anyone here?"

The kitchen must be soundproofed or something. She couldn't hear him at all while she was in there. Stepping out of the kitchen, she says, "Hello, I'm so sorry about that, I popped off for a cup of coffee and didn't realize I couldn't hear anything from inside the kitchen."

"Oh really? That's interesting," he replies, a smile plastered on his face. He waits for her to put her coffee down then extends his hand to shake.

Shea grabs his hand, then feels something in her palm, like getting her finger pricked when she had passed out on campus a few times.

Pulling her hand away, she sees a small dot of blood, where she felt the prick.

Looking at the man, she begins to demand what that was, but the words won't come out. Her head is fuzzy, and the man is blurry. As Shea loses consciousness, she can hear the man chuckling.

00031 🌲🌲 Nurse John

Looking at her in her weakened state, saying that to him, brings tears to his eyes. There's so much he wants to say to her, and if she gets any worse, he'll lose it. He gently places her head onto his leg and strokes her hair, watching her sleep. "I'll take care of you, Shea, we'll get you better," he promises.

Propping her up slightly, he starts to remove her clothing, working not to jostle her too much. Once she's disrobed, he bridal carries her to the bathroom, switching to a one-armed carry. He leans over the tub to run the water cool. Once the tub is full enough, he gently lowers Shea into the water.

She gasps deeply, "FUCK," and begins thrashing in the water.

"I know, I'm sorry, Shea. But the cool water will help with the fever. Sit back, relax, I'll be quick," he soothes.

Using antibacterial soap, he lathers up a washcloth and begins washing every inch of her. He is careful in sensitive areas, but ensures he's being thorough. Using his fingertips, he gently washes her face with the same soap, taking it up into the hairline and carefully scrubbing around her wound. After rinsing her off, he props her head up with a towel and runs back into the room for her toiletry bag.

Rushing back, he picks her up slightly and turns her body to face the other way, so her head is now closer to the faucet. Running the water to a much warmer degree this time, he cradles her body with her head under the faucet, careful to avoid the wound. After washing and conditioning her hair, he drains the tub and pulls two towels down from the rack—one for her hair and the other for her body. He carries her to the couch to keep the bed dry.

Looking down at her, he sees that her skin is covered in goosebumps and her teeth are chattering, but her eyes are closed. He takes his time getting the knots from her long hair. Pulling out a pair of her pajamas, he puts them back immediately, deciding that's not the best idea right now. He picks one of his softest t-shirts out for her instead. Lying her back in her cocoon, her shivering starts to slow. He gathers his IV supplies, and a few minutes later, the saline bag containing antibiotics is hanging from a screw that was previously holding up a landscape picture.

He climbs into the bed next to her, sliding into the middle of the cocoon. For once, he's the one to cuddle her. He pulls her onto his chest and holds her there. As he slowly relaxes, it seems like she does too. Her shivering stops all together. He stays there, holding her, calming his frantic heart, for a couple of hours—awake—wanting sleep so badly. But he still needed to let the antibiotic run, pull her stiches out and wash out the wound.

Once Shea is deep asleep, and the antibiotic has finished—somewhere in the wee hours of the morning—John throws on a shirt and disconnects the IV line. He leaves the IV access in Sheas arm in place, caps it off and wraps her arm fairly loosely in Coban. He grabs his gun and runs down to the parking lot. He finds the truck is gone, and in its place, a 1973 GMC Jimmy, painted orange and white. Satisfied, he heads back to the room.

He carefully turns Shea in bed, lifts her head and places a folded towel under it. He takes out his small scissors and runs a lighter over them, so he can carefully cut at the strings. Then, he takes his tweezers, again running the lighter over them before use, to pull all of the strings out. All without Shea stirring at all. Next, is the hard part—using the tweezers, he pushes at the flaps of skin and sees pockets of pus all along her skull. This is the worst possible news—if the infection spreads past that plug, Shea could die. He takes an irrigation syringe full of sterile saline and pushes the plunger hard and fast in the wound, breaking up the pockets of pus. Shea starts to stir as he does the same over and over again. Finally, he takes a gloved finger and wraps it in gauze and uses it to roughly wipe every surface of the wound.

"That hurts," Shea says. "Will you come back to bed? I'm cold."

"Yes, I'll be back with you in just a minute. I just need to dress this first."

"K."

He takes a cup and adds a bit of sugar from the coffee station and mixes in betadine, creating a thick paste. He spreads this inside and on top of the wound before covering it with gauze taped to her forehead. He places one of the headbands he washed earlier over her head, ensuring her ears are free. Climbing back into the bed next to her, he grabs her and places her on his chest. She doesn't feel as warm as before, so that's, at least, a good thing.

John is so exhausted, his body begs him for sleep, but the men who were after them tonight will not give up, and Shea's condition is too fragile to sleep now. As he stares into the darkness, he hears Shea mutter, "Thank you, God, for this man."

Twin Pines

00032 🌲🌲 At last

■ ■ ■ ■ ■ ■ □ □ □ □

Gregg is doing great with the new team, quickly adapting to his role and impressing his team with his innovative ideas. The researchers have been able to figure out the right delivery method and materials for synthetic neuro pathways within the brain. During his first hour in the building, he has already come up with three options. The other scientists are now scrambling to get him all the materials he requested.

As he's refining his three options with the required math and such, he hears the doors seal and lock. Several large red lights flicker on, accompanied by a loud siren and a voice. The voice repeats, "Please stay where you are, guards are on their way," over and over again.

Gregg stands frozen at his desk, wondering what could possibly be happening. His mind races as he thinks about Shea and Todd, hoping they're safe.

About ten minutes later, a team of armed men in suits enter the hallway. Gregg can see them because like the main lobby, this room is entirely made of glass, which kind of makes him feel like 003. The guards open the glass doors and signal to the scientists to remain silent. One of the guards approaches Gregg, reaches for his lanyard, and scans it.

"Mr. Marsh," the guard whispers. "When the all-clear is sounded, the CEO would like you to meet him at the main-level entry desk. Nod if you understand."

Gregg nods, his mind racing with questions he's unable to ask

About twenty-five minutes later, the building is cleared, and the intercom announces, "All clear, all clear, all clear." As the all clear sounds, the locks release on the doors, allowing Gregg to leave his area. He hurriedly makes his way out of his glass enclosure and dashes down the stairs to the main floor.

When he has visualization of the main floor, he is overwhelmed. The entire building appears to have been called down to meet with Todd. There are also police and paramedics everywhere. Gregg pushes his way through the crowd to the desk, where he spots Shea on a stretcher. She's hooked up to an IV and wearing an oxygen mask, she appears to be sleeping.

Todd sees Gregg and waves him over to where he stands. When Gregg fights his way over there, Todd pulls him close, leaning in to whisper in his ear.

"This has not been a great first day for Shea. Tina was supposed to come and train her earlier, but got stuck by the same guy. Luckily, Shea read her binder and pushed the panic button on the way down. The guy had already hit ten of my buildings," Todd explains.

Gregg looks at him shocked. "I'm sorry, hit?!"

"Yeah, long story. One of my competitors was testing out a nearly invisible injector, that he placed on his palm. Shea went to shake his hand, to be friendly, got dosed with Fentanyl—not enough for an overdose but enough to incapacitate her," Todd says. "Now, as much as I want to be there for her right now, I have nine other directors in the same situation. I can't look like I'm playing favorites. I need to check on Tina, as soon as possible—she is my sister after all."

That's a revelation Gregg was not expecting. "Tina is your sister?" he whisper-screams at Todd.

"Okay, Gregg, you gotta focus. I heard you've already made a lot of progress today in the little bit of time you've had—so, I need you to go with Shea to the hospital and be there for her. I'll stop by later and bring you some more clothes that you can have."

"Right, Shea. Is she going to be okay?" Gregg asks anxiously.

"They think so, but I want you with her. I already told the medics that you'd be following in your car. They're waiting for you to leave. So, go tell them you're ready, and get out of here. The golf cart key is hanging right by the front door," Todd says.

Gregg is amazed by how well Todd is doing under all this pressure. He nods at Todd and jogs over to the stretcher where Shea lies. "Shea, my annoying best friend, I'll be with you, don't worry," he murmurs.

Looking at the medics, he says, "I'm going to take a golf cart to the front building, get my car, and I'll be right behind you."

"No problem, our ambulance number is 41, there are about ten ambulances on this property right now and we're not all going to the same place. Make sure you follow 41," the medic says.

"Got it," Gregg says. He presses a kiss to Shea's forehead before turning and walking out of the building.

When Gregg exits the building, he sees that the property—as far as he can see—is crawling with suited guards, medical personnel, and police. He hurries to the SUV, his eyes scanning the crowd for the ambulance carrying his friend. Once he spots it, he pulls out and follows 41 all the way to a local hospital.

Parking near the emergency entrance, Gregg jogs to the ambulance bay and walks into the hospital at Shea's side. As they take Shea back, hospital staff pull Gregg away from her and ask him to fill out some paperwork. Oddly enough, Gregg knows every answer—allergies, medications, even last menstrual period (he's a little embarrassed about that one), and of course address and insurance information. He gives the clipboard to the woman at the desk, asking if he can please go back with Shea now.

"I'm sorry, sir, but because you're not family, we can't accommodate that. Does she have a next of kin? There's none listed here," she responds.

"Shea has no family, except for me. I am her family," Gregg protests.

"Do you have proof? Anything in writing?" the woman insists.

"Actually, we just filled out paperwork at work that had a whole page about emergencies. I can call the CEO and get him to have it faxed over, does that work?" Gregg asks, already pulling out his phone.

"Yes, that would be perfect."

Gregg calls Todd immediately, "Hello? Gregg? Is everything okay? Is it Shea?" Todd sounds mildly panicked.

"I'm sorry, man, she's in the ER now. Can you have her emergency paperwork faxed to the Cape Canaveral hospital? Like, right away if you can," Gregg asks urgently.

"On it now," he says, and the line goes silent.

Gregg lingers by the desk waiting to hear the fax machine, the knot in is stomach growing each second.

"Sir, I got her paperwork from… Crowned Skull Labs, is it?" the woman asks.

"Yes. Thank goodness, am I listed? Greggory Marsh?" he asks, peering over the desk to catch a glimpse of the paper.

"She has here, that in the case of an emergency, Greggory Marsh is to be contacted and given all decision-making capacity. You're also listed as next of kin. Nurse Kelly will meet you at that door there," she points around the corner, "and take you to your family member."

"Thank you so much," Gregg says. He feels deeply touched that Shea put his name for all of that, maybe he means almost as much to her as she does to him.

Gregg meets nurse Kelly, and she walks him to the desk within the ER. Once there, they learn that Shea has already been sent to a room. Kelly gives him directions and bids him farewell.

When Gregg gets to Shea's room, he feels as if his knees will buckle. The air leaves his lungs, and his heart feels like it misses a beat or two. Shea is lying in a bed attached to heart monitors and IV's, and she's also intubated. Gregg tries to keep his composure as he goes to her bedside and takes her hand. "Shea, I'm here. I'll be here until you're better. I love you, Shea," he whispers in her ear.

Heading to the nurse's station, Gregg demands to speak to Shea's nurse or doctor, then he feels bad and says please and thank you, and 'at your earliest convenience'.

Walking back to Shea's room, he sits and holds her hand. Grabbing the bag that her personal effects are in, he pulls out her phone and opens her playlists. Scrolling through them, he sees two that he's unfamiliar with—one says 'Todd <3' and the other 'Gregg <3'.

A small smile sneaks up on him as he selects the playlist that is the obvious choice. Selecting the shuffle option, he turns the volume to a low level and places the phone next to Shea's head. The room goes from being filled with mechanical noises to a song that makes curious uncertainty crawl over his nerves, *At Last by Etta James*.

Thinking there must be some kind of mistake, he grabs the phone, checking to see which playlist he selected. It's the right one, so as it plays, he looks through Todd's playlist, which contains songs like, *Sexual Healing* and *Let's Get It On by Marvin Gaye, Pony by Genuine*, and *I Can Tell by 504 Boys*.

Feeling hope, disbelief, and curiosity, Gregg places the phone back next to Shea's head and goes back to holding her hand. Soon, the second song in his playlist begins, *Your Song by Elton John*. Gregg sits, passively running his thumb over the soft skin of her hand, thinking. As her playlist continues for hours, he doesn't even look at his phone or the TV, he just thinks about what all of this could mean.

If all of this is true, then why is it Todd who gets her affection?

After a while, Todd pops into the room. He immediately looks taken aback by Shea's condition. "What happened? She was breathing on her own before," he says, his voice tight with concern.

"I asked to speak with the doctor a few hours ago, but no one has come in here. Not even a nurse—come to think of it—that's weird," Gregg answers, his gaze fixed on Shea.

"Are you playing her love songs, Greggy?" Todd asks, with one eyebrow raised high.

"Ah, yeah, I just picked a playlist, thought it might help," he says.

"She does love her playlists. She must have been thinking about me when she made this one, then," Todd gloats.

Gregg just smiles softly and says, "Hey, do you maybe wanna try to scare up someone I can talk to?"

"I can talk to them too, I'm her boyfriend after all," Todd says, sounding like a child who is waiting impatiently for their turn with the toy.

"Actually, they are really strict about that. Shea listed my name for everything, so they will talk to me. You can listen though," Gregg says, with a smirk.

Todd stares at him for a moment, then stomps to the nurse's station. Gregg can hear him from the room, he's not as nice as he was about it all. He continues to hold Shea's hand, and says, "Whenever you want to wake up, I'm here, Shea, you need to come back to me."

As if in response, one of Shea's fingers twitches, but Gregg thinks it must be some sort of reflex. Marching back into the room with Shea's doctor in tow is Todd, appearing to be ridiculously pleased with himself. Gregg stands, releasing Shea's hand to reach out to shake the doctor's hand. "Hello, doctor. I'm Gregg," he says, pressing pause on Shea's phone.

"Gregg, nice to meet you," the doctor says, shaking his hand. "Sorry I couldn't get here earlier. I was pulled into emergency surgery. I happened to be at the desk charting that surgery, when your friend here caused a scene."

Gregg laughs through his nose.

"So, Miss Murphy here was dosed with Fentanyl, but not regular, run-of-the-mill Fentanyl. At first, we thought with the assumed dose given, she should have been awake, or at least semiconscious, after the doses of Narcan she received from EMS. However, within minutes of being in the ER, she lost her airway, like she was still getting dosed. She had pinpoint pupils and wasn't responding to pain. They attempted several more doses of Narcan at that time, to no avail. It appears that the drug has been altered in some way, and all we can do now is continue administering fluids in an attempt to clear the drug faster—which is why she has the catheter."

"There were several others dosed, and they are all recovering at home now. Is there really a need for her to be intubated?" Todd asks.

The doctor looks to Gregg, who nods before the doctor responds, "In all honesty, I haven't tended to those other patients. I have no idea the difference in patient or drug. What I do know, is that Shea is currently stable, but I don't want to say that she is out of the woods yet. We honestly don't know what might happen."

"Doc, I was holding her hand, talking to her, and her finger twitched. That's just a normal reflex, right?" Gregg asks.

"Could be, or she could be closer to the edge of consciousness, keep talking to her—she might be able to hear you," the doctor answers.

"Thank you, sir," Gregg says, sitting back down and taking Shea's hand.

The doctor leaves, and Todd moves closer to the side of the bed. He leans down and kisses Shea on the cheek. "Alright, I have to head out. Text me if there are any changes. Oh, and I have a bunch of stuff for you in garment bags. I put them in your car—you left it unlocked," he says.

"Thanks, man, I appreciate it," Gregg says, wondering why that is what Todd is focusing on at the moment. "Real quick, before you go, how did this mystery guy even get on campus?"

"His name is Neal. He's a competitor that I occasionally collaborate with," Todd answers, running the back of his fingers over Shea's long hair. "I had a meeting scheduled with him this morning at ten. He had a new product he wanted me to see. So, I put him on the list for the gate. He arrived like two hours early and told the gate not to announce him because he didn't want to disturb me until it was actually time for the appointment. The idiot in the guard box listened to him, so I had no idea something was off, until the alarm went up. I can't believe nine other directors went down without hitting the button. Thank God Shea made it that far in her binder—she saved not only herself, but all the others too. Neal was caught and arrested, he'll probably spend the rest of his life in prison."

"So, the guard in the box?" Gregg asks.

"Big time fired. Because of him, Neal managed to get my sister and my girlfriend, plus eight other directors in one fell swoop."

"Well, I'm glad everyone else is okay," Gregg says, looking at Shea's unconscious form and smiling. "Shea just needs a bit more time, go figure."

"Yeah," he says, looking down at her face and dropping a kiss on her forehead. "Well, I gotta get going. I'm glad she has you here with her, man. I appreciate it."

As soon as Todd leaves, Gregg restarts the playlist and takes her hand in his. After a little while, mostly out of boredom, he begins recounting the work he did today, before all of this happened. As dawn approaches, he scoots his chair closer, resting his head in her lap—still holding her hand tight.

00033 Did You Pee?

John must have dozed off, he wakes up in a puddle of what he believes is sweat—whether it's his or Shea's, he has no idea. He carefully looks down at her, lying across his chest. Her hair is splayed out in every direction, with some seriously impressive volume, due to John's lack of knowledge of hair products. She's breathing rapidly and making faint noises—this must be what woke him. Touching her forehead, he curses softly and begins to carefully get out of bed, allowing Shea to slide off his body and onto the bed.

As soon as he is up, her whimpering grows louder. John curses himself for falling asleep as he prepares her antibiotics, pain meds, ibuprofen, and the supplies to clean her wound and change the dressing. Calling in a breakfast of bacon and eggs, he hangs up the hotel phone and starts trying to rouse Shea. He thinks she must be in a fever dream because she is not reacting to his attempts, at all. Bile rises in the back of his throat, and he starts to shake her a little more violently, repeating her name over and over again. Finally, right before he resorts to smacking her, she opens one eye, just a little bit, and asks, "Did you pee the bed?" but makes no moves to get out of the puddle.

"No, you weirdo. I'm pretty sure it's all my sweat from your hot body," he says, chuckling, because in the face of all she has been through and continues to go through, she remains the same.

She smiles weakly up at him, and says, "You think I have a hot body?"

"You're incorrigible, Shea. You are literally burning alive. We have a few things to do, then we can go back to bed, after breakfast, of course." He sits on the edge of the bed, next to her, taking in her sickly appearance.

"Bacon?"

"Of course, but first meds," he says.

She looks down at her chest, and says, "The Beatles? Right on. Um, John, how did I put on this shirt?"

"YOU didn't do anything, you were an inch from death last night. I had no choice," he says.

"Look how far we've come," she says, scooting away from the middle of the bed.

"How are you feeling, anyway?" John asks, hanging her IV of antibiotics and handing her the pain meds and ibuprofen.

"I have no idea, I kind of feel like I'm still dreaming," she says.

"Well, we need to get some food in you, especially with these pain meds. Puking will put a lot of pressure on your head and probably feel like torture. Can you stand?" he asks.

"I think so," Shea replies.

"Come to this side. Watch your IV line. Wait—your foot is stuck! Don't grab that, it'll fall. You know what? Allow me," he says, scooping her up and depositing her on the nearby couch. He tosses her a dry blanket from the bed and pulls all of the sweat-soaked linens off the bed, tossing them in a pile by the door.

As he's placing fresh linens on the bed, there is a knock at the door. "Must be room service, cover yourself better with that blanket, please." Shea pulls the blanket up under her chin and leans back on the couch. John stops to pull his gun out of his duffel on the way to the door. He opens the door—the four inches that is possible with the hotel chain lock. Seeing a hotel employee with a tray, he slides his gun into the waistband of his pants and opens the door wider. Reaching an arm through the gap, he takes the tray from the employee and asks if more blankets can be brought up.

Putting the tray on a table and pulling it in front of Shea, he reveals a plate piled high with eggs and bacon, with a side of syrup. There isn't much excitement from Shea, but he will make sure she eats at least half of it.

"Shall we dig in?" he asks.

"I guess so," she replies, eyeballing the plate. "It doesn't look tasty, my tummy just doesn't feel right," she says.

"I'm sure it doesn't, that's why you need to eat, otherwise you'll yak," he says, handing her a fork.

Shea does manage to eat her half and drink some water. John helps her to the bathroom to do her business, carrying her IV bag behind her and then draping it over the shower door handle. While she's in there, he sets up wound care supplies, preparing to take the best possible care of her infection. When he hears Shea call out his name, he stops what he is doing and rushes to her aid.

He knocks a couple of times before entering. As he tries to open the door, he feels it butt up against something—or rather someone. Through the gap, he asks, "Are you okay, Shea?"

"Yeah, I was trying to get up, but my legs went to Jello. I couldn't stand back up on my own," she explains.

"Okay, can you scoot on your butt so I can open the door to help you?" he asks.

"Yeah," she replies, which is followed by noises of effort, then he feels the door give.

Looking down on her, he sees how pale and sickly she looks under the fluorescent lighting. Keeling beside her, he says, "Great job, now I'm going to just pick you up, okay?" he asks.

"Please, this floor is freezing," she says, trying to put herself in a position to make it easier for him to pick her up.

He's sure his face looks like he swallowed a bug when she says it. As he carries her to the couch, she asks, "Why did you make that face when I said the floor was cold?"

"It's just… the heat is set to seventy-five degrees, that's why I was sweating so much last night."

"So?" she asks from the couch.

"So, the vents in Alaska are on the ground, like in Ohio, and you were sitting right next to one," he informs her.

"Oh, is that the fever? Because I am really cold," she says.

"I believe you, I'm just worried it's sticking around," he says.

"Weren't we supposed to leave today?" she asks.

"Yeah, but it's okay. I just need to make a few calls after we get you in bed." Looking at her, he realizes she had been holding her IV bag in her lap, and the part of the line closest to her arm is now filled with blood.

"Here, gimmie that," he says, taking it back over to hang it on the screw.

"How come it's got blood in it?" she asks, pulling the blanket he gave her earlier up to her chin.

"The bag was lower than your IV site. It's okay. It's clearing up already. Let me make the bed so you can lie down and warm up while I clean your wound," he says.

As soon as he starts to secure the bottom sheet, there is another knock at the door. Forgetting he had asked for blankets, he goes on high alert again, grabbing his firearm. This time he asks through the door, "Who is it?" He keeps wondering why there's no peep hole.

"It's Carl, sir. You asked me to bring some blankets earlier," John hears through the door.

"Right, sorry," he says. He again puts his gun in his waist band and opens the door a few inches.

Carl hands him a stack of four blankets, and says, "These just came out of the dryer, so they're nice and warm."

"Wow. Thanks, Carl. This is really above and beyond. Can you wait here a sec, I'll be right back," John says, grateful.

Carl's response is muffled by John closing the door. He tosses the still-hot blankets at Shea, who moans in delight. He then grabs his canvas backpack and pulls out a one-hundred-dollar bill. He opens the door again and hands it to Carl.

Carl smiles kindly, and says, "This isn't necessary, sir. I'm happy to help."

"I can tell, that's why you deserve this," he says, tucking the bill into Carl's breast pocket.

When he makes it back to the bed, Shea is snuggled under the warm blankets, fast asleep on the couch. He chuckles to himself and makes the bed. She still seems very sick, but at least she is more with it today.

He deposits Shea in the middle of the cocoon he made for her and takes off her bandage. The wound is looking much better—swelling has gone down considerably, redness receded. Grabbing the supplies from the table, he again irrigates the wound. The paste is doing its job, the wound has dried up and there is far less pus today. Since she slept through the whole exchange, as soon as her IV is finished, he wakes her to tell her that her that her gun is on the table by the bed, just in case.

He makes a quick call alerting his team of the need for increased security, then steps out of the room with his canvas bag and one of the twenty-five burners he packed, when they left Florida.

Walking down to the front desk, he sees a different clerk from last night. He mutters "Crap," under his breath and gets in line.

When it's his turn, he explains the promissory note and that they won't be able to leave today, asking if there's anything he can do to extend it.

"Sir, we have the note here, but there's no expiry date, so you guys are good," the clerk says. "The only thing I'd advise is that if you're going to continue to get room service, you should probably put a little money in a room service account with us. Earlier, the resort tried to run a credit card that we don't have, so it ate into that five-hundred dollars. Which, technically, puts you out of the agreed-upon terms of the promissory note. Now, I'm not going to do anything about that, but I do recommend bringing that back up to five-hundred and also starting a room service account—that the resort can pull from for those services," he explains.

"Wow, thanks for letting me know, man," he says, reaching into the bag. He pulls out what feels like about a thousand dollars in one-hundred-dollar bills. Stacking two on the counter, he says, "For the note." He then lays five down, and says, "For room service." Finally, he takes whatever is left in his hand and puts it on the counter, saying, "For you, but I need a favor."

"I'd be happy to help, sir," the clerk says, gathering up all the money, which totaled fifteen hundred dollars.

"We can't leave because my traveling companion acquired a wound, which is now badly infected. I need a doctor to come look at her, but it needs to be a private practice doc who does house calls and is knowledgeable in wounds and antibiotics. They also need to know how to keep their mouth shut. You know a guy?" John asks.

"Actually, I think I do," the young man says.

"Well, if you can get them over here today, there might be more where that came from," John says, lifting his head in the direction of the cash behind the desk.

"You can count on me, sir. Should I have them go right up, or should I ring when they arrive?" he asks.

"Ring first, please. I may be out of the room. If I don't answer, please call back in five minutes. I'll make sure I check in regularly," John says.

Leaving the counter, John walks out of the back entrance and heads to the fire pits. Sitting there, he wishes he could share this moment with Shea, but he shakes it off to make his calls. After he is done, he breaks the phone in half and tears it into pieces. He considers putting them in the firepit and setting them aflame but knows that would ruin the firepit and stink something horrible as well. He settles on tossing it into the closest garbage can.

Twin Pines

00034 In the Closet

Gregg gently sways in the hammock between dream and awake, floating happily, when he hears his phone ding. Opening his eyes, he then feels fingers stroking his hair. Shooting up in the chair, he looks at Shea. Her big, beautiful, brown eyes are open and alert. She has also already been extubated and is smiling at him. Her playlist continues to play, but her phone is now on the other side of her lap.

"Hi, beautiful. How are you feeling? How long have you been awake?" he asks.

"I feel like I took a long nap, and now my throat's scratchy. I woke up around six this morning, called the nurse, and they took the tube out. I asked them not to wake you—you looked so peaceful," Shea says.

"Shea, I was so worried, I would have been lost if something worse… if you had…" Gregg tries to tell her how much she means to him, but he's tongue-tied at seeing her awake. He feels his throat tightening and a prickle behind his eyes.

"I know," she says softly. "Just like I know, that you know, about my secret playlists. I can explain."

"It's okay, Shea. I know you don't feel that way about me. I just thought the playlist might bring you back to me…to us," Gregg says, not wanting to hear the heartbreaking words from her.

"Gregg, you don't know anything… in fact… *You know nothing, Jon Snow*,'" she says, as she scoots to one side of her bed. She pats the spot next to her, and Gregg takes off his shoes to slide in with her. She immediately takes his arm and hugs it tightly.

"If I don't know anything, can you enlighten me?" Gregg asks, scared shitless but curious.

"I could, but what fun would that be?" She smiles looking up at him, mischief in her eyes. "Gregg, I care for you, and I trust you with my life, obviously. I know how you feel… I heard you. You know?"

"You heard me?" Gregg asks, confusion written on his face.

"Yes, I heard you," she says, and with that the topic is dropped. She snuggles as close as she can to him and closes her eyes.

"Well, well, well, look what we have here," Todd says, standing over the two forms.

Gregg hears the voice and jolts awake, shooting up into a sitting position. Looking at Todd, he says, "Hey man, sorry, she wanted some comfort, I think."

"I'm right here, and Gregg did nothing wrong. He slept in that chair all night for me," Shea says, giving Todd evil eyes.

"Whoa, I'm not mad, babe. It's all good. I couldn't be here because nine other directors were affected too. I was all over the place checking on everyone. Plus, I had Tina at my place with her little rats that I had to deal with," Todd says.

"Is Tina okay?" Shea asks, her voice thick with concern. Gregg smiles because that is so Shea—always caring about others first.

"Yeah, she was just milking it. No one got it as bad as you, we're still trying to figure out why, but no more handshakes allowed on campus," he says.

A couple of days of recuperation at home by the pool, and on the beach have Shea feeling better than ever. Gregg took the time off too, to be there for her, and she rewarded his care by wearing a bikini around the house for a couple of days. Todd joined them and he also enjoyed the view. They watched more of their show and ordered takeout every night. Shea and Todd also made Gregg perform a fashion show of all his new clothes, and Todd spent hours explaining what "tumble dry low" and "hand wash only" mean.

"Hand wash means hand wash, Gregg. Take it to the sink, plug the sink, run some warm water, add a little soap, and just wash it!" Todd says, while Gregg looks on like a lost puppy. "Here I'll show you. Go get some detergent."

Shea watches as Todd takes off his high-end button-down and tosses it toward the sink. Looking back at her, he smiles and gives her a wink.

I could wash the shirt on those abs...

With Gregg providing the soap, Todd instructs him on how to proceed, "You don't want the water too hot now, we're hand-washing for a reason, dude."

"You're telling me, you do this every week, with all of your clothes?" Gregg asks, mildly frustrated.

"Of course not, man, I'm rich. I either have new ones delivered every week—which is how your wardrobe is so much better now—or I just have Tina drop them off at the cleaners. It's only a few hundred dollars a week," he says, smirking at Gregg. "You can afford it now. You could just send them out."

"Dude, do you have any idea how expensive swords are?" Gregg asks him seriously.

Shea bursts out laughing from her spot on the couch, holding her side and really giving it her all.

"Shut it!" they holler from the kitchen. She then sees them bump knuckles and continue on their shirt-washing journey.

"What happened to (mockingly) 'I can't man, that's my girl'?" she teases.

"What? What are you talking about? I have your back always, but you love my man Gregg's sword just as much as he does, so don't start with me," Todd says seriously, to the delight of Shea.

Gregg and Shea laugh for what feels like forever to Todd, but really it had only been a few minutes before Shea is able to speak enough to get out, "I do love his sword."

Todd stands there, confused for a moment, then they can see the light bulb go on. "Oh, what-ever, you know what I mean."

Later, Gregg tries to talk to Todd privately regarding Shea's pictures, but doesn't really get anywhere. Gregg feels like Shea is kind of putting it in the back of her mind. To not think about it, because it's too painful—it makes Gregg want to fix it for her.

When they return to work, Shea gets properly trained at the front desk with Tina, and Gregg dives into his project, which is moving along quickly—in true Gregg fashion. Most days, the three musketeers find a way to get off campus for lunch together. As the days turn to weeks, the three of them get into a routine after work. Shea grows more and more attached to the men in her life.

One morning Shea wakes up next to Todd, nuzzling her face into his neck, she whispers, "Good morning, sleepy head."

"Good morning, my love. What time is it?" he asks.

"About six-fifteen. We need to get up and get ready for work. I bet Gregg is already making us breakfast," she says, standing and putting on her robe.

"Wait, don't go yet," he says, rolling toward her. "Come back to bed for just a little longer."

"Mr. T, what-ever could you mean?" she teases, pulling the robe off and jumping into the bed beside him.

They hear Gregg's voice call from the kitchen, "I'd like you to recall that the walls aren't that thick, and if the bacon goes cold, it's not my fault!"

Giggling, Shea gives in anyway, it's easy to lose herself in Todd.

At work, Gregg is killing it in his lab. He decides not to name his new rats, as these implants are completely new to him, and he couldn't bear the heartbreak if he had to leave them again. Instead, he uses Crown's coding system—Crown followed by the number of the rat—rat one is named C1, rat two is C2, and so on.

Gregg spends many hours engineering and testing to identify the perfect material that would work as a biologic, able to integrate seamlessly with both the brain and the body. But also, be able to behave in a smart manner, driven by the chip it's attached to. After weeks of intense work, he develops the first prototype, which is implanted into a synthetic brain containing interactive nerve centers to simulate the very real reactions a brain will have. Unfortunately, this prototype, as documented by Gregg, "ran too hot, burning up the synthetic fibers from the implant and the brain's nerve centers."

Several versions and a significant portion of his budget later, he believes he's done it. It takes him a longer while still—of vigorous testing with positive results—to trust the implant in C1 through C5.

Though it's a grisly task, Gregg insists he perform the implantations himself. He uses a mild sedative, both for the comfort of the rats and to minimize wiggling. Carefully, he makes a small incision in the scalp, using tiny retractors to hold the area open. Doing this by himself, he wedges the ends of the retractors into blocks of fake brain to keep them steady.

Taking a surgically sterilized Dremel with an impossibly small attachment, he drills through the skull, just deep enough to expose the dura layer. He then carefully drops the chip into the hole, and watches the magic.

Tiny, shimmering, almost microscopic, hairlike protrusions gently unfurl from the chip. He watches, the beauty of it is over in an instant, but captivating. These protrusions smartly target certain areas of the brain—control centers for eyesight, memory, and hearing. The protrusions easily pierce through the dura layer and into the areas of the brain that are preprogrammed into the chip. Utilizing a form of X-ray and live brain mapping, he watches the protrusions settle into place, the appropriate areas in the brain lighting up in response.

Once the implant is in place, Gregg fills the hole using a medical-grade, two-part putty and carefully sutures the rats scalp. Once the rat is off sedation, he's up and around like nothing happened.

The chips aren't designed to control the rat—or the humans they'll eventually be implanted into—but to allow for sharper senses. And in humans, the ability to have a heads-up display (HUD) with the ability to link their phones, map applications, and even Netflix to their brain. With just a thought, they'll be able to navigate or to watch shows and movies. One lingering concern of Gregg's is that, deep in the programming, is the ability to recall memories to an outside device. So, for now, he has opted out of implantation on himself.

While Gregg is busy in the lab, Tina is teaching Shea different dialect accents, which days the hottest delivery drivers show up, and—as time goes on—Tina becomes increasingly insulting to Shea. Shea just attributes Tina's actions as being her sense of humor, but it is starting to wear on her.

"Morning, Shea," Tina greets her, as she walks into the building and around the desk. "Is your coffee full? You're going to actually have to work today, so you won't be able to visit the kitchen every hour like you normally do. Oh, and no off-campus lunch, either."

"Yup, I'm ready for the day. And Mr. T comes to get me every day to go off campus, so I can't offend him by declining his offer, right?" Shea asks, with maybe a little bit of attitude thrown in.

"Well yeah, but he'll be busy today too, so don't hold your breath," Tina replies cooly.

"So, what has us so busy today?" Shea asks, keeping her cool.

"Not us, you," Tina corrects. "I'll be manning the desk while you escort today's driver to your bestie, Gregg. There are a ton of boxes coming in—supplies for human trials. So, you get to build new shelves in the supply closet and then properly organize everything."

Tina's voice drips with malice, though her face and tone remain steady.

Shea simply nods. This is actually a perfect task for her, she likes building things and loves organizing. Plus, she gets to hang out with or near Gregg all day—win-win.

Shea takes phone calls and schedules meetings for Todd for the first part of her morning, as Tina observes in silence. As soon as hunky

Brad walks through the door with a dolly full of boxes, Shea jumps to her feet.

"Hey, Brad, is that for the lab?" she asks, eager to get away from the desk.

"Yeah, I got, probably seven or eight more loads this size. You got the elevator access?" he asks.

"Yeah, follow me," she responds, leading him to the elevator and using her key card to open the doors. When they get to Gregg's floor, she directs Brad to leave the boxes just outside of the glass-walled lab. "I'll carry them in, or have Gregg help me."

She rides the elevator up and down a total of eight times, and on the last load she keys in and has Brad ride down alone. She's not stupid, she watches the floors pass overhead, ensuring he actually goes to the ground level.

Gregg sees Shea watching the elevator, absolutely surrounded by boxes, just outside of his glass sanctuary. Walking over he peeks his head out the door, and teases, "Hey, butt munch, you get a little carried away on the home shopping network?"

"Home shopping network? What are you, eighty? It was Amazon. Now, come be my pack mule," she retorts with a grin.

Gregg looks at her with one eyebrow cocked and stands his ground.

"I'm sorry, Greggy-poo, will you please help me? I'm weak and frail and need a big strong man," she playfully exaggerates, smiling at him.

Keeping a straight face, he says, "You think you're funny, but you really do need the help of a big strong man, so…" He milks it because she really does need him.

Shea eyes him, as he stands in the doorway, he's wearing an outfit Todd picked—and it seems she's admiring it. He's standing with his hands on his hips, biceps slightly flexed—they're impressive without flexing, but with the way she's looking at him, he feels like an absolute unit wrapped in a tailored Prada button-down and slacks.

"Fine, could you be my truest and bestest friend and help me, please?" she asks. She seems sincere, but it always comes out moderately sarcastic.

"I accept," Gregg says, walking over to her, propping the door open behind himself. "Where are we taking these, pretty lady?"

"Oh yeah, where's the supply closet?" she asks him.

"Uh, we have, a small supply rack in the middle of the floor. But I assume that isn't what you're talking about?"

"Nope. Let's go investigate," she says.

Looking behind every closed door that they can open, they keep coming up short. Finally, Gregg smacks the side of his head, mushing his curls. "I'm an idiot. Come this way."

Shea follows him across the floor to a door that literally reads, 'Supply Room'. She gives him a deadpan look. "Really?"

"Hold on, don't judge! The sign wasn't always there, and up until recently, there was a comfy napping couch and a microwave on a milk crate in there."

"Well, let's see if it's nap time or shelf-building time. When do you nap? You're like the busiest person here."

"I know, but when I was in development, there were times I literally just had to wait. So, I'd power nap it," he says, putting his keycard against the sensor to open the door.

Looking around the door, Shea's eyes widen in shock. The room is huge, this isn't a closet—it's a damn warehouse. There are already forty boxes—at least—inside, plus the boxes containing the materials to build the shelves. "Well, Tina undersold this job," she says, incredulously.

"Yeah, what's up with her lately? Real wacky pants," he says, shaking his head.

"Wacky pants? Gah, I love you, Gregg," she says, laughing in spite of herself.

"Alright well, all the rats are being monitored currently, and I have some free time. Would you like some help?" he asks, sincere.

"Gregg, you are literally the best ever," she says, grinning brightly.

Gregg decides it's better to build the shelves and sort out what's already in the room first. Shea watches him move and stack boxes with ease, admiring his strength. Curious, she tries to lift one when his back is turned, just to see if she can—she thought she was going to shit her pants. Too much effort for her taste and ability.

They work diligently for hours, after Gregg tracked down a tool bag. The shelves are professional quality and come with mounting hardware, so they are even properly secured to the walls. Around noon, Todd calls her cell phone.

"Hey, what up, boss?" she asks.

"Hey, sweets, are you too busy for an outing today?" he asks.

"Tina told me I'm not allowed to go off campus today, but if you could order us a couple of pizzas, Gregg is working really hard helping me."

"Well, I outrank Tina. So, what if I still want to take you out?" he asks.

"I'd actually rather stay in. We haven't even started unpacking the boxes, and I don't want to be trapped in this closet all week. I mean the company is great, don't get me wrong, but…"

"Okay, I know what kind of pizza you both like, so I'll order it. I have a lot to do too, so I'll just see you after work," he says, then hangs up.

Shea and Gregg move along, quickly getting through the boxes that were already in the room. Shea admits to Gregg that she couldn't lift them, so he goes out to grab the others by himself. Shea is breaking down boxes when she sees him come in, carrying two at a time.

"Way to show off, Gregg. Geez, I feel like a true weakling now," she says.

Gregg chuckles, putting the boxes down. "These are different. I could probably lift ten of these, but they're too awkward. You will for sure be able to lift at least one," he says with a teasing smile.

Shea follows him out to the area near the elevator, and watches him stack four of the boxes, sliding them toward the door. "Just lift one, you can do it," he encourages.

"You go ahead, I'll be right behind you," she says, watching him walk through the lab, casually sliding the boxes with one foot as he goes. She didn't want to embarrass herself in front of him, so when he's gone, she really tries to lift one. Expecting the box to be heavy, she is caught completely off guard, when it's not. She lifts it with so much effort she almost falls backwards, flinging the box over her head. But she rights herself and chuckles, carrying the box in.

They move all the boxes into the room by the time the pizza arrives, and although the pizza is welcome, Tina delivering it just isn't.

Shea and Gregg are laughing while stocking the shelves, listening to another one of Shea's playlists when suddenly, something slams onto one of the boxes behind them. They both turn around, and Gregg says, "Damn, Tina, you scared the crap out of me."

"Is that any way to thank your own personal delivery woman?" Tina says, her voice dripping with sarcasm.

"Thanks, Tina, we're all good here," Shea says, keeping her cool.

"Oh, are you all good? Did you even do any of the work, or did you just rope Gregg into doing it all? You know what? I already know the answer to that. Enjoy your pizza," she says with a smirk.

"Hey, Tina, what's the issue lately? We were never really friends, but the way you treat Shea now is out of line, and frankly, super awkward for her to try to deal with, considering you are Todd's sister," Gregg says.

Tina laughs, a creepy, maniacal laugh. "Sister? Is that what he told you?" she says, her eyes glinting with something dangerous.

Gregg and Shea are too stunned to answer. They stand in silence for a moment, unable to process what just happened. Tina turns on her heel and vacates the area.

The two stand there stunned, not able to even put into words what this could mean. They decide to just move on and open their pizzas. Each box has only half of a pizza inside, and Shea's box contains a greasy, pink, sticky note that reads, "*You don't need a whole pizza, little piggy.*"

Furious, Gregg takes a picture and sends it to Todd along with a full account of their interaction with Tina. Gregg and Shea continue working, late into the night, finishing the whole room together. Gregg never hears back from Todd. Shea doesn't hear from him that night either.

The next day, Todd approaches Shea. "It's now time for phase two of your employment. You'll be moving to the top floor in building twenty-five." He continues, explaining that her real adventure with Crown is about to begin. She will now be working on their most top-secret project. Todd also informs Gregg that he will be moving to the top floor soon, once he has a couple of weeks of successful human trials. His role would be changing drastically but would still be scientific.

None of them addresses the elephant in the room.

00035 DR. P

About twenty minutes later, he's back in the room with a coffee for Shea and another plate of bacon for himself. That first half plate of bacon was cute and all, but he needed more than that to feed the beast. Shea must have heard the door this time because she is sitting up, with her gun in her hands, watching for someone to come around the corner. As soon as she sees it is John, she puts the gun back on the table.

"Coffee and bacon! For me?" she asks cheerfully. Her color has returned, and John thanks his lucky stars—it looks like she's improving.

"Of course, for you! I ordered more food with room service, but wanted to get this to you first, myself," he says, smiling.

"You're the best," she says, slipping from her cocoon and walking to the couch to eat at the table. "Truvia?"

"What do I look like? Of course, Truvia, in French vanilla coffee," he says.

"Thank you so much. I feel like this will make me feel human again," she says, sounding more like herself.

"Sure. Here's the remote. I'm just gonna call downstairs and check on the food, be right back," he says. From the bathroom he orders another plate of bacon and two cheeseburger meals with fries. Plus, if she doesn't eat it—more for the beast.

Leaving the bathroom, he finds Shea watching *The Office* and is cringe-giggling while eating 'her' bacon.

"Ooooh, John, what else are you getting us? I'm so hungry."

"I'm glad to see my medical skills are paying off, you feel better?" he asks her.

"Yeah, honestly, I feel almost like my normal self. Just a bit cold and my head is really sore, but much better."

"Just in time, I guess. I called for a doctor to come see you this afternoon," he says.

"Is that safe? In our current predicament?" she asks.

"We shall see."

After gorging themselves on their room service cheeseburgers, Shea mentions feeling the need for a nap. John sits with his back against the headboard next to her, as she snuggles into his side, seeking his warmth. Taking the remote, he finds a rom-com that's playing, and selects it, tossing the remote onto the nightstand.

"You like rom-coms?" Shea asks, looking up at him.

"They're okay. Just wanted to pick something I thought you could fall asleep to," John says.

"Suuuuuuurrreee, use me as your excuse," she teases, settling back into her cozy position.

Within fifteen minutes, Shea is lightly snoring beside John. He sits, watching the movie, but the longer he sits there, the more disgusting he feels. He has been so worried about taking care of Shea, that some of his hygiene has seen better days. Gently sliding out of the bed, so as not to disturb Shea, he grabs his toiletry bag and heads to the bathroom. Unsure if taking a shower now is a good idea, he settles for a wipe down, teeth brushing and changing the contacts he's been wearing for several days. Feeling a bit better, he claims his spot next to her, turns off the TV, and doses off.

At 2:30 p.m., the resort phone rings, into the silence. John, groggy, reaches for it. Clearing his throat, he answers, "Hello."

"Mr. Doe, the physician you requested is here at the desk," the clerk from earlier says.

"Oh great. What am I looking for?" he says.

"About five foot eight, dark eyes, dark hair, curvaceous, wearing scrubs and carrying a backpack," the clerk reports.

"Name?" John asks, picturing a curvaceous man for only a couple of seconds before he realizes the doc is obviously a woman.

"She goes by Dr. P. Do you want me to send her up or do you want to come down to escort her?" the clerk asks.

"Uh, send her up," John says, thinking he could use the time to tidy up.

"Yes, sir. Just to let you know, she will leave her invoice for services rendered here at the desk by tomorrow," he says.

"Perfect. Thanks man," John says, hanging up the phone and jumping from the bed.

Shea remains deep asleep and is looking pale again. John tidies up the room and grabs everything he's been using on Shea, placing it on a table. Lastly, he throws on a hat, just in case.

The knock at the door isn't a surprise this time, but he still doesn't immediately open it. He opens it as far as the chain will let him, peering at the woman on the other side. "Dr. P?" The clerk described her perfectly, he just left out the fact that she's gorgeous.

"Yes, Mr. Doe, I presume?" she says.

"Ah, call me John. Please, come in," he says, closing the door to release the chain and open the door wide. He ushers her into the room and leads her over to where Shea is sleeping.

"There are a couple of things we need to discuss before we move forward," John says.

"Sure, what are your concerns?" Dr. P asks.

"I need you to understand how important our privacy is. Nothing that happens in this room will leave this room. No documentation, no talking with colleagues—nothing," John says, his voice serious.

"Well, John, I strictly adhere to HIPAA guidelines, so I wouldn't discuss the case with anyone you hadn't approved. I can forgo documentation or just have you hold onto it in case I need to see her again," she responds, calm and confident.

"I'm not trying to scare you. I think you're actually being genuine, and I hope you can help my friend, but I need reassurance in your ability to keep our business private, even under duress," he says.

"I am a professional, the kind who actually cares about their patients. I would never put the lives of two people in danger, even under duress," she answers, firmly.

"Okay, well, here's what I've been using to treat her. I guess just do your thing, I'll answer what I can," John says, pointing to the table piled high with medical supplies.

"Is she not rousable?" Dr. P asks.

"She was this morning, but she has amnesia. She doesn't remember the last year. I just got her a few days ago," John says.

"Got her from where?"

John looks at the doctor carefully and decides the less he tells her the better, for everyone's safety. "From where she was. Sorry doc, that's all I can say."

"Okay. Give me the history, and then we'll wake her up," she says.

John spends about ten minutes explaining just enough of what happened for Shea to get the wound and infection. He then takes a couple of minutes to outline what he's done for her so far.

"Great, well, the broad-spectrum antibiotics you've been administering are probably making a dent, but from here, her pallor doesn't look great. If she is worsening again, the antibiotics might not be what's needed," Dr. P says.

"Yeah, her color got a bit better earlier, but we fell asleep, and now she's pale again," John says.

"Okay, let's wake her. I want to get a good look at her and ask her some questions," Dr. P says.

Twin Pines

00036 🌲🌲 Playing Dumb

■ ■ ■ ■ ■ □ □ □ □

Shea's first day on the top floor has her feeling nervous—and not the cute, shaky kind, but the several bathroom visits kind. Not only did she have to sign what felt like a hundred privacy contracts, but mostly because Todd has been so tight-lipped about it. Standing at the desk next to Tina, she waves goodbye to Gregg, who heads up to his office to begin work on getting the next round of neural implants into human subjects with the medical team. Tina shares that she'll be getting the neural implant as soon as she can.

"Ah, here are my two favorite ladies," Todd says, strolling in through the front door.

Shea turns to face him and freezes, mouth agape.

"Weird, isn't it? It's like a whole different creature," Tina says.

Todd chuckles and walks over to Shea, wearing what looks like a full spandex outfit, complete with athletic cup. He places his arm around her waist, snapping her out of her shock.

"Mr. T, we're at work," she says, gently pushing him away. "And what's this about? Not that I'm complaining or anything—just curious. What's about to happen?"

"Well, phase one of the new project is training, and you'll be meeting your personal bodyguard," he says.

"Training? I need a bodyguard? Seriously?" Shea says, feeling like she is completely unprepared for today.

What the hell kind of training do I need? How to be a Director?

"Look, we're gonna go up and have a talk about a couple of things, then training, okay? It's only for your safety, Shea," Todd says. "Oh yeah, and here is your new key card, so I don't have to escort you every day."

"Thanks," she says, taking the keycard before falling into step with Todd toward the elevators.

When they step onto the elevator, Todd instructs Shea on the protocol to get to level five, which involves a card swipe and fingerprint scan. When they arrive on the fifth floor, Shea is shocked by how different the layout is compared to other levels. Whereas all the other floors are open with all-glass walls, this floor is like a high-ceilinged warehouse, with different areas partitioned off by large metal cubicles.

"Okay, I know this is different, but eventually you'll see why. Let me radio your guard so you two can have some time to bond. Go ahead and head into that first cube on the left; it's a kitchen and conference room. I'll send him in to meet you as soon as he arrives," Todd says.

Shea walks over to the cube and opens the door. Inside there's a table full of bagels, donuts, and several carafes of different flavored coffee. She walks over to the table, spreads cream cheese on an everything bagel, and pours coffee from the carafe labeled, "French vanilla." She sits down, eating her bagel, when the door opens, and (another) tall, and handsome man walks through it. He's also wearing whatever athletic, military hybrid outfit Todd had on.

"Hello, Miss Murphy. It's great to meet you. I'll be your personal bodyguard, trainer, and hopefully, friend," he says, walking toward her and offering his hand.

"Look, I'd love to, but I'm not allowed," she says, pointing at his outstretched hand.

"I'm so sorry. I totally forgot. I was informed not to shake your hand. Crap, not out to the best start, huh?" he says.

"You're doing great. Wanna sit? Todd said we should get to know each other a bit," Shea says, leaning back in her chair. She looks up at this handsome man, with his well-kempt beard, and asks, "What's your name, by the way?"

"My name's John, ma'am. It's a pleasure to meet you."

"John, hi. Great to meet you. So, while I eat my bagel, can you tell me what this training is going to look like?" she asks, taking a sip of the coffee she poured. "Yuck, ugh."

"What's wrong with it?" John asks.

"It's hazelnut. I'm not a fan. The label said French vanilla though."

"Well, do you want me to try the one labeled hazelnut?" he asks.

"That would be amazing, actually," she says, smiling at him.

He takes one of the disposable cups and pours a little bit of the coffee labeled "hazelnut" into it. He swirls the cup and takes a sip like he's tasting wine, making Shea giggle. He makes a face of contemplation, and says, "French vanilla, definitely."

"Well, you're my hero of the day," she says, grabbing a new cup and filling it from the "hazelnut" carafe.

"I will wear that as a badge of honor," he says, smiling at her.

"Okay, back to business. The training?"

"Right, well, today and probably for a week, we will be working only on defensive stuff. But eventually, we will be doing offensive stuff, hand-to-hand training and even weapons," he explains.

"Wow, I'm so curious to see what this project is about… it's making me a little nervous," she says.

Why the hell do I need weapons training and a bodyguard?

"Yeah, Todd should be in here any minute, and we'll learn more about what we're doing," John says.

"So, you don't even know?" she asks.

"No, I was working as a guard on the property, and Todd asked me to move here. I've been with Crown for a long time, so maybe he thought I deserved a promotion? I don't know. But I'm glad it's guarding you. You seem really cool," he says.

"Oh, I'm the coolest. Maybe we can have you over for dinner one night, make you part of the gang," she says with what she hopes is an inviting smile.

"That'd be awesome."

"Hey, guys. You feel acquainted?" Todd asks, walking in the door.

John immediately stands, his feet shoulder-width apart, his hands clasped behind his back.

"Relax, John. Take a seat. Besides, although I pay you, Shea is your boss now. She's the one who deserves your attention," Todd says.

"Apologies, ma'am," John says, sitting.

"Alright, you two, we're going to go over the basics today. Then we'll slowly bring you further into the fold," Todd says. "Remember, everything discussed on this floor stays on this floor. It's like Vegas that way. Even if it's just us, hanging out at Shea's house, we can't discuss it. You need to remember this," Todd says.

Shea and John both nod, curious about what the walls could possibly hear.

"Okay, Shea, and John by association, the project you will be working on is called, 'Twin Pines', hence the silhouettes on the building."

"Great Scott!" John exclaims, referencing Doc Brown, making Shea giggle.

"Alright, we have a lot to go over. I have a binder for each of you, but now isn't the appropriate time," Todd says. "I do have a few pairs of our high-tech training clothes for each of you though," he says, handing them each a butcher paper package wrapped in twine.

"Before you go get changed, Shea, there will be several stages to this part of your employment. In the end, you'll see it's easier that way. What I can tell you is that you'll spend quite a bit of time training. You'll need to be prepared, but after that, you'll get everything you need to know to move forward. Another thing is, as Gregg finishes the human trials for the implants, you will be requested to get one. This isn't necessarily a requirement, but for your position, it will be highly useful. Now, go put that juicy butt in that uniform and meet us in pod 5. You'll see the number on the side. Oh, and you can just use the bathroom in here to change," Todd finishes, leaving Shea questioning if she made the right decision coming here.

She opens the package and pulls out a black sports bra, black compression bodysuit, and leggings-like bottoms and a top. She goes into the bathroom to change, turning this way and that in the mirror once she's changed. The clingy fabric really isn't her best friend. It's not horrible, but it's not great.

I look like a busted can of biscuits…

Her confidence is pretty low as she walks over to pod 5 in her training suit and stilettos, carrying her clothes and other training suits. As she presses her keycard to the pad to enter the pod, she sees something in her peripheral vision. Turning her head, she spots Gregg, standing in a training suit and looking like a freaking piece of carved marble.

"Oh, what the fuck? Now I feel really bad about myself," she says to him.

"You shouldn't. You look hot. I don't want to hit on my boy's girlfriend or anything, but the shoes with that outfit are really doing it for me," Gregg says.

"Alright, alright. What are you doing here anyway? I thought it was going to be weeks?"

"Yeah, after your meeting, Todd came to the lab and said that the medical team are the ones performing the implantations. I just have to check the data every day. So, he wanted me with you and John, so we're able learning at the same pace," Gregg explains.

"Well, at least I'll have you. I'm glad," she says, tapping her keycard again and stepping into the pod.

John is standing just inside the door and rushes to hold it open for her and Gregg. "Thank you, John," Shea says.

Shea keeps to the concrete rim around the mats that are situated in the middle of the room, waiting for Todd to look her way. When he does, he smiles and shakes his head softly. He points to one of the benches on the concrete floor, where she sees a pair of socks and shoes for both her and Gregg. They walk over and change their footwear, then look to John for guidance.

"I think we're supposed to have an instructor, but until then, we can do some blocks. Shea and Gregg, stand here facing the door, and I'll pretend to punch you. I want you to block it like this with your forearm," he instructs, demonstrating the action.

Gregg and Shea stand a few feet apart, mirroring John's stance. John comes straight at them, he obviously and slowly throws a punch at Gregg. Gregg deflects it perfectly, then glances to Shea, eager to see how she does.

Don't make me look like an idiot… please don't make me look like an idiot

John throws the punch at Shea—again slow and obvious—and she also deflects it smoothly, just like John had shown them.

"I know it's kind of silly, everything really slow and obvious like that, but it's how you learn, ya know?" John remarks.

Todd, who's been observing, approaches and places a hand on both Shea's and Gregg's shoulders. "Well, it looks like you guys don't even need me! Great first exercise, John."

"Thank you, sir. I figured we could learn some basics while we waited," John says.

"Absolutely, great thought," Todd agrees. "Now, I will be going through a bunch of moves quickly with John. Just watch and don't get overwhelmed. The names of the moves will always be displayed on that TV, and I will demonstrate them every day," he says, turning to John. "John, that gives you the burden, most days, of training, though I will try to be present whenever possible, if that's okay?" he asks.

"Of course, sir. I've taught it all before, so it's no problem," John answers.

"Great. If you would step into the defensive position, we will go through the list and I'll get out of your hair," Todd says, shifting into a fighting stance.

Gregg and Shea decide to park it on the closest bench, fearing they would be in the way otherwise. Shea is so focused on the moves and trying to commit them to memory that she doesn't even realize she's only been watching bums for a few minutes. Tapping her chin, Gregg leans in close in, and whispers, "You had a little drool there."

She smiles at him, showing him one of her fingers, then turns back to witness the clash of the titans.

John is a great guy, and if you asked Shea, she would tell you that herself. But currently, she is icing her forearms, butt, and calves because of that drill instructor. Gregg is sitting on the couch next to her, in a semi-catatonic state, just staring at the wall. When Todd arrives, they're both so exhausted that they praise his name when he walks in with the gift of food.

"Thank you so much, man. We are wrecked," Gregg says.

"No problem. Give it some time. You'll be in shape in no time," Todd answers, heading to the kitchen to plate up the food.

"I thought I was in shape man. I mean…" Gregg says, lifting his shirt to reveal his abs.

Todd chuckles. "C'mon, Gregg you are. You're just working different muscle groups for this, that's all."

"I may not be in shape, but I am a shape. Amiright?" Shea says, jovially.

"A beautiful shape—wouldn't change a thing," Gregg says.

"I agree. I just want to tone the shape a little bit, so you can defend yourself—that's all," Todd says, serving them both plates with Crown and Cokes to drink.

Sitting up, Gregg and Shea eat their dinner. Shea holds her fork like an inmate, due to the pain in her arm. When they're about done, Gregg clears his throat and summons the elephant.

"Hey, Todd. I know you saw my texts the other day, and since then, you haven't really been around. I feel like it's only fair that you address this, for Shea. What happened was completely wrong, and what was said needs to be addressed—especially because Shea is your girlfriend. I'm not trying to overstep any boundaries, man, but enough time has passed," Gregg says, his voice serious.

Shea looks over at Gregg and like he feels her gaze, he returns the look. She mouths, "Thank you, love you." He grabs her hand, kisses it, and continues to hold it as they both turn expectantly toward Todd. Todd is 'chewing' and puts up a 'hold on a sec' finger.

Shea is expectant and hopeful that after this conversation, they can be back on the right track, of love and all that stuff. Though the longer Todd sits there with his stupid finger up, the more Shea wants to reach over and break it off.

"You're right," Todd finally says. "I should have addressed the problem head-on that night. And I want you to know, Shea, I did talk to

Tina right away about how inappropriate she was with you that entire day. She's been asked to keep her distance, and I hope you will let me know if she doesn't. I should have handled the entire situation better. I just found it difficult, considering my relationship with all three of you," Todd explains.

Though Shea's face remained neutral, Gregg can tell there's a fire underneath—not only because he knows her so well, but because the bones in his hand are currently grinding together. "And what would that relationship be, Todd?" she asks, her voice icy.

"You're my love, you know this babe. I made a mistake. Please forgive me," Todd says.

"Not that relationship," Shea responds.

"Tina is my sister. I thought I told you that," he says, glancing between Shea and Gregg.

Shea looks at Gregg, her expression asking, 'Am I crazy?' He gently shakes his head, silently telling her she's not. Feeling like he needs to provide her with some backup, Gregg says, "C'mon, man. I told you exactly what she said that night. Playing dumb really doesn't look good on you."

"PLAYING DUMB?" Todd roars. "Whatever she said to you was obviously a lie. Meant to get under Shea's skin, a way to mess up what we have, because she is a jealous, needy, heartless bitch. It doesn't matter what Tina has to say because I found someone else to work the desk in twenty-five!"

Shea shrinks back into the sofa, leaning into Gregg. He wraps his arm around her shoulder and holds her close, which seems to set Todd over the edge.

"Why are you two questioning me when you live together and touch and play all the time?" Todd demands. "I don't ever give you a hard time because I trust you, Shea! This is completely unfair, especially because we both know Gregg is in love with you. I'm starting to question if the feeling isn't mutual."

He stands with his dishes, drops them in the sink, and hollers on the way to the door, "Meet John in the training pod at 8 a.m. tomorrow."

Instead of running off to her room like she wants to, she decides she and Gregg are going to have a self-care night. Face masks, manicures, and several drinks are included in the plan. Gregg informs Shea that he had no idea how far up cuticles could grow before this experience. He also mentions he is now thinking about growing a beard, because she likes John's so much.

00037 L.T.

John moves to the side of the bed and gently rubs Shea's back until she wakes and turns to him.

"John, I'm cold, please lie with me," Shea says.

"I will, I promise, but for now, we have a guest. Dr. P is here to check you out, so try to stay awake, L.T.," John says, hoping she picks up on the use of her 'nickname'.

"I'll try."

John nods to Dr. P, and she takes his place at Shea's bedside.

"Hello, L.T., I'm Dr. P. If you're able, I'd like to ask you a few questions," she says, gently.

"Okay," Shea says, using her whole body to turn more fully toward the doctor. She can't stop shivering but makes an obvious effort to look awake.

"Are you in any pain?" she asks.

"Yes, my head and my side," Shea responds.

"Okay, can you give each of them a numerical value, from one to ten, for me?" Dr. P asks.

"Ummmm, head like a six, side has been getting way worse today. It's like a nine right now," Shea says, wincing slightly.

"Any severe tiredness, swelling, or decrease in urination?" Dr. P asks, listening intently to Shea's answers.

"Well, I've been sleeping a lot. My legs went to Jello last night, and I peed this morning, but it was just a little bit," Shea says.

"Okay, L.T., just try to relax. I'm going to listen to your heart and lungs." Shea nods, and Dr. P commences with her exam. John is on the other side of the bed and watches the doctor like a hawk.

After taking off her stethoscope, Dr. P lightly touches Shea's side. Shea's reaction is violent and immediate and seems to even surprise herself. John lifts an eyebrow at the doc, who covertly gives him a look that says, 'We'll talk soon'. She then presses her fingertips into Shea's lower leg, lifting her hand to reveal small pits in Shea's flesh that remain for a while.

Next, she takes gloves and some gauze out of her backpack. Bending over Shea, she wipes the paste from Shea's wound and inspects it. She lifts the jagged flaps of skin and uses her gloved finger to feel the surface of the skull. Shea remains quiet and still for the inspection.

When she is done, she stands back up, and says, "L.T.?"

When no response is given, the doc looks at John, and says, "Can we take a walk?"

"Yeah, sure," John says, stepping toward the door. Shea has a gun if needed and she has plenty of security—she'll be fine. He leads Dr. P out to the back, where the firepits are, though they don't sit, it's a pleasant place to walk.

The doc is silent until they're outside and out of anyone's earshot. "Alright, first of all, you made the right call taking the sutures out. The wound is looking almost free of infection, but it's difficult to tell because of the Betadine dying the tissues. The real problem now is, I think she might be septic. It also appears that the stress of the antibiotics might be impacting her kidney function. In your current situation, there's only so much I can do, but I'll do everything possible to keep her out of the hospital. I'll draw lots of labs today, including blood cultures. I'll also culture the wound. I'll be as thorough as possible. As soon as I have results, I'll have antibiotics delivered that are sensitive to the bacterial infection she has."

"I waited too long, didn't I?" John asks, now incredibly worried about Shea.

"This is not your fault. There are a ton of unknowns, and you were travelling. You did the best you could. We do need to max out her anti-fever meds around the clock though. I'll leave you my thermometer so you can track her temperature. When I just checked her, it was 103°F. We need to get that under control, maybe another cool to cold bath," Dr. P says.

"Okay, so you want me to not give her any antibiotics, and wait for the labs?" John asks.

"Yes."

"What about her wound dressing?" he asks.

"I'll apply some packing today, and I'll return in a couple of days to change it. Just keep it clean and dry," Dr. P advises.

"So, rigorous travel is out of the picture for a while, huh?" John asks, concerned.

"I'd say so, but I'll do everything I can to get her up and running.," Dr. P responds determined.

John nods, and they head back up to John's room. Dr. P cleans and dresses Shea's wound, gets her to take medication to reduce her fever, and draws enough vials of blood to fill the Ziploc bag marked Biohazard that she holds.

Twin Pines

00038 🌲🌲 Double Vision

For the next several days, they train with no sign of Todd whatsoever. When they arrive one day, to a bunch of knives on a table in the middle of the pod, Shea does a small happy dance and a smile lights up Gregg's face, which is already scruffy with a few days' growth. Todd is actually in pod five, with his back to the door. Turning slowly, he reveals a dozen black roses in his hands. He walks slowly across the pod toward Shea. Gregg thinks it looks like he's auditioning for a men's cologne ad.

When he gets to Shea, he hands her the roses and offers a fist bump to Gregg. Gregg and Shea both feel like he's trying to act like the other night never happened. But, of course, there is more to it, which becomes clear as soon as Todd opens his mouth.

"Shea, these beauties are for my beauty. Listen, as we're progressing quickly here, so is the lab, which I'm sure Gregg could tell you all about. The human trials have been nothing but successful. Tina got hers a few days ago and loves it. We really feel like your position moving forward requires it at this point, so what do you think?" Todd asks, handing her the flowers, and spinning the ring on his finger.

Grabbing her crucifix, she says, "Well, I guess if it's required... I mean, I don't want to lose my job or anything."

"I'm not threatening your job, love. It's just that it would be best. I won't force you," he assures her.

"Okay, yeah, sure. When is this going to happen?" she asks.

"Actually, right now. I'll take you over to the medical building, and they'll do the procedure. You already ride with Gregg, so he will just need to drive you home afterwards," Todd says, looking toward Gregg.

"Oh, okay, sure," she says.

"Todd, if it would be okay with you, I'd like to walk over there with Shea," Gregg says.

"Yeah, I figured you were coming, Greggy. Let's go."

"No, I mean, I'd like to walk over there with her—just the two of us. I want to make sure she understands what this means," Gregg says firmly.

"I mean, do what you want, but we plan to go into great detail with her. But, she trusts you most, obviously, so I'll meet you over there," Todd says. "But John will be following close behind for security."

As Todd walks away, Gregg turns to Shea, and says, "Listen, shorty, I know you just want to do a good job, and the money is great, so it's hard to say no. But this implant goes into your brain, Shea—not just one place, but all over. We still don't know if it can ever be removed, and if it can, there might be irreparable damage. I also read that they might be able to access your memories through the system," he says, glancing at her while walking toward the medical building.

"Wow, well, I already said I would. I'll be okay. I'll always have you to figure it out, right? Plus, why remove it?" she asks flippantly, though her hand is wrapped tightly around her crucifix.

"It might seem that way now, Shea, but you don't even know what this project is. Is it really worth it?" he asks, every word dripping with concern.

"I'll be fine, Gregg. Thank you for looking out for me, but really, it'll be fine. I have a feeling," she says, handing him her flowers.

After the medical team leads Shea to their treatment chair, they start to prep and drape the area. Gregg sets her flowers on the ground next to where he stands. He and John both stand outside the glass wall and watch, both anxious for her. One of the doctors speaks close to Shea, Gregg can't hear them but sees her shaking her head no. He looks over at John, who is also watching intently.

"I think they just told her that they need to shave her head," John says.

Gregg laughs in response, watching the nurse part her hair at the incision site, then scrub it with betadine. From behind the medical team, Todd approaches with a clipboard and a pen. Shea reads the form, and seems to ask a couple of questions before quickly signing the form. Shea is antsy, her legs keep wiggling in the chair. Finally, the nurse starts an IV and administers a mild sedative. When Shea's legs stop moving, they make the incision. The rest of the procedure goes just like it did for Gregg with the rats—overall, a fairly quick process.

Once they're suturing her up, Gregg looks over at John, who's leaning on the glass, looking white as a sheet.

"Are you okay, man?" Gregg asks.

"Yeah, just, uh, a little woozy," John replies.

"Hey, since we're, like, done for the day, do you wanna come over? You can help me watch her, we can have some drinks, watch some TV?" Gregg offers.

"That sounds great, actually. Should I bring anything?" John asks.

"Well, only if there's something special you want, but we keep it pretty well stocked," Gregg says.

"I don't mean this to sound rude, but isn't it weird living with her, like just as friends? She seems so badass and really nice, isn't it hard?" John asks.

"Yes, yes, it is, John. Being close to her is like getting pulled into her orbit, but being in the outer orbit—not quite close enough—is just plain shitty, to be honest. Watching her love someone else isn't fun, but she relies on me. She calls to me when she needs something and gives me more attention than I deserve, to be honest," Gregg admits.

"You love her?" John asks.

"Yeah, I do. Maybe one day she'll see me. I don't know how close you are with Todd, but if you could just keep this between us, I'd really appreciate it," Gregg says.

"Yeah, I don't talk to Todd like that anyway," John says, turning more toward Gregg. "And I see how you don't recognize it, dude, but she sees you. Everyone else sees it too."

"Really? How do you mean?"

"Dude, I watch you two all the time in training. Anytime she makes a joke, she looks over at you—to see if you laugh. Even when you're focusing on something else, she watches you—looks to you to know what to do. And I've only been around you guys for like a week," John says.

"I never noticed. Thanks for saying all of that," Gregg says, looking through the glass to see how it's going for Shea. "Oh, look, they're putting her in a wheelchair. Shit the car is at twenty-five. Listen, can you go and bring it around? I want to be here for her when they bring her out," Gregg asks.

"Of course, man. Toss me the keys, I'll bring it right out front. I know where the guards keep the pillows and blankets for when they're working doubles, so I'll grab one of each on my way," John says.

Gregg hands John the keys to the SUV. "That's perfect, thank you so much. If you want, just follow us out of here and over to the house afterward?"

"Yeah, sounds good. I'll be back."

The nurse brings Shea around to where Gregg stands. "Alright she's going to be a little out of it, so no operating heavy machinery, obviously. Watch her when she eats and drinks to make sure she doesn't aspirate, and keep her head at least slightly elevated when she lies down. Watch for any heavy bleeding. Mild swelling in her face is normal, but make sure there isn't a lot of swelling around her airway. I know you know what to look for, Gregg. Just take her to the ER if anything, okay?" she says.

"Got it," he says and leans down to look at Shea's face. "How you feelin', beautiful? Ready to go home? John is going to come hang out with us."

Shea blinks slowly in his direction, like she's trying to clear her eyes. "Okay, Greggy. I feel sleepy, and I see two of you. I like John, he's a good one," she says, leaning her head this way and that.

"It's okay, butt munch, it could just be the drugs. Let's not worry about it too much, okay?" he says.

"I don't know. It wasn't like this until I saw you. You're just so handsome you give me double vision," she slurs.

The nurse looks at Gregg and giggles. She then looks back at Shea, and says, "Actually, she didn't get much at all. Saying silly things is normal, but I'm not sure about the vision." She holds up two fingers, and asks, "Shea, how many fingers do you see?"

Shea looks at the hand, and says, "I know there are only two fingers up, I just see a blurry double of it." Hearing this, Gregg has a light bulb moment.

"Hey, Shea, I'm gonna take your glasses off so you can lie down in the SUV, okay?" he asks.

She nods in response, and Gregg walks up to her, carefully pulling her glasses free of her face. He folds them up he puts them in his breast pocket. He kneels to get on her level and asks, "How about now?"

She looks up at him, and smiles. "There you are, Greggy."

Gregg relays to the nurse his belief that the implant improves eyesight and hearing. He recommends they try it out with anyone else they implant, before the person leaves, for research purposes, if nothing else.

John comes in and walks to stand behind Shea's wheelchair. He looks to Gregg, and says, "We ready to roll?"

Shea tips her head back as far as she can and looks up into John's face, and says, "Hike!"

Gregg chuckles, and her smile grows as she continues to look at John. He smiles back at her, and then asks Gregg, "What does that mean?"

"She watched a documentary on dog mushing. She's commanding you to go," Gregg says, reaching down to grabs Shea's roses.

"Alright, I'm Hike-ing!" John says, gliding the wheelchair toward the front door.

John had already set up the pillow and blanket in the backseat. Gregg and John gently lift her into the SUV, get her comfortable with her head elevated, and Gregg places her roses next to himself in the front passenger seat. They head out of the Crown property and to the house, with John following behind.

Once the reach the house, Gregg and Shea sit in the car park until they see John pull into the driveway. Gregg gets out quietly. Shea had been snoring lightly the whole way home, and he doesn't want to disturb her, just yet. Gregg walks over to where John is and asks if he'll help carry Shea inside. John, of course, agrees. So, Gregg quickly unlocks the house, grabs a couple of pillows and Shea's favorite blanket from her room, depositing them onto the couch. He jogs back outside and sees John gently rubbing Shea's leg to wake her.

Unfortunately for John, his training has been going a little too well. He startles Shea, causing her to react by throwing a punch directly at John's throat. As he coughs and backs away from her, Gregg can see that her face is a mask of horror.

Gregg runs over to the SUV. "John, dude, are you okay?"

John is bent over, hands on his knees—he looks up at Gregg and nods his head.

"Why don't you go inside and grab yourself some water or soda? I can carry her alone," Gregg says.

Walking over to the SUV, Gregg keeps his distance at first, looking in on Shea. When she locks eyes with him, there are tears welling in her eyes, and she reaches out for him. Gregg climbs into the SUV and holds her as she cries on his shoulder.

"Beautiful, please stop crying, you're going to give yourself a headache. John is fine, he understands. We need to get you inside," he says, gently.

In between sobs, she stammers, "I don't... know why...I did that...what if... I really hurt him?"

"He'll be okay. You can apologize yourself once we get you inside, alright?"

"I'm so embarrassed," she murmurs, sniffling.

With Gregg's help, she slides to the edge of the seat, closest to the door. "I'm sure I can walk now. You don't have to carry me," she says, wiping her eyes.

"Just because I don't have to doesn't mean I don't want to. Get over here," he says, picking her up into a bridal carry. "Grab your flowers," he says, leaning her into the front seat. She grabs them and puts them onto her stomach. He carries her into the house and gently deposits her on to the couch, arranging the pillows and blanket for her, before going back outside to close up the SUV.

When he returns to the house, he sees John sitting next to Shea on the couch, talking to her.

Gregg goes to change out of his training clothes, switching into a form-fitting t-shirt and a pair of basketball shorts. Walking back to the living room, he sees John hug Shea. "We all good now, guys?" Gregg asks.

"Yes, John is a literal angel, just like you," she says, face relaxed.

"Ah, I try. Speaking of being an angel, I know you want those clothes off, so let me get you to your room, okay?" Gregg says.

"You know me so well," she says, smiling at him.

He again carries her to her room and sets her—in a sitting position—on her bed. She teeters for just a second, then finds her balance.

"Alright, girlie, I'll just leave you to it. Do you need me to get anything out for you?" Gregg asks.

"Nah, I think I'm good. Oh, do I have to keep a bra on because John's here? No, right? Oh also, do you have my glasses? I don't know where I put them," Shea rambles out.

"First thing, your boobs equal your business, but we are home, so I just assumed you'd let 'em hang."

Shea makes a face.

"I'm sorry, I meant hang out, like free. Not hang hang— your boobs are always where they should be—not that I'm looking. I just mean…" He's struggling and can feel the fire in his face.

"It's okay, Gregg, they don't have ears," she says, feeling quite witty in her drugged state.

He knows he is beet red, when he says, "Well, if you feel like you should because of John, then you do that. Also, do you feel like you need your glasses right now?"

"No, I mean, I normally take them off at home anyway because I can see well enough. I just want to make sure you have them, is all," she says, still slightly slurring her words.

"No, Shea, do you need them? Like is your vision blurry?" he asks, probing.

She ponders for a moment, and says, "No—actually I can see really well—like better than with my glasses, even."

"Yeah, it's a perk of that implant. I'm gonna go hang with John while you change. Holler if you need me," Gregg says, walking out of her bedroom, and pulling the door closed.

"Oh, Gregg, will you toss those Roses? I'm not the biggest fan of them in the first place. I prefer pink lilies, and Todd's an idiot, so…"

Gregg walks out to the living room and sees John touching one of his swords. "Hey man, you like the swords?"

"Yeah, these are awesome. I know where most of them are from, except for this one. I've been standing here for, like, ten minutes now and still can't figure it out," John admits.

"Ah, the one next to *The Witcher* sword?" Gregg asks.

"Yeah, this one here," John says, gently stroking the sword's grip.

"That's from *House of the Dragon*, I just got this one, actually," he shares.

"Oh, nice! I haven't seen it yet, but these are all beautiful man. And actually sharp, I wasn't expecting that," he says, extending the fingers of his left hand for Gregg to see.

"Oh, man, you need some Band-Aids? I don't want ya bleeding on the couch," Gregg jokes.

"I rinsed it and put pressure with paper towels. It seems to have sealed off already," he says, again holding out his hand.

Gregg is about to agree, when he hears, "Grrrrreeeggggggg, I need help, I'm stuck, pleasseeee help me, keep your eyes closed though."

John grins at Gregg. "Here's your moment, bro. I'll just be out here, admiring your swords."

Gregg shoots John a look and heads to Shea's room. Placing a hand over his eyes, he opens the door and steps inside. "Okay, Shea, here I am. I don't know how I can help you with my eyes covered… but I'm here," he says.

"Gregg, I don't want to alarm you, but I am currently stuck in my sports bra, and I'm stuck in a way that I can't cover myself. So, I need you to try," she says, humor in her voice despite her predicament.

Taking a deep breath, Gregg uses muscle memory to get to Shea's bed. He reaches out his free hand and lands on something soft and squishy.

"Gregg, I need you to bring that hand north about twenty inches. You are currently grabbing my right breast," Shea says.

Gregg immediately turns bright red and apologizes profusely, before estimating twenty inches and reaching out. He feels an elbow and follows it down with his fingers until he feels cotton. Just as he's about to grab the bra, she giggles and pulls away from him.

"Shea, I almost had it! What's the problem?" Gregg asks, flustered.

"Your hands are just so soft. They tickled me. I'm sorry! I'll be good. Keep your hand there, I'll try to come to you," she says.

He finally feels the bra and wrenches it upwards. As soon as she's free, Gregg hears her pull something off the bed near them. "You can open your eyes now, I'm covered. Can you just let me hold your elbow or something? I can walk," she says.

Getting her out onto the couch, Gregg leaves her with John, who fluffs her pillow and covers her with the blanket while Gregg grabs her a bottle of water.

"Guys, you're both so sweet, but really, I'm good. It's not like I had brain surgery this morning or something," she says. Gregg sits down next to her, and she leans against him.

John laughs and plops down on the other side of her, peaking over at her bandage. "Hey Gregg, you guys have first aid supplies?" he asks. "Shea's bandage is looking soiled. I think getting a new one on is probably a good idea. You two look comfortable, I can go get it if you tell me where it is," John offers.

"Yeah, man, it's right there in the kitchen, under the sink. Todd and I are really good at burning ourselves, so we keep it close," Gregg says.

After John changes Shea's bandage, the three of them spend the night getting to know each other better. They find that he is a great fit with them. He even stays the night on the couch after they all receive a text message from Todd, informing them they have the next three days off. When the three days are up, they'll learn more about their roles—as they cannot train again until Shea's sutures come out. Todd explained that it was because he wanted to keep them all on the same path.

For the next three days, no one hears from Todd other than their group text about work. John basically becomes the new and improved Todd. It's fairly hot outside, but Shea has sutures, so they don't have any pool time. Instead, they spend time watching *The House of the Dragon* and testing Shea's new superhuman sight.

Gregg stands at the opposite end of the house, holding up a playing card. Shea is able to see it clearly. They make a game of testing her vision with several other things. John has one of his pins from the military on his backpack and holds it up. She knows the shape and colors but not what it means.

Gregg thought he'd win the game, when he pulls out a small piece of metal the color green, shaped like a four-leaf clover. It has super small writing on it—he's pretty sure he'll stump her—but if she can read it, she will know the surprise he has in store for her.

"Oh man, I think I might have to squint a little to read it," Shea says, leaning forward from where she stands to see the item better.

John stands next to her, also leaning forward and squinting, trying to see it. "Nope, Shea. You know the rules. Do you give up?"

"Wait, wait! Across the top… the text is a bit larger. I can make out 'Animal Hospital.' Is it some sort of animal tag?"

Gregg pockets the charm with a grin and nods. Walking toward his hallway, with a quiet, "Well, come on."

Gregg can hear Shea and John jostle each other the whole way across the house to the door, laughing all the while. Shoving each other, they make it into the room to see Gregg sitting on his bed, his comforter over his lap. He smiles up at Shea, who stands in front of him, and says, "You're my best friend, Shea. You know I love you, right? I just didn't want you to feel alone ever again." He lifts the blanket slowly, watching her face the whole time.

A small puppy has its body pressed against Greggs folded legs, its head resting sweetly on his foot. Gregg watches the realization spread across her face and sees that John is also watching on with a smile on his face. She steps up to the bed, and before even petting the puppy, she leans over and places her hands on his legs for balance. She kisses him on the cheek.

John doesn't see it, but she also leans in, to whisper in his ear, "You're the most incredible man. I love you, Greggy."

He feels the boiling blood rush into his face as he watches her bend down and gently stroke the sleeping pup's paws. Looking up at him, she asks, "Is it a boy or a girl?"

"Boy."

"Oh, my goodness, I love you so much! I'll always take care of you," she murmurs softly to the pup. "Does he have a name?" she asks Gregg.

"Nope, he's been waiting for you, beautiful. What do you think?"

"I think John's a solid name," John says, stepping up to the bed and reaching out to pet the pup.

"Well, let's see," she says, looking at his small face and petting his nose. "I can tell you'll grow up to be big and strong, and that you'll protect us, no matter what. So, I think a name that reflects that would be best. How about Diesel?" she asks the sleeping pup.

"Diesel?" Gregg asks, one eyebrow raised. "That's not an ex of yours or something, is it?"

Shea chuckles, rolling her eyes. "No, Gregg. You really think I'd do that? No. He just looks like a badass in the making. I can just tell."

"Alright, well, pick him up. I have a bunch of stuff for him under the bed—toys, a dog bed, food and water dishes, that kind of stuff," Gregg says.

Shea picks up her little Diesel, and cuddles him to her chest, while Gregg and John grab the pups new accessories. Together they head to the living room. Laughter now fills their home, and Shea never feels alone.

John continues to keep a close eye on Shea's sutures, and the boys learn how to wash her long hair in the sink. On their last night of freedom, while they sit around talking about how none of them would ever marry their uncle, Gregg brings up what's been going on with Tina. After relaying all the events and Todd's reaction, Gregg sits back, watching John intently.

"Wow, that is really weird. Have you guys ever Googled either of them?" John asks.

Shea immediately whips her head in Gregg's direction. Although she hadn't thought of that, Gregg's definitely the type that would do that.

"I know what you're thinking Shea, and yes, I have tried. But it's like they've had the entire internet scrubbed. Plus, we don't even know Tina's last name, and if it is Donoghue, then I can't find anything," he says.

"John, you said you have been working there for a long time, right?" Shea inquires.

"Yeah, I mean, when I started, there were only like ten buildings. Tina hadn't even started there yet," John says.

"Really? How long has she been there? Do you know anything else about her?" Shea presses.

"Honestly, when she started, I never really saw her, because I was doing patrols outside of the buildings. But I did see her leave with Mr. T a bunch of times, but if he's telling the truth, that wouldn't be so weird, right? People hang out with their siblings all the time," John reports.

"I wouldn't know…" Shea says, then immediately slaps a hand over her mouth, regretting it. She hates the looks of pity people give when she slips.

In true Gregg fashion, he says, "Count yourself lucky. My little sister used to put gum in my hair all the time just to watch my mom lather me in peanut butter and use a comb to try and get it out—making me howl for hours before she finally just cut the damn chunk out."

"That's brutal, dude," John laughs. "I actually have a twin, an identical twin. He liked to play pranks on our parents and get caught. Now you're thinking, 'Well, it could have been either of you, right?' You'd be wrong. Whenever we were in trouble, we would wait for our mom to yell the other brother's name, then take off, hoping to get them in trouble. Because she knew this, and because he knew she knew, he would wait to hear his own name and then run. I was always in trouble," John says.

Shea feels a deep appreciation swelling inside her, and she hopes it's showing in the look she gives them both.

"Well, we will just have to pay close attention at work. The three of us should be able to figure it out," Gregg says.

"Speaking of work, I think I'm going to finally get out of you guys' hair. We have to be up early tomorrow, and my bed has been calling my name," John says.

"Aw, well, thanks for taking such good care of me. I really appreciate it!" Shea says, standing to give him a hug.

After he leaves, Gregg tells Shea goodnight, and she heads to bed. Laying there with Diesel curled up beside her, with nothing but her thoughts. She isn't able to fall asleep for what feels like hours. All of these issues with Todd are making her feel, for lack of a better word…icky. She wonders if this is a relationship she really wants to be in or if she stays because that's what is easier.

00039 🌲🌲 Cold Man

After Dr. P leaves, John takes Shea to the tub, repeating yesterday's routine. Shea is more alert today, though, and her attitude about the whole situation is a mix of anger and embarrassment. Before he lets her return to dreamland, he makes her drink some water and eat some bland, low-sodium chicken and roasted vegetables.

Once she's settled back in bed, he takes another temperature, hoping the medication and the bath will have helped. He reads the result and feels mixed emotions—her temp is 101°F, which is lower, but also still a fever.

John steps out for only a moment, to make a few calls, letting their contacts know they would be held up for a bit, and alerting the team he has watching the perimeter of the resort to beef up security. He spoke to the team not only because they had a visitor today, but because they would be here for longer than expected.

After his calls, he cracks the phone in half, tossing the remnants, and lies down next to Shea. He gently rubs her hair, and thinks, 'She has to get better, I can't show up without her.'

John wakes up to the alarm on his watch. He sets one every few hours to wake him to stay on top of Shea's temperature. Looking down at her, he feels her forehead with the back of his hand—still hot. He gently rolls toward the nightstand, grabs the thermometer, and checks Shea's temperature in the darkness. Checking the reading, he sees 104.9°F.

"Shit, shit, shit, " he mutters, reaching for Shea. He shakes her gently. "Hey, Shea, you gotta wake up for a little bit, okay?"

"What is it, Todd? Has Gregg already made breakfast?" she murmurs, eyes still closed. John knows she's hallucinating because of the fever, but now he's wondering if she remembers more than she's let on.

"Shea, it's me, John," he says, again shaking her gently.

"John. Oh, thank goodness. Is snow getting in the tent? I'm freezing," she says.

"Shea, we're in our room at the resort. Come back to me."

"Okay," she says, then goes silent.

John, knowing he doesn't have time to be tender, scoops Shea into his arms and heads to the bathroom. Running the water at the coldest setting, he plugs the drain and reaches for the medication they've been using to combat Shea's fever. After the tub is full, John turns off the water and looks from Shea to the tub. In her current state, there is no way he'll be able to prop her up enough to keep her above water, while still having enough of her body submerged to make a difference in her fever. He reaches a decision he despises but knows he has no choice.

Stepping into the tub with Shea still in his arms, he curses under his breath at the frigid temperature of the water. Orienting himself, he slowly sits in the tub. He turns Shea, so she's parallel to his body and attempts to submerge her whole body at once. He expects a reaction from her, the water is so cold it is making his teeth chatter. But, as the water laps over her breasts, she remains silent, even as her full body shivering increases.

After a few minutes, John slides Shea to the side of his chest so he can inspect her face. He sees dark circles under her eyes, and still healing bruises, but most alarming is the slightly blue tint to her lips.

John reacts on instinct and slaps Shea across the face—hard.

"Ah! What?" she says.

"I needed to make sure you're okay. We've been in the bath for a while, and you haven't made a peep," he says, his voice tight.

"And you couldn't leave me be? Now I'm freezing," she says, eyes fully open, the familiar Shea charm present again.

Calming her anger, Shea says, "John, am I going to be okay?"

"Yeah, of course. The doc will be back the day after tomorrow and we'll get you fixed up," he says, pushing her hair out of her face. She lazily lifts her mouth into a smile, teeth chattering and all. Clearing his throat, he asks, "Hey, do you remember what you were dreaming—or hallucinating—about before?"

"I had a dream about a dog and a man—well two men. One was cold, and one was warm. I remember the cold man doing things to get close to me, but something wasn't right. And the warm man was there to protect me—always looking out for me. I think he loved me. They were both tall," she says.

Smiling to himself at her descriptions, he says, "Oh, alright. Have you been remembering more?"

"I get flashes. I'm not sure if they are memories or dreams… A green, metal, four-leaf clover; a small hand; fire…"

John is taken aback. There are no people, but she is definitely getting some memories back. "Well, do you wanna get out of here?"

Shea holds her arms to her body, and says shakily, "Please, I'm so cold."

"Okay," John says softly, turning her so she is again perpendicular to his body. He stands in one fluid motion, their clothing clinging to their cold, wet bodies. He steps from the tub and then steps to the towel rack so Shea can grab one. She seems much more alert, so John says, "Do you want to get ready by yourself? I can bring you another soft t-shirt, and I'll be right outside the door if you need me for anything."

"Well, maybe if you put me down, I can make an educated decision," she says.

"Oh, right," he says, gently placing her feet on the floor. He keeps his hands gently at her sides, just in case.

She stands there for a moment, searching for her balance. Once stable, she nods at John. He fully releases his grasp on her, stepping back. "I'll go grab that shirt. Do you want me to grab any of your things?"

"Please, just bring my whole toiletry bag," she says.

John quickly gathers her toiletries and a soft shirt and delivers it to her. Gently closing the door when he's done. He then hurriedly changes out of his soaking wet clothes. Once dressed, he stands guard at the bathroom door, hearing Shea talking to herself inside. He hears, "Get your hair out of your armpit," and he laughs.

A few minutes later, the door opens, revealing Shea. She's brushed her hair and applied some oil to define her waves. She wears the shirt he gave her, though he hadn't realized how worn thin it was until now. The material is see-through in places, and nearly see-through in all places. He looks away, not wanting her to think he's a creeper.

"Don't worry," noticing his discomfort, "I've got nothing to hide. I know you saw it all last night," she says.

John chuckles awkwardly. "Let's get back to bed. Any minute now, you'll be feeling that fever again. We can watch a movie," he says, trying not to be awkward.

"Sure, but I get to pick this time," she says, sauntering over to her cocoon.

John stops her just before she gets into bed, handing her two bottles of water to chug. "Hey, have you peed at all since you've been up?" he asks.

"Geez, take a girl to dinner first, would ya?" she teases, smiling, "I did pee—it was more than earlier, but still a small amount."

"Okay, drink those, then we'll cuddle and watch a movie," he says, walking around the bed and getting in.

Shea drinks all the water and returns to her cocoon. More alert now, she doesn't allow him to pull her onto his chest. She pulls his left arm close to her, tucking his hand between her legs. He passes her the remote with his right hand. Scrolling through the TV menu, she quickly decides, selecting a movie before tossing the remote onto the bed and snuggling into John.

When John sees the title come up, he looks down at Shea and smiles. *"Thor Ragnarök* again? You've seen this like a thousand times."

"I can't help it, I love it," she says, looking up at him

"Hey John, I trust you—something, whether my gut, intuition, or subconscious, is telling me you're trustworthy. So, I know when I ask you this, you'll tell me the truth. Before…did you ever try to hurt me in any way? Was there ever a time I didn't trust you? Are you the cold man?" she rattles off.

John's heart clenches. "I could never hurt you, Shea. We've always trusted each other, and no, I am not the cold man," he answers firmly.

Satisfied with his response, she wiggles as close as she can get to him, with her arms around his arm. She rests her head on his shoulder and closes her eyes.

"Good night, beautiful," he says softly, kissing her forehead and closing his eyes.

Twin Pines

00040 🌲🌲 Welcome to Crown

■ ■ ■ ■ ■ ■　■　□ □ □

The following morning, things are routine as usual—other than Shea wearing a power suit with tennis shoes. She figures she has an excuse, so she's not wearing heels. She also gave up on trying to style her hair in a way that covers the bandage—she just doesn't care. Gregg, of course, tells her she looks beautiful, and she starts her day with a smile.

As soon as they walk through the door at 25, Todd and John are standing at the front desk, waiting for them. Shea and Gregg exchange a quick glance, but when they look at John, he gives them an, "I didn't say anything" look.

As soon as they're within talking distance, Todd says, "There she is! I'm sorry I didn't visit. I've been preparing for your come-back."

Shea offers him a small smile, and asks, "Well, what are we getting into today?"

"We're all heading up to the top floor. Gregg will be learning about his new job, and you and John will be learning about yours," Todd replies. "Of course, I need to remind you both—that nothing can be cross-discussed or discussed at home."

"We got it, Todd, my man. We're zipped in the lip region," Gregg says, walking toward the elevators.

When they all get up to the top floor, Gregg is escorted to a pod far in the back by a woman in a lab coat and a man carrying about ten different weapons. As he looks back at Todd, Shea, and John, Todd blows him a kiss.

"That seemed kind of ominous, man. Is he going to be okay?" John asks.

"Oh yeah, he's fine. I was just trying to be funny. Guess I failed," Todd says, grabbing and spinning his ring.

"Well, Shea—John and I will be your escorts. We're heading to the largest pod on the other side of the floor," he says.

When they reach the pod, there is not only a card swipe, but a retinal scan and a DNA scanner. Todd walks Shea through the process—having her slide her card, position her eye in front of the scanner, then pulls a hair from the root and places it in the slot. Her checks all pass, and the door unlocks. John doesn't have access without her, so he has to just follow behind.

Walking into the pod, Shea is awestruck. It definitely looks bigger from the inside—she doesn't even have words to explain what she's seeing. Todd smiles at her awe of his creation and leads them down a hallway. Shea and John follow, trying to take it all in. At the end of the hallway is a door, opening it Todd ushers them inside.

The room is large, but has very little décor, it's painted a rich royal blue (purple). A large dark wood desk sits at the center, with one of those red leather office chairs with all the buttons. It looks rich and fancy in Shea's opinion. This office also has visitors' chairs, and this is where John and Shea deposit themselves.

Meanwhile, Gregg walks into his pod after completing the same security checks. Inside, he finds a small lab and a room that resembles one that could be found in a medical office, with three small glass rooms to the side. Confused, he looks closer at one of the glass rooms. It appears the walls are electrified on the inside, and although he can't tell if it's glass or something else, the walls appear to be about a foot thick.

Stepping back from what he now realizes is a cell, a loud bang suddenly echoes from the last cell in the row.

Gregg whips his head in that direction and sees that inside the cell is a small child, sitting on the ground with one of their feet against the glass.

At around the same time, Todd sits in his red leather chair and leans forward over the desk, looking right into Shea's eyes, he says, "Shea, there is so much to go over, but what if I told you that traveling to the past is less science fiction and more science fact?"

Shea sits staring at Todd, speechless, for a long while, like a seriously long time. Just staring at him, like he has eight heads.

"Okay, that didn't go great. Is there anything I could have said differently to make that easier?" Todd asks.

"Time travel? You're expecting me to be okay with the revelation of time travel?" Shea asks, dumbfounded.

"Well, maybe not okay, but maybe more open to the idea," he says.

"Wait, twin pines…" John starts, piecing it together.

"What can I say, I have a flair for the dramatic," Todd says, grinning. "Though Project Salt N' Vinegar was catchy too. But seriously, anything better I could have done?"

"You want to go back and change how you approached me, don't you? I can't believe this. How much have you changed since I met you?" Shea asks, feeling her anger rising.

Shea feels John's chair scoot into hers, with a gentle hand to the back of her arm, she can feel his support.

"We're getting off track. We have a lot to go over," Todd says, pulling two binders out of a drawer in his desk. He hands a three-inch binder to Shea, and a one-inch binder to John.

"What's up? You think I don't read good?" John asks.

"Most of the contents in hers is explaining how to properly use her implant, and run other departments as Department Head, as was agreed upon in her offer letter," he says to John. Then looking to Shea, says, "Looks like you're healing nicely."

"Yeah. I'm a miracle. Listen are we just going to read these, or is there some sort of preamble you need to spew first?" Shea says, snarkily.

"Shea, we may have a personal relationship, but I cannot tolerate this blatant disrespect and insubordination," Todd responds firmly.

"I apologize. My brain doesn't feel like this is real life. I'm trying to get it together," she says.

John reaches over and pinches the fat on the back of Shea's arm. "Ahhhh, dick! What was that for?" Shea shrieks.

"Well, you're not dreamin'," John says with a teasing smile. Shea slightly turns her head toward John, narrowing her eyes, but she can't help herself—she bursts into giggling fit.

"Okay, this is off the rails. I want you two to read your binders today. They cannot leave this pod, so I'll show you to your office, Shea," Todd says, standing.

Across the floor, in another pod, Gregg stares at a child's foot pressed against the glass. He starts to walk toward the cell when the

woman who'd escorted him to the pod, says, "You're not quite ready for that yet, Mr. Marsh. Why don't you come with me? I'll show you to your office."

"Sure, but can I ask questions about…that?" he asks, nodding toward the cell.

"You won't need to once you read your binder. That's today's objective—to get started at least," she says.

"So, are you my boss?" Gregg asks.

"No, not at all, Mr. Marsh. In fact, in the grand scheme of things, you're my boss a few times over. I've been up here from medical for the last eight weeks, just getting things settled in, until you got here," she says.

"What will you do now that I'm here?" he asks.

"I'll stay on to assist you until you feel you're ready to be alone," she says. At this point, they had reached a nook in the wall containing a door. Stopping, she opens it, and gestures for him to step inside.

The office is a good size, furnished with a comfortable-looking couch and a bookcase on one wall. There's a standing desk with scientific instruments on the other, and on the back wall—a beautiful desk holding a computer.

He walks into the office, and his 'assistant' walks in behind him, stepping over to the bookshelf. She pulls down a three-inch binder and hands it to him.

"Absorb as much as you can. The sooner, the better. Once you're done, the real work begins," she says, and with that she leaves, closing the door behind her.

Shea's office is identical, except for the scientific set up. In its place is a second couch with a small, over-the-lap table, holding a laptop. John's name is on a card placed on top of the laptop.

"Look, John, your very own space," Shea says.

"Sure, but if I could, I'd like to read your binder with you. I wanna know all the deets," he says. Shea pulls a face at John, unsure if this is a good idea, but he continues, "I'll read mine too, don't worry, and I'm a real fast reader, so I'll keep up."

"Fine," Shea says. Taking her binder over to her couch, she takes off her shoes and gets comfortable. John sits on the side where her feet are not, and she opens the binder. As they begin reading, Gregg does the same.

Welcome to Twin Pines!

A project ten years in the making. Through our engineer's and scientist's tireless efforts, this idea has come to fruition. Your role in this project will help propel Crowned Skull Laboratories into the next millennium. As you move forward into your onboarding binder, we would like to remind you that all events are true, and none of this is a work of fiction. Welcome to the team.

From there, the binders get very different. Shea's, being read by herself—and John—was something like what follows.

You were scouted to fulfill this position because of your history in administration, your outstanding work ethic in previous projects and your ability to keep people on task while also showing care and compassion.

In your new position you will be expected to train regularly, either in the gym provided for you here or at home. The expectation for this position is that a neural implant has already been implanted, as it will prove to be invaluable in the field.

"In the field?" Shea asks John.

"No idea. Keep reading," he says.

The neural implant is an amazing innovation. By taking a picture of the QR code on this page, the link provided will take you to a secure website that offers an application download that pairs with your implant. By downloading the application, you will then be able to access previous memories, the implants HUD function, and, as the implant evolves, many other features. The application will guide you through its functions with videos, tutorials, and written PDF's.

The memory function allows you to rewind through your days. This will come in handy when writing reports after a day in the field. The HUD function offers maps, streaming services, communications and other functions of your cell phone, all projected right in front of your eyes. While in the field this will be essential as you will be visiting times and places you will be unfamiliar with.

The technology that allows Twin Pines to take a step into the past is not so different from the concepts in some of the movies you might have seen. By producing hydropower at the rate we have in our facility, we caused a rip in our reality. Utilizing a satellite telescope, we were able to ping off a celestial body from the time and location we wished to travel, creating an unstable portal. That's where our team came in—stabilizing the portal with structure, and making it possible for us to lock in on particular dates, times and locations.

To begin, a location, date and time are entered into the touch screen module. The portal will become active, and you step through to your mission. No items of modern times can be taken through the portal, which is why the HUD is so essential. Clothing will be provided prior to the mission, allowing you to assimilate into your surroundings. The portal will be closed as soon as you are through and will only be opened again when a code word is provided over comms. An alternate code word will also be provided in case something goes awry and the mission is compromised.

Which when used, will cause the portal to remain closed while the mission's operatives seek shelter and wait for a better opportunity.

Detailed reports will be expected within one day of the mission, no excuses. No communication regarding the nature of the mission may be shared. If deemed necessary by two or more board members, your memories may be accessed.

The following two hundred pages detail the construction and science behind time travel.

"Yeah, let's skip that. We'll have this thing done today!" John exclaims.

Shea gives him some side-eye, then begins turning pages.

As Gregg opens past the first page of his binder, he pushes his thick glasses up his nose and thinks that there is no way he will be done with this today. He charges forward.

You were scouted to fulfill this position because of your scientific knowledge, exceptional work ethic in previous projects, and your undeniable caring and compassionate nature. Though the nature of your new position is quite different than your past work in development, we are challenging you to push yourself into the future with groundbreaking research.

Within not only this pod, but many pods, and many buildings on our campus, scientific breakthroughs are occurring every day. We look to you to propel us into new and uncharted territory. Your objective is to study a child with a supernatural ability—through DNA sequencing, stress testing, and any other tests that you can imagine. We look to you to replicate these, or other abilities, during your time at Crowned Skull Laboratories.

Your charge is a seven-year-old male child, whose origin is unknown. Since arriving at our facilities, he has remained non-verbal but has other ways to communicate. Through this method, we have come to learn his name: Christian Lee. Christian is gifted in touch—a single touch to any building, person, land or object allows him to see everything that has ever happened to whatever he has touched, and around him. Asking Christian about specifics, he is then able to filter through all of the information, extracting exactly what you are looking for. To relay this information, he will then lay his hands upon the asker, showing them the answer.

Christian has an incredible gift and is utilized by Crowned Skull Labs to uncover treasure, long lost to time. These missions will only take a couple of days out of his week, leaving the remaining time with Christian in your care for scientific study. Due to the nature of some experiments, we recommend ensuring that all of your skin is fully covered during research.

"What the fuck?!" Gregg pushes out. He abandons his binder and heads back to the cells.

Christian Lee is right where he was last time Gregg was in here.

"Christian Lee?" he softly questions, standing in the front of the cell. Gregg thinks the boy looks small and thin for his age. He has light blonde hair, cut into a bowl-cut style. He looks afraid.

"I'm not going to hurt you. I just wanted to introduce myself. My name is Greggory Marsh, you can call me Gregg though," he says—then feels like an idiot when he remembers the kid doesn't talk.

The child glances up through his long lashes, almost inspecting Gregg. His piercing blue eyes pin Gregg with his gaze.

"Are you hungry, Mr. Lee? Want some food and some juice?" he asks.

Christian's lip goes up slightly on one side, apparently finding Gregg calling him 'Mr. Lee' funny. Christian docilely looks toward Gregg. Gregg is sure this will take a little time because the kid is in a cage.

Gregg moves forward and presses his keycard into the door's electronic locking mechanism. The door releases and slowly opens outward. Christian looks up at Gregg, who holds out his bare hand, to guide him. As soon as Christian grabs it, Gregg's head swims, but he feels normal otherwise.

Suddenly, Gregg's vision goes dark. Then, in an instant, a scene explodes before him. Looking down to see if Christian is still with him, the boy gives Gregg a single nod and points to a building about thirty feet from where they stand. Looking around, Gregg can see that they are in the outskirts of a city—New York, if he were to guess. The building Christian pointed to is multiple stories with beautiful architecture. While Gregg remains rooted to the spot, Christian begins walking toward the building, tugging on Gregg's hand with quiet urgency.

Following the child across the street, Gregg begins to notice that the people around them are dressed in clothes from another time. Women pass wearing beautiful dresses—some with ruffles, others more form-fitting—all carrying parasols or hand fans. Their large, elaborate hats adorned with feathers, flowers, and ribbons. The men are dressed in three-piece suits in natural colors, each adding their flair via a hat. Gregg is amazed at how many different styles he sees: bowler hats, fedoras, top hats, collegiate hats and boater hats.

As they near the building, Christian begins tugging on Gregg more insistently and pointing with urgency. Stepping up to the building, Gregg realizes it's an orphanage. Several women in outfits that Gregg thinks look like something a nurse might wear—all white dresses with aprons. Christian begins pointing again, looking in that direction, Gregg sees a tall man talking to one of these women, who has a haggard appearance that makes it look like she's worked there for a while.

Gregg follows Christian and hears the woman tell the man, "Yes, sir. We've had him since he was just a year old. No one will take him because of the claims from other children and carers. Word has gotten out."

The man passes the woman a ten-dollar bill, and asks, "Can I have a moment with him?"

"Sure thing, sir," she says, bowing slightly at the waist and walking away.

Gregg notices, behind her is a child sitting on what looks like a hay-filled sheet, on the floor. The child is the spitting image of Christian—in fact, it is Christian. Gregg looks down at the child still holding his hand. Christian just nods and points at the man again. Looking closer, Gregg realizes that the man now approaching the child, is Todd.

"What is this place?" Gregg asks, looking over at Christian.

Christian just points at this version of Todd. The man is now squatting down next to the child. He offers the other Christian a large smile, and says, "Show me," extending his hand out toward the child.

The other Christian places his hand in Todd's. As soon as the other Christian makes contact, Todd's back goes ramrod straight. Gregg blinks, and a new vision swims in front of him. He's now standing in a shack, made completely of wood, no bigger than ten by ten feet. A cold draft caresses Gregg's face, making him shiver. He is still in shock at seeing Todd here, in this other time. He is now amazed he can feel the cold wind, as if he is truly there.

In one corner, a mattress lies on the floor. Next to it, there is a woman, naked from the waist up, sitting in a rocking chair, breastfeeding a baby. She is sitting unnaturally straight and holds the baby tightly to her breast.

Christian doesn't show him, but somehow, Gregg knows this is Christian as an infant, and that as he feeds, he is giving his mother visions from when he was in the womb. As soon as the baby releases his latch on his mother's nipple, the mother's posture drastically changes, she seems to cave in on herself. She weeps as she swaddles the baby and burps him.

Gregg is then propelled forward in time. He can't explain how, but he just seems to understand what is happening. When the vision clears, the woman is standing in the middle of the shack, her night gown hangs off her frail frame. She is extremely emaciated, with her hair falling in clumps around her face. A toddler sits on his knees next to her feet. She begins to shake, and tears stream down her face, as he reaches out a tiny hand toward his mommy.

The scene again changes. The young mother has her toddler bundled up, all his skin covered. She holds him as she steps out of the shack in a patchwork dress and walks him over to the building Gregg entered earlier. There, she speaks with one of the carers. Gregg and Christian watch as the young mother hands the baby to a carer, crying and continually shaking her head no. She runs from the building, leaving her child behind.

Gregg looks over at the Christian still holding his hand and watches a single tear roll down his cheek. Gregg gives his hand a gentle squeeze, keeping his eyes forward as the scene changes again.

Years of different adoption opportunities, all lost, when the potential parents would grab Christian's hand to leave. Rumors spread, children call him names, they spit in his face, and worst of all—everyone around him refuses to touch him. This vision ends with a carer talking to a creepy man in a long coat about setting up a transfer for the child, for a long-term solution, at the asylum.

The vision clears, and Gregg finds himself back in the orphanage, looking at Todd holding Christian's hand. Todd shakes his head and stands, chuckling, he asks, "That's a pretty cool gift, kid. But where is this from?" He holds out a lava rock.

Christian touches the rock, then touches Todd's hand. The interaction lasts for only a couple of seconds, before Todd says, "Perfect," and walks out to the carer. "Keep the child here for a while longer, I will come for him."

The vision again shifts in time and Gregg is again in front of the same building. Two tall men in long coats walk along the sidewalk, dragging Christian in between them. Out of nowhere, Todd runs up behind them, shouting for them to stop. When he catches up to them, he demands, "Who gave you this child?"

The men sneer at Todd. Gregg can't believe his eyes. It's like something out of a movie. "The orphanage has been begging us to take him off their hands. There was another incident earlier today. They insisted we come get him."

"Well, I guess that's handy for me. I was just coming to take him to his new home. I think this deserves a reward, for all your hard work up at the asylum, helping the child's mother, until her untimely demise, that is." Todd reaches into his pocket and pulls out two twenty-dollar bills, shoving one into each of the men's breast pockets.

Todd takes the child's hand in his gloved one and walks back the way he came, disappearing behind a building.

When Gregg's vision clears, he finds himself back in his lab, with his assistant glaring at him. "You cannot take the test subject out of the confinement cell."

"Oh, well," Gregg says, glancing down at the child next to him. "No, sorry. I'm sure you've done a great job, but this is my department now. I'm taking Christian to get some lunch and some juice—just like any seven-year-old should have. Test subject or not, everyone deserves to be cared for. It seems no one has offered that to this poor child." Gregg strides past her. Feeling his anger bubbling below the surface, he turns to her, and says, "In fact, I don't even want a person on my team that would keep a child in a cage twenty-four hours a day, seven days a week. I'll find my own assistant. You're dismissed."

Landing on the next topic in the binder, Shea and John read.

While traveling to distant lands and times, you will be escorted by John, who will serve as your bodyguard and assistant during missions. You will

also be escorting a seven-year-old boy to these locations. This boy has a supernatural power of touch. When touching a person, item, or place he is able to see the entire history of that item, place, or person. He will then touch your hand, transmitting the information to you via a vision. Your skin must remain fully covered at all times when around the child, until you are ready for an answer to a question. The child's name is Christian. He was born in 1901 and rescued in 1908 from an insane asylum. In order to be a great chaperone to Christian, you are required to get back to training, including weapons training as soon as possible.

John sits forward on the couch, placing his elbows on his knees, and his face in his hands. Shea reaches over and gently pats his back.

"Well, now we know what we're doing, right?" she says.

00041 ⛄ angel among us

The resort phone rings at 10 a.m. the next morning. John jolts awake, freaking out—he forgot to set a new alarm for Shea's temp.

" Hello," he answers.

"Hello sir. Front desk here. The physician you saw yesterday just arrived and is demanding to go up immediately. Is that okay?"

"Yes, yes, let her up, thanks," John says quickly, then hangs up the phone. He walks to the door, opening it to the width the chain allows, before Dr.P can knock.

"Good morning…" he starts, but she pulls the door closed so he can undo the chain. When he opens the door fully, he only gets out a confused, "What…" before she cuts him off.

"John, hey, how is she?" Dr. P asks, walking in with purpose and heading straight to Shea's bedside. She drops her backpack beside the bed.

"I'm okay," Shea says softly from her cocoon, looking up at the doc.

"Oh, that's great, I'm glad you're awake today. The cultures we took yesterday already had some growth. We're looking at a fungal infection, and since there's a broad-spectrum type of treatment, we're going with that. I'll also need to perform a debridement of the wound—cutting away all the infected tissue in hopes of clearing the wound infection. It is a hefty diagnosis, but treatment begins now."

"Whatever you need from me, I'll be over here, just let me know," John says, sitting on the table near the couch.

"Yes, I have a lot to go over with you, but first, L.T., how are you feeling? How's your urine?" Dr. P asks, with a straight face.

Shea smiles, though she looks kind of delusional, when she answers, "I woke up in the tub late last night… John had me drink a couple of bottles of water, and I've felt better since. A few hours ago, I got up and had to pee really bad, it was a large amount of urine," she says.

John stands from his perched position. "L.T., why didn't you wake me?"

"I felt like I had it on my own. It was a bit slow going, but I got it figured out," she says.

"This is great. Well, I want to get John set up with your treatments, and then I'll be back to debride your wound," Dr. P informs her.

"Okay," Shea says, sitting up a little more to watch what they are doing.

"Hold on a second—she's going to cut away at your wound and no whining, no begging, nothing?" John asks, thinking she must still be sick.

"No, John, because I was going to ask you to sneak me whiskey. You dolt," she says.

John stands there, just staring at her. Dr. P, ever the professional steps in, and says, "Actually, we're trying to spare you organ damage, so no alcohol. But I did bring injectable lidocaine and lidocaine jelly to numb the area, so no need to worry," Dr. P says. "Since I'm thinking about it, let me put the jelly on you now. We'll let it sit while we're doing this."

"Thank you. Finally, some professional service," Shea says, chuckling at John's face.

After she applies the jelly on Shea's wound, Dr. P grabs her backpack and heads to the table that John occupies. "Alright, I brought enough IV bags and medication for the full course of treatment. I don't recommend you move her for at least a few days. Make sure she tolerates the treatment well first. Plus, that will give me time to debride it at least twice," Dr. P says.

"Okay. I have to mix it?" John asks, focusing on Dr. P's instructions.

"Yes, you will, but I'll show you how," she says. Reaching into her backpack she pulls out a twelve-pack of vials, in a cardboard container wrapped with plastic, and places it on the table. She then pulls out several IV start kits, chlorhexidine—to better clean the site, saline bags, a cool collapsible IV pole and a small IV pump. "As you can see, all of this is pretty travel-friendly. You'll just have to make sure nothing breaks," she says.

"Wow, thanks for all this," he says.

"No problem. I want to make sure she gets the care she needs. That drug can have really severe side effects, so you'll need to medicate her about thirty minutes before you start the IV—with Tylenol, Benadryl, hydrocortisone and ibuprofen."

She pulls a pillbox, set up with twelve days, out of her bag and places it on the table.

"Should we give her one of these now?" he asks.

"Yes, have her drink a good amount of water with it," she says.

Once Shea takes the medication, John returns to the table, awaiting further instructions.

"Since this medication can cause inflammation in the vein, you'll have to watch her IV site closely. I've given you enough IV start kits for all twelve days, just in case. The first three days, the dose will be a bit higher, so you'll run it really slowly. Today, we will do a test run for the first thirty minutes, before running the whole dose. If there is no reaction, just make sure she gets it around the same time every day—let's call it 11 a.m.," she says.

John nods, and watches the doctor walk over to Shea.

"L.T., do you still have an IV in your arm?" Dr. P asks her.

"No, John pulled it out since he knew there would be a break in my IV's," Shea says, holding both of her arms straight in the air as proof.

"Alright, that's great," she says to Shea, then turns to John. "Go ahead and get us access, then."

John gathers everything he needs and walks over to Shea's bedside, setting everything up on the nightstand. Taking her right arm in his, his eyes rove over it, looking for the best option. Once he finds it, he quickly gets the tourniquet on her arm.

"Alright, L.T., you know the deal if you watch, I won't."

Shea quickly turns her head to the side. With the doctor standing right behind him, he expertly accesses her vein, braces it with gauze, and applies Tegaderm film. "Alright, you're all done. You did so great," he says, quickly using a syringe to make sure, they are, in fact, in the vein.

"That was your best little prick yet," she teases.

Dr. P smiles at the two of them, and John coughs a few times. "There's the girl I know and… tolerate," he says, turning to throw away the garbage.

Shea rolls her eyes, and Dr. P steps closer. She now has the nightstand covered with a drape and instruments. "Okay, I'm going to test you to see how well the jelly worked. Let me know what you feel."

John watches on as Dr. P picks up a tweezer-looking instrument and lifts a wound flap with it, pinching it between the pincers lightly. "Anything?" she asks Shea.

"Uh, I'd describe it maybe as pressure, but not much, and no real pain," Shea answers.

"Perfect. I'm going to get started while John gets you hooked up to the medication," Dr. P says.

"That stuff is amazing. Would have been nice for you to pack me some of that!" Shea says, looking at John.

"I raided as many supplies as I could before I bailed. Beggars can't be choosers," John says, not looking at her, but instead at the IV supplies on the table.

"I brought some extra that you can take with you, just in case," Dr. P leans close to Shea to tell her, and to begin debridement.

"How did I just realize there's an angel among us?" Shea says, unmoving.

Dr. P smiles down on her from behind a mask, and says, "I do what I can."

As Shea's wound is being debrided, John is getting the IV pump programmed and priming the tubing. With her head tilted toward John, giving Dr. P better access to her wound, she watches as he clamps the pump to the pole. He turns toward her with the tubing in hand, and Shea reaches her right arm toward him. He hooks her up to the line and looks to Dr. P for the thumbs up to start the treatment.

"Everything looks good. Let's just do thirty minutes then pause, so we can watch for any adverse reactions," she says. Then, looking down at Shea, says, "You still doing okay with the debridement?"

"Yeah, everything is fine. A little worried I'll have a horrible scar and no hair, but I'm survivin," she answers.

"Well, I can't make any guarantees about the scar, and I'm sorry about that, but I will do my best. With this IV, there is a chance of some side effects, so I want you to let us know if you start feeling any different, okay?" Dr. P says to Shea.

"Sure, so far so good," she says, eyeing the fluid in the IV line.

Thirty minutes later, Shea is freshly bandaged and her IV is on hold. She hasn't had any reaction so far, so they decide to push ahead. Dr. P says her goodbyes, "John, call if you need anything, I'll be back around the same time tomorrow."

That evening is quite different from the previous, for Shea and John. Shea is able to take a shower by herself, with a bag taped over her IV, so she doesn't get it wet, and a shower cap to keep her wound dry. She feels like a new person when she gets out, and sassy as ever. "Alright John, my pits and poon smell like desert cedar, and I'm starving!" she announces, striding out of the bathroom in only the resort robe.

John chuckles, looking her up and down. "Alright, I want to go down and grab the invoices. I'll order some food while I'm down there. What are you thinking?"

"Those cheeseburgers were really good, but I think I want something different. Can you choose?"

"Sure thing. I'll be back in a jiffy."

Shea takes the time while John is gone, to tidy up the room, clearing all the medical supplies so they can eat at the table. When she's done, she moves to the window to admire the beautiful landscape. She second-guesses her eyes when she spots John sitting at a fire pit. Then, she feels rage pour through her body when she sees he's talking on a cell phone.

00042 🌲🌲 Secret Love

■ ■ ■ ■ ■ ■ □ □ □

Shea and John decide they've had enough for the day. Leaving their office, Shea texts Gregg.

Text to Gregg at 5:22 p.m.:

> < Hey can you leave yet?

Text from Gregg at 5:23 p.m.:

> > Leaving my pod now

"Come on, let's head over his way. The sooner we grab a drink, the better," Shea says, pulling John along by his sleeve.

"Oh, I'm invited?" he asks, voice overly excited.

"Of course you are. I need someone to drive us home," Shea teases, smiling at John's reaction. "I'm just kidding, bud. We'll make Gregg do it."

"You mean we'll get a car, right?" John asks with a knowing voice.

"Yes, I have an executive account, after all."

"Fancy. Can we get a limo?" John asks.

"I dunno, we can try!" she says. She feels her face fall as she watches Gregg walk toward them with a similar look on his face.

Meeting them, Gregg says, "Let's go. I really need a drink."

"Better call that limo, Shea," John says.

"Already did. I have an app. I don't know if it'll be a limo, but it'll take us to the bar anyway."

"We going to Lou's?" Gregg asks.

"Sure, that way we can add good music to our night of libations," Shea responds. "Oh, also, the vehicle is out front. Let's go."

Finding no golf cart key, they decide to drive to the gate and park their cars there. When they park, they spot a small limo on the other side of the gate. They line up, scanning their cards, and walk out the gate. Once all three of them are safely in the limo, they collectively release a sigh of relief.

At that same moment, Shea's phone dings in her hand. After reading the message, she shows it to the boys.

Text from Todd at 5:36 p.m.:

> Getting a limo on company dime, to go out, with not one, but two men, and not even an invite to your boyfriend? Doesn't look great for you, Shea.

"What an ass!" John exclaims.

Gregg gives John a look of warning, and says, "Don't forget, Shea's wearing a wire."

John's face pales, but Shea's face hardens with determination as she responds to the text.

Text to Todd at 5:36 p.m.:

< I thought you trusted me?

She then turns her phone off completely. Leaning forward, she speaks to the driver. "Hello, I'm so sorry. We'd like to go to Lou's. My phone just died, so I'm going to need you to park and wait outside until we're ready to go. Can you do that?"

"Yes, ma'am, I'll do that," the driver replies.

Entering the bar, they grab drinks and head upstairs. They stand around a table, all three of them exchange glances, each with no idea where to start.

This sucks. I should have listened to Gregg, now I'm stuck with a wire…wait…

"Gregg," Shea says, breaking the silence. "I'm just wondering… for no particular reason. Does the chip have access to my internal voice?" Shea asks.

Gregg looks at her, runs his hands through his hair, creating a fluffy mane and drains a good portion of his drink before answering. "Honestly, I'm not sure. That wasn't a specific target, but those tendrils adapt and burrow. I'm thinking it's probably fine. This is why I advised against it."

"Yes, Gregg, I know. I told you so, right?" Shea says. She reaches for her glass and downs her drink.

"I'll go get three more. We gotta figure this out," John says.

Gregg stands closer to Shea, presses his hand to her lower back, and whispers in her ear, "Beautiful, you're going to need to trust me for a while, if you don't understand what I'm saying or instructions I'm giving, just follow along, okay?" Shea nods her head and remains still in Gregg's arms. "Run and touch up your make up, meet us on the dance floor, we need to dance our troubles away."

Gregg watches Shea's retreating form, then quickly looks for John. He spots him making his way back from the bar, carefully carrying three drinks. As John approaches he sets the drinks down and sees Gregg flash him something small. John nods—barely—to let Gregg know he saw it. Gregg then places the small object in his ear and then passes John one.

John continues to watch Gregg, who silently shows him a dot on his finger, about the diameter of an unsharpened pencil. Gregg presses the dot into the skin behind his ear, then hands one to John, who does the same.

Gregg barely moves his mouth, but John can still hear him clearly. "We're going to take Shea dancing. The background noise should drown us out. Keep her with a drink—that'll be even better. We have a lot to talk about."

"Okay, I feel bad leaving her out like this, man," John says.

"I know, but this is temporary. I'm working on a plan for something, so we can talk to her, too. She's waiting for us. Let's go down there. We'll talk more," Gregg says, picking up two of the glasses and heading down the stairs.

When he reaches the bottom step, he turns and scans the dance floor until he spots her. She's slowly swaying from side to side in the middle of the dance floor, sipping a bright blue liquid from a straw. As Gregg walks toward her, he hears a voice in his ear, "Guess you don't need to worry about getting her liquored up."

When Gregg reaches her, her face lights up with a smile. He smiles back and pulls her close, spinning her, so she's facing away from him, he rests his hands—each holding a drink—on her hips. Noticing he's holding two drinks, Shea takes one and replaces it with her now-empty one.

"Where you at, John?" Gregg says, soft enough that Shea won't hear him over the music.

"Dancing up a stacked little blonde. Thought it might be better for our purposes," John responds, his voice clear over the coms.

"Yeah, great. So, did you guys get through your binders?" Gregg asks.

"The main points, yeah. I can't imagine what your role is now," John says.

"Nothing," Gregg replies, his voice tense. "I won't do what they want. I am however going to get that chip out of her and get her out of here."

"Might be some kinks in your plan, man. This will take longer than you think. You need to keep that chip in her head as long as possible. You'll have to find another way."

"What aren't you telling me?" Gregg asks, placing the empty glasses he holds onto a passing server's tray. He continues hold lightly onto Shea, so that she will remain facing away from him.

"Dude, I wanted to let you two talk about all of this. This isn't fair," John says, his voice heavy with guilt.

"I know, John. But we have to figure things out, and we can't do that if we don't know everything," Gregg says, determined.

"They have a time machine," John blurts out.

"I figured."

"Dude, how? Some kid is gonna go with her to random places to find treasure," John says.

"Yeah, I'm in charge of the kid. He somehow showed me his past today, and Todd was in it. I wasn't sure it was time travel, but I believe you."

"So, what's the move? I'll do whatever I can to help," John says.

"We need to do a lot of planning. I'll text you tomorrow, and we can meet up. Keep the tech—it has good range. That way, we can talk and know what's going on while at work," Gregg says.

"Alright, man. This is gonna be difficult," John says, voice laced with dread.

"You got that right," Gregg says, then turns Shea to face him. Looking down at her, he knows they have to figure this out.

Shea looks up into Gregg's face, feeling the weight of those drinks, her eyes take in every hair of his beard. She watches as his mouth stretches out into a smile, showing his beautiful white teeth. Her eyes flick to his, seeing concern, mischief, and love there. She stands on her tiptoes but is still far away from him.

Gregg chuckles, and says, "What do you want, beautiful? Use your words."

"I don't know, Gregg. And I can't talk to you about it. I just… feel so alone again," Shea admits.

"Beautiful, I'm right here. You're not alone. Plus, Diesel is at home waiting for you. We're going to get this all figured out. I've got you," he reassures her.

"I know you do, Gregg," she says and buries her face in his chest.

Gregg gently grabs the sides of her face and looks into her eyes. "I love you, Shea. I know I shouldn't say that. I know you're with Todd and don't feel the same way… but I adore you. And I'll make sure you're taken care of."

As he finishes speaking, she feels a tear slip down her face, which he brushes away with his thumb. They stand this way for a while as she cycles through different emotions, until one emotion settles on her face that she has never shown him. Shea pulls her index finger toward herself, and Gregg leans closer. She stands on her tiptoes to make up the distance.

Putting her mouth next to his ear, she says, "I know you love me, Gregg. Your actions show me that every day. You treat me better than anyone else ever has. I've taken you for granted, and didn't see what was right in front of me. And now… I'm trapped. And it's too late. I'm so sorry, Gregg. And I do love you."

She drops back, her feet landing flat on the floor, and bolts for the door.

The words weren't hard to say—she's known for a while—but it's all too much. Her heart feels like its cracking apart, sending sharp, tingling pains into her arms, making it hard to breathe, as if her lungs refuse to expand. Tears race down her face, blurring her (now perfect) vision, she can feel snot on her lips and taste it in her throat. And she runs from all of it—from herself, from Todd, from Gregg, from the look John gave her as she ran past him.

Gregg is too stunned to move. He hears, "Holy shit, dude. Are you okay? Should we go after her?"

Gregg over at John, seeing a look of serious concern written on his face. "I'm okay. Let's go."

As they walk toward their waiting car, John keeps looking over at Gregg. Finally, John says, "Gregg, man, what are you thinking? Isn't this huge?"

Gregg looks at him, his expression unreadable. "It is. But right now, I'm more worried about her safety. I need to move this as fast as possible." He reaches the car, and opens the door, sliding further into the seat to make room for John to get in after him. When John gets in, Gregg nudges him and holds his index finger to his lips, tipping his head to the other seat.

John looks over and sees Shea curled up, using her purse as a pillow, fast asleep. He smiles at Gregg, and speaks quietly, "Tell the driver to take us to your place. We can grab the cars tomorrow. That way, you don't have to wake her twice."

Gregg nods his head and gently kneels on Shea's seat, quietly giving the driver instructions. When they pull into the driveway, John gets out while Gregg wakes Shea just enough, to help him get her out of the limo and into the house. In her room, he lays her in bed and pulls the covers over her. Diesel wines, wanting to lie with her but John steps in, taking the dog outside to go potty first. Pulling her phone out of her purse, he puts it on the charger and turns it on. As he turns to kiss Shea on the forehead, he hears her phone ding several times. He picks it up, seeing that all the notifications are all from Todd. He clicks the text thread.

00043 🌲🌲 E99-celent

John, having ordered them some calzones, picked up the invoices and called his people to update them on their plan to leave Monday, walks back into a tidied room. "I'm back, I ordered us some calzones, they should be up soon," he says, to what he realizes is an empty room.

Instantly, panic rises and he begins tossing the whole room, ruining her tidy job in one foul swoop. He checks the bathroom and closet, but she is nowhere to be found. He takes a couple of deep breaths to compose himself, and begins to walk back to the door, when the satellite phone rings.

Confused, he digs in his bag and grabs the phone, looking at the caller ID. The number shown is one that is attached to one of his burner phones. Holding the sat phone in his hands, he remembers it has his old number linked to it, she's trying to call him.

Feeling emotional, he flies out of the room and straight to the desk. He gives the desk clerk Shea's description and begins searching for her himself. Just when he thinks she was most surely abducted, he sees her crumpled shape, sitting just under the awning in the back.

He rushes out to her, unable to believe she would come out here in her bathrobe—it's cool and windy. Placing a hand on her shoulder, he says, "Shea, what are you doing out here? This is dangerous. I know it sucks being cooped up all the time, but it's for your safety. We need to move inside."

"I saw you…sitting there…talking on the PHONE!" she starts out quietly but ends up standing and screaming at him. "I thought we couldn't have phones. I thought it was too dangerous. Or is it just that you don't want me calling anyone for help?" she says.

John feels like he's been punched in the gut. She has no idea how much she wounds him. "Shea, I have those, so I can update the people who are helping us, along the way. I called them because I'm hoping we can move on Monday. I had to tell them. You're not my hostage, or my prisoner, Shea. I have done everything I can to help you, that's all. After this is over, and you remember everything, you can go wherever you want. I promise," he says, the last part with a quiver in his voice.

The wind seems to leave her sails. "Okay, I'm sorry, John, I just feel so lost," she admits quietly.

John sighs, his voice soft with understanding. "I can't imagine what you must be feeling, Shea. I'm sorry. Maybe I wasn't the right man for the job."

"You've done an amazing job. I just… I got upset, and I'm sure I overreacted. I really do appreciate you."

"Did you call anyone?" he asks, curious to hear her answer.

"I don't know… I just wanted to feel safe and comforted. A number popped into my head. I called it, but no one answered. I don't even know who it belongs to," she says.

"Okay, no harm done then. We just have to destroy the phone. Let's get back to the room, okay?" he says.

She stands from the fire pit, snaps the phone in half and hands it to him. On the way in, he tosses it in the trash. When they reach their room, they find a tray outside their door containing their dinner. John picks up the tray, and Shea holds the door for him, ushering him inside. When they sit to eat, they both apologize and forgive each other. But John feels like Shea isn't quite herself. He wonders if he'll need to start pretending to be asleep again.

When they go to bed that night, Shea still snuggles close, but John feels distance. Turning on *Brooklyn 99*, he keeps his eyes closed but never sleeps. At 9 a.m. the next morning, he finally decides to get out of bed. He quietly sets up the supplies he'll need for her treatment on the table by the couch.

He decides he needs a shower before Dr. P arrives but has anxiety about Shea trying to leave. It reminds him of the anticipation he felt thinking about how she would act when she first woke up. Looking down at the watch on his wrist, he remembers—within the plug he placed in her skull, there is a tiny tracking device. The watch allows him to pull up her current coordinates at any time, which gives him just enough confidence to get his stinky ass into the shower.

As soon as the water starts, Shea startles awake. Her dream— more like a memory—slips away quickly. Assuming John is in the shower, she decides to get up, brush her teeth, and make herself more presentable. The thought of leaving never crosses her mind. Once she feels freshened up, she orders them breakfast.

She watches as he leaves the steam-filled bathroom, clad only in a towel.

"Mornin', sweet cheeks," he says, flashing her a smile.

"Good morning, John. I brushed my teeth and braided my hair. I didn't want to scare you away with my dragon breath."

"Well, I appreciate that," he says, his smile widening. He sets out his toiletry supplies, and within a few minutes he has brushed his teeth and hair, conditioned his beard, cleaned his ears and changed his contacts.

After stepping back into the bathroom to dress, he walks over to Shea, and says, "What'd you order for breakfast?"

"It's a surprise!" she says happily.

John raises an eyebrow, then hears a knock at the door. "Perfect timing," he says, turning to answer it. He's gotten lax in room security, opening the door without the chain and without his gun. He chats with the hotel employee for a bit as Shea tries to angle herself to watch John's face.

When he closes the door, he turns to face her with the tray. There's a large mischievous grin on his face. Placing the tray on the bed, he turns to clear the table again.

"Would it be okay if we lounge in bed together to eat? It's okay if not, I just think it would be fun," she says.

"I think that would be a great idea. Let me put the pillows against the headboard, so we can be comfy," he says.

Shea responds with a large smile, and walks around to the other side of the bed, waiting to jump in. They settle into bed, and get comfortable, with their backs against the pillows. John pulls the tray closer, carefully handing Shea her coffee, then sliding the tray between them.

"So, what made you decide to order this spread?" he asks.

"Well, the orange juice is because I saw some in your fridge before we left Florida. The plate of bacon is because of our flight and I ordered cheesy omelets because, well… you are egg-celent, and you make me cheesy!" she says, finishing the last bit in a mumbled rush.

John chuckles and pops a small piece of bacon into his mouth. "Well, I think you're egg-ceptional and make me feel all melty and gooey."

They lounge and eat, and before they know it, Dr. P is knocking on the door. The three of them fall into the same routine as the previous day. When Shea finishes all her treatments, she feels worn down and craves a nap. She lies down and invites John to nap with her. His own exhaustion propels him into the bed, and Shea's body clinging to his arm guides him into a deep sleep.

They both needed the rest, apparently, because they sleep until the phone rings the next morning.

Twin Pines

00044 🌲🌲 I Lost Count

■ ■ ■ ■ ■ ■ ■ ■ □ □

Text from Todd at 5:38 p.m.:

> Trust you Shea? You're proving right now that my trust was ill-placed.

Text from Todd at 5:40 p.m.:

> Really mature turning your phone off. Text me when you grow up

Text from Todd at 6:30 p.m.:

> Why does it seem like you're trying to hide things from me

Text from Todd at 8:35 p.m.:

> Really? Big Dorkus McGee, Gregg? You love him now? You realize this is cheating, right? Why is it always Gregg? I've seen how this plays out, Shea. You never end up together.

Text from Todd at 8:45 p.m.:

> You're angering me. Reevaluate, before you're met with consequences you will not like.

Gregg sighs, disgusted by how truly unhinged Todd is revealing himself to be. He moves to put the phone back on her nightstand when it dings in his hand.

Text from Todd at 9 p.m.:

> Get out of her business Gregg. Isn't it enough that she professed her true feelings tonight? Acting like the whore she truly is, cheating on ME?

Gregg drops the phone like it burned him and quickly turns to Shea's open eyes, staring at his back. He sits on the bed next to her, and says, "Get a life, Todd," right before he leans down, and softly kisses Shea's lips.

They hear her phone ding a few times as Gregg gets up and wishes Shea sweet dreams.

"Ignore the phone. Get some rest, beautiful. I'll see you in the morning."

"Night, Gregg. Thank you," Shea murmurs.

"Oh, don't forget this." John says, carrying a still whining Diesel to the bed. As soon as he's enveloped in Shea's love, he falls deep asleep.

When Gregg returns to the living room, John is practically dancing in anticipation, for the story of what just happened. "Dude, dish."

Gregg walks over, and says, "I keep forgetting about the damn mic. Todd just blew her phone up all night. I was reading through the texts when she opened her eyes behind me. I didn't know, and then he texted immediately saying nasty shit. Makes me think all he's doing is watching her memories like a live feed. Makes me sick."

"Wait, he can't. The option to watch back her memories has to be approved by the board, or a couple of members. I forget, but why would they approve a live feed?" John says.

Gregg shakes his head. "Come on, man. He doesn't need approval. I'm sure he has them all by the balls, with personalized threats of things he can go back and change, if they don't let him do whatever he wants."

"Damn, that's horrifying," John says, removing his shirt. "You got a blankie I can borrow?"

"Yeah, man. Lift up the cushion against the wall. It's full of blankies. Night, man."

The next morning, Shea wakes up earlier than the guys. She stays in her room, using the time to read all of the texts from Todd with her tiny emotional support buddy.

This is insane. I made a huge mistake getting this implant

As she's reading through all the texts, her eyes start watering. She feels similar to how she did after her parents died—alone, with no one to talk to.

Text to Todd at 7:30 a.m.:

< We need to talk. I've ignored a lot because I truly cared for you, but there's just too much to ignore now

Text from Todd at 7:30 a.m.:

> I'll call you in a couple of minutes

Shea gets up and uses the bathroom with her eyes closed. She uses the same technique while getting dressed. Looking in the mirror, only to braid her hair. Returning to her bed, she gets comfortable and waits for her phone to ring.

Because she hasn't heard either of the guys up yet, she decides she wants to go outside for the call. She turns her ringer down, and sneaks silently from her room to their back porch-pool area.

Sitting at the edge of the pool, she slides her legs into the water. Taking deep, steadying breaths, she watches Diesel sniff around and fiddles with her necklace. She tries to calm her nerves, as her phone lights up with a call.

"Hello," she answers.

"Shea, good morning. Have fun last night?" Although the words cause a shiver to pass through her, he sounds normal, pleasant even.

"Todd, I'm done playing cat and mouse. Why are you watching my memories like a live feed? That wasn't in the agreement, or the binder for that matter."

There is a short pause before he responds, his tone mildly taunting. "Well, it's standard practice to observe team members who have just learned top-secret information about my company. It's a security thing. Therefore, it's an exception to your contractual terms."

I'm glad I didn't poop with my eyes open.

"Okay, Todd, what about Tina?"

"What about her?"

"Who is she really? And don't feed me more lines. I'm not an idiot. Our situation is obviously over anyway, so just tell me the truth," she says, trying not to beg him to tell her she isn't crazy.

Hearing the sliding glass door open behind her, she remains facing away, her cross in her hand.

"Things are over when I say they are, Shea. You don't get to decide to cheat on me and then drop me," he says, his voice hardening.

It doesn't matter what I do. He'll never reveal all of the truth

"Todd, you don't seem very fond of me anymore, and you heard how I feel last night. So, why would you want to continue with this farce?"

"Every interaction we've had has been carefully curated and customized to get the necessary results, for my project. You were most likely to accept my offer, therefore, bring Gregg with you, when you were told that Tina is my secretary. Then, when I blew you off for her while you were in the hospital, it was more believable for you to hear that she was my sister. But I didn't feel bad, because while I was blowing you off,

Gregg was denying that you could ever possibly love him, shoving his own feelings of love and adoration for you, deep down inside."

I feel like a lab rat

"Alright, Todd, you're the master of time and knew how we felt before we could admit it to ourselves. Still doesn't answer my question," she says, trying to keep her voice steady as she stares at the ripples of water coming off of a pair of hairy man legs next to hers.

A hand reaches out, taking her hand from around her cross and holding it in his. She's momentarily distracted by the butterflies she feels.

"…think you're, just, so smart. I guess it doesn't really matter anymore. You both already signed your contracts."

Shea presses the speaker phone icon on her screen, and Todds voice comes through loudly. "Tina is my wife. She got upset when she learned we had been intimate—it wasn't in my deal with her, but I thought it would help you both get here. I did what I had to. No offence, but you're not really my type. Tina was so upset that she worked with a competing company to take you out. But you remembered to hit the button on your way down. If you hadn't, you would've probably gone down for the long nap."

"Oh, well, lucky me. I guess attempted murder is no big deal. Makes sense. I'm not offended about not being your type, but why did getting Gregg and me here require so much work?"

"It's too much to go into now, but basically, there was always something that got in the way of you two deciding to relocate. When I didn't get involved with Project SNV, it meant Gregg and that other girl got more serious, and he didn't want to leave. When the two of you don't get together—even just as friends—you become a loner, and self-destructive. Not wanting to relocate because you couldn't let go of your house, because of your parents. Look, it's always something. I had to insert myself, and now that you're here, we need to just move on and complete missions, like you were poached to do."

The past six months have all been orchestrated by Todd…

"How many times did it take?" she asks, looking down at the hand holding hers, running his thumb along her skin.

Todd's tone is almost indifferent. "I lost count. It was a couple of years' worth, though. I'm not restarting again, so you and Gregg can love each other all you want, as long as you do your jobs—the jobs and terms outlined in your offer letters."

"Got it. See you Monday then," she says, desperate to get off of the phone.

"Meet me in my office at 8:30 a.m., Monday morning," he says, then hangs up.

Shea's arm drops to her lap, her phone clutched in her hand. Gregg sits quietly beside her. She assumes he is giving her time to process everything she just heard. Although she didn't put the call on speaker until the end, her phone is crazy loud on its own anyway, so he heard everything. As they sit in comfortable silence, Shea's eyes start watering again.

"Beautiful, don't let that guy affect you like this. He isn't worth it," he says.

She looks at him, unshed tears fill her eyes. "It's not him. It's that you could have had a different life—probably better if it wasn't for me."

"Shea, I know it seems that way, but come on, I wouldn't want a life that you aren't in. However we got here, I wouldn't change any of it. You're my best friend, and my favorite person. I just hope you're at least okay with how things have turned out."

"I feel selfish. I'm happy he's married, and I'm happy that, however many times it took, we got to where we are now. You're the guy that gives me butterflies, and I didn't even truly realize it until I woke up in that hospital bed and you were sleeping on my lap. The only person there for me…"

"Well, things are different now, new beginnings, right?"

"Right. New beginnings."

"Come on, I'll make breakfast. John is trying to be polite, but I know that big boy's hungry."

Getting up, they go inside and make breakfast. While they eat, they debrief John on the situation. Shea can feel Gregg watching her as she stares into space, pushing her food around on her plate.

"Shea, I was wondering if you could order a regular car for me, after breakfast?" Gregg asks.

"Sure, where are you going?"

"We're going to get our vehicles, and then I'm gonna run a few errands. John is coming back, though, he signed up for play time with Diesel, and whatever you want to do."

"Oh, sure. Am I not allowed to know the errands that you're running?" Shea asks, as John and Gregg deposit their plates into the sink.

Gregg takes the plate out of Shea's hand, passing it over the bar to John. "Shea, I never want to have secrets from you, but I have no choice right now. I'm sorry."

"I understand," she says, wrapping her arms around his torso.

Looking down at her, he sees that look again. He leans down and she rises on her toes to meet him. Not wanting to be assumptive, he kisses her forehead and releases her waist.

Oh no you don't

Shea grabs the sides of Gregg's face, pulling his head down toward her. She softly lays her lips on his. It takes Gregg a second, but once he's back in this universe, he turns the kiss into something that makes Shea's toes curl.

This is so different. Gregg kisses like he went to university for it

John clears his throat, and they both return to earth, breaking apart. "Sorry, guys. I am so excited for the two of you, but I figure we should probably get the car ordered, right?"

"Yeah, you're right," Shea says, opening the app and hoping Todd didn't bar her from using the corporate account.

"Okay, it says twenty to thirty minutes."

While they wait, Gregg showers and changes in a fitted polo and boot-cut jeans. John tries to distract her from her thoughts, but even his best efforts are ignored. "Hey Shea, you want me to stop at the store on my way back?" he asks.

"I don't think so. How long do you think you'll be?" she asks.

"I'm just coming straight back, as far as I know. I'll ask Gregg when he comes out."

"Ask me what?" Gregg asks, walking out from his wing, gel still on his fingertips, which are currently running through his curls.

"Are you gonna need any help before I head back here?" John asks Gregg.

"No, not today, anyway. I don't know how long I'll be gone—it could be until dinner. Keep Shea safe and entertained while I'm gone." He walks over to Shea, casually leans down and brushes his lips against hers. "Be back before you know it. I promise I'm doing all of this for you. Be patient with me, okay?"

"Okay," she agrees, then gives him another peck for the road.

After they leave, Shea takes Diesel on a walk, trying to clear her head. But the whole time, she's distracted, wondering about what Gregg could possibly be doing to get them out of this situation.

Later that afternoon, as John plays tug-of-war with her pup, she asks, "Look, I know you can't tell me specifics, but can you tell me if you know what he's doing?"

John waits a second to respond, listening to his earpiece, he hears Gregg's voice. "Tell her it's safer for both of you not to know. That way, Todd can't do anything skeezy to either of you."

John relays the message to Shea and watches her face change to understanding—and fear.

"You don't think Todd would hurt Gregg, do you?" she asks.

"Not on my watch," John says.

They spend the rest of the afternoon running through training drills. John thinks it is the best use of their time, considering. In the late afternoon, they decide to run to the grocery store, getting ingredients for a salad, some steaks, and potatoes.

John gets confirmation that Shea's mind is elsewhere, when she doesn't even try to connect her phone to Bluetooth.

Shea and John are rinsing lettuce and other vegetables, when Gregg walks in the front door. John watches Shea's face light up at the sight of him.

"Hey guys, you taking my job now?" he asks, putting the keys down and resting his forearms on the bar.

"Nah, man! We left the steak and potatoes for you—rinsing veg is easy," John says.

Shea continues to look at Gregg with adoration and desire. John chuckles, because Gregg doesn't notice it at all. Walking away from the two of them and tucking himself into the pantry, he whispers, "Look at the way she's looking at you, man! She wants you to kiss her, grab her, hold her tight. Do something!"

Shea watches Gregg struggle to hold back a smile, then he looks at her more intently, like he hadn't truly seen her before.

"What is it?" she asks, her voice soft with curiosity.

"I just can't believe how dumb I've been, standing on this side of the bar, when you're over on that side of the bar," he says, then confidently walks over to her. Pulling her into his arms, he tries to pay attention and decipher what her face says, but he still can't tell. "Tell me what you're thinking, truly, so I know what this face means."

Shea chuckles. "I'm thinking that you look sexy today, and that I can't believe I can kiss you any time I want, and…" she trails off, feeling the heat rise into her cheeks and ears.

"And? Don't leave me hanging, beautiful," he replies, flush rising into his cheeks as well.

"And that I love you. I love you, Gregg, and it feels weird to say it, but it also feels like I've been waiting forever to say it, too, you know?" Shea answers honestly, her voice soft and steady.

"Wow, I do know. And that's a face I'll definitely be looking for from now on," he says, a slow smile creeps over his face, and then he nuzzles his face into her neck, before kissing her lips deeply.

"Alright, you two. I wanted to give you plenty of time to have your moment, but I'm coming out of the closet!" John says, then fabulously steps free of the pantry, facing Gregg and Shea.

That night, after dinner and their show, Gregg follows Shea to her room—letting John stay in his room, if he wanted to. Gregg kisses her good night, and they snuggle close together. He doesn't put his glasses on the nightstand until Shea is already asleep, not wanting to miss a single second of her face.

Gregg and John leave the next day after breakfast. Shea decides to take the time she has to herself, to look for that little leather notebook she packed. She decides she should document this craziness, but once she finds it, she hesitates. Writing it down and having Todd witness it, is probably the worst possible idea. Luckily, the boys get back right when she starts to look for something else to do.

They're near the front door, speaking in hushed tones, when they see Shea come from her wing.

"Hey guys, can I be out here?"

"Of course, beautiful," Gregg says with a smile.

Twin Pines

00045 🌲🌲 I Know

AFTER

"**Hello?**" John answers.

"Hello, Mr. Doe. Dr. P is already on her way up," the front desk clerk informs him.

John immediately hangs up the phone, shaking Shea awake. "Wake up, Dr. P is almost here, and our nap turned into sleep-sleep," he says.

Shea launches out of bed. "Oh my gosh, we slept so long! I have to pee so bad!"

John chuckles as she rushes to the bathroom. He tries to smell his own breath by doing that hand-in-front-of-mouth—exhaling and then sniffing thing. He doesn't smell anything but maybe that's a good thing, because he doesn't smell shit either. Shea comes out of the bathroom, and is in the process of re-braiding her hair, when there is a knock at the door. John answers it, letting Dr. P into the room.

"Good morning L.T.! It's nice to see you sitting on the couch, you look great. How're you feeling?" Dr. P asks.

"Yeah, I feel great today. I was really run down after your visit yesterday, so I slept a ton, but I feel so much better today," Shea says.

After the treatment, Dr. P sits next to Shea on the edge of the couch. John leans against the wall beside Shea's side of the couch, sensing something significant must be happening, because he's never seen Dr. P sit before.

She looks at Shea and smiles, placing her hand on Shea's arm. "Well, I have a feeling this will be the last time I see you," she says. Shea looks over to John who nods almost imperceptibly. "You have already had a remarkable recovery, and I think you're in good hands for the rest of it. I brought supplies with me today to give you both, to take care of that wound. I know you'll be traveling, but it's important. I won't be able to come to you, but I put my number in the bag. If you have questions or need advice, don't hesitate to call or text," Dr. P says.

"Thank you so much for everything you've done for me," Shea says, her voice thick with emotion and her eyes welling up with tears. "I'm certain I would have died without you."

"You're welcome. But I'm certain you would have been okay either way. I believe John would have done whatever he needed to—to get you help—even if it meant putting himself in danger. Isn't that right, John?"

"Yes ma'am."

"Well, I'll get out of here. Goodluck you two, I'm truly rooting for you," Dr. P says, getting up and walking to the door, but she turns just as she reaches it, and looks to John. "Oh, and I don't want to be that guy, but can we settle my invoices before I leave?"

"Oh yeah, of course. I don't have one for today though," John says.

"I have it here," she says, handing him a piece of paper.

Looking through all of the invoices, John does some quick math in his head, and then excuses himself to the large walk-in closet, where he had put the canvas bag last night, for this reason. The total for all Dr. P's visits, medications, supplies and procedures comes to fifteen thousand dollars. John knows some people might think this is way too much, but the cost of saving Shea from the infection and avoiding a public hospital, has no limit. Taking the money out of the bag, he proceeds back to the entryway.

"Here it is. Feel free to count it," he says, handing her a couple of banded stacks.

"I'm good, I know who you are," she says with a knowing smile.

Shea looks from John to Dr. P, watching this exchange, then looks at Dr. P with pleading eyes.

"L.T., you will remember. And when you do, you'll be grateful I didn't spoil it. I promise. You have my number—if you feel differently when that happens, just give me a call." She opens the door and steps out. Right before it closes, John catches a glimpse of the very serious look on her face and the solemn nod she gives him before the door swings closed.

"Pack up, we need to leave before dark," he instructs Shea. "I have to go make a call to our security detail, to let them know, and I also need to call ahead to where we are parking, so they can get everything ready. Should only take me like ten minutes."

Shea nods, grabs her handgun and settles into the couch, preparing to wait for his return.

Twin Pines

00046   COLLATERAL

■ ■ ■ ■ ■ ■ ■ ■ □ □

Monday morning, Shea walks over to Todd's office. Checking her phone for the time, it's 8:25 a.m. Figuring it's better to be early than late, she knocks twice before letting herself in.

"Well, come on in, Shea. We're all friends here, right?" Todd says, as John vacates one of Todd's visitor chairs. "Remember what we talked about, and be in the training room at 10 a.m., you're dismissed."

"Yessir. Thank you," John says. He passes Shea on his way out and doesn't even glance in her direction.

What the fuck, is he a plant?

Shea sits in a visitor chair and waits for Todd to speak, her mind racing.

"Alright, Shea, let's not let things be awkward between us, okay? I received a report from medical, your incision healed perfectly, thanks to some Crown innovations. You're cleared for normal duty. So, although we do still have more training to do, your first mission is today. Are you capable of maintaining professionalism?" he asks, eyes glinting.

"Of course, Mr. Donoghue. I'm here to work," she says, keeping her voice steady.

"Good. Is there anything else you'd like to address?"

Shea, while thinking, looks around his office. She notices a box next to him, behind his desk. She only sees a sliver of cardboard but she's sure it says 142. "Yes, now that I think of it, what's that box next to you?"

Todd chuckles, in a maniacal way. "Well, Shea, you're so smart— you tell me?"

"Todd, I thought the games were over. What's in it?" Shea presses.

"You're right, Shea. No games. This is the box of your pictures. I took them from your house in Ohio for safekeeping during the move. I was going to have them reframed. But now, let's call it collateral. Do your job, do what I ask of you, and you'll get them back—eventually."

Her stomach drops. "Todd, my family is dead. Those pictures are all I have left of them. I can give you something else as collateral, please."

"I'm sorry, Shea. But no. Now, that's all I have. Be in the training room by 10 a.m." Todd instructs.

Shea has to resist every urge in her body that tells her to punch him in the face. She grits her teeth, and says, "Yes, sir." Then stands and walks calmly out of the office. She doesn't even know where she's going, she just sees red. As she mindlessly storms the halls, she begins to hear her name being called.

"Shea! Shea! Come on, Shea! Wait up!" she hears behind her. Turning around, she sees John standing behind her, both hands cupped over his crotch.

"Get. The. Fuck. Away. From. Me," she spits at him, seething.

"Please, it isn't what you think. Please, just wait until you know more before you pass judgement."

"Okay, go ahead," she says.

"I can't, Shea. I know it sounds like a lie, but I promise, when I can, I'll explain"

"Okay, bye." Shea turns and walks to the training room. She may be early, but she decides to use the time to punch something. She spends her time imagining John's face on a target that she punches and kicks. Then, on a target she flings ninja stars, daggers, and bad energy at. She's beginning to feel moderately better, when her alarm for 10 a.m. goes off. Turning toward the door, she sees John and Todd, souring her mood once more. She walks over to them, wanting to get this over with.

"Alright, Shea. You two are going to head to the weapons room. You're going to pick out a firearm, and then you'll do some target practice. Go with John," Todd orders.

She follows John into a large room lined with shelves that are filled with so many different firearms. "Pick them up, feel the weight, find the one that you think will work for you," John instructs.

"Eat a bag of dicks," she mutters under her breath. She holds and inspects different guns, but she doesn't know what she's doing, so how can she pick one? "Alright, you're here, so give me some instructions. Show me how to check if it's loaded and how to properly hold and aim it."

"Sure," he says, picking up the gun closest to himself. He runs her through all of the things she asked for.

"Okay," she says, picking up one of the guns close to herself, she releases the mag and pulls back the slide quickly, catching the 9mm bullet that flies out. Holding it with good trigger discipline, she slowly raises it to shoulder height, aimed at John. She thought of John like a brother. He laughed and joked with them, knew Gregg's secrets…and now she just feels it in her gut— he's telling Todd.

"Shea, whoa! You never point a gun at a person, loaded or not, unless you plan on pulling the trigger," he says.

She just stares at him, then slowly drops her finger to the trigger, "Who says I'm not?"

"Shea, stop. It's not what you think. Please stop."

"Sure. This is the one I want." She drops the gun to waist height and reloads it.

"Okay, come on, let's go shoot it," John says, leading her to the indoor range, his back stiff as a board as she follows. They work for a couple of hours, during which time Shea quickly becomes accurate with her new weapon. Afterward, they find a couple of different holster options for her, so she is able to carry her weapon on missions.

Meanwhile, Gregg makes sure Christian eats a good lunch, to have energy for today's mission. He tells Christian about Shea, and how he loves her. So, Christian needs to take care of her—for him. The small boy nods in agreement, smiling up at Gregg.

"You're gonna love her too, bud. She's kind and loving and beautiful— like really beautiful," Gregg says.

Christian offers his hand to Gregg, who immediately gives it to the child. Gregg goes into a vision of a shadow of a man he's never seen before, who asks, "Think of her. Show me."

Gregg calls Shea to mind—in her PJ's rubbing something into her face, in a stunning sundress and bare feet, and her looking at him with 'that look'. Christian lets go of Gregg's hand and looks at Gregg with a shy smile.

"Beautiful, isn't she?"

Christian nods his head vigorously.

Around 12:30 p.m., Shea follows John, not too closely, to where they're to meet for the mission. As they get closer, she sees Tina, Todd, Gregg and a child waiting there. Shea hears Todd whisper closely to Tina, "She's armed. Keep your mouth closed."

Shea slaps on a smiles and raises a hand, moving it around, saying hello to everyone. When she gets back to John, she changes it to just one finger. She blushes, and mouths, "I'm sorry," when she sees Gregg's hand cover the child's eyes and Gregg whispers in his ear.

Hey kid! I'm an asshat! Fuck!

"Alright, we're all here. Just a reminder: while not in the training facilities or on a mission, your weapons are to remain holstered at all times," Todd says, eyeing Shea's weapon. Shea rolls her eyes violently and places her elbow on the weapon holstered at her side.

"Shea, John, and Christian, please step over here for costume and make up," Todd orders.

Christian clings to Gregg, unwilling to go to Tina. Shea sees Gregg point to her and whisper to Christian. Christian slowly nods his head and walks hurriedly to Shea's side. His small face is upturned, watching her, so she sticks her tongue out at him and then smiles.

Tina remains silent during their fitting and make-up—making the time go by much smoother than Shea thought it would. Christian and Shea sit watching *Spiderman* on her phone, waiting for John to be done.

Christian reaches out his small hand for her's, and she freezes. She remembers the binder's warning—only touch him when absolutely necessary. But, he's looking around, making sure no one is watching and shaking his hand at her.

Shea takes the child's hand, and nothing happens. She sits there, holding his hand for a minute, when suddenly she hears—well no, she doesn't hear it—when Gregg's voice is in her mind.

"Beautiful, it's me. Listen, you promised to do what I ask of you. Please, stop with John. He is your friend. I promise, I'll explain more when I can. Just trust me. Please, don't push away one of the only people you can trust, especially while leaving for another time. I love you. Take good care of the kid."

Christian pulls his hand away as Tina walks past them announcing, "Let's go. Places, people. Time to go!"

Shea, John, and Christian stand in front of an arch, while technicians type information into the large module.

"Okay, today's mission shouldn't be too dangerous. You'll be visiting California, in the year 1855. This is about the time the gold rush started to slow down in that area. Christian will find where all the large deposits of gold were, and you'll call for return. So, our teams can excavate the larger deposits, prior to the rush. Shea, do you have your HUD up?" Todd says.

"Oh, you're not currently viewing it?" she says with serious snark.

"No, Shea, I'm not. Yes or no, please," Todd replies, not amused.

"No, I have no idea how to do that."

"Okay, well, it was in your binder. Paul, go ahead and activate her HUD, please," Todd orders.

Shea blinks as the HUD overlaps her vision, just like when she used to play *Halo*. A mini-map of their destination appears, with a floating icon marking their mission area.

"Now?" Todd asks, impatiently.

"Yes," Shea answers.

"Alright, fire it up, Paul! Shea, you'll call for return by using the command, 'Call homebase, Toddie the Hottie,'" Todd says, mockingly.

Just as Shea's about to make a retort, John grabs her and Christian's hands, walking them through the arch. They are deposited onto a dusty, sandy, hill-covered, California landscape, in 1855.

"Okay, kid. Do you need anything from us?" John asks.

Christian shakes his head no, walking a few feet away. He squats down, his palm pressed to the dry earth and he closes his eyes. In just a few seconds he absorbs what he needs, the location of the largest deposits of gold. Brushing his hands off on his pants, he turns back toward the adults and gives them a thumbs up.

"That's it? Why does he even need an escort, then?" Shea asks.

"Shea, this one was easy. But I saw a mission on the books in a couple of weeks from now—to Auschwitz," John says.

"What?" Shea asks, a sick feeling in her gut.

"Yeah, Auschwitz," John says, his voice filled with disbelief.

"But he can see everything that has ever happened in a place—that would be horrific and traumatizing. He's just a kid!" she says, looking at Christian's sweet face.

"I know…" John says, pain etched into his features.

"That son of a—"

"Shea! Use the call sign and take us home already."

"Ugh, fine. Call home base, Toddie the hottie," she says robotically.

Christian chuckles, and an arch appears in front of them. Stepping through, they are back on the tile floor, standing in front of Gregg, Tina and Todd.

"John, please take Christian to Gregg. He can get the coordinates and email them to me," Shea says.

John, sensing the gravity in Shea's voice, jogs to Gregg. They vanish out of the main door to the pod.

"What the fuck is wrong with you?" Shea's voice shakes with fury. "I mean, I recently realized you're fucked in the head, but Auschwitz? Do you realize the pain, suffering, death, starvation, and nudity you'll be exposing that poor kid to? What the fuck is wrong with you, just for a few bucks?" Shea feels the words fall out of her mouth like verbal diarrhea.

"It appears this has really upset you," his voice ice cold. "I suggest you get over it and do what you're told. Otherwise, your collateral will burn up like the rest of your family."

"Fuck you!" Shea spits at him like venom, storming off to her office.

Twin Pines

00047 Remember Us

As John showers, Shea gets her things ready for her shower and packs up the rest of her things. While packing, she notices that the butterfly bandages John applied to her hand are peeling at the edges.

Project Salt N' vinegar... was a chip... in my hand

Shea continues to ponder the matter when John walks out of the bathroom, dressed from the waist down, rubbing a towel through his hair. He walks toward her, and says, "Alright, it's all yours, if we hurry, we should be able to get there before dark."

When Shea doesn't respond, he says, "Hey, what's up?"

"My hand," she says, holding it out to him.

"What's wrong? It looks okay to me," he says, scanning her hand.

"I had a chip right there, didn't I?"

"Yeah, you remember?" he asks, trying not to get too excited.

"I remember that I had a chip for a program called Project Salt N' Vinegar, and it was implanted right here," she says, pointing to the red skin under the butterfly bandage. "It was done by a fuzzy-haired man in thick glasses."

"Wow… Well, you're getting somewhere."

"Did you cut it out?" she asks.

"No, it was an open wound when I got to you."

"Okay," she says, turning to gather her things to take a shower. "Well, I guess I'm one step closer. It's something. I'll be quick."

"Shea, it is something," he says. "It sounds like you saw a face."

"Kind of," she admits. "It was mostly just magnified features, but yeah, you're right."

John packs his bags, carefully wrapping the glass vials of Shea's medication in his clothing. He methodically inspects the room for any garbage or belongings, even stripping the bed to go through the linens. He empties all of the trash cans in their room and leaves the garbage bags open on the couch. He grabs the bottle of cleaner and rags that he pilfered off a maid cart earlier, to wipe down all surfaces. As the water turns off in the shower, he is wiping down the bedside table and the remote.

The bathroom door opens, and Shea steps out in her bra and underwear, covered by a towel. She looks over at him, and seeing that he's cleaning, says, "Don't do it all by yourself, I'll be ready in just a sec."

"No problem, I'm just getting started. The sooner we finish, the sooner we can get on the road," he says, looking up at her. She had dropped the towel and was braiding her long hair, twisting it against the back of her head and pinning it into place.

Once Shea is dressed in warm clothes and snow boots, she packs the rest of her belongings and zips up her pack. "Okay, tell me what I can do," she says.

"Double-check for garbage around the room, then tie off the bags. I've got another one for the linens—if you want to stuff the sheets and bedding in there and tie that bag off, too," John instructs.

Shea moves quietly through the room, searching for garbage while John continues wiping down every surface. About twenty minutes later, John is carrying the luggage to their new—to them—vehicle, while Shea carries the bagged garbage and linens. While he hoists the luggage into the back, Shea stands with her bags. "Where are we going to put these?" she asks.

"Throw them in," John replies. "We'll burn the garbage and use the linens later."

"Isn't that stealing?" she asks as she tosses them in.

"Um, I'm gonna say, gray area."

"Okay," Shea says, shaking her head and chuckling.

"Go ahead and jump in. I'm gonna run in and settle the bill. Oh, did you grab your gun? Your holster should be in your bag too. I'd like you to wear it," John says.

"I didn't see it before, but I'll look again."

"Climb into the back though. The less you're out in the open, the better."

"Will do," she says, climbing into the back. She inspects her pack, checking for zipper pouches she might have missed before. After a couple of minutes, she finds one along the side of the pack. Unzipping it, the pouch reveals the holster. As she pulls it out of the pocket, a small rolled-up piece of paper falls to the carpeted floor of the Jimmy. Opening it, she sees unfamiliar handwriting.

Remember us
We love you.

She looks at it, but feels no pull to her memory—this could have been written by anyone. She notices that it seems to be written by three different people, with one looking almost childlike. She rolls the note back up and slips it in her pocket. Putting on the holster, she then grabs her gun out of its pouch and slides it into place. Getting back into the passenger seat, she sits just as John opens the driver's side door.

Sliding in, he hands her two aluminum foil packages. "Did you get your gun and holster?" he asks, then pulls on his seat belt and starts the Jimmy.

"Yeah, I've got it on. What are these?" she asks, holding up the warm foil packages.

"Breakfast burritos. Figured we'd probably get hungry on the way there."

"Ah, smart thinking," she says, placing one of the packages into his cup holder.

Looking down at the burrito, John mutters, "Ah, shit." Taking off his seatbelt, he opens his door, hops to the ground, and reaches his arm up to the roof. A second later, he climbs back in, handing Shea a cup of coffee.

Smiling, she takes it from him and takes a sip. "John, I found another note…in my holster," she says.

John, in the process of pulling out from the resort, shows no reaction on his face. "Oh, really?" he asks, tone flat.

"Do you know who it's from?" she asks.

"You know I can't tell you that, Shea. I don't even know what note you're talking about."

"Sure. I know, I need to remember on my own," Shea says, feeling let down. She just wants to know who is out there, loving her.

"Wanna pick a playlist after I make a couple of calls? We'll be on the road for a few hours," John says.

"Sure, I'll look while you call."

John pulls out the burner that he'd tucked in his pocket earlier. Dialing their first contact, he hits send. "Hey, have you seen? The geese are traveling north, they should be in your area in about three hours," he says, hanging up to dial the next number. "The geese are flying, the hunter is in orange, V flight pattern," he says, hanging up, he breaks the phone in half and throws it out the window into the other lane, in hopes that the traffic will further obliterate it.

As soon as he tosses the phone, Shea plugs in her iPod. Starting the playlist titled, *An Alaskan Adventure,* she leans back in her seat, eating her burrito and sipping her coffee. She's uncertain about what was going to happen, but relieved they are finally on their way.

Twin Pines

00048 UP IN FLAMES

Shea sits working on her report for the mission, distracted and upset. Not needing her memory footage, she permanently deletes it from the log.

John walks into their office about half an hour later, with Gregg and Christian in tow. Shea stands, and upon seeing their faces, asks, "What's going on?"

"We don't know. Todd has a bunch of people waiting in the mission area. He called for us—ordered us to come get you. Whatever is about to happen, it's probably best to just keep your mouth shut, okay?" Gregg says.

"Yeah, okay," Shea says, filled with dread. She sets one foot in front of the other until they reach the staging area.

"Alright, ladies and gents, everyone is here. Now we have an audience," Todd announces, his back to the arch.

Standing shoulder to shoulder with Gregg and John, Shea watches, wondering what's about to happen. Feeling something brush against her side, she thinks nothing of it, until she feels her firearm being pulled from her holster. Spinning around, she sees Tina standing behind her, a wicked grin on her face and her stolen gun pointed at Shea's chest.

"Go on, up by Todd. You're the woman of the hour, after all." Tina says, motioning her forward with her gun.

Oh God, is he going to burn my pictures?

Todd stands near the module, typing in a location and time, which is obstructed from Shea's view. He looks back at Shea and flashes her a grin, before he moves in front of the arch. "Ladies and Gentlemen, the arch will remain open. Feel free to watch the festivities."

Tina bumps the barrel of the gun against the back of Shea's head. "In front of the arch, with Todd."

As she takes her place, she looks over her shoulder at Gregg. Not knowing what is coming for her, she wants his face to be the last that she sees. She finds him, with John, being dragged by several guards, out of the pod door. Gregg's face is pure rage, until he sees Shea looking his way, he mouths, "I love you, meet me at Lou's."

Christian, who is left alone, hides on the other side of Tina, watching Shea from a safe distance.

Shea's heart hammers in her chest, turning her attention back to Todd as the arch comes to life. She watches as Todd steps through, onto a lush green yard, in front of a beautiful home. Shea's knees give out and she collapses to the floor, dropping so fast that Tina's grip on her arm tears at her skin.

Realizing what's about to happen, she sobs uncontrollably. Seeing Todd's back move closer to her childhood home, she jumps to her feet and sets out for the arch. But, a sharp, searing pain strikes her lower back, and she crashes to the tile, sprawling on her stomach. Tina digs her stiletto heel into Shea's back and steps down.

"Stay put, little piggy," Tina says, her voice dripping with malice. "but watch closely—the fun is about to begin."

Tina reaches down, grabbing a fistful of Shea's hair, and yanks her head up, forcing her to watch. Every time Shea squeezes her eyes shut, Tina digs her heel deeper into her spine, leaving Shea, no choice…

But to watch.

Watch, as he kicks down the front door.

Watch, as he uses a large misshapen vase—the one Shea had made for her mother when she was six—to hit her father on the back of the head, dropping him instantly.

Watch, as he laughs while her mother frantically tries to staunch the bleeding, and her father struggles to sit up, to shield her mother.

Watch, as Todd pulls bottles of clear fluid out of his coat pocket.

Tina leans down and whispers in Shea's ear, every word dripping with venom. "Ever wonder how they never found an accelerant? Or any evidence? What he's got there is an accelerant made right here at Crown. It burns so hot that it leaves no trace. Watch how well it works."

Watch, as he douses her parents with the liquid.

Hear, their broken, pleading cries, begging him to stop.

No… No… No… Oh God, I can't breathe

Watch, as he pulls a lighter from his pocket, flicking it with his thumb, a small flame flairs to life.

Watch, as he presses the flame to her father's chest, igniting both of her parents in one motion.

Hear, both of her parents scream in pain.

Watch, as he throws back his head and laughs.

Watch, as her mother stumbles, trying to extinguish herself, only succeeding in spreading the fire around the house.

Watch, as Todd exits the burning home, and saunters back down the driveway, as her parents and their home, blaze behind him.

Watch, as Christian darts through the arch, touches the grass, and returns, hiding.

Tears stream down Shea's face. She's hyperventilating, gasping so hard it feels like she's suffocating. The cool air of the pod chills the sweat and tears that cover her skin, making her shiver.

There are no thoughts or feelings within her now, as Todd steps back through the arch, allowing the view of the blaze to continue, searing it into her mind.

Numb, she stares into the fire, hypnotized, eyes disassociating. At some point, Tina had let her go, and everyone cleared out, leaving her lying on the tile floor, with her cheek in a puddle of her own tears. Closing her eyes she tries to remember what her parents looked like… before he got there.

Shea doesn't realize it, but hours have passed, and Christian can't handle her pain any longer. He ran in for these memories for a reason. Sitting next to her leg, he tries not to startle her, gently placing his small hand on her exposed calf. Shea is sent into a vision, this time.

She stands in her front yard, Christian beside her, holding her hand. As she stands there, she hears the infectious giggle of a little girl, who runs from behind the house. Chasing her, is a younger version of the father she remembers, growling, "I'm gonna get ya!" as he catches and tickles the little girl.

Then, a girl riding her bike falls, skinning her knee, a young mother's kiss, and a Band-Aid fixing the young girl's booboo.

Then, a young teen fiddling with her dress before a dance, smiling when her mother pins the straps, so they won't fall.

Then, both parents help her carry boxes to a used station wagon, hugs and tears exchanged before she gets in and leaves for university.

Memory after memory pour like an elixir down Shea's spine, releasing the tension the day had caused. She looks to Christian and squeezes his hand. "I think I'm doing better, kid. We can go now."

He shakes his head no, and holds up a finger that says, 'one more'.

As the scene again changes, Shea realizes this must be right after she left that spring break—the last time she saw them.

Shea's mother has her head on Shea's father's shoulder, as they sit on their front porch steps, holding hands. It's dusk—the sky pink and gray. There is a light breeze, little insects and frogs have just begun their concert for the evening.

"We did good, didn't we?" she asks him, her voice filled with quiet pride.

"Honey, we couldn't have done better. I mean, her coming home drunk as a teenager wasn't much fun, but she figured it out."

Shea watches her mother smile, a single tear falling onto her husband's shoulder. "You think she knows?" she asks him, a quiver in her voice.

"Knows what my love?"

"That she's amazing, and strong, and so ridiculously smart… that she's unconditionally loved?" Another tear falls, tracing the line of her jaw.

"No, I don't think she does," he says gently. "But I have a feeling one day she will."

He kisses the top of her mother's head and the vision fades.

Leaving Shea sitting on a tile floor, tears streaming down her face. Christian sits beside her, trying to comfort her by gently rubbing her back.

Twin Pines

00049 | | Be Ready

"**Are** you serious?" Shea snaps at John.

"I'm sorry, we're kinda in the middle of nowhere."

"Why did you buy me a coffee and a burrito?" she asks.

"I wanted you happy and not hangry. Sorry!"

"So, what are we going to do now?" she asks, squirming uncomfortably in her seat.

"I have toilet paper. I'll pull over, and you can go," he says.

"On the side of a damn highway?"

"I'm sorry, Shea. I can stand guard if it makes you feel any better."

"BETTER?" she shouts. "No, that will not make anything better."

"Ah, I see. You need to make a deposit?"

Shea stares at him for a moment with a glare that could kill. "What did you just say?"

"Don't be embarrassed. That burrito was greasy."

"Oh my… can you please stop talking about my bathroom habits?"

"Oh, here. I know this spot. You can climb down this walkway, and you'll be hidden from all sides. Just keep your gun on you, just in case."

"Gun? Got it! TP?" she asks, holding out her hand.

"Got it," John says, placing a whole roll on her outstretched hand.

As soon as the Jimmy is in park, she flings her door open and runs down the pathway. John looks over at her still-open door and chuckles to himself—some things never change. With only about an hour until they reach town, he decides to use the sat phone to make an important call, while Shea is indisposed.

"Yes?" the person answers.

"It's today," John responds.

"Seriously?"

"Seriously. No real memories yet."

"Damn, okay."

"How's things there?"

"Bagged a moose this week, learning cursive, and chasing varmints," the voice replies.

"Good. Be ready, okay?"

"You got it, man. See you soon."

Hanging up, John tosses the sat phone back into his duffel bag just as Shea crests the hill of the walkway.

As she gets closer to her open door, John leans over, and calls to her, "Feel better?"

She climbs in and smacks his arm. "I wish that never happened," she says, mortified.

He opens the glove box and pulls out a travel-sized bottle of hand sanitizer and hands it to her. "It's not cool or sanitary to walk around with shit hands. So, here."

She snatches the sanitizer from him. Speaking under her breath, she mutters, "I don't have shit hands."

He chuckles and pulls back out onto the highway.

Twin Pines

00050  Take a nap

■ ■ ■ ■ ■ ■ ■ ■ ■ □

A woman comes for Christian, to take him back to his cell.

Shea finds the strength to rise and pull herself together at the same time, so that she doesn't add more stress to the poor kid. She gives him a weak wave as she trudges to the pod door. Making her way outside, she scans the parking lot and finds her and Gregg's vehicle still parked out front. Without a thought, she gets in and drives herself to Lou's—she doesn't even turn on the radio.

When she arrives, she parks next to John's vehicle. Before she goes inside, she pulls down the visor to check her mascara-streaked face. She wipes at it with her fingers in an attempt to look presentable, and heads into the bar.

Looking upstairs, Shea sees Gregg and John huddled close together at a table. She slowly climbs the stairs, her eyes feel like they are covered in broken glass every time she blinks. Walking up to the table, she walks straight into Gregg's arms and buries her head in his chest.

"Fuck, Shea, we've been so worried," he says, rubbing her back. "Please, tell us what happened."

"We love you, Shea. We're here for you," John says from behind her.

Shea unburies herself and looks at them both before starting the horrific journey through this day, again. Leaving nothing out, she unburdens herself. Sobs wrack her body when she is finished. "It was Todd, all this time… it was Todd."

He's orchestrated my whole adult life

Gregg and John look at each other, neither saying anything. Gregg gently rubs her back, and John holds her hand. They sit like this for at least an hour, only moving once Shea says, "Let's go home. I need sleep."

The next morning Shea is up early and ready for work, well before the guys. She heads out to the kitchen and starts taking out eggs and bacon for breakfast.

"You unhand those precious breakfast ingredients immediately!" Gregg calls out, walking over to her, giving her a hug and some brief kisses. "Beautiful, you are not going to work today. In fact, none of us are. It's only one day, and Todd didn't give any argument after the day we had yesterday."

"I'm sure," Shea responds, her words dripping with venom. "I don't need time off. I need to stay busy—distract myself."

"I'm sure I can come up with a few ways to distract you, for a few minutes anyway," Gregg teases lightheartedly.

"Gregg, I'm serious. I can't just sit around all day."

"And you won't. I want you to remember something I told you recently—when I tell you to go to your room, put on some comfy clothes, bra optional, put that relaxing eye mask on, and relax for a little while."

"Gregg, I just got up…" she starts, but seeing his face, she stops. "Okay, I'll be napping if you need me."

"Alright, love. That's probably best. I'll see you in a bit."

While relaxing, she hears Gregg and John's hushed tones, smells breakfast, and then—absolutely nothing for a while.

Did they just leave without me?

All of a sudden, she feels arms slide under her upper back and legs. Just as she is about to ask what is going on, she hears, "Shhh, just relax, Shea. I'm just going to cuddle you for a little while."

Shea remains quiet, confused as to why John was carrying her throughout the house, then holding her in the same way as they get into a vehicle. He continues to hold her through the drive and slowing at a new location a few minutes later, then hears a garage open and close.

John and Gregg are silent as they take her through the house and to a room behind a false wall, in the master bedroom closet. They have to be careful maneuvering Shea, because both men also have to duck to enter the closet room. As soon as they are all in, Gregg steps back out for a moment. Returning, he gives John two thumbs up, no signal to her implant seen.

John places Shea on a hard chair, then steps back to allow room for Gregg to get close. "Shea, you can take off your mask now," Gregg says.

She pulls the mask up and off her head, squinting at the brightness of the room. Gregg knows her pupils will take a moment to constrict enough to see her surroundings in the sun-lit room. Although the windows are tinted with a mirror finish so no one can see in, they still let in a ton of light. Gregg watches her realize that she's sitting at a wooden dining room table with John and Gregg, who are both smiling at her.

She inspects her surroundings, and can't help but notice, that covering all the walls and the ceiling of the room—is a cage.

"What is this place?" Shea asks them.

"We have a lot to catch up on, which is why this place exists. This is a Faraday cage. Todd can't access your implant from here, I made sure. It basically cancels out any outgoing or incoming electromagnetic waves, to simplify it. Because we had you 'nap,' the footage Todd sees should just look like you've been sleeping. We can't hang out here forever, though, so we need to talk about some stuff."

"Right, okay. So, I'm not a 'wire' in here? I can speak freely?" Shea asks.

"Yes, Shea," Gregg responds.

She takes a deep breath, appearing to gather her strength. "I know I need to know what's been going on. But first…I love you so much. Forgive me," Shea says, then stands abruptly.

Without warning, she screams, every obscenity Gregg knows— and then some—regarding Todd and Tina. Every word is filled with emotion and anger. When she finishes, she slumps back into the chair, her chest heaving.

Gregg lets the silence linger only for a second, before he says, "Well, I don't think I needed to know that about Todd's wang, but I guess it does make me feel better about myself. You good now?" he asks.

"Fine, I'm listening."

"Shea, we have to do something. The way they treat Christian is appalling. After what happened yesterday, it's clear we need to get off the grid. All of us. So, I rented this house—which no one knows about—and built this Faraday cage so we can communicate until we can get that implant out safely. In the meantime, we need to figure out where we're going, how we'll get there, false ID's, everything," Gregg says, watching her face to ensure she is paying attention and absorbing what he is saying.

"Okay, I totally agree. We need to get out. I'm grateful to you both for doing all this work so I can be involved. When are you thinking about leaving?"

"Depends on how well we can get things set up, and what we figure out about your implant," John pipes in.

"Okay, so what's on the agenda for today?" Shea asks, curious.

"Well, this was more, to update you, test the cage, get your thoughts," Gregg says. "But for now, I think we need to get out of here. I don't want to spend more time here than we have to. We don't want to raise suspicions. I'm Sorry, Shea, but you have to put the eye mask back on. Same procedure as before, until we get you home and in your bed. Once there, you can 'wake up' and play with Diesel or whatever you want to do," he says, using air quotes.

Shea stops her protestations before they start, "Okay, eye mask on," she says, pulling the mask over her face and relaxing her body to make it easier to carry her.

As soon as she hears the small door open, John and Gregg remain silent. The ride back to the house is also silent, but as Shea is carried through the front door, Gregg and John begin to chatter. Seeming to be obviously rehearsed.

"Dude, what's in the box?" John asks, curiosity in his voice.

"A huge surprise for Shea. I've been working on it while she slept. I plan to give it to her when she wakes up," Gregg responds.

Shea, still lying limply in John's arms with her eyes closed, listens as they continue their conversation. He holds her limp body like it's nothing.

"Man, well, I'm glad I could help where I could. I'm sure she'll love it," he says, and with that he starts to walk again.

"Hopefully, but honestly I'm more worried about Shea loving me," Gregg says the last word as John deposits her onto her soft mattress.

Why is Gregg worried about me loving him? Does he not realize how much I love him… I need to tell him!

Shea sits up quickly, tearing the mask from her eyes. When she is able to take in her surroundings, she sees John standing at the end of her bed with Diesel in his arms. She doesn't see Gregg, although he was just talking.

"Ah-hem," she hears from the side of her bed, near her nightstand.

When Shea's eyes land on Gregg, he is on one knee. Her hand flies to her mouth and tears flow down her cheeks.

Seeing her reaction, he is a little more hopeful in her love for him, so he says, "Shea, you are the most amazing woman I have ever known. At every turn you've surprised me, and with each day I fall more and more in love with you. I don't know what the future has in store for us. I can't even begin to imagine it, but I know that I want to be by your side through it all. I know we haven't been together for very long, and it's not exactly the best timing, but my heart and soul tell me you are the one for me. I thought it was my turn to surprise you, for once. Would you do me the honor of being my wife?" Gregg finishes by opening a small velvet-covered box.

Shea remains motionless, soaking in every scent, sight, and feeling within this moment. She tries to process what is happening. How could someone love her this much? And how had she gotten lucky enough for it to be Gregg? The man that had never let her down, was offing her a life she never thought she would have. Her emotions overwhelm her.

Meanwhile, Gregg feels like he might shit his pants. She's been quiet for far too long, this has to mean no, right? He glances at John, who smiles and lifts a shoulder in an "I don't know what's going on" gesture. Gregg works to calm his nerves and steady his breath, but the feeling of unease grows.

"Shea, it's okay if you aren't ready. I shouldn't have pushed you, I'm sorry," Gregg says, closing the small box and standing, he turns to walk away, a tear escaping his long lashes.

Reaching out, she firmly grabs his forearm and pulls him down on top of her. Her face, only a few inches from his now, he sees all the emotion there, and there's that look again.

"Gregg, I'm sorry. I was in shock and trying to soak it all in. I would be honored to be your wife, and excited." After the word excited, she kisses his face. "And happy," she kisses his nose. "And safe," she kisses the corner of his mouth, "and know that I am always loved," she softly brushes her lips against his lips.

"So, your answer is…?" Gregg smiles down at her.

"YES! Of course, yes! I love you so much, Gregg!"

Gregg pushes his mouth onto hers, taking her tongue with his. He forgets all the bad things going on in their lives and just pours his love into his kiss. Shea moans softly from under him, and John quietly says, "Pardon me," and walks out of the room with Diesel. Which, of course, makes both of them laugh, breaking the kiss and the spell.

"We will finish that another day," Shea says, pointing at her head.

"Better believe it," Gregg responds, again opening the small box and holding it out to her.

The ring took Gregg a while to pick, it has a main cushion-cut diamond, accented with diamonds down the band. With it, is also another band of diamonds. Gregg reaches out to her for her hand, and she places her left hand on his. He gently slides both rings onto her left ring finger, a perfect fit. Shea admires her finger for a moment, then says, "Why a band too?"

"I don't plan on having a long engagement, and I didn't want to misplace it before then, it's better if people think we're already married anyway," he says, smiling at her.

"I love you, Gregg," she says, standing taller on her knees to reach his face. She takes his face in her hands, and whispers, "To new beginnings." Her lips press gently against his.

"I love you, too, beautiful. Now, come on, I have something to show you," he says, climbing down from the bed and holding out his hand for her.

"There's more? Geez, Gregg, I'm gonna have a heart attack if you keep this up." She laughs, shaking her head.

He smiles at her and walks her out of her wing. Standing quietly beside her, letting her take everything in. First, she sees John lying in a large dog bed with Diesel. A small bin of brand-new toys next to them, which John keeps dipping his hand into, picking out each one to introduce to Diesel. Diesel, however, is only mildly interested—at best—in the toys. Instead, the pup is hopping around, energetically attacking John's long beard—his new favorite toy.

Looking to the bar, she sees that it has been cleared of all of their junk and is now set up with different celebratory items. An ice bucket, which is chilling a bottle of Champaigne, a fancy platter holds chocolate-covered strawberries—in milk and white chocolate—and a bunch of different Chinese take-out containers. There is also a banner taped to their kitchen cabinets that reads, "*Congratulations.*"

"When did you do all of this?" she asks, turning to Gregg with wide eyes.

"Well," he begins, voice light, "before we left, when I told you to lie down, that's when the bulk of the prep started, but I quickly finished it when we got home—timed the delivery of Chinese just right," Gregg says, still holding on to Sheas hand.

"This is amazing, guys. Thank you."

"Well, Gregg did all the hard work, like stealing you away from Mr. Psycho. I just had to learn how to drizzle some chocolate," John says, Diesel hanging from his beard like an ornament.

They all make plates, piling on the goodies they want and take them to the couch. They put on a movie and eat in relative silence.

Throughout the night, Shea can't stop herself, she stares at the ring on her finger, contemplating where this life will lead them and if she's got the guts for it… (balls, she wonders if she's got the balls for it).

After they eat, Shea invites the pup onto the couch. She spends the rest of the evening sitting with her back against Gregg's side, teasing Diesel into chasing a scrap of ribbon. As the night dwindles down and she begins to feel sleepy, she asks, "Are we going to work tomorrow?"

"Unfortunately, yes. So, you'll probably drive home alone at the end of the day. John and I will be busy the next few days," Gregg says.

"Oh, right, okay. No problem, I'll teach Diesel some tricks."

Twin Pines

00051 🌲🌲 Toilet god's

When they arrive in town, John knows where he needs to park but decides to give Shea a little time to just be a human. They both end up getting ice cream and sitting on a bench to people-watch.

"You're really testing the toilet gods today, huh?" he teases, watching the red rise in her cheeks.

"Ugh, you're such a guy, thinking toilet humor is so funny," she says, rolling her eyes.

"Ha!" John laughs.

"What?"

"I don't think you've ever referred to me as 'such a guy', before," he says, continuing to eat his ice cream.

"Well, there's a first time for everything!"

"You done?" he asks, reaching out his hand.

"Yeah," she says, depositing her empty bowl into his hand.

"Good, it's already getting darker, so I'd like to get going."

"Going? I thought we were staying?" she asks, climbing back into the Jimmy.

"No, this isn't our final destination," he replies, pulling a few streets further and parking. As soon as they get out, several men in military uniforms rush over to them. Without a thought, Shea pulls her gun and levels it at the man closest to John.

"Whoa, whoa," John says, moving to place himself between Shea and the man. "It's okay, Shea. They've been helping us all along. They're our friends."

Shea immediately drops her arms and holsters her gun. "Sorry, I didn't know."

"No problem, Shea. Nice reflexes, though," the military man says.

"Okay, guys, focus. Where's the rig?" John asks them.

One of the men points to a four-wheeler, fifty or so feet away, that is hooked up to some sort of trailer that looks like a four-wheeler sized bucket. "How packed is that meat wagon? Will our bags fit?" he asks.

Shea raises her hand, and when John nods and chuckles in her direction, she asks, "What is a meat wagon?"

"See that trailer hooked up to the four-wheeler? That's just what people call it, a meat wagon," the military man tells her. "Here in Alaska people use them when hunting, to haul out their kill—their meat."

"Oh, okay, thanks." She hopes there was never a dead animal in that thing.

"We left room. We'll go load them in now," the same guy says, taking their bags from the back of the Jimmy and loading them into the meat wagon. Shea continues to stand next to the Jimmy, watching everything unfold. She watches John take the canvas bag and hand it to the man. Shea is unsure if this is for their services rendered or a way to ensure their silence.

"Alright, Shea, say goodbye to town," John says, smiling as he hands her a pair of safety glasses, gloves, and a small snack to keep in her coat. With that, he climbs onto the four-wheeler. Holding a hand out to Shea, he helps her on to the vehicle as well, and she then straddles the seat behind him. He starts the four-wheeler, and it vibrates to life. Shea can't even hear herself think—she kind of likes it. The smell of burning fuel surrounds her, and she can feel the heat from the exhaust on her right leg. With everything in place, John starts out on the trail that begins their thirteen-mile trek through the woods.

Twin Pines

00052 I'm Not Sold

The next day at work, Shea feels like everyone is treating her like she carries some sort of disease. No one will even come near her. Since the mission to Auschwitz got rescheduled to next week, she makes sure to complete all of her other duties. After a few hours, she finds herself back in the training facilities with John, boxing with a bag and working on target practice with her gun.

Sometime after lunch, she remembers what Christian did for her—getting those memories and comforting her. Feeling deeply grateful she treks over to Gregg's pod. On her way there, in a hallway alone, a chill runs down her spine. She stops and looks around but sees no one. Standing still, she tries to listen for approaching footsteps, but the blood rushing through her ears is making her deaf to any other sounds.

"Miss Shea, fancy seeing you here. Considering your pod is in the other direction," comes a deceivingly friendly voice from the shadows. "I was looking for you. To congratulate you on your engagement. I found it odd, though, considering you and I only broke up, what, a couple of weeks ago at most?"

Her veins feel like they are filled with ice water, but she takes a deep steadying breath. "Thank you. Gregg and I have been friends for a long time, so admitting our feelings and moving forward all felt very natural."

"Ah yes, friends," Todd says, this time with the malice clear in his voice.

"Well, if that's all, I would like to go give my thanks to Christian for comforting me the other day," Shea says, the palm of her hand moving to rest on her weapon.

Todd's eyes narrow. "Just one more thing. Is Gregg a virgin, you think? It seems odd to me that every time you seem to be into what he is doing, he immediately stops."

Her face hardens. "I honestly don't know, Todd. But it doesn't matter, either way. He stops because he's a gentleman who knows I don't want you watching what he and I do behind closed doors. It's no one's business but ours," Shea retorts.

"Wait," Todd says, chuckling he continues. "You're telling me, I'm the reason he hasn't given it to you?"

"Are we done here?" she asks, her hand still resting firmly on her weapon.

"Yeah, fine, go do what you want," he says dismissively, walking away from her.

As Shea walks to the end of the hallway, she can hear Todd talking loudly to someone on the phone. "Babe, guess what? That little virgin boy is afraid I'll see his tiny pecker, so he refuses to fuck Shea!" After which Shea hears, "Yeah, even he probably thinks she's unfuckable, I guess."

Shea ignores his words.

The opinions of mice don't matter to Sheas…or something like that

She continues her walk, requesting entry to Gregg's pod. When the door opens, she finds Gregg and Christian sitting at a table, playing chess.

Looking at the board, she turns to Christian, and asks, "You know how to play?"

He nods his head vigorously in the affirmative.

Smiling at him, she says, "I just wanted to come down and thank you for being so brave and comforting me the other day."

He looks at her and nods once, smiling.

At this point in the conversation, Gregg says, "Oh, you know what bud, I forgot to tell you something. I asked Shea to marry me yesterday. Guess what she said?"

Again, Christian nods his head vigorously, excitedly looking at Shea.

"Of course!" Shea says, holding up her left hand to show him the ring.

Christian's smile grows, and he covers it with his hands. Shea sits, watching them play a few rounds and by then it's time to leave for the day. Shea looks at Christian, and says, "Can I give you a hug? It's okay if you aren't comfortable…"

Before she can even finish, Christian plows toward her, wrapping his arms around her, and hugging her hips tight. His small face looks up at her with compassion and love.

After work, Gregg is gone for most of the evening. Shea works on teaching Diesel some tricks and mentally cataloging everything she didn't want to forget when they left. She had been instructed not to pack anything—as it would alert Todd to their escape.

The next two weeks pass in much the same way. Shea couldn't shake the dread of their upcoming mission, though she looked forward to her next trip to the Faraday cage—which hadn't happened yet. Diesel was growing rapidly, and Shea had actually gotten permission to bring him in to work with her, as sort of an emotional support animal. She is super excited for that to start.

Leaving work on Friday, Shea already knows the deal—she's going home to feed and love on Diesel while the guys prepare some things. She was going to take a nap at around seven, and hopefully "wake up" in a cage.

What an odd life I have…

Shea hadn't been napping long when she feels strong arms scoop her up. There's nothing but silence, right up to the moment the sleeping mask is pulled off her face. The cage has a much different feel today—there are several stacks of paper, money, and envelopes scattered on the table in front of her. Looking around, she says, "Okay, guys. What's up? What's the plan?"

"We've got all the passports, deeds to a property, and people lined up to help. I have a real marriage license here that we will submit before we go, and false adoption papers in case we're stopped," Gregg explains.

"Okay, what's your plan for my implant?" Shea asks.

"I'm thinking I'll deploy an EMP in our building, simultaneously killing the implant and Todd's favorite toy," Gregg says.

"Will that be safe?" she asks.

"I think so. Honestly, it's the best move we have."

"I'm not sure about that. But what's the rest of your plan?" she asks.

"We have flights and everything figured out. We'll all stay late one night, steal your pictures, break Christian out, and disappear," Gregg reports matter-of-factly.

"Sounds great, but if we all leave at once, aren't they going to be right on our asses?"

"We'll be off the grid, so it won't matter."

"It will, though, Gregg. If my implant is still in place, EMP or not, it needs to be removed. You can't remove it safely off the grid," she says, looking into Gregg's eyes, she uses hers to plead with him to understand.

"We can remove it and leave immediately after, Shea. We will take care of you," he tries to reassure her.

"There's no guarantee that I'll even be conscious, and no guarantee that I won't be brain dead. You can't risk everyone else's safety!" she urges.

"So, what exactly are you asking of me Shea?" Gregg asks, his high-alert status coming through his voice.

"Leave me."

"What?!" John and Gregg both exclaim.

"I'm serious. Let me distract them. It'll give you guys time to get out and get to safety. Then, when it is safe, I'll figure out a way to get out too."

"No, absolutely not! I'll stay!" John says, "We're not going to leave you behind."

"John, it has to be me because of the implant," Shea explains. "If you guys really think about it, you'll see that this is the only way." Her voice quivers and she swallows hard to remove it. She needs to be strong now. "I'll either be incapacitated for God knows how long, brain dead, or unable to remember anything. Or worse, you leave the implant in and I lead them straight to us!"

"You're suggesting that we get Christian out, then once you eventually somehow escape, we can meet up?" Gregg asks.

"Yes," Shea says, determined.

"There's one major problem with your plan, Shea," Gregg says, his voice cracking. "I love you, and I know you're just trying to help everyone else, but they will lock you in a glass cage and beat you until you talk. You'll never leave that place." Desperation dripping from his voice.

"I realize that. But I have something they want. I am the only link to the three of you, they won't kill me, I'm sure of it. Then, when I don't talk, they'll get mad and sloppy, and I'll make my escape," she says.

"Then what? As soon as you leave, they'll have tracking and a live feed. They'll pick you up immediately," John says, his voice tinged with disbelief.

"Actually, no," Gregg interjects, "they won't, as soon as we leave, I'll deploy the viruses, and they'll be pretty much dead in the water electronically. But that doesn't mean they won't track her manually. Depending on how long she's there, they might have some programs back up, though," Gregg says.

"Well, either way. I'll leave my implant in until I'm somewhere safe—somewhere we decide together, is our meet-up point. Then I'll remove it on my own. It might help them think they have the upper hand," Shea adds.

"Well, we can talk more about this later. I'm not sold. I'll get those nasty viruses in the works, in the meantime," Gregg says, then pauses, his face earnest. "Shea, I don't think I can just leave you here."

"Same," says John with determination, his eyes never leaving her.

"Well, what either of you does once Christian is safe, is your business," she says, walking over to John and kissing his cheek, then moving to Gregg, for a kiss on the lips. Sitting herself on Gregg's lap, she asks, "What was that you said about a marriage license?"

Gregg grins and looks to John. "Hey, you ready?"

John stands in front of the two, dramatically clears his throat and says, "Dearly beloved Diesel, you and I are gathered here today to witness the marriage of Greggory Marsh and Shea Murphy. A reuniting of Thor with his hammer, if you will. Two halves are becoming whole today. Do you?"

"Yes," they both say.

"Then, by the power of the internet where I was ordained this morning, I now pronounce you husband and wife. Kiss her."

Shea leans into Gregg, turning her head to meet his. John leaves through the small door to allow the Marshes some privacy to consummate their marriage. He decides to take Diesel for a nice, long, walk outside.

Shea wakes up on cloud nine the next morning, her husband breathing softly at her back.

My husband!

Hearing John and Diesel playing in the living room, Shea leans over and kisses Gregg until he wakes up. Once everyone is awake, they all get dressed and ready for the day. John excuses himself to do some shopping.

"Okay, beautiful, take a nap while I do some cleaning," Gregg says, leaning in to kiss her and softly touch her face.

As Shea lays down for her nap, she whispers to herself, "It was like Thor's hammer. Definitely not a virgin." A shit-eating grin crosses her face, and she hopes that asshole heard every word.

About thirty minutes later, inside the cage, Gregg says, "Alright, Shea, make that list we were talking about, and I'll bring in your pack so you can load up what you can."

"Don't forget to add the pictures when you get them, please," she reminds him.

"I know, babe. We got you."

Shea spends a few hours in the cage, trying to ensure she sets herself up for success after her implant is removed. Before she leaves, she places letters to herself in strategic places and slips her crucifix in an envelope, tucking it into a zipper pocket. Unable to hold it together any longer, she silently calls out to God.

Please, let them get away to safety. Please God

Drying her eyes, she calls out to Gregg, "Okay, I think I've gotten everything done that I can."

"Be right there," Gregg calls through the house, which Shea will never see because she cannot risk their safety.

Entering the cage, Gregg says, "Okay, I have both viruses loaded onto separate USB drives. I'll plant them both the night we leave with Christian. When we go, we won't really be able to say goodbye. You know this is killing me, right?"

"I know, and it's killing me too, but we have to do what's best for everyone. But Gregg, I know we can accomplish anything together. We will get through this," she says, reaching out to hold his hand.

Gregg reaches for her and holds her tight, kissing the top of her head. "I wish I could keep you here forever. Okay, naptime."

Gregg and John spend all day Sunday out of the house, leaving Shea alone to try and subtly put things out that she won't be able to pack herself. As the day winds to a close, she keeps reflecting on how insane her life has become since Project SNV.

I hope the implant doesn't rip out my whole brain

"Honey, I'm home," John calls through the house.

"Hey, finally! I've missed you guys," Shea says, walking out from her wing.

"Sorry, we were gone all day, babe," Gregg says.

"It's okay, I've been playing with Diesel and doing random stuff around the house. Had to keep myself away from the living room. I wanted to watch our show, but I waited."

"We should get to bed. I'm sorry, babe, but John got an update from Todd earlier today. You're going to need your rest," he says.

"Why? What's happening?"

"Auschwitz has been moved up to tomorrow. Todd did say you can still bring Diesel, though," John answers.

"Oh, well isn't he… thoughtful?" Shea says.

"I know, beautiful. I'm sorry, but we have to do what we have to do, right?"

Shea nods, pouting all the way to the bedroom.

Monday morning, Shea walks into work with Diesel. Gregg and John had already left when she woke up, so she set out for Crown early, to introduce Christian to Diesel. At this hour, the building was pretty empty, so no one bothered her or stopped her on her way to his pod. A care worker had to be on-site with Christian twenty-four hours a day, seven days a week, so Shea knew she'd have someone to let her in.

Once in the pod, she asks the woman on duty to let Christian out, but she refuses, explaining that only Mr. Marsh has the authority to access the boy. Shea brings Diesel over to the glass of Christian's cell and taps it to get his attention. As soon as he sees Shea and Diesel, his face lights up, and he stands pressed against the glass. Diesel sniffs at the glass and whines, sitting in front of it.

"Looking for me?" Shea hears.

When she turns to the voice, she's unsure what's happening. She is sure her face shows her confusion.

"What?" he says, smiling.

Recognition finally dawns on Shea, and she gasps, "Oh my gosh! I didn't even recognize you!"

He cut off his beautiful curls! And no glasses!

He walks over and opens the glass of Christian's cell, allowing the boy to pet Diesel. "Kind of like a disguise, huh?"

"Uh, yeah," Shea replies with a teasing grin. "You better get away from me, sir—my husband could be here any minute."

"Is it bad?" Gregg asks, running his hand over his head.

"No, it's hot! Really hot!" she says, mesmerized by the change, until she hears giggling at her feet. Looking down, she sees Diesel licking Christian's face, while the boy giggles.

"Well, I don't know how big of a disguise it is, but it works for *Superman*, right?" Gregg asks, smirking.

"Yeah, but contacts and a haircut are really a big difference. You should try to stay more hidden at work for a while. What made you decide to do this?" Shea asks.

"John talked me into it—not for the reasons you might think. He suggested it so that when we're on our travels, we are less distinguishable from each other. If you think it looks good, that's just a bonus."

"Oh, it looks really good," she says, salivating over her hunk of a husband.

He smiles at her, and they sit together, watching Diesel and Christian play, until they are due in the meeting space for their mission. Shea walks there with Diesel and Christian, leaving Gregg behind in his pod, so fewer people would see his new look. Todd spots her approaching with her dog and the child and walks to meet her.

"Ah, look what we have here." As soon as he gets about three feet from them, Diesel steps out in front of Christian and Shea, growling low.

Todd throws his head back and laughs, like a cartoon villain. "Little guard dog, huh?"

"Do we need make-up? Clothes?" Shea asks.

"Yeah, Tina's over there," he says, lazily flinging his arm in Tina's direction.

When they get over to the costuming area, Shea takes a second, getting on her knees and petting Diesel, she coos, "You're such a good boy. Good job protecting us from the big bad Todd. Yes, good boy."

After clothes, hair, and makeup, Shea, John, and Christian line up in front of the arch, with Diesel at Christians side.

"Okay, same rules as always," Todd says. "Call-back sign for today is 'Du bist mein." He flashes a mega-watt smile at Shea.

Shea rolls her eyes at him.

"You will be emerging in the middle of the year 1945, inside the camp. John and Shea, you two will be looking for caches. Christian will evaluate for anything the previous residents might have stashed, that no one knows about," Todd explains.

"Keep it together," John whispers to Shea.

Twin Pines

00053 Tickle Tickle

Sitting behind John on the four-wheeler, Shea makes an effort to hold on to various parts of the vehicle, but with the bumpy terrain, she only feels safe and secure when she holds on to John. She is also completely blocked from seeing anything in front of them because of John's height. She makes the best of it, though, looking out to the sides of the trail. There are so many different kinds of tall plants on either side of the trail, most of them have tiny thorns that whip across her hands and lap. As the venture deeper into the woods, she sees dense forests of spruce pines, cottonwoods, and birch trees. She's thankful for the protective gear John gave her, before they set out. About fifteen minutes into their ride, John shoves her hands down to his belt.

This is a little forward…

Feeling a bit uneasy about it, she moves her hands back up to his sides. After another couple of minutes, John pulls the four-wheeler over to the side of the trail. Turning to her he says, "I'm not trying to be fresh, you're tickling the shit out of me."

"Oh, I'm sorry!" Shea says, embarrassed.

"Just hold my belt. You can hold it on the sides if you want, just please, stick to the belt."

"Okay, sorry."

With that, she grabs his belt at his sides, and they continue along the trail.

00054 It's Today

As soon as the arch flairs to life, their group marches through, landing on a path between tall brick buildings. The portal quickly closes behind them. Shea can see that no one in their party is ready, so she attempts to be cryptic, saying, "We all know we don't want to be here, but try to imagine that this is the last one you'll ever have to do. When we leave here today, things will get better, okay?"

"Yeah, okay. I'll go look for any caches. You stay with Big C for his part," John says.

Shea looks to Christian, her heart heavy. Seeing his face, she says, "I'm sorry. I promise it'll be better."

He nods at her and holds out his hand.

"You already did it?" Shea asks.

He shakes his head and keeps his hand out. Shea takes it and hears Gregg's voice in her mind.

"It has to be soon. Something's off. If you agree, just say, 'Hey John Snow,' to me, and I'll put everything in motion. If it's a day that you bring Diesel, just put him in your office when you leave—we'll get him. Remember me. I love you. See you soon."

Shea dabs her eyes and nods once at Christian. With Diesel close and Shea closer, he reaches a hand to the ground. Immediately, Shea senses something is wrong. After just a few seconds, sweat rolls down his forehead, and he fights to remain crouched, his knees buckling. Diesel watches Christian and whines.

Shea reaches over and tries to pull his hand from the earth. After a moment of struggle, he finally lets go. As soon as Christian is free of the earth, he begins convulsing.

"JOHN! Get here now!" Shea shouts.

"Coming!" he yells, running toward them.

"Homebase, we're ready. Du bist mein! Have a medic waiting," Shea tries to sound calm.

Christian continues to convulse in her arms. As he does, she accidentally comes in contact with his skin—flashes of the horrors of the past play in her mind.

"Where's the arch?" John asks.

"I don't know! This isn't funny!" she yells. Then she tries again, "Homebase, Du bist mein!"

Shea hears a voice inside of her head, cruel and cold. "What if I just left you there? What would you do?"

Stunned, Shea's response comes out raw and furious. "Your asset is seizing. So, if you don't want him to be braindead, OPEN THE FUCKING ARCH!"

The arch appears in front of them. John picks Christian up and helps Shea to her feet. They all sprint through the arch, with Diesel running and growling ahead of them. A medical team meets them immediately, taking Christian from John and placing him on a stretcher. The entire medical team starts running, pushing Christian toward his pod. John watches all of this, then looks at Shea. She nods to him—Christian needs him right now, not her.

Todd saunters over to Shea, a knowing look in his eyes. "What did you do?"

"What? Nothing, it was the freaky download of a horrendous history that did it."

"Not that. Why is it that you have blank spots in your memory? Gaps of darkness in the middle of the day?"

"Blank spots? No idea. How would that even happen?" Shea asks, feigning confusion.

"Don't play coy. If you're planning something, I suggest you stop. I would hate for a young Gregg or John…or Christian, to have an 'accident.'"

"Todd, I really have no idea what you're talking about. I've been taking a lot of naps, but other than that, nothing new."

"Fine. But if you step one more toe out of line, someone will get hurt," clearly not a threat—a warning.

"Got it," Shea says, then turns and walks toward Christian's pod, her mind racing. She hopes she can get even a partial report from Christian, and to see Gregg one last time. Today had to be the day.

I wish I could tell him off, but I'm not taking the risk. I've already lost too much

When she reaches the pod, Gregg is sitting outside Christian's cell, with Christian asleep inside. "Hey, is he okay?" she asks, her voice filled with concern.

"Yeah, he got some meds to stop the seizures. They knocked him out," Gregg answers.

"Can you open it just for a second? I need at least a partial report."

"Yeah," Gregg says, his voice heavy. He opens the glass and picks up the boy, bringing him over to where Shea sits. "He's really out, babe. I don't know if this is gonna work."

"Well, it has to. I need it. I'm so sorry, John Snow" she gets out, in a heart-breaking whisper.

Gregg studies her for a few long seconds, his gaze filled with something she's never seen. Then, he nods and works on shaking Chrisitan, to wake him.

When Christian rouses a little, Gregg says, "Bud, Shea needs the report. Today is the day we talked about."

Christian slowly reaches out a hand, and Shea grabs it. The moment their skin touches, a flood of images rush through her. Whatever she thought she knew, didn't even come close to the horrors he was showing her.

Piles of skeletal-like bodies, frozen together, while guards throw more onto the heap. Women in a barrack, piled on top of each other, some in stages of dying, some already dead, some with massive infections from having their ovaries forcibly removed the day before. Bodies so emaciated, it makes no sense that they still held life. Women and men are herded into showers, where they take their final breaths. Smells so foul— infection, death, shit, urine, decay and the foul stench of grease and ash from the cremation process.

Her stomach clenches so violently, she worries she might throw-up. Unable to hold it in any longer, Shea's cries turn into weeping, and she reaches out to hold the rest of him. Pulling him into her arms, she slides to the floor, they cry and hold each other for a while. Diesel lies next to them with his head on her lap, whimpering.

Gregg gives them space at first, but after a while, he picks them both up off the ground and places them on the couch. He leaves for a while, and when he returns, John is with him. John immediately walks over and grabs Christian from her arms.

"I'm sorry, Shea," John says, his voice thick with emotion.

"You need to go write your report. I'll see you later, I love you," Gregg pleads with her.

"I'll see you later. You're in my heart, alongside John, Christian, and Diesel," she says, her voice shaking.

John nods at her, a tear in his eye. Gregg finds it impossible to move away from her, he seems glued to the spot he stands in.

"Dude, I know. But we have a lot to get done before work tomorrow. We need to go," John urges.

Standing, Shea kisses Gregg's forehead and walks across the floor to her pod. She leaves all of her loved ones behind, in that small pod. Once she is in the quiet safety of her office, she breaks down crying. Forgetting about the mission report entirely, she curls up on her couch and falls asleep.

Shea is jolted awake by someone firmly grabbing her shoulders and slamming her into the bed over and over.

"Gregg? Alright, I'm awake. What's wrong?" she mumbles, her eyes still closed.

"Nice try, bitch," she hears.

Instantly, Shea is reminded of where she is and what has hopefully happened. Her eyes snap open. She jerks to a sitting position, heart hammering in her chest. Todd, who had been holding her shoulders, releases them with a sneer. In her office, she sees Todd, Tina, and about fifteen guards.

Todd squats down to her level, getting in her face. "Tell me what happened. Right now."

Shea can tell there is a rage about to boil over, but despite the danger, she can't help but to feel pride and happiness for her comrades.

"I don't know what you're talking about," she says calmly. "I got tired and fell asleep here. I thought I had until the day after the mission to do my report?"

Todd's mask slips further. "Shea, you are testing the very thin amount of control I have right now. Where. Is. Gregg?"

"What time is it?"

"It's ten in the morning. We didn't even realize you were still in the building until a couple of minutes ago. Gregg, John, and Christian— are unaccounted for, and there has been some sort of breach. That took out all of our systems and my FUCKING TIME MACHINE! So, tell me what you know, right now."

"I don't know anything, Todd. I hope they're okay," she says, with no emotion.

Todd stands and brushes off his dress slacks. Shea watches him intently, fearing the worst. She doesn't even see it coming when he pulls back his right hand and backhands her across the face. The blow is so sudden, so brutal, that her head snaps sideways and bounces off the couch.

She clutches her face in reflex, to cover what he had just done. Blinding pain radiates across her cheek and jaw, so severe it feels like it might explode. She drops her hand from her face and sees that it is covered in blood.

00055 🌲🌲 overwhelmed

Shea is really tired of getting smacked with all this foliage, she wonders if John is too. While contemplating this, she watches as John's hand suddenly snaps up to his face, followed by all the power leaving the four-wheeler. She jerks forward, her chest slamming into John's back.

"I'm sorry, I wasn't expecting that," she says.

"FUCK!" John yells, jumping from the four-wheeler, infuriated, and storms away.

Following him with her eyes, she watches as he digs around in the meat wagon, a gloved hand still pressed to his face. "Are you okay?" Shea asks, concerned.

"A stick the front of the ATV pushed over, flung back, and got me right in the eye," he mutters, frustrated.

"Oh no! Do you want me to look at it?"

"No, we're almost there. We just have to cut by the river, and we'll be there. I'm just going to rinse it out really quick," he says, putting the contact solution bottle next to his eye.

After he has rinsed it a few times, Shea can tell it's still bothering him. He walks back, not delaying their arrival any longer. He gets back on, and they head on their way.

Shea can hear the river and see the wake from it coursing over rocks. As they turn toward the cabin, cottonwood trees that are bigger than a car at the base and ferns that are taller than her (by over a foot) surround them. She sees fresh blueberries, raspberries and watermelon berries growing everywhere. John begins to slow, and Shea looks around. To her right, she sees a cabin on stilts, with a huge overhanging porch. There is a man on the porch, with a rifle slung across his back and a pair of binoculars in his hands. He opens the front door to the cabin, and a small boy and a dog barrel down the stairs to where John is parking.

Dismounting, John turns to Shea. "Hey, I'm gonna fix this," he points to his eye. "None of them will hurt you. They are all friends." Then he half turns and calls out to the man, "Hey, man!" as the man descends the stairs to stand near them. Then he looks at the boy and says, "No touching yet, got it?" The boy nods in response.

Shea feels overwhelmed, the smells of forest and fish accost her nasal passages, her butt and thighs are killing her from the ride, there's a thick layer of sweat covering her face and body with tiny bugs stuck in it. Her underwear and pants are soaked through with sweat in her crotch. The cool breeze hits her sweaty face, making her shiver.

She just stands there awkwardly while John rinses his eye and the three new members of their party inch closer, eyeing her curiously.

"Is that your dog?" she asks the boy.

He shakes his head and looks to the other man, who is now at his side.

"He doesn't speak. But no, Diesel is not his," the man says.

"Oh, okay. Well, hello. My name is Shea. It's nice to meet you all."

"Nice to meet you too," the man offers with a crooked smile.

"Alright, any chatter?" John asks the man.

"Nah, we're good. I've been on watch twenty-four-seven, I'm glad you're finally here. I'll sleep for a week."

"I'll do whatever I can," John responds.

Twin Pines

00056  Shit Stained

Todd laughs, "Oh, I must have forgotten to take my ring off. Tsk, tsk."

Oh God, he just now realized I wasn't missing with the boys. This is not going to be fun at all

Shea keeps her head bowed, hair curtaining her face, refusing to meet his eyes.

"Maybe you'll remember something later. After you spend some time in a cell." Todd nods to the guards and they shackle her wrists to her feet in a hogtie. As the guards walk across the floor between pods, Shea hangs painfully between them, the shackles biting at her skin.

She tries to focus on the silver lining—they made it out safely and she would sit in a glass cell, that reminded her of her loved ones. Except they walk past Gregg's pod, then board a back freight elevator and descend to a sublevel. When they get off the elevator, Todd walks out in front of them and leans down so that Shea can see him.

"These are not our normal accommodations," he says, grinning like a vulture. "But seeing as all of our systems are down… maybe a stay down here will change your mind about talking."

"I am willing to talk to you. You just haven't asked me anything I actually know."

Shea feels his rage in the silence that follows, just before a man's dress shoe, size thirteen, connects with her ribs. All of the air leaves her, and she feels like a fish on land as they drag her over to the dark underground cell. She is almost certain she is dying when they toss her into the cell, landing on the mud-crusted floor. They pull the door closed, sealing her in utter darkness.

Once she can breathe again, she attempts to look at her new home. The cell is only five feet by three feet, making it easier to take it all in. Shea tries to look at the bright side, but the only one she can find is, at least she's short. Trying to wiggle around on her stomach, Shea finds that there is no bathroom bucket, no water available, and the door is so well fit that she can't even tell where it is. Pure darkness surrounds her with a frosty temperature as its brother.

Her optimistic viewpoint only lasts for a few hours. Shea has no idea how much time has passed when the door next opens. All she knows is she is so hungry, she feels weak, her tongue is glued to the roof of her mouth, her lips are cracked and bleeding, the skin under and around her shackles is raw and sore, and her joints and muscles feel locked in place. There is also a large pile of excrement in the corner that she has wiggled through several times.

But, most of all. That she hates Todd. She thinks it could have been anywhere between five days and two weeks.

As the small sliver of light gets larger, her eyes adjust. Which allows her to realize, that although she thought she was shitting in the back corner of the cell, it was in fact, right against the door. When the door opens all the way, she looks up, squinting, to see Tina standing there.

"Well little piggy—look at you now," she sneers. "Get her up. Get her to the shower room, she's covered in shit. And unshackle her."

Shea cries out when the shackles are removed—her joints and limbs are so stiff. It feels like they would rather be in the position they had been, the last… however long. She sits in a room full of shower heads, alone. She decides to crawl over to the controls, desperate for water, and a shower would be great considering she is covered in her own… well. The sound of Tina's heels approaching makes her freeze, deciding to stay where she is on the floor.

Tina comes into view, brass knuckles gleaming on each hand.

"Well, girl, I've been waiting for this day. Before I do what I want, I'm supposed to ask—got anything you want to say?"

"About what?" Shea asks weakly.

"Oh, I don't know. Your doofy hubs? The weird kid?"

"Oh, then no."

Tina laughs—cold and cruel. She walks up to Shea and punches her at the top of her nose, in a downward motion, breaking it and immediately beginning the darkening of both eyes. Shea keeps her reaction to a minimum, remaining still as blood pours out of her nose and in her mouth. It pours down her throat, making it almost impossible to breathe.

Tina leans over and inspects her work—apparently unsatisfied—she hits Shea in the side of her head, making Shea fall over sideways, confused. Before she can recover, a firehose is turned on and aimed at Shea. Tina laughs as the guards hose her down with the high-pressure water. Shea fights to breathe under the relentless torrent, unwilling to drown via firehose.

Shea is dropped—dripping wet—back in the same dirty cell. Before the guards leave, they toss in two liters of water and two wrapped sandwiches.

Could be drugged… I really don't care

She sits and eats a whole sandwich, slowly sipping the water. Before long, sleep claims her. When she next wakes, she's no longer in her cell. Instead, she finds herself naked, strapped to a cold metal table with a screen in front of her. Behind her, Todd's voice cuts through the silence.

"Sorry, Shea, but I need you to cooperate. I'm not above removing body parts or teeth, but let's start with some home videos."

On the screen, a baby appears in its mother's arms, she watches the mother waste away to almost nothing, terrified of her child. Then Todd steps into view, taking a child and locking him in a glass case. Shea cries silently, her heart aching, but not for the reason Todd thinks. She cries because she knows Christian just wants love, and that he has been refused it for so long.

Then, Todd burning her house to the ground, but she refuses to feed into his sick game.

"Come on, Shea. That's your family! Aren't you angry?"

"Remove what you want. I don't know anything."

Angering him is not a great idea, but she can't help herself, and neither can he. He swings and lands a punch on her jaw, splitting skin that had started to mend. "Shea, you need to talk."

"I don't know anything. I slept here one night, and everything fell apart. I have no idea what is going on."

"I'M NOT AN IDIOT!" he roars, seething with rage he grabs a pair of pliers.

Before Shea can even come to terms that this is real, he's already pulled one of her back teeth free. She lies back on the table with blood pouring down her throat and surrenders. She knows Todd's anger, and she knows her end might very well, be now.

God, please watch over my boys. Let them know I tried

Todd looks at her with disgust and spits in her face. "Another week," he says, addressing the guards.

She offers no resistance. She enters her cell willingly. The food and water from before are gone, it's just her and her shit. She has no idea how much time passes, —to her it feels like over a month before someone opens the door fully, again. During that time, her waste pile continued to grow, taking up more and more of the little space she did have. She is fed more regularly, estimating their visits about every other day. To pass the time she sleeps as much as she can, but when she can't, when she's really awake, she sings her favorite songs. She imagines the playlist she made just for this occasion—*Firey Black Hole*.

Before the guard's arrival today, she was singing her new favorite song, *Oblivion by Softspoken*. She is again taken to the shower room and hosed off, then given clean clothes and led to Todd's office.

Sitting across the desk from him, his eyes cold, he speaks in a voice that says, 'there will be no more fucking around.'

"Shea, this will be the last time I ask you about this. Where are they?"

"I. Don't. Know."

"Guards," he snaps.

Everything after that is a blur for Shea—she is brutally beaten, kicked, spit on, and knocked out cold.

When she comes to, she is face down, deep in the garbage dumpster in the back of the building. It takes her a moment to get her bearings and remember what to do. Climbing out of the dumpster, she glances down at her bare feet, noticing a large shard of glass next to them.

Picking up the glass, she takes off running—through the pain, starvation, and exhaustion—toward what she hopes will be freedom. She knows they expect her to lead them to her people, but her people are long gone at this point.

She makes it to Lou's, running to the alley between the parking lot and the bar. Dropping to her knees, she steels herself—this is going to suck. After talking herself into it, she takes the glass and slices open her left hand, feeling around for the chip. She pulls it out and crushes it with the blunt end of the glass. Now for the hard part.

Shea doesn't know it, but as soon as the bouncer—the one who regularly works there—sees Shea running, he immediately calls the number he was given several months ago.

"Yeah, she came in hot just a second ago," he says into the phone.

"Thank you. I'll take it from here," the voice replies.

A car she doesn't recognize pulls into a spot shaded beneath a tree, hidden from her view.

She kneels on the cement, face and body battered, bruised, and broken, blood pouring from her hand as she reaches into her hairline and finds the scar.

With trembling fingers, she guides the shard of glass to her scalp and begins to cut.

It doesn't happen all at once. She has to start and stop, darkness clawing at the edges of her vision.

The man in the car watches. He holds his breath, and watches.

She continues to make cuts with the glass, deeper and deeper, until she finally feels the bone under the glass.

Using her fingers, she feels for the plug that she knows is there. The blood makes her hand slippery, and she can no longer hold on to the glass. It falls from her fingers.

She folds herself in half, sobbing, questioning all of her decisions. She's on the brink of just giving up.

The man in the car makes himself stay seated, fists clenched. "I can't help her yet, not if there is a chance the system is up."

Minutes drag by, Shea gathers her strength. She reaches up and finds the plug.

Getting a fingernail beneath its edge, she yanks it free.

With only one more step to go—knowing that there is a chance she might never wake up from this or just die all together from ripping part of her brain out of this tiny hole, she whispers, "Thank you for this life, God. Thank you for Gregg, and for John, and for Christian, and for Diesel. Thank you for the laughs. Thank you for a true love I could never deserve."

As soon as she finishes her thanks to God, she feels where the plug once was. The chip is down in the hole, and she is unsure how to get to it.

Panic bubbling up, she feels overwhelmed—she can't do it. But, if she doesn't, she will never see them again.

She takes her bloody finger and presses it over the hole, creating suction—pushing down and pulling up, over and over— working the chip closer, little by little.

Finally, she feels it. She tightly grabs it and counts to three. "One, two, three." She yanks the chip hard and all of its tendrils follow.

As soon as the chip is free, her body gives out. She face plants, unconscious, on to the cement.

The man wipes a tear from his cheek and gets out of the car.

He picks her up and places her in the backseat.

Without a word, he leaves and never comes back.

Twin Pines

00057 Eyes for You

Shea steps back from the interaction, watching the boy play with the dog. She feels like there is something familiar, but it's probably just that photo she saw at John's house.

"Shea, you okay? You hungry?" John asks.

Pulling her out of her stupor, she looks to John for the first time since they've been here. She suddenly feels confused and the earth is wobbling. "John?" she asks, her voice trembling. She looks from him to the other three, all of them stare back with concern on their faces. Time slows to a crawl, and she watches all of them move toward her with deepening concern. She realizes she's falling and has no control to stop it.

"John?" she says, again looking over to him, trying to make sense of what's happening.

He makes it over to her just in time, guiding her gently to the ground, her upper body resting across his lap. Her eyes rove over his face, never settling anywhere.

"What's wrong, Shea? Are you okay? Can you hear me?" He looks at his companion, who smiles and shrugs.

"When did you get glasses?" she asks, her voice distant.

Her body goes still, and her eyes remain fixed. She continues to hear the world around her, as memories slam into her from all directions.

"What's happening?" the man asks.

"I think my glasses are making her remember, give her space," John says.

Shea remains in the same position, staring into space, for almost fifteen minutes. In her mind a frizzy haired man with thick glasses blushes at her. A tall man with a hint of evil in his eyes, spins a ring on his finger. The man with thick glasses holds her when she cries. Another tall man makes her laugh until her sides hurt. A puppy. A boy. A ring. And love. So much love. Then, darkness and pain and blood.

She hears John say, "She's coming out of it," just as tears begin sliding down the sides of her face.

When she blinks and opens her eyes, she knows that he knows.

John Doe is Gregg! It's Gregg!

"Is that my beautiful wife?" he asks her.

"Gregg? I can't believe I didn't know it was you," she cries. She reaches up to caress his face, feeling moisture from shed tears and his beard, so long and soft now. "I love you so much. I've missed you, so much," she rambles, no longer overwhelmed by her senses. Instead, overwhelmed by the memories and emotions.

He smiles down at her and helps her to her feet. She sees her friend (from work), John, standing over all of them, his eyes full of relief, and Christian and Diesel playing nearby. Shea breaks down harder, inconsolable, remembering all they'd done for her, and all she had done for them.

John, seeing the change in her, calls over the others. They all pile on top of each other, on the ground, hugging, crying, and laughing.

Gregg stands nearby, watching them play, listening to the sound of Shea's laughter. He knew she could do it—make it out of captivity— but a part of him thought he'd never hear her laughter again.

EPILOGUE

In a large office, a man sits in an opulent chair. The phone on his desk rings, and he reaches over to answer it, a ring prominently on his right ring finger.

"What?"

"Sir, we've made progress on the computer system. The tracker went live two hours ago."

"Excellent. Deploy the black hawks and at least fifteen men."

"Yessir. Anything else?"

"Bring them in. Do not fail me. The child and Gregg must be brought in alive. The other two targets…dealers' choice."

Twin Pines

THANK YOU
FOR
READING

BE SURE TO LEAVE
A REVIEW ON
AMAZON or GOODREADS

Twin Pines